CASTLE BEACH

CASTLE BEACH

Kathleen Jablonski

ISBN 978-0-615553-030

For my Parents

With the exception of the mention of historical figures and events, this book is a work of fiction.

Vermont, early 1980s . . .

I

Jeremy watched the yellowing leaves let go of the tired branches and spin on the breeze. They twirled and tumbled and caught the sun as they fell. He tried to run and catch as many as he could before they reached the ground, but it was difficult because his mother had dressed him in a heavy wool coat and bulky mittens. Several times he looked around to see if she were paying any attention to him. If she happened to be looking in the other direction, he would slip off the gloves and push them into the pocket of his coat and then work frantically at his task. He had made up this game and mittens were not a part of it. He secretly felt that somehow he had saved the life of every aging leaf he intercepted on its journey to the ground. But the subject of his rescue attempt soon met a fate far worse than nature had intended. Jeremy would wait until he had what he considered to be a respectable amount. Then he would crumble them up in the palms of his hands and toss the tiny fragments up into the wind where they would shimmer and dance like orange confetti before settling torn and motionless around his feet. He would laugh with wild joy at this small celebration and then begin the game once more.

Dori watched her young son amuse himself while they walked along in the bracing autumn morning. The sun was big and brilliant but almost totally lacking in warmth this time of year. As Dori walked through the grove of birches the rapid play of light and shadow gave the entire scene the feeling of an old movie where the churning camera made normal body movements appear short and jerky. The thin, sharp air stung her nostrils. But it was not an unpleasant sensation, and she breathed deeply, watching the small clouds of breath as they escaped her mouth. Though she had grown up here and had seen almost every fall as it arrived with the same steady procession of glowing color and quickening wind, she had never tired of observing summer as it reluctantly acquiesced to the stronger newcomer.

Jeremy had stopped and was sitting cross-legged by the base of a large maple as he watched a fat, thick-tailed squirrel scratch up the trunk and dart and leap from branch to branch, much to the child's delight. The boy, red cheeked, turned in Dori's direction. "Look, mommy, he's showing off for us."

She smiled and he turned his gaze again upon the animal, who seemed to know that it had an audience. It leapt from tree to tree with grace and ease. Jeremy applauded at each new feat of daring undertaken by the small acrobat. Finally, perhaps realizing the unproductive nature of its folly, the squirrel dropped to the ground and rustled off into the underbrush. Jeremy sighed in disappointment and took Dori's hand as they continued their walk.

They rounded a corner on the trail and entered a large open space. Brown stubby grass rose up in unruly masses, and the low cut stumps of trees dotted the entire field. Jeremy dropped his mother's hand and ran methodically from stump to stump, pounding his feet upon the flat surface of each one as he strained to hear the important sounds. At once he had a new game. He was sending secret messages to all of the creatures in the forest.

Dori was not looking at her son now. She had lifted her eyes to the large slope at the opposite end of the field. Mechanical ski lifts sat idle and waited for snow and the migration of the skiers from the hot, stuffy office buildings of New York and the crowded college libraries of New England. Dori shuddered involuntarily as she stared at the machine, which almost seemed to be standing in silent defiance. She did not try to fight the memories any more—that was futile, and at least as painful as reliving them. She had hoped that by allowing herself to experience that day over and over again she could somehow exorcise the terror and agony from her body and mind. She hoped that perhaps the intolerable sorrow would shrink and vanish. But now, as she stood here again and thought of that afternoon in late December, she realized that time had not padded her emotions. The feelings were still rough and raw, and she ached with the same intensity as always. The faces, the names, the smells, and the sounds of that day—nothing had muted into a half-light. It was almost as though the events of that afternoon were a play constantly being performed in her mind, becoming more immediate through repetition. She sensed it beginning its cycle again.

It had been such a perfect morning. She and Chris had driven up with Jeremy from New York the day before. Dori's parents still lived near the town of Fairlee in the lovely old farmhouse where she'd been raised. It was late when they arrived, and Jeremy was sound asleep in the backseat of the car. Chris carried him up the dimly lit porch steps and into the house. Dori's mother flashed a big grin and silently took the child from Chris' arms and upstairs to the small bedroom that had once been Dori's.

Dr. McGee helped Chris and Dori with the luggage, and then put another log on the waning fire.

"I thought you were only coming for the weekend. You've got enough stuff to outfit a wagon train."

"Well," Dori defended the excessive suitcases. "We've been invited to a big party tomorrow night after skiing and I have three outfits with me. I probably won't be able to decide what to wear until the last minute."

Mrs. McGee was descending the stairs and heard her daughter. "If I know you, you'll change clothes in the middle of the party." She turned to Dori's husband. "Chris, did I ever tell you about Dori's high school graduation pictures?"

Chris nodded that he hadn't heard.

"Well, she couldn't decide what sweater to wear right up until the photographer was ready so she had three different pictures taken and changed her sweaters between shots."

"Not in front of the photographer, I hope," teased Chris.

"Oh, enough of this please," pleaded Dori in a melodramatic tone. "Dad, why don't you fix us all a drink? We have some important news."

Beth McGee winked at her husband.

"No mother," Dori cautioned. "I am not pregnant."

"And neither am I," said Chris.

"Well, if this is going to be a celebration, let me get some champagne from the cellar." Dr. McGee lifted a rug from in front of the fireplace and climbed down a deep set of stairs into the small wine cellar he had fashioned from a portion of the basement.

Dori's mother shook her head. "That thing is more trouble than it's worth, but Andy loves it."

"Here we are!" he announced, emerging from the floor. "This is the best I've got, so it better be really good news."

Beth retrieved the crystal champagne glasses from the cabinet in the dining room while her husband skillfully uncorked the cool, dusty bottle and poured the liquid deftly into the waiting glasses.

"Oh, who knew your intricate surgical techniques would serve you so well in retirement, Andy?" Chris grinned at his father-in-law. They all raised their glasses and Dori looked over at her husband.

"Should I tell them?" she asked.

Chris winked. "I believe so. Modesty prevents me."

"Oh you." Dori made a face. "Very well then. Mom and Dad, you are now in the presence of the man who might very well be the future junior senator from the Empire state. I give you the honorable Christopher Patrick Dugan." Dori studied her parents' faces for their reaction. Their response seemed to be almost in unison. Their eyes widened. They sat very still for an instant before they both stood up laughing and smiling, full of congratulations and questions.

"When did all of this happen?" Dr. McGee asked.

"Tell us the whole story," Beth demanded urgently. "Don't leave out a thing."

So, for the next hour Chris and Dori chronicled the series of events that led to Chris' tentative decision to run. He was an attorney in private practice in Manhattan dealing mainly in corporate law. He had earned the reputation of possessing honesty and fairness, commodities in short supply lately in the political arena. His Republican backers convinced him that he was their best hope against the ultra left Democratic incumbent. "Anyway," Chris concluded, "Dori and I are going skiing tomorrow with some of the supporters behind his plan. That's what the dinner is about tomorrow night; meeting some of these people will give us the opportunity to consider things with our eyes wide open and to make sure it is something we really want to do."

Dori looked warmly at her strong, young husband. She was not afraid of whatever decision they would make simply because it would be their decision, one they would make together. Suddenly, Dr. McGee jumped up, put on his fleece lined jacket and leather gloves and grabbed the heavy ax by the fireplace and headed for the front door.

"Where are you going?" Chris asked.

Dr. McGee's eyes glowed with mischief and his mouth broke into a playful grin. "Why, I can see the handwriting on the wall. I'm going out right now to build the log cabin you were born in."

It had been a wonderful evening. They all stayed up and talked and just enjoyed the close company and the festive champagne. Chris rebuilt the fire and it glowed on far into the night. But the following afternoon it was all to end.

Dori and Chris had been skiing all morning with three other couples from New York. One of the men was a partner in a firm that was always trying to recruit Chris, and the other two were independent businessmen who were very active in the local Republican Party organization. The other wives were not very good skiers and Dori rather enjoyed their envious glances as she traversed the hills with confidence and style. But having lived in Vermont most of her life, skiing was not only a sport but also many times the only means of transportation. The sky had been clear during the morning but as they all sat in the lodge having lunch huge gray clouds materialized from nowhere and crowded out all but a few narrow strips of blue. And with the clouds came a wind and faint traces of misty snow.

"Well, that does it for my skiing," said one of the women as she stirred a steaming bowl of tomato soup. "I'm bad enough without trying to battle the elements."

Another of the women was in full agreement. "To quote *Alice In Wonderland*, 'Things are looking curiouser and curiouser.'"

"Yep," her husband added. "Seems like I am going to spend the rest of the day doing a little mahogany skiing."

"Doing what?" asked Dori

"Glued to the bar, my dear." Everyone laughed.

"Hey," said Chris. "Dori's dad is a doctor. Maybe he could make a fake cast for you so you can sit by the fire all weekend nursing the sherry and getting sympathetic glances from the bevy of passing coeds." Chris looked at Dori. "What about you honey? Are you up for a few more runs?"

She really wasn't but Chris was enjoying himself so much she didn't want to stay behind and let him ski alone. "Okay, but just for a while; I really think we are in for a storm."

"You better listen to her," Chris said addressing the table. "She was born and raised in these woods."

"Honestly, Chris." She looked at the group. "It's true folks, and I rode to school everyday on a big blue ox."

They left the group of laughing people and headed back outside. The temperature seemed to have dropped at least twenty-five degrees since they went in for lunch. They climbed aboard the chair lift. The morning crowd had thinned out and only the ardent skiers remained.

"Having fun?" Chris asked.

"Yeah I am. But I have skied so much today I feel like I am trying out for the Olympics."

"Me too," Chris agreed. "We have been pushing it. Somehow when I am in the office all week I feel like I have to make a weekend count for a whole vacation. One more run and we'll call it quits." They were reaching the end of the ski lift.

"Did I ever tell you that you are beautiful?" he asked.

"Not nearly often enough."

"Well, I'll make a note of that."

"Campaigning already?"

He grinned and pushed off down the hill. The snow was really beginning to fall now and in a few minutes Dori lost sight of the bright red parka and gleaming metal ski poles. Suddenly she became very frightened. She looked over at the ski lift operator, "My husband is a much better skier than I am and I…"

"Don't apologize lady; ride the lift back down."

"Thanks." She climbed into one of the seats and with a lunge the chair was lifted from the snow and began its slow grinding descent down the mountain. Freezing sleet beat against her face and goggles obscuring her vision. Attempts at wiping the snow away with her wool gloves only smeared the lenses and made things worse. But halfway down the hill she saw a group of people huddled over an object in the snow. She could make out little else. When she arrived at the bottom she heard the sound of a siren and saw several young men wearing snowshoes and the bright orange vests designating them as members of the ski patrol start back up the hill carrying an empty canvas stretcher between them.

A crowd of curious people had gathered on the deck of the lodge to watch the proceedings. Dori unbuckled her skis and ran up to where her group of friends was huddled.

"What happened?"

"Skier down," one of them said.

"Where's Chris? Dori looked all over for the familiar red jacket and blue wool cap.

"Didn't you come down together?" asked Tom Stephens, Chris' friend from the firm.

"No, Chris skied down ahead; I decided to take the lift and—" Suddenly, the men carrying the stretcher emerged from the wall of snow and sleet. Chris lay limp on the canvas mat, his face grey and pale. Dori screamed, rushing up next to him.

"What happened? Talk to me," she pleaded.

An attending physician was waiting at the ambulance. Dori climbed in beside him and stared down at Chris while the whining siren yelled into the wind and the gathering darkness. The chained tires bit into the road. The physician hovered over the stretcher for several minutes; then made a gesture to the driver and soon the siren stopped completely. Dori looked at the doctor with bewildered terror.

"I'm so sorry," he said softly. "He was blinded by the snow. He struck a tree and suffered a massive head trauma and a broken neck. He was dead within minutes."

As simply as that, it was over. In the weeks that followed she had been paralyzed with grief and shock. Chris' family flew in from Los Angeles for the small funeral. Many of his friends came up from New York to aid her in the grim task of burying her husband. Dori had spent evenings before the funeral explaining to Jeremy what had happened to his father.

"God decided that he needed daddy more than we do now, so we can't be sad forever." She used all the tired old clichés deemed valuable in explaining death to children. All were grossly inadequate. She cloaked truths in euphemisms not so much for Jeremy's benefit as for her own. The jagged reality was something she felt totally unprepared to accept.

"Mommy, I'm cold. Let's go home." The persistent tug at her coat sleeve catapulted her thoughts momentarily back into the present.

"O.K. But put your mittens on or your hands will get chapped again and sting."

The child obeyed and skipped ahead of his mother in the direction of the McGee farmhouse.

For a while after Chris' death Dori had tried to go on with her life in New York. She kept their apartment and hired a live-in nanny for Jeremy. Then she returned full time to her work as an interior decorator. She was doing quite well. At first, people gave her small jobs to keep her from dwelling on the past and to occupy her time. But soon, because of her genuine talent in the field, she did not have to rely on the charity of friends for assignments. Her work spoke for itself and shortly she had acquired some of the wealthiest and most influential people in the city as her clients. She was trusted to decorate everything from huge penthouse flats to small but elegant summer homes in the Hamptons.

She found great satisfaction in her work and immersed herself in it completely, to the exclusion of any kind of social life as well as to the exclusion of her son. On the few occasions Dori would let Molly have the weekend off, Jeremy would cry and beg her not to leave. His mother had become a stranger to him. Dori irrationally resented his behavior and refused to understand it. She would scold him and he would sulk on his bed.

But on one such rainy Saturday morning Jeremy emerged from his room with puffy eyes and tear-streaked cheeks holding an old scrapbook. Dori was sitting by the fire going over cost estimates for some fabric she was purchasing for a client. The child approached her chair silently and opened the book in her lap on top of her papers. There was a yellowing photograph of Chris when he had been about Jeremy's age of six. Jeremy had seen the picture and the entire album many times.

"What is it, honey?" Dori looked at her son. The small boy took a long ragged breath and stared up into his mother's face.

"I look like daddy did when he was little. That's why you hate me, because now I'm here and he's not and it makes you mad to see me."

Dori felt as though she had been physically assaulted. The words hit her with such force. This tiny child had exposed the ugly truth she had found too horrifying to face. She pushed her papers to the ground and gathered her son up in her arms and began to cry, something she had not even done at her husband's funeral. By denying herself emotional release she had thought that she could protect herself from the facts of it all. Jeremy tucked his face close to Dori's neck and cried too. But he wasn't sad anymore. For the first time he was starting to feel that maybe things would be all right again.

It was shortly after that that she made the decision to move back to Vermont with Jeremy. It was summer now and the city heat was unbearable. But aside from that she had had enough of trying to live up to the façade of easy self-assurance and independence she had erected. She needed a rest from her job as well as from the excessive number of blind dates her friends had recently talked her into accepting. And most of all she needed time to become reacquainted with her son and herself, time to assess things as they were and to choose a new direction for their lives.

, She watched Jeremy skip ahead of her on the trail. They had been here now since June, almost five months. Dori's parents loved having their daughter home with them. Jeremy was an added joy. Dori had been an only child born to the couple rather late in their lives. She even suspected that perhaps she had been an unexpected change-of-life baby. Yet growing up she never felt as though her parents had been old. They were both so engrossed with the sheer fascination of living. "It's one big adventure," her father used to say. Up until several years ago he had been a pediatric surgeon in a small hospital near Middlebury. It was not far from the college Dori had attended before transferring to Parson's School of Design in New York. But now he had gone into semi-retirement, practicing general family medicine. He had turned his den into an office where his patients came for consultations. But he secretly still preferred to make house calls. He loved to drive the old rural roads and visit with people in their homes. There would always be a pot of coffee brewing and some cookies or cake offered to him.

"Your father has gained ten pounds since he retired," Dori's mother announced. "I'm beginning to think that most of his house calls are spent in the kitchen."

Watching how Jeremy was flourishing here protected by the secure loving home of his grandparents, Dori realized what a very special and unique childhood she herself had enjoyed.

The past five months had sped by rapidly with one week blending into the next. Dori had spent most of her time helping her mother manage the small gift shop she had opened near the college. She called it "The Quilted Pine." Basically it carried handicrafts made by the local residents: patchwork quilts, reproductions of early American furniture, homemade maple candy, and a few baked goods. Students from the college came often to select gifts with a genuine New England appeal to be sent to their families in the west or south. Dori's mother had run the shop since Dori had been a freshman in college. She did it mostly for fun but it was surprisingly profitable. Recently Dori had convinced her to carry a small but exclusive line of collegiate girls' sportswear, which had met with great success.

Jeremy had been enrolled in the first grade at the only public school near them. His classmates were all the children of the local merchants and farmers. There was a private progressive school, which had been opened by a group of New York ex-patriots of independent means. They had come to settle in the backwoods of Vermont to engage in pseudo-intellectual endeavors. Dori had seen enough of them and their children in Manhattan. The men all wore tweed sport coats with leather patches on the elbows while the women looked like they were attending a Vassar reunion, class of '58—long skirts, loafers, and tightly drawn and very sever expressions. Most of them feigned resentment for the trust funds off of which they lived. The locals tolerated these invaders quite well, recognizing them for what they were. Thus, no one felt threatened by their presence.

Dori looked up. Jeremy had reached the front porch steps of the house well ahead of his mother and was motioning with giant waves of his arms for her to hurry up and join him.

"Just a minute," her shout cut the air. "Go on inside and see if you can help grandma with anything. I'll be along soon." Jeremy made a face of frustrated resignation and then disappeared behind the big front door.

Dori walked around to the far side of the house. A large sawhorse stood beneath the branches of a thin birch tree. The toy had been Dori's when she was small. She loved the fact that her dad had saved it all these years. She climbed aboard and straddled the wooden beast remembering the many Saturdays she had spent in the saddle galloping over imaginary prairies in search of "outlaws." The morning was evaporating into afternoon and by four o'clock the sky would start to darken in preparation for evening. Everyone had been expecting the first snow any day. Talk of the weather occupied much of the conversation in these small country towns. Dori closed her eyes and for an instant wished that she and Jeremy could be brother and sister, that she could be little again and grow up all over in this fine warm house, being tucked into bed at night and playing in the snow and falling asleep by the fire waiting for the sound of Santa's sleigh on the roof. Pretending came easily here.

The sad insanity of her wish made it less difficult for her to accept the truth of what was happening. Life here was becoming too comfortable, too secure, too isolated from reality. And she knew how simple it would be for her to surrender to all of it and live here with her mother and father and her little "brother," for that, indeed, was what he was becoming. Dori's parents treated them both like their children. At first, they had babied Dori. She had assumed it was because of her loss. But their hovering concern had increased in the last several months. While welcoming their attention in the beginning, it was now starting to annoy her, and several times when Jeremy had called Dr. McGee "daddy," Dori was quick to remind her son that "daddy" was gone and that this was "Grandpa." She did it as gently and calmly as she could, yet she saw the hurt expression on her father's face.

"What harm can it do?" her mother would ask. "Just for a little while anyway."

Dori heard the front door slam and the sound of Jeremy running down the big porch steps. He circled the house and stopped short when he saw his mother astride the sawhorse.

"You look silly."

"Jeremy, this horse belonged to me when I was a little girl."

11

Jeremy stuck his bottom lip out, thinking. "But you're too big for that now," he theorized, having obtained an instant perspective on the whole situation. Dori sighed and dismounted.

"You are right. Have you had your lunch yet?" she asked.

"No. Grandma is making tomato soup and grilled cheese sandwiches but we're waiting for Grandpa. I'm going back inside. It's cold."

Just then the familiar sound of Andy McGee's old red Jeep filtered across the breeze. Jeremy ran around to the front of the house and hollered back to his mother. "Grandpa's coming. Bye." And he disappeared in the direction of the cloud of rising dust on the driveway. Yes, everything was becoming too patterned and too routine and too easy. She knew the period of adjusting to her husband's death was over. If she did not fashion some kind of a life for herself now, she could very well grow old and die right here, secluded and safe but numb to the experiences of life as well.

She looked down at her hands. They were red and she could barely bend her fingers. She had been outside longer than she had imagined.

"Dorothy!" Dr. McGee came around to meet her as she headed for the house. Jeremy had his grandfather by one hand and was proudly carrying the old man's medical bag in the other. "Jeremy tells me that you two went for a long hike this morning and that you saw several ferocious grizzly bears." Dori looked at her son who was grinning happily.

"Well dad, the bears were really quite a bit smaller and had a strange resemblance to squirrels and there was only one, but other than that, everything Jeremy told you is true." Andy McGee laughed and tickled the little boy.

"That's about what I figured."

Dori kissed her father lightly on the cheek and they headed in for lunch. If she were going to make a change, it would have to be soon. Leaving now would hurt her parents enough, but if she waited much longer, the strain on all of them would be even more painful.

The following morning Dori worked at The Quilted Pine helping her mother decorate the windows for the coming of Christmas just weeks away. When she returned home shortly before five, the phone was ringing. She struggled with her key and made her way into the house. It had been snowing off and on for several days and sometimes the wind would blow snow flurries against the door and temporarily bury the lock. With a mittened hand Dori angrily picked up the receiver. "Hello!" she snapped into the mouthpiece.

"Dori?" she heard a man's voice meekly ask. "Don't tell me," he continued. "You've been out taming the wilderness all day and you're beat."

Dori recognized the voice now. It belonged to Logan Hart, one of her previous clients. He owned an exclusive resort in Hilton Head, North Carolina, and one in the Adirondacks, which she had decorated for him several months before Chris' death. This was the first time she had heard from him in over a year.

"Logan, what in the world are you doing?" she asked.

"Right now?" he said. "Well, if you must know, I'm at the Plaza, submerged in a marble tub filled with warm champagne while six naked women dance around the room. You know, same boring stuff."

Dori laughed, despite the fact that she was cold and wet and her nose was running. And despite the fact that with Logan Hart everything he was saying could be true. "What in the world possessed you to call me?" she asked honestly.

His tone became more serious. "I'm sorry about Chris. If it's any consolation, everyone thinks he would have made a terrific senator."

Dori shook her head. That's Logan Hart. She lost a husband and he lost a candidate. "Well, thank you, Logan."

His voice was light again. "But that's not why I'm calling. I have a proposition for you."

Dori laughed loudly into the receiver. "Sorry, but I don't think I can compete with six naked dancers."

"No, not that kind of proposition. Business, strictly business. The whole thing is really quite exciting."

Dori had removed her coat and had flung it over a chair. She pulled off a tight, wool knit hat and ran her fingers over her damp blond hair. "I'm listening; tell me about it."

"Not over the phone. Could you come here?"

"Only if you promise to be out of the tub when I arrive."

"Really, I'm serious," he insisted. "How about coming into town tomorrow night for dinner? I'll book a room for you here. Then I can explain things to you more fully." Dori had to admit, the prospect of an evening in the city was sounding very appealing at this point.

"O.K., Logan, I'll come. I'll be driving, so don't expect me much before six."

"All right, my love. I shall be keeping sentry at the Oak Room bar."

Dori hung up the phone and peered through the front window. The snow seemed to be slackening. That would mean that the plows would be out clearing the roads soon. If the weather held, the drive tomorrow would be pleasantly relaxing. She smiled at herself in the front hall mirror on her way upstairs. Her blond hair was cut in a gentle oval around her face with thick bangs just brushing her eyebrows. Her complexion was so fair that she was often thought to be of Swedish ancestry, not Scottish. Though almost thirty-five she still looked like a college sophomore. She bounded up the stairs in much the same fashion she had done years before. All at once, for no particular reason, she was happy that she had made the decision to travel to New York, if even for an evening. At least she was doing something to break up the monotony. Logan Hart was wild and unpredictable. She knew that. But she also knew that he was never dull, so the evening was bound to be exciting. What she didn't know was that it would also change her life completely.

The drive into the city took Dori a lot longer than she had expected, and it was anything but relaxing. She had left the house at five in the morning. Dr. McGee was up and put Dori's overnight case into the trunk of the small Fiat that had belonged to Chris. Her mother hovered around with coffee and orange juice and warnings to drive carefully. The scene was almost identical to the many times Dori had been leaving to return to Parsons after spending the holidays at home, with the exception of Jeremy. He was sitting curled up in a flannel sleeper on an overstuffed chair in the living room, observing all of the activities and reminding his mother at ten second intervals to "bring me something."

At last she was off, with a light snow just beginning to float through the icy, blue-grey morning sky. She was forced to follow a snowplow for what seemed to be forever before she could leave the two lane back road and hook up with the Interstate Highway just outside of Middlebury. The drive to Albany was arduous and she was certain that chains would be necessary before the trip was over. But miraculously she escaped without having to struggle with them. She stopped at one of the innocuous chain restaurants along the way for a quick lunch of a club sandwich and coffee.

Why did they call it a 'club sandwich'? she thought. She had never had one in a club. The driving made her tense and her shoulders felt tight and ached. Why didn't I fly? No, I had to drive, to commune with nature, to wax poetically to myself on the splendor of a New England winter. Walt Whitman, where are you when I need you? She sighed, paid the check, and resumed her sojourn.

Surprisingly, the remainder of the drive wasn't bad. The snow had stopped falling and the roads, though wet, were smooth and clear. By the time she reached the city she was feeling very smug about her accomplishment. And as she pulled up in front of the Plaza she imagined having finished first in the La Mans and was only slightly disappointed to be greeted by an aging doorman rather than by a tired and defeated formula one driver.

The lobby was warm and smelled of perfume and leather. It was filled with guests in various stages of arriving and departing. The Christmas decorations were up and traditional holiday carols were being piped into the huge foyer. Large ornate chandeliers hung majestically from the ceiling. Dori registered and gave her luggage to the bell captain to take to her room. She then took a quick trip to the Ladies' Lounge before proceeding to the bar at the far end of the lobby. She glanced at the massive grandfather clock in the hall. Six-thirty. Not bad! As her eyes adjusted to the rose and rust light in the bar, a waiter came up and stood politely and expectantly in front of her.

"I'm to be meeting someone here," she said.

The waiter glanced at her wedding ring. "Your husband?"

Dori was startled and shot a look at her hand. It had never even occurred to her that she should no longer be wearing her wedding ring. Why had all of the men she had previously dated failed to mention it? Too polite? Too indifferent? "No," she turned her attention to the waiter. "I am meeting—"

"Dori!" It was Logan. He had emerged from somewhere in the recesses of the room. "I have been waving to you for the last two minutes. I was beginning to think that you wanted a drum roll to announce your entrance." He kissed her lightly on the cheek and took her arm. The thin waiter had discretely vanished. "You look amazing." He was guiding her to his table. "Widowhood agrees with you."

"Logan, please!"

"I apologize. That was a thoughtless remark. But it has been almost a year. You are not a dowager you know. Mourning is meant to be a temporary state. Life does go on."

"I'm here, aren't I? Although at this point I am beginning to wonder why." The same unctuous waiter appeared from the darkness and gave Dori the glance of someone who is privy to a clandestine rendezvous. She ignored his expression. "I'll have a scotch on the rocks." Her tone was abrupt.

Logan stared at his empty glass. "And I'll have whatever it is I've been having." He took her hand. "Forgive me for teasing you, Dori. I really am happy that you came and I have an idea, I think, or should I say I hope, you'll find as exciting as I do. I've pretty much been keeping the lid on the whole thing until I could talk to you because my future plans will depend a great deal on what you have to say."

The drinks arrived. Dori took a long, slow swallow. The scotch was strong and burnt her throat but it tasted good. "Honestly Logan, enough of the courtroom dramatics. I was married to an attorney remember. I am dangling on your every word." Though her manner was flip, she really was more than just mildly intrigued now. Logan stirred the ice around in his glass with the tip of his index finger.

"Well, here it is. As you know I have a resort in Hilton Head and the one in the Adirondacks that you so exquisitely appointed. Not exactly a chain yet but I do hope to acquire and build some more soon, but I want all of them to be of the most exclusive nature and only in the most desirable locations. I want them to be so lavish that there will constantly be a waiting list to book a room regardless of global economic conditions. Remember, the rich as well as the poor shall always be with us."

"That's easier said than done, Logan. A lot of the large hotel outfits are in big trouble. They are hemorrhaging money all over the place."

"That's because they got too greedy. They all expanded too fast, spent all of their money on land and then just built mediocre facilities right next to each other like gas stations on all four corners of a block. They all look alike. Someone needs to show them how it's done. And I modestly propose that that someone is me."

Dori smiled and shook her head at her companion. "Conrad Hilton will not sleep well tonight." Logan ordered another drink for each of them.

"I shall not comment on that cheap shot." Logan continued. "I have just acquired one of the finest stretches of beach property in the entire Atlantic. I have mortgaged my soul and it will be worth it."

"Where could it be?" Dori asked. "The Bahamas and the Virgin Islands are already exploding with hotels."

Logan finished chewing an ice cube. "It's a little farther south than that." He paused and took a sip of his drink. He winked. "It's in Miranda, in the West Indies."

"The West Indies?" Dori looked directly across the table at him. "You can't be serious, especially Miranda. Isn't that the island where they had a big native revolution about four years ago?"

"The same," he said with a wry smile.

"It was a political hotbed. The tourists left in droves and all of the hotels went bankrupt."

"That's why I have been able to pick up the land so cheaply now."

"You're mad!"

"Not totally. Things have settled down. The island has won its independence from the British and it is now under native rule. The new black Prime Minister is eager to bring tourism back to the island on a grand scale. He wants Miranda to be a showplace as much as I do, to set an example for the other islands, to let them know that it can be done. Because aside from their exportation of nutmeg, cinnamon, and a few other spices, their entire economy is supported by tourism. I bought two of the vacated hotels. One was a Madison Norwood development. The other belonged to the Paradise Inn chain. I picked them up in a kind of distress sale, so to speak."

17

"So to speak." Dori chorused.

"Those poor bastards," he continued. "They had spread themselves so thin that even now, when the time is right, they don't have the necessary capital to reopen them themselves."

"Well, don't forget, Mr. Hart, perhaps they haven't had the benefit of your Cornell education."

"Education my ass!" Logan barked. "A group of third graders could have done a better job of management. But that is beside the point now."

"I don't think so," Dori insisted. "What makes you think you can do any better?"

"Well, for one thing, the political climate is entirely in my favor, and secondly," he took a hesitant breath, "I am hoping that I will have you to help me."

"What?"

"Now don't say anything until you hear my idea. I want you to move to Miranda as part of the team I'm assembling to renovate the hotel. I have already hired a top-flight architect to redesign the area between the two so that they can be joined together. I have three landscape geniuses down there already, studying the local agriculture and terrain, making sketches and proposals. They will have them finalized and to me by the first of the year. I want you to be in charge of decorating the entire place. You will have cart blanch. You can hire as many assistants as you need, but with the understanding that they shall all be under your direct supervision. I have total faith in your taste and judgment. If you want to do the whole thing in shades of black and blue, then go ahead. Whatever you say goes. I'll give you a budget generous enough to redecorate Windsor Castle. I want this resort to be the shining star of the Caribbean."

"You don't want a hotel. You want a monument."

"So what?" Logan became defensive. "If it works, it works."

"And if it doesn't?" Dori asked quietly.

"That is a possibility I refuse to even consider."

He was serious. Dori examined his face. The mellow, easygoing expression had vanished. The angles of his square jaw seemed more pronounced and exact. His grey eyes looked enormous and defiant, but beneath it all, Dori sensed a current of fearful desperation.

"Logan, exactly how much do you have riding on this deal?"

He drained his glass. "Everything," he said simply. "I have put all of my proverbial eggs into one basket. If this thing flops, Chase Manhattan will own my holdings in the states and I'll be lucky if I can land a job managing a flop house in the Bronx."

"Then why are you doing all of this?"

"Dori, I am forty-seven years old. Last year my wife ran off with a philosophy teacher from City College because, she said that life had, to quote her, 'ceased to have meaning.' Now you tell me what the hell am I supposed to get from that? I have two kids in college who only bother to get in touch with me when they max out their credit cards. And I have a nymphomaniac for a secretary whom I screw on Tuesday and Thursday afternoon because those are the only times she can fit me in, pardon the pun. I don't know if it's male menopause or what, but I've got this dream and I am going to play it out. I've got nothing to lose but millions of dollars and my remaining shred or two of sanity."

Dori had really not been prepared for this type of soul-bearing confessional, and though she realized her questions brought it on, it made her feel awkwardly uncomfortable. "I'm sorry, Logan. I didn't mean to press you into telling me all that. Forgive me."

He looked up from his glass at her. "Forget it. It's not your fault. "I had this need to unburden myself and," his face brightened and his mouth spread into a slight smile, "now that I have your sympathetic compassion, you may find it more difficult turning down my offer."

"Why you…"

"Ah-ah-ah. Everything I told you is true. I just scheduled the timing of the story to my advantage, I hope. Come on now. Think about the opportunity this would be for you. You would have an entire resort upon which to vent your creative spleen. Think of frolicking in a tropical paradise. No more tight-assed matrons with the taste of chorus girls telling you to do everything in tones of hot pink and green velvet. You wouldn't have to deal with anymore nouveau-rich gay guys who order marble statues of little boys squirting water out of their cocks."

"Logan!" Dori teased. "You certainly know how to turn a phrase!"

"Oh come on. You know it's true. In your business the only people who can afford your services are so obnoxious I am amazed you are not mainlining Valium just to keep going."

"I worked for you, remember."

"I am the exception to the rule."

He was right of course in his descriptions of the vast majority of her clients. She was trying to recall what working for him had been like. As far as she could remember he had given her pretty much of a free hand. "But Logan, I have given up my career. You know that my son and I are living with my parents now."

"And what are you going to do for the rest of your life? Wade around in buckets of maple syrup and predict the weather by your bunions?"

She burst out laughing. He went on. "I could tell when I talked to you yesterday that you were about ready to hang yourself from your gingham apron strings. Thomas Wolfe said it best: 'You can't go home again,' not for more than a couple of weeks anyway."

Suddenly Dori's eyes swelled with tears and she began to cry softly. "I guess I've had too much to drink."

"Or maybe I've hit a nerve?" Logan asked, reaching across the table for her hand.

"Yes, you have and you're right; I wanted so much to be happy there like I was as a child. Jeremy adores my parents and he feels that he belongs there." She had stopped crying now but her eyes were wet and shiny. They were royal blue. Logan had never seen anything like them before.

"Your son belongs where you are; kids are a lot more resilient than we give them credit for. They can adjust and make friends in almost any surroundings as long as they feel secure. And I am sure you give him feelings of security and would wherever you go. You can't isolate him in a pinecone-covered bubble forever. If you're doing something that makes you happy, he'll be contented too. But if you sacrifice everything for him and are miserable, he'll sense it and bear the guilt. Listen to me." He shrugged his shoulders. "My own family life has gone down the tubes and I'm sounding like an authority on domestic bliss lecturing a room full of expectant mothers." Dori squeezed his hand.

"Don't be too hard on yourself. I know what you are saying is right. I have felt it for a long time. I am going crazy in Vermont. I know now that I need my career, such as it is. Chris knew that. But since his death I've felt that I should devote myself to Jeremy to make up for his loss. But it isn't working." Her voice trailed off.

"The Mary Magdalene of Montpelier, huh?" Logan chided gently and Dori smiled at him.

"Does sound kind of grim, doesn't it?"

"Kind of."

He let go of her hand and sat up straight. "Dori, accept this job. Come to Miranda and bring your little boy. Give it a try. Just for six weeks. If you hate it, you can come back. New England will always be there, and at the very least you'll return with a fantastic tan and Jeremy will have the greatest collection of seashells in Vermont. He'll knock them dead at show and tell."

The same small ingratiating waiter appeared at their side with his usual bad timing. "Sir," he announced. "The table you reserved in the main dining room is now ready for you and your guest."

"Thank you," Logan said.

Dori stood up without saying anything and followed the waiter and Logan into the large rosewood-paneled dining room. A gigantic lighted Christmas tree dominated the center of the room and the air hung heavy with the mingling scents of pine and coffee. A heavyset Italian waiter lumbered over to their table with the menus. He was smiling as though everyone in the place were guests at his private party. "I can honestly say that all of the entrees on the menu are excellent this evening." He winked at Dori. "Our chef is a magician."

Logan grabbed the menu out of Dori's hand and returned it to the startled waiter. "The lady will have bread and water," he announced sternly. Then he turned to Dori who was sitting in stricken silence. "Unless you have decided to accept my offer, then I can expense this dinner." Dori sighed and shook her head addressing the waiter.

"In that case," she began," please bring me the Beef Wellington." Logan beamed a satisfied smile.

"Just bring me a yellow canary. Only kidding, old fellow. I'll have the same as the lady."

Dori was anxious to discuss the specifics of their new business arrangement but Logan was not. "The sales pitch has worn me out. Mind if we just relax for the rest of the night and pretend that we are on a normal date?" He did look emotionally drained. "I promise I'll go over all of the details with you tomorrow."

"O.K. I'm a bit wrung out myself but my mind is whirling with questions."

"Tomorrow," he said softly. "Be patient; just enjoy the evening."

They did. The waiter had been right about the chef. The dinner was delicious. The Wellington had been cooked to perfection. Dori hadn't realized how hungry she had been. They both had strawberry-filled crepes for dessert.

"Where in the world do you think they got such fresh berries this time of year?" Dori wondered.

"Oh, I saw them arrive this afternoon."

"You did?"

"Yeah," Logan winked. "A flock of two hundred carrier pigeons were flying in from Australia holding each berry by the stem."

"Logan, I am sure that lines like that killed vaudeville."

It was close to midnight when they left the dining room. "Would you like to go sit by the fire in the bar and have a brandy?" Logan seemed to be getting his second wind.

"No, I think I have seen enough of that leering waiter for one night."

"Well, then let me have a bottle sent up to your room, just one drink to toast your very wise decision."

Dori found herself agreeing to Logan's suggestion even though she was exhausted. "Alright, but give me a few minutes. I haven't even had a chance to wash my face. I feel as though I were born wearing these clothes."

"Fine. I'll take care of the arrangements and be up in a bit."

Dori had a lovely room on the tenth floor overlooking Central Park. She kicked off her shoes and rubbed her feet for a minute before going into the bathroom. She dipped a washcloth into hot steaming water and ran it over her face, breathing into it, creating a warm soothing vapor. It felt fantastic and she longed to take a bath. She looked in the bathroom mirror shaking her short hair into place.

When a knock came at the door a few minutes later she was feeling strangely rested. She opened the door to find Logan carrying a tray with two brandy snifters and a bottle of Courvoisier. He had placed a white linen towel over his arm.

"Funny how all of the people in this hotel look alike," she said. "Can't tell the guests from the help."

Logan came in and set the tray down.

"Oh, the guy in the bar started giving me some routine about how it would be an hour before they could get the stuff up here. Just another glaring example of poor management." He opened the bottle and poured them each a generous serving. They went into the adjoining sitting room where Logan proposed a toast.

"To the coming of the new year and to the success of Miranda." Dori touched her glass to Logan's and took a sip. Like the scotch earlier, it was warm and soothing. Logan lit a few logs in the small fireplace and they both sat down in forest-green leather wingback chairs in front of it. The wood was dry and burnt easily, crackling and hissing, sending soft tentacles of amber light into the room. For quite a while neither of them said anything. But it was a pleasant kind of easy silence. Finally, Logan leaned over the arm of his chair.

"You haven't slept with anyone since your husband died, have you?"

Dori was taken aback and instantly angry.

"Do you screen all of your perspective employees this thoroughly?"

He ignored the question.

"Well, you haven't, have you?

"No," she answered flatly. "Not that it's any of your business."

"Then sleep with me."

"I don't love you."

"Do you like me?"

"Up until this minute, yes."

"Then that's even better. The first time you make love again any man will be a disappointment. Better a friend disappoint you than a lover."

"This conversation is absurd. And even if your demented logic holds some merit, I am not ready yet. I think I've made enough decisions for one day."

"Can I take that to mean that we won't be spending the night together?"

Dori couldn't help laughing. "You are perceptive, Logan."

"Then I guess I'll have no need for this." He extracted a long, narrow, small gold box from the breast pocket of his blazer. Dori looked at it with a puzzled expression. He snapped it open to reveal a nylon bristle toothbrush with a gold handle matching the carrying case.

"Dunhill's. My secretary gave it to me for my birthday."

"What a thoughtful girl," Dori said sarcastically, leading Logan to the door.

They made arrangements to meet for breakfast at ten the following morning. Logan had just started down the hall when Dori called to him. "Just remember, Tuesday afternoon is just around the corner. Your secretary will be waiting."

"Be still my heart," he said dramatically, and disappeared into the elevator.

Dori slept a deep, dreamless sleep and awoke feeling relaxed and renewed, even if a wee bit hung over. From her bed she looked out of the far window to see flurries of snow descending. It had probably been falling all night long. She sighed and pulled the covers up around her neck, trying not to think of her drive back to Fairlee. She took the hot bath she had been too tired to take the night before and dressed warmly in a pair of wool slacks and a pullover sweater.

Logan was already in the dining room having coffee and reading the *Times* when she arrived. He too looked as though he had slept well. He was casually dressed in a pair of brown corduroy pants and a navy-blue pinstriped shirt. If he had not revealed his age to Dori, she would have guessed him to be much younger than forty-seven. He had thick, shiny auburn hair that looked as though it belonged on the head of an English schoolboy, as well as deep brown eyes and an attractive angular jaw line. When he saw her approaching his table he stood up smiling expansively at first then scowling. "You look terrific," he said sadly.

"Well don't sound so disappointed."

"It's just that I have been getting such comfort thinking that you had probably been up all night pacing the floor fighting the impulse to rush to my room."

Dori sighed and sat down, shaking her head. "Oh Logan, please, enough." She said it gently but he got the message.

"O.K. Sorry. Now, how about some orange juice and an order of eggs benedict?"

"Sounds delicious. I'm ravenous."

They discussed the logistics of the new arrangement over breakfast. He wanted her to be prepared to leave at the beginning of January.

"There's a kind of eccentric American couple who have lived on the island for the last twenty years running a small hotel, more like a series of bungalows, really, nothing elaborate but clean and comfortable. It's on a hillside overlooking the beach and the property I now own. Anyway, I'll rent one of the places for you and Jeremy. You'll have a local native girl to help with everything, of course, and I'll arrange for you to have some kind of car. The roads on the island resemble the General Motors proving grounds I'm afraid."

"What about school for Jeremy?"

"Believe it or not, there is a fine small English school there. Even though the island is run by an independent black government, the British still have a diplomat living in the old governor's mansion. He has no power of course. He is a figurehead essentially. He entertains visiting officials and the Prime Minister tolerates it all fairly well. It would serve no purposes to burn bridges. I'm getting off the track. The school is there for the sons and daughters of the group of permanent European and American residents as well as for the children of the island. The English governor has two of his children attending. I think you will be very pleased with the place. And Jeremy will be able to walk down the beach to school. I've given up the lease on my apartment and am living here until after the first, when I will move down to Miranda—lock, stock, and barrel. I am hoping you will be ready to leave then, too."

"That's less than a month."

A waiter came over and poured them more hot coffee.

"There's so much to do."

"Like changing your mind?" Logan asked.

"No. I'm not going to do that. I may have accepted your offer on an impulse but your arguments were persuasive and logical. Jeremy and I will be ready by the first."

"Good"

Dori glanced down at the front page of the paper lying by Logan's plate. "Blizzard hits New England," she read out loud. "That's just swell; I can't drive back in that."

"Don't," Logan said. "Leave your car here. I'll take care of it for you. Soon you won't be needing it anyway. We can store it here. I'm keeping a corporate suite here all year because I know it will be necessary for all of us connected with this operation to make trips back to the city periodically. You probably most of all, in the beginning at least. Maybe you will want a car here then. After you get a feel for the place and talk the plans over with Phil, you'll have to come back and meet with some suppliers and order fabric and...."

"Wait a minute." Dori cut him off in mid-sentence. "Is the architect you hired by any chance Phillip Graham?"

"Why yes. Do you know him?"

"Don't be cute Logan. That's like asking if I've ever heard of Frank Lloyd Wright. People frame Philip Graham's napkin doodles. He is one of the most innovative, creative young building designers in the country."

"Well. Now maybe you'll believe me when I tell you I'm serious about this deal."

"I believe you," she said softly.

After breakfast Dori went up to pack while Logan took care of the plane reservation. While collecting her things in the bathroom she saw her plain gold wedding band lying on the side of the bathtub. She had lost a little weight recently and the ring had been fitting her loosely so she removed it whenever she bathed or showered. She didn't realize until this instant that she had forgotten to put it back on when she dressed earlier. She picked it up and began to slide it back on her finger and then stopped. She thought of the irritating waiter in the bar the evening before as well as of the things Logan had said. She put the ring in a small satin jewelry pouch sewn in the lining of her leather suitcase. Then she went over to the window and looked out again at the cascading snow. It was the same snow she had romped through as a child, shrieking with delight, falling on her back, moving her arms and legs making the impression of angels. It was the same snow that had, with vicious silence, killed her husband. She turned away and pulled the curtain angrily and began sobbing. She had had enough of it. She had had enough of this constant tension produced by trying to separate the painful memories from the pleasant ones. The past, she realized now, like her wedding band, had to be put away for safekeeping. In a few moments she stopped crying, finished her packing, and left the room. She was smiling, almost excited for January to arrive.

II

It was the third morning without sun, just the constant cloud cover making the air heavy and damp. Claire Rutledge stood on the terrace of her bungalow, which was built into the hillside overlooking Castle Beach. Her eyes started at the far stretch of land and worked their way back across the sand, past the two vacant resorts until her gaze settled upon the thatched roofs of the changing rooms and garden bar of her own hotel. She watched as Thelma, her corpulent West Indian maid, snapped orders at the beach boys to set up the deck chairs and supply the changing rooms with fresh towels. She spoke to them in that unique blend of English and Creole French, which the natives reserved for their own use. Unlike other nationalities that appreciated and applauded the foreigner's attempts to struggle through in the local vernacular, the natives of Miranda resented outsiders even partially mastering their language, as though it were something that could be stolen from them and sold. Thus, through the years they had complicated it to the point where they themselves had difficulty at times understanding each other; Claire knew this and never attempted to deal with them in their own tongue, though she was certain that she could. Nevertheless, she rarely tired of listening as they bantered back and forth in the strange rhythmic dialect.

Thelma looked up and saw her. She cupped her short plump fingers around her mouth before calling. "I will be right up to fix you coffee as soon as I am sure that these jackasses are working. Two cruise ships expected this afternoon. Nellie brought in some nice fresh sweet bread from town. I'll bring it up when I come, if I don't eat it all first!" She laughed loudly at her own joke and then turned her attention back to the young boys. They too had caught sight of Mrs. Rutledge on her terrace and quickened their work pace, lining up brightly colored canvas deck chairs on the grassy slope near the bar. When they were finished four neat rows of red, yellow, and blue chairs faced expectantly toward the bleached sand and softly churning turquoise sea.

Claire went back inside and closed the sliding screen door behind her. She went into the bedroom and climbed back into her unmade bed. She watched as a small bright green lizard climbed up the wall opposite her bed. She remembered how terrified she used to be of them when she first arrived. But now, they had just become part of the décor, coming and going at will and impossible to keep out. There was a calendar hanging on the wall above her chest of drawers. She squinted up at it from the pillow. It was the last Saturday in November. She sighed and closed her eyes. Another Thanksgiving had come and gone. She had cooked a turkey, as usual, for herself and her husband and for their small circle of American and European friends living on the island. But the turkey was the only relation the day had to any of the traditional Thanksgivings she had experienced growing up in South Carolina. In Miranda the most significant thing about Thanksgiving was that it marked the beginning of the tourist season, such as it was. This past dinner the talk had been of the impending arrival of Logan Hart and what his investment would mean to the island.

"This is really going to be the start of something very good for all of us," Howard, her husband, had said. "They're gonna need me. I know how to deal with these natives. Plus, I know all of the charter boat captains around. Yep, this might just be the break we've been waiting for." He paused to pour himself another glass of champagne. He was such a huge man that he made the fragile glass appear as though it had been stolen from a child's dollhouse. "The publicity this whole operation will bring to Miranda, well, it's the kind we need." He was animated and excited and drank an entire bottle of champagne himself.

Victor and Allison Trent, the British governor and his wife shared, to a degree, Howard's optimism. But they were a bit more skeptical. "We'll just have to wait and see," Victor cautioned. "We really have no alternative at this point." His wife shook her head in his direction.

"Well, she added, "any activity will be better than this state of limbo we're all walking around in."

Frank LeBeau, a French writer in residence on the island for the past five years, was also intrigued by the prospects of "new blood," as he referred to the promised influx of Americans.

"Speaking of blood," interrupted Ransom Turner, "this will mean a whole new batch of tourists to treat for all of the mysterious island maladies. At a hundred dollars per visit I ought to do quite well." Turner was an M.D. with a somewhat vague past who had been living on the island ever since Claire and Howard had arrived. It had been rumored that he left the states under questionable circumstances. But whatever reputation he had fled from in America, the islanders held him in the highest regard. He performed numerous kinds of minor surgery in a small clinic. He also administered medicines quite freely. Thus the natives claimed that he could cure everything. When the cruise ships were docked he would dine with the ship's physician. Claire had required his services upon occasion for some recurring migraine headaches. He was always quite professional in his manner and appeared to be extremely competent.

Yes, it seemed that everyone was very eager over the prospects of the two abandoned resorts being restored and reopened. And they were all ready to welcome the new comers to Miranda. The only person who had not been caught up in the spirit of the evening had been Claire.

A sharp knock on the door caught her by surprise and she bolted up in bed. "Yes, What is it?"

"It's just Thelma. I have your breakfast. You want me to set it up on the terrace? You can watch the cruisers coming in."

Claire felt the slow steady pounding behind her eyes begin again. "That will be fine Thelma. I'll be out shortly."

"O.K." Thelma began to hum gaily as she retreated from the doorway.

Claire reached for the small glass bottle on the nightstand. It was filled with capsules of some kind of powerful painkiller. Dr. Turner had "prescribed" the medication to treat her headaches. She didn't ask him where he got his drugs and he never offered to discuss it. She was just grateful that he had found something to provide her with a short respite from the relentless pain. She went into the bathroom and took several of the pills, looking at herself in the mirror as she swallowed. She was in her early fifties, but due to the constant exposure to the harsh sun and sea winds her skin was rough and creased, with countless lines around her eyes, causing her to look much older than her actual age. She dyed her curly hair red with various concoctions prepared by the natives and applied in the single-chair beauty shop in St. Phillips, the nearby capital city. Her hair was shoulder length and unruly. It flew about her face and she was always brushing it off her forehead with a gesture that had become habitual. She wore the look of someone who had once been remarkably attractive, perhaps even beautiful. But a stranger meeting her would know from her face that life had not been easy or pleasurable for her.

Yet the face reflected in the mirror this morning, and every morning, was not the face that Claire Rutledge saw. She always saw the same pretty young girl with the soft creamy skin and the wavy auburn hair that shown in the light like a glass of rich brandy. And she would stare into the mirror for long periods of time just taking comfort from the lovely, gentle countenance smiling back at her. And along with the perfect face she had also managed to idealize her past in her mind as well. She would tell each new visitor to the island, for she had already told all of the current residents, about the fabulous career she had abandoned in Hollywood to move to Miranda with Howard. "The studio was livid. I broke my contract and packed up and left right in the middle of casting for *The Graduate*. I was told later that I could have had the part that went to Katherine Ross if I had stayed. I mean I would have had much more screen chemistry with Dustin Hoffman than she ever did." Then she would sigh in the middle of her story and throw her head back. "But this whole thing was so important to Howie that I really had no choice at the time."

Most of the natives believed her since she kept an old Bell and Howell projector and would run movie clips for them in which she appeared most often as a nonspeaking extra. None of the tourists believed her but they found her stories colorful. And after several drinks of the heavy rum punch served at the garden bar, they wanted to believe her. Howard never spoiled her tales with the truth, though at times her exaggerations and distortions of the facts (he would call them lies) frightened him. When they had first moved to the island he had encouraged her to elaborate and embellish upon the lives they had left behind in an attempt to gain the acceptance and respect of the locals. But he had always been certain that Claire knew it was all pure fabrication. But now he wasn't sure that she did know.

Claire Cambert left South Carolina in 1948 when she was seventeen years old. She was the youngest of four children. Her father was an accountant for a tobacco firm in Charleston and her mother was a seamstress. Her brothers had all gone off to the service before she was fifteen. Although two of them had died overseas, Claire always envied them and the exciting lives they must have led up until the end. She would read the letters they sent home over and over, imagining all of the places they had been while her jumpy mother just wrung her hands and whined and prayed for their safe return. Claire really didn't know them well, and was only mildly sad in a detached way when they died. But she used the occasions of their deaths to swoon and take to her bed vowing never to forgive the world for its injustice. She saw immediately that her feigned despondence produced rapid results. Relatives hovered around her with gifts and offers of rides in the park and dinners out to "cheer her up." It was then that she made the decision that she would go to Hollywood, where people believed in the romantic spirit and lived it.

When she first arrived in Los Angeles she took a job in a hospital as a night telephone operator; during the day she went from one sleazy talent agency to another. She slept with anyone who would offer to get her an audition. She had no qualms about her actions. They were all part of her dream of becoming a great actress. She went out on every possible interview and even spent a month's salary to have a portfolio of photographs taken. Eventually she managed to get enough work so that she could boast that "acting" was her career. But her big break never came. She was never discovered, not by anyone except Howard Rutledge anyway.

Howard had been a great college football player for the University of Southern California during the late fifties. He had even played a little pro ball, but resulting knee injuries forced him out of active participation in the sport. He knew that he wanted to remain close to the game in some way so he borrowed enough money to open a sporting goods store in North Hollywood. Some of the movie studios used him as an advisor when they were making pictures in which there would be a football sequence, usually the college-coed-meets-the-college-athlete type film. It was as an advisor on one of these pictures in 1963 that Howard first saw Claire Cambert.

By that time Claire was over thirty, too old to be cast as one of the campus innocents, but she had the role of faculty sponsor in one of the girls' dormitories. In one particular scene she was required to escort the girls to the bleaches to watch football practice. Howard was showing several of the young male actors how to throw a pass and make it look as though they knew what they were doing. After several practice throws the director decided that it was time for a take. Howard came over to the make shift bleachers and sat down next to Claire.

"Boy, working on this set really takes me back to my school days," he offered by way of introduction.

"I never went to college." Claire said, and then added bitterly, "As you can see, I was too busy becoming a famous movie star."

Immediately, Howard felt protective toward her. "It's not easy making it in this town. Not in this racket. Anyway, some people just don't know when they see perfection. I think you're more beautiful than any of these girls," he concluded surveying the rows of ingénues.

"Really? Tell that to the director."

"I did." Howard smiled.

Claire liked him right away. He treated her as if she were made of fine porcelain. They had gone out to dinner three times before he kissed her. He would drive her from audition to audition. And when she didn't get a part he would try to bolster her ego by telling her repeatedly that the only women who made it had to put out for everyone in town. She feigned shock and embarrassment at his remarks, and he would apologize for being so indelicate. From the very beginning their relationship wove itself into a tapestry of deceit, she pretending to be the unblemished puritan, he attempting to personify strength and subdued power.

On one occasion an agent sent Claire out on an audition for what he promised to be "the job" to get in Hollywood this season. As it turned out the picture was to be a soft porn film done by a couple of backyard producers with one thirty-millimeter camera and a lot of flesh. Claire didn't shock easily at this point. But at last she was forced to come to terms, momentarily, with what she had become: a woman bordering on middle age who had nothing to her credit but a plethora of bit parts and the last vestiges of a few hopes.

"Take off your clothes, sweetie," one of the "producers" said to her as well as to several others in the small dirty room.

All of the women hesitated a bit at first. Then one shrugged her shoulders and stripped and the rest reluctantly followed her example. Claire had to admit it wasn't the most bazaar thing she had been asked to do in this city. Still, she knew she could never allow Howard to know what was happening in this dark apartment while he waited outside. Both of the young bearded men involved walked by the group of naked females several times, like medical examiners at Ellis Island, looking for imperfections. Finally the older, and more repulsive of the two, came up close to Claire. His eyes were vacant and impersonal. He smelled of strong, cheap tobacco and mint chewing gum. "You can split sister. We ain't making *Lassie Come Home*."

Claire's entire body went rigid. Suddenly she felt more degraded than she thought possible. She had been set up. Her agent let her walk into this. Her eyes welled with tears and her throat ached. She threw on her clothes and ran out into the bright afternoon sun to the welcoming sight of Howard's blue Chevy convertible, double-parked, waiting for her. "It wasn't for me," she said and Howard understood.

It was that night that they took hamburgers from a take out restaurant and went up to park on Mulholland Drive like a couple of teenagers. Howard had stopped and bought a bottle of red wine and a carton of Dixie cups. The sun was just setting when Howard maneuvered the car into a choice space high above the San Fernando Valley. From this vantage point they were also able to see all the way to the beach at Santa Monica. The radio was playing and Johnny Mathis was singing, "It's not just for what you are yourself that I love you like I do, but for what I am when I am with you." That was the night that Howard proposed and Claire accepted.

They went to Howard's small apartment off of Sunset Boulevard and made love, for the first time. Howard proved to be an adept and passionate lover, but equally tender. That night he made love to Claire tenderly as if she had been a virgin. She realized that he must have known that she wasn't. But he never asked and she never told him anything.

A Justice of the Peace in Pasadena married them the following week. For the next few years Claire continued to look for acting roles while Howard managed the sports shop. He was still supportive of Claire's ambitions and shared her minor triumphs and colossal defeats. Their lives had settled into a kind of routine. But late in 1967 things changed abruptly.

Most of the major movie studios had come to the realization in the early sixties that television was not going to go away like a bad dream, and that if they wanted to survive in the industry they had better kiss and make up. Thus the larger companies were developing television subsidiaries of their own: Universal, Paramount, Warner's, and others. And new theatrical companies were being spawned every day. One such company was Associated Artists Incorporated, a slick outfit comprised of many of the old-time film stars and Los Angeles business heavy weights.

They had bought up most of the existing vacant land in the area and were literally cranking out television series by the gross; some of them sold to the networks and some of them didn't. But the successes exceeded the failures so they were expanding their operations constantly, constructing sets literally overnight. But they needed one more piece of prime real estate to make their coup complete— Howard Rutledge's sporting goods store and an adjoining field and running track he also owned. He used the track to coach young kids who were interested in playing football. It was the only section of land in the area that remained uninvolved in the workings of Hollywood. In effect, it served as a kind of buffer zone separating the Western set of Paramount from the World War II set of United Artists.

All of the studios wanted the property and were willing to pay Howard far in excess of its worth. Claire had been urging him to hold out until she had time to decide the perfect way in which to reinvest the money. "Don't worry, Howie," she would say. "They want it. They'll wait!" But Howard wasn't as certain as his wife and was very eager to accept one of the offers. Yet, he was smart enough to realize that Claire possessed real business sense. So, he reluctantly abided by her decisions. At last she made up her mind what to do with the money.

She had returned early one afternoon from her weekly rounds of booking agencies. But unlike most days she did not seem depressed or upset. "Close the store, Howie. I want to talk to you right away."

Her husband made apologies to the young couple he was outfitting with ski equipment, asking them to return in a half hour. "What's the matter?" he wanted to know once they were alone.

"Nothing. Now look!" she demanded, thrusting a group of pamphlets at him. The name of a real estate company was rubber stamped on the front of them.

"So what are these?"

"Well, read one," she snapped in annoyance.

Howard sighed and opened the front flap of one of them. He read out loud. "For Sale: Ten acres of land and a charming cottage on the lovely island of Miranda in the British West Indies. Asking price: $50,000. "What about it?" he asked, still mystified.

"This is it honey. Let's buy this place. The fellows at the reality company said this spot is going to be the new playground of the rich, a whole chain of islands, with beautiful calm seas, trade winds, and friendly natives. We can build a hotel there. I can entertain the guests and manage the rooms. You can teach the tourists scuba diving and sailing, and even football." She giggled like a schoolgirl. Her face was flushed, her eyes wide and shining.

Howard said nothing for a very long time. He didn't even know where the West Indies was exactly. But Claire's travel log description sounded wonderful. To him, her idea was sheer madness, but no more insane than the amount of money the studios were willing to pay him for his tiny store and dusty field. He pictured himself sailing and swimming. And he pictured Claire hovering about, taking charge of all the guests and loving it.

He didn't allow himself to think about the actual execution of her plan, the logistics of the deal. He just knew that somehow things would work. He would be happy to get his wife out of this environment totally and forever. The last several years had been particularly hard on her. She was competing for jobs with girls who were still in their teens and newer to town than she was. He knew that she had suffered in countless ways. Perhaps now she might even consider having a child. He grabbed her by the hand. "Come on, let's go to Associated Artists and tell them the good news."

So, a few months later they moved to Miranda, with the deed to the property they had never seen and seventy thousand dollars in cash left after the sale of the store and track and the purchase of the island property.

At that time Miranda was still under British rule. The whole of the West Indies had a rather strange history. Each of the large islands and the majority of the more insignificant ones had been colonized in turn by the Spanish, English, French, and the Dutch. These foreign sailors had come across most of the islands by accident on their way to explore other parts of the world. It had often been argued by scholars that journals from Columbus's travels indicated that he was perhaps the first explorer to stumble upon Miranda. The proof was never definitive enough to warrant a universal acceptance of the theory.

What was known was that the English had established the first settlement of any lasting importance in St. Phillips, the principal harbor of Miranda. In the ensuing years it was learned that the island had been inhabited since 1400 by a race called the Caribes, a nomadic group of warlike people who had wandered by land and sea from South America. From accounts of their victory battle celebrations over neighboring tribes, it was generally agreed that the Caribes were, initially anyway, cannibals. They would eat portions of their prisoners of war taken capture in battle.

The French were the first Europeans to gain total control of the island. They ruled from the middle of the seventeenth century to the middle of the eighteenth, when at last the British fought for and won dominance of Miranda. But the battle for control was to go on between these two rivals for many years to come, with the British ultimately left in possession of the island.

Many fortunes were made and lost in the West Indies during the nineteenth century. Sugar cane plantations flourished, managed by powerful Englishmen and worked by the native Mirandans. And even after the Act of Emancipation freed the slaves in the 1860s, a colonial system of government endured with a rigid economic organization focused on one crop: sugar.

But the British had more to contend with than simply the natives. They had to dominate the elements as well. There were always threats of hurricanes and volcanic eruptions. Nevertheless, the soil was so fertile and the climate so generally favorable that the yields were great. And the island flourished.

Yet, even after the Second World War, when the earth settled into a type of nervous peace and prosperity, and the vacation resorts were beginning to boom in the Bahamas and in the northern Caribbean, Miranda remained untouched by big developers.

The towns were small and comprised mainly of the natives, all of whom were connected in some way to the British plantations. The architecture of the island reflected the combinations of European styles: the red tiled roofs and arched windows and doors inherited from the Spanish stood next to small Georgian Colonial structures, complete with columns and domes. Many of these places might be furnished with smatterings of French provincial furniture, some copied, some authentic. The French had left much behind when they fled the island after defeat at the hands of the British.

, The homes of the natives had a brick or stucco exterior painted in soft shades of pink and lime green or other mild pastels. The English on the island lived well, with maids and houseboys and every possible convenience that they could bring from home, down to bulky English furniture and countless silver tea sets. But although they tried to cling to their regimented and tightly structured lives, they found the weather too warm and the lavishly abundant and colorful vegetation too seductive to resist. Thus the pace of life on the island was slow, hypnotically rhythmic, and peaceful. It was into this environment that Claire and Howard Rutledge came.

, They arrived in a single-engine plane, which flew between Barbados and Miranda once a week carrying mail and the occasional passenger. The flight had been noisy and rough, but the landing had been worse. The "airport" at St. Phillips consisted of a small wooden hut and a short, rocky runway, which dropped off abruptly into the ocean. When Claire felt the plane descend to approach the dirt landing strip she dug her fingernails into the palm of her hands and closed her eyes. Howard wasn't concerned at all, and in fact had managed to keep the young ex-Navy pilot engaged in conversation the entire trip, although that necessitated both parties constantly shouting to be heard above the engine noise.

They were met at the plane by Dr. Turner. He had been friends with the previous owners of the property and had generously offered to help the Rutledges get settled.

"You two got a steal. That land is going to be worth a fortune someday. I would have bought it myself, but I've been a bit strapped since I moved down." He was short and overweight and was perspiring excessively in the hot afternoon sun. He kept blotting his forehead with a handkerchief as he spoke. "I've been here close to ten years now. Hard to believe. Time passes so fast. And at the same time it feels like it's standing still. Know what I mean?"

He drove them to their new home in some kind of a small French car. The roads were as rocky and dusty as the airstrip had been but the doctor maneuvered the car gracefully around the tight curves. It was well after they had passed through the harbor of St. Phillips before Claire realized that the few cars here drove on the left side of the road.

"That's the only way the Brits know how to drive," Turner explained. "And the natives don't pay any attention to traffic laws anyway. They just jump behind the wheel and go, trying not to hit anything." He laughed good-naturedly.

"Claire! Claire! Come here!" Howard's voice pierced her thoughts and startled her. She dropped the bottle of pills in the sink. Fortunately the cap was on and none were lost to the drain. She returned to the bedroom to find her husband standing in the doorway holding a huge crate filled with bottles of dark rum. "I'm taking this down to the bar now. The cruisers are arriving. I already saw one of the transport boats being lowered over the side. The first group of people will be here any minute." He came further into the room and rested the crate on the edge of the bed. "Hope there will be enough fellows for a little game of touch football. You coming out? Thelma said you haven't eaten your breakfast."

Claire was tying her hair back into a brightly colored scarf. "I'm sorry, Howie. I've just been sitting here remembering when we first came. And I've been thinking about Hollywood and…"

Howard knew what was coming and sighed deeply, shifting the weight of the carton back to his arms. "Look, this thing is heavy. I've got to get it down there. Mandy is setting up the bar. Please get dressed and come outside. The weather is clearing." He turned and left, leaving the door to the bedroom open.

Claire followed him and stood on the terrace watching as he carried the liquor down the steep wooded steps leading from the house to the lawn and to the beach below. He was dressed in khaki Bermuda shorts and a dark blue short-sleeved cotton shirt. He was tan. And although he had put on weight over the years he was still handsome and athletic looking. Claire was his junior by five years but appeared to be the older of the two.

She walked out to the terrace and poured herself a cup of the coffee Thelma had set out. It was lukewarm and too strong but she drank it anyway. Resting inside the shelter of the small bay she saw the huge cruise ships. From the flags and the markings on their sides one was probably Norwegian, the other French. They always dropped anchor in the middle of the bay and lowered dinghies to bring all interested passengers onto shore for the afternoon. This was the first group of tourists who had dared to come since the revolution and the change in power. Howard, along with the rest of their small staff, was anxious to make a good impression. That hadn't always been so necessary.

Claire remembered when the waters had been dotted with boats of all descriptions, from luxury cruisers to the smaller private yachts of the floating rich. She and Howard had started with one small bungalow. Over a ten-year period they had built twenty of the airy, spacious units. Each one had two small bedrooms, a bath, a compact functional kitchen, and a comfortable living room with a terrace overlooking the spectacular bay. They were decorated modestly with things she had been able to acquire on the island, or persuade the natives to make. They had spent the majority of the money they had on advertising in the more prestigious glossy travel magazines. Slowly they built up a loyal clientele who would lease a bungalow for the season, beginning in December and ending in June. And even when the two new hotels on the beach began opening, their old guests still preferred staying at the Cinnamon Inn, as they ended up naming their resort. Though less modern and flamboyant than the newer facilities, the cottages were private and secluded. There was a pervading atmosphere of a little friendly compound of semi-permanent residents.

Every Sunday Howard would organize putting contests on the lawn above the beach. It had been Claire's idea to build a group of changing rooms next to the garden bar for use of the daytime guests, coming to the island from the cruise ships. They charged ten dollars for a room, towels, and showers, use of their private stretch of beach and one tropical rum punch from the bar. The drinks cost three dollars after that, but no one stopped after only one. The whole operation brought in a respectable stream of revenue. Things were really going along well. And Claire and Howard were contented, Howard with his sports and Claire with a fresh captive audience to entertain each day. She was busy making plans to construct a little theater on the island. She would offer drama classes to all and perhaps even produce small plays.

But in the early 1970s the revolution came without warning. The natives struck against English domination and fought for their independence. They terrorized the foreigners and declared a state of siege, ordering the hotels to evacuate their guests from the island. Even Claire and Howard, though they had made friends with the natives, were forced to take refuge in the Governor's House with the Trents, Frank LeBeau, Ransom Turner, and the rest of the ex-patriots.

For a few weeks the eyes of the world were on this small speck of earth in the Atlantic. It was because of this focus of attention on the tiny emerging nation fighting for its independence that England acquiesced to the demands of the insurgents. The people of Miranda were granted their freedom from three centuries of British control. And while the natives celebrated in the streets of St. Phillips, the real casualties of the war, the hotel owners and charter boat skippers, packed up and left. All except Claire and Howard Rutledge. They had no place else to go.

They had worked so hard to build up Cinnamon Inn that it had become their surrogate child, demanding all of their attention, devotion and resources. So they stayed. Allison and Victor Trent also remained. They were invited to stay by John Salter, the newly appointed black prime minister of Miranda. He felt that the Trents could be useful in helping the island make a seamless transition to self-rule. Victor's superiors in the home office agreed that it was a good idea for him to maintain the Government House and to watch over the considerable British interests on the island.

It was during the next three years that Claire's attitude began to change. She started to hate all of it—Cinnamon Inn, the island, and their entire way of life here. They still advertised. But no one came. Their regulars canceled en masse. No cruise ships ventured into the harbor; the pristine white sand beaches and polished turquoise waters were deserted. Claire would walk up and down Castle Beach staring into the windows of the empty shore front hotels. The flat glass stared back like the eye sockets of a thousand dead men rotting on a battlefield. When she would get to the far end of the beach she would turn around and look up at the side of the hill sprinkled with the white stucco cottages of Cinnamon Inn. The vacant terraces were gaping mouths, wide and laughing, mocking. It was then that the headaches had started.

They went through most of the money they had saved just to maintain the units and grounds and to support themselves. They couldn't sell because there were no buyers. But Claire had almost convinced Howard to take what they had left and move back to the states, holding on to their property until something changed and it could be sold. "There's a big market for good character actresses now, you know," she would tell Howard. "I bet I could get some fantastic parts that would not have been open to me before."

But while Claire came to loath the place, Howard fell more in love with it, protecting and shielding it as one would a frail child. Yet he also knew that the money was running out and that they would have to do something soon. He had grown tired of his wife's whining and was almost persuaded to give her plan a try when word came of Logan Hart's purchase of the two vacant hotels.

"Well, there you are!" Thelma approached Claire on the terrace. "I was beginning to think you were going to stay in bed all day. Want me to make you some fresh coffee?"

Claire looked down at the cup of uninviting, cold, black liquid in her hand. "No thank you, Thelma."

Down below on the beach the small boats were docking, spilling their human cargo onto the shore. Fat old men with flowered bathing suits and pale, white skin plodded their way across the sand carrying shirts and cameras. Middle-aged women in huge straw hats toting bulging purses stopped on their journey to the changing rooms to buy small spice baskets peddled up and down the beach by little island girls. The woven containers were filled with fragrant nutmeg, mace, cinnamon, and saffron, all of which flourished on Miranda. The steel bands were setting up and Mandy, the bartender, was pouring deep-amber rum punch into waiting glasses. Thelma squinted down at him. "That boy is sure mixing with a mighty heavy hand. I'll go down and tell Mr. Rutledge. Otherwise, all that rum'll be drunk up before it's paid for." She started toward the steps leading to the lawn then turned to Claire. "Sure is nice to see all this activity again, huh?" Claire looked down at Howard who was busy signing up people for the putting contest. She didn't answer.

III

Claire Rutledge was not the only one watching the tourists returning to the island. In the Prime Minister's office, high above Castle Beach and Cinnamon Inn, John Salter looked down from his window at the activity below. He watched intently as the dinghies from the luxury liners brought streams of people into shore, where they would splash in the water, lie on the beach, drink rum, and inevitably spend money. He sighed and smiled. It had been a long time. He greeted the return of the tourists with ambivalent feelings, although he knew his approval of the sale of the hotels to Logan Hart was instrumental in their renewed presence. The people needed the revenue generated by the visitors. No one would argue with that fact. Yet he wished that spice, sugar, and banana industries on the island would be enough to sustain the natives. He wished that the people could survive without the exploitation of the travelling wealthy. He closed his eyes and messaged his temples. That was visionary and totally impossible. But he was determined that this time the game would be played according to his rules. After all, he had spent his life to get to this position. And this was only the beginning of what he had planned for himself.

He heard the shouting and laughter of the schoolboys in the street outside his office. He walked out of the front door of the ministry and watched them file past the wrought iron gates. They were on their way to the sporting fields adjacent to the government buildings. All of the children were about twelve or thirteen. The majority of them were black. He did notice Victor Trent's two sons among the group on their way to play cricket. Their uniforms were direct copies of those worn by the young athletes at Eaton, modified only slightly to adapt to the tropical climate. Three centuries of British colonialism would not die easily. The boys shouted a greeting to the tall, robust black man as they passed by. He waved and urged them to play a good game. "I'll be down to watch perhaps!" he called after them. They turned a corner and disappeared into a thick grove of fat, short palms, whirling dust trailing after their footsteps.

He thought of the excitement of the cricket matches. Had it really been so long ago? He sat down on a small marble bench facing the cobblestone street. He had been born on this island in a tiny wooden shack near the largest of the banana plantations, where his parents had worked. They had accepted their station but wanted more for their only child. So John studied at the English school run by the British government. His teachers saw immediately that he was exceptionally bright. By the time he was ten he could speak fluently in English, French, and German. He was also extremely handsome and very well coordinated, even for a child.

He remembered one day in particular when he had been playing cricket with some of the English boys. Bradley Trent, Victor's father and owner of the largest sugar plantation on the island, stopped by the field to watch them play. Victor was only about five at the time and rode atop his father's shoulders. All of the other boys greeted Trent and his young son casually, while John did not say anything and kept his eyes down cast.

"I must say, that's a sharp game of Cricket you fellows play. I'm afraid you would disgrace them in London." He addressed the group in general but was paying special attention to the young, intense-looking black boy. Trent walked over to him, extending his hand. John sensed that this man was sincere and that the gesture was not condescending.

"How do you do sir," John said looking up into the smiling face of the tall Englishman.

"Hello" little Victor said, inserting himself into the conversation. "I'm taller than all of you lads," he proclaimed and the group began to laugh. It eased the tension felt by John, and perhaps by all of the boys.

From that time on Bradley Trent was John Salter's friend. He hired him to tutor his young son not only scholastically, but in the area of athletics as well. Unfortunately, Victor lacked the size and natural rhythm of movement necessary to really excel in sports. But he was an amiable boy and enjoyed the Camaraderie more than the game anyway.

Often, John would accompany Victor and his father when they went to the Governor's Mansion. Bradley would sit in a huge wicker chair on the massive stone veranda overlooking all of the harbor of St. Phillips. John and Victor would play hide and seek with Victor's two sisters in the lavish formal gardens below. Upon one occasion Mrs. Trent had the houseboy bring some lemonade and cookies out to the children. John saw that the boy was one of his classmates in school. For some vague reason he felt uncomfortable when he saw him approach with the tray.

"Hello, Marshall," he said brightly, trying to sound off handed. Marshall looked at him with cool indifference, pouring the fruit juice into tall glasses.

"Just call me if you want anything else, sir. I'll come running. On my knees if you prefer." Marshall glared at John and his grip on the silver pitcher tightened. "My mother and father said that young John Salter was going to be the leader of this island one day and devote himself to his people. They will be distressed to learn that you are not Mirandan anymore. You're as bloody English as the queen." He said the last with an exaggerated cockney accent. "Drink your lemonade. What is there for you at home anyway? Your parents still have four more hours in the fields." He turned and walked quickly back in the direction of the house.

The other children had heard it all. John stood silent; he was shocked and humiliated. He looked down through gathering tears at the fine crystal glass he was holding. Suddenly he threw the goblet to the ground, shattering it. His companions looked frightened and baffled. "I hate you!" he screamed. "I hate all of you!" He bolted away down the steep path that led from the gardens to the road below the mansion. Bradley Trent had heard the breaking of glass and stood up in time to see John running blindly away from the others. Victor came up on the veranda and confronted the puzzled man. "John doesn't want to be an Englishman anymore father."

John Salter recalled that day as the beginning of his drive to be the leader of a free and independent Miranda. But he was not foolish enough to bite the hand that was feeding him. Not yet, anyway. He allowed Bradley Trent to pull some strings to get him into a private English academy where he excelled. From there he went to Oxford. He continued to distinguish himself in the classroom and on the sporting green while at the university. The islanders of Miranda were following his career very closely. His parents were afraid that the exciting and vibrant pace of life in London would appeal to him and that he might decide to remain there after graduating. But they worried for nothing. Any time their son spent away from his island home was devoted to the acquiring of knowledge. John was aware from his study of the past that one must know one's enemy and understand him if success were to follow. He obtained his PhD. in history from Cambridge, writing his thesis on Winston Churchill. He viewed many times the recordings of Churchill's addresses to the people. And what he watched, as well as the man, was the reaction of the crowd to his words.

He had never seen one man command such loyalty and devotion. They trusted him explicitly, as though they were under some kind of hypnotic trance. Indeed, perhaps they were. At the time England was in deep trouble and desperately needed this charismatic and brilliant statesman. The world seemed to have a sense of the frightening, terrible history being played out before them. Churchill represented all that was good. Hitler embodied all the attributes of evil in its most raw and savage state.

Both men were larger than life, and their influence godlike. Each man could have ordered his troops to march into the sea, and the soldiers would not have even broken stride in their journey to a sure and certain death. More than the terrifying blitz in the streets of London, more than the constant screeching air raid sirens and the pounding of combat boots in the night, more than any of the horrors endemic in war, it was the sheer power and complexity of character of these two men that left a lasting impression on the young black student from Miranda.

John Salter returned to his homeland upon completion of his studies and began his struggle for power. He organized the anxious natives and forced England to provide all of them with a better standard of living. He was instrumental in breaking up some of the large plantations and dividing the land among the natives. England was preoccupied in becoming, once more, a military and economic juggernaut. She lacked the motivation to fight this slow but steady take over of this small piece of land. In 1970 Salter had been elected as the Prime Minister of Miranda. Though the island was still under

British control, subject to its laws and regulations, the crown realized that it was Salter who had the real power with the natives.

And Victor Trent, now the English Governor of the island, knew that his childhood playmate was waiting, like a leopard in the jungle, to strike when the time was right and demand independence for his people. Although the two men maintained strained, but cordial working relationships, both had a silent understanding of the situation.

Slowly, the West Indies was beginning to be discovered as a vacation retreat. Salter had resented the fact that the two huge American chain hotels had opened up on Castle Beach since the revenue from the sale of the land went directly to the crown. "But John," Victor would argue, "they provide a sponge for the local unemployed. Jobs are an essential part in improving life here. You know that."

"That's all well and good, Victor, and on the surface very noble. But let us not deceive each other. The real money remains in the sale of the property. Had that capital been dumped directly back into the island economy the people would not have to be working for the slave wages doled out by the benevolent Madison Weston corporation and that other bloodsucking conglomerate."

John Salter watched with frustration and disgust as the hotels flourished and the English shared the spoils, while his own people swarmed around like ants, fighting each other for the most menial of jobs. The islanders thought that what they were experiencing was the dawn of prosperity. They were thankful for all that their own leader had done for them, but his open hostility to the American businessmen and tourists worried them. Soon, small splinter groups composed of the more powerful native landowners and merchants formed to vocalize their opposition to Salter's stand on certain issues.

This open challenge to his power both infuriated and disturbed the prime minister. He knew that to succeed there must be no resistance to his authority. His tactics in wiping out any dissenting groups were swift and brutal. He organized the "Kangaroo Brigade," as it came to be called by the islanders. This was a group of heavily armed secret police that would infiltrate the meetings of the dissenters and take down names. Suddenly there was a fire, an "accident" in which four of the leaders died. The prime minister attended the funerals and grieved with the relatives at the tragic fate of their loved ones. After that Salter's power became strong and absolute once more.

In early 1975, after months of organizing and planning, John Salter knew that it was time to make his move. One particularly lovely evening when a full white moon illuminated the alabaster beaches around the two big resorts, a large group of American and European tourists danced with carefree abandon to the loud, penetrating beat of a steel band. The whirling figures were silhouetted against the thick flowering hibiscus bushes and sprawling banana trees. The smell of rum and pineapple hung in the motionless, balmy night air. A circle of tiny yellow light bulbs formed a halo like canopy over the dance floor. Then totally without warning the underbrush exploded in a flurry of rapid rifle fire lasting only seconds. When the echo of the bullets drifted out to sea eight people lay dead on the beach. The white sand became a red blotter, drawing the blood from their bodies.

Many tourists fled the island as news of the attack spread. When the wandering gangs of militant natives grew larger and heavily armed, the remaining foreigners left, including the staffs of both hotels. It was then that Salter ordered the Rutledges and the few others he had encouraged to stay to join the Trents in the Governor's mansion. In fact, he even provided them with protection from the mobs that were determined to storm the grounds. For although he wanted independence for Miranda, he realized that any more bloodshed would hurt his cause, especially if it were to be the assignation of a British official. And aside from that, he genuinely liked Victor, and had not forgotten what his father had done for him. The natives loved Dr. Turner. And the Rutledges were harmless enough. At least Howard was. He was not certain about Claire. He did not know her well. But they were both good to the natives, and their small hotel was clearly not a threat to the economic restructuring of the island.

As fast as the rebellion had started, it was over. The crown granted independence to Miranda in July of 1975. John Salter rode through the streets of St. Philips in a stately convertible limousine. The islanders swarmed around the car to cheer their leader. The

Kangaroo Brigade had filtered through the city making certain that the prime minister's reception would be without incident. It was hot and windless and Salter sweated in his suit under the relentless afternoon sun.

He looked out on the crowd of Mirandans waving as his entourage passed by. School children stood in groups singing patriotic songs. They were all still dressed in the uniforms issued to them by the British government. Their British teachers stood near them. The faces of the children were vibrant and healthy, a result of the medical attention and vitamin supplements allotted to them by the crown. All at once John Salter was uneasy and he felt an icy chill pass over his body despite the excessive heat. In two or three months when the last of the financial aid from England was depleted, would these cheering, happy natives still be satisfied with the sheer wonder of independence? Would he still be hailed as the engineer of their precious freedom, or vilified as the architect of a new and more devastating poverty? The answer depended on what he did now. For although he planned on maintaining a cordial trade relationship with England, he knew that with independence came the loss of direct assistance. He prayed that the island could weather the agonizing transition to self-government.

But two years later the island was suffering. It was completely void of tourists. The hotels remained empty. The only people to occupy the bungalows of Cinnamon Inn were the ex-patriots in residence. Local merchants were practically starving. Gangs of unemployed young men roamed the island vandalizing stores and terrifying the people. The well-educated Mirandans started to leave the island, applying for professional jobs in the United States and Canada. Those who remained were discontented and restless.

Unfortunately, the colonial regime left by the British as a legacy was marked by a crippling lack of a stable economic infrastructure. The island was in the precarious position of producing what it did not consume and consuming what it did not produce. John Salter had watched as Trinidad traded its independence from foreign control to dependence upon foreign corporations. He did not want this to happen to Miranda, though at times he felt helpless to prevent it. But he was ready to face the facts. What Miranda had to sell was herself—her beauty, her restfulness, and the healing powers of her climate. The whole world was frantic to escape from itself. Well then, let it come to Miranda.

Hence, for a myriad of reasons, Salter promoted and approved of the sale of the two vacant resorts to Logan Hart. He volunteered to help with the beginnings of the new enterprise, with certain caveats. Every islander employed by the hotel would have to be eligible for a kind of profit sharing. Salter had convinced Hart that if the natives felt that they were in some way benefiting from the success of the venture, then they would work harder at their jobs. "Human nature, sir," he had told the American investor, "knows no color or language barriers." Hart readily agreed. The principle had worked well enough in the states. It was also made obvious, though nothing was overtly stated, that John Salter himself would get a big share of the action. "To be used for the betterment of Miranda, of course."

"Of course," Hart responded softly.

Salter was determined to put Miranda on the map in a favorable light. With independence he had given the island black political power. Now he was obligated to give her black economic power. The other small islands in the Atlantic were all watching to see what he would do now that the apron strings with England had been severed. Next year there would be an election to choose a president of the newly formed Organization of West Indian Islands.

Suddenly a large parrot swooped down and perched on the iron gate near the bench on which Salter had been sitting. The bird's plumage was brilliant in shades of orange, yellow, red, and deep blue, as though it had flown through a sunset capturing essences. The black man rose and stretched. He glanced up at the afternoon sun. It was hot, but not vicious. He motioned to the guard to open the gate. He would walk down to see if the cricket matches were still being played. Then he would return and dress and have his driver take him to the Governor's house. There he would have a drink with the Trents and celebrate the return of the tourists. He tucked in his shirt and smiled. Hart and his group would be arriving in a matter of weeks. Yes, it was going to be an interesting new year.

IV

"How much longer until we get there mommy? I feel like I am going to throw up." Jeremy stared out of the window of the plane. His skin was pale and perspiration dotted his cheeks. The plane had hit air pockets and for the last five minutest the effect had been like riding on a roller coaster. Dori reached for a small pouch under her seat and removed the white airsickness bag. She opened it up for Jeremy. She hoped that he would not have to use it, or that she wouldn't either for that matter. The little boy held the sack to his face and just sort of coughed into it, but nothing more. He sunk back down into his seat. A small amount of pink color began returning to his face. Dori took a deep breath and tried to relax. The plane finally left the turbulence behind. "We ought to be there very soon. Why don't you try and take a short nap now?" The suggestion was unnecessary. The child was already asleep. It had been a long two days. They had caught an early flight out of Kennedy to Miami, then on to Puerto Rico where they spent the night. In the morning they flew to Barbados, then proceeded on this small island hopper to Miranda.

The islands were so close together now that the plane had very little time to gain much altitude, so that the views from the windows were often quite spectacular. The chain of West Indian islands was green and lush looking from the air. The beaches seemed like an artist's conception of the mythical Atlantis. In between the landmasses the iridescent turquoise sea was sprinkled with ships of every size and description, from the most massive of ocean-going yachts to small utilitarian fishing trawlers. Staring down at the panorama passing below it was hard for Dori to believe that just less than forty-eight hours ago she had been standing in the falling snow saying goodbye to her parents.

They had taken the news of her plans very well, with almost a philosophical reasoning. "You grew up and went away once before,"

Dr. McGee said. "We knew that your recent stay with us was just to be a temporary hiatus, that you would eventually be ready to leave again. All we have ever wanted was your happiness. But you have to decide where you will look for it." So the maudlin, tearful Christmas Dori had expected was filled instead with a spirit of fun and joy and excited anticipation of the coming months. Logan had sent Jeremy an intricate model sailboat. "To put him in the mood," he had told Dori. The toy now rested on the seat between them.

They had been flying now for about thirty minutes without another piece of land in sight. Then suddenly the plane flew into a ridge of white clouds. When it emerged a few seconds later, Dori looked down to see the outer coastline of what she knew must be Miranda. It was magnificent and even greener, if possible, than the other islands they had been flying over. It was also far bigger than the rest with a very mountainous terrain. Logan Hart and Phillip Graham had flown down earlier in the week. Logan had cabled her that he would meet her plane.

The landing was rough and hard and its abruptness woke Jeremy. "We're here honey," Dori announced. "Gather up all of your things." The youngster obediently tucked his sailboat under his arm and picked up the array of games and comic books Dori had bought him before they left New York. While the plane was bumping to a stop Dori glanced out of the window to try and catch a glimpse of Logan. She saw only native men and boys scurrying about outside of the one room terminal. The only other Americans on her flight were a group of Marine Biology students from the University of Florida who had come to gather information on West Indian sea life. They would be staying a week at the invitation of the prime minister. They were all carrying sleeping bags and backpacks.

When at last Dori, with Jeremy in tow, managed to file out of the small aircraft after the students she was hit immediately with a wave of warm perfumed air. She at once felt ridiculous carrying her wool coat over her arm. She looked around for Logan but he was nowhere in sight. All of the young Mirandans were busy with the arrival of the college students. She approached one of the men unloading the luggage from the plane. "Excuse me," she said. "Do you know how I might get to Cinnamon Inn?" The man stopped for a moment and looked up at the blond woman and the boy then continued his work.

"In a minute. I biz now, you see?" The sentence was spoken so fast it sounded like a single word run together. Dori was just getting ready to try again when she felt a tap on her shoulder.

"Logan," she spun around. "Where have you— Oh, I'm sorry," she said, seeing that the smiling face did not belong to her new employer but instead to an extremely handsome man who appeared to be as new to the island as was she.

"Hello, I'm Phillip Graham. Logan is meeting with the prime minister this afternoon and couldn't get away. Allow me to apologize for him."

"Oh, that's O.K. How long have you two been here?"

"Since Monday. I really don't know my way around the island yet, but there are only so many roads on an island, and only one leads to the airport, such as it is. It wasn't hard to find my way back here today." They were walking toward a car. At once Dori saw that it was the Fiat she had left with Logan in New York. It seemed right at home surrounded by the tiny box like French and English automobiles driven by the locals.

She laughed, "Logan wanted you to be met with a few of the old familiar things from home." Phillip said.

"What a sentimental eccentric he is."

"Not really. He also figured out that it was cheaper to ship this here than to buy you one of the other imports."

"With all of the cash he is dropping on this deal you would think that would be the least of his worries."

"Penny wise and pound foolish, you know. By that singular act of thrift he has cleansed his soul. Now he can be excessive in other areas without feeling guilty."

Dori introduced Jeremy to Phillip, who admired his sailboat and there by became a fast friend. As they climbed into the car and started down the narrow twisting road away from the airport, Dori was interested in learning more about her new co-worker. "Why did you take this job?"

"The same reason you did."

"I doubt that."

"Well I don't. It's a challenge, an adventure, a chance to create what could be one of the world's most lavish and elite resorts. You have no idea what it means for an architect to be able to have a free hand to renovate a structure that is to be totally devoted to pleasure. Plus, it doesn't hurt having a natural surrounding like this to work in." They were passing through a forest of ferns with leaves of deep green, almost blue. Bright red bougainvillea flowers lined the dusty road. They looked like miniature elephant ears. Wild multi-colored birds perched lazily in the trees.

"I suppose that is why I am also here. I want to work with the natural materials on the island as much as possible to decorate the hotel. I want it to look as though the rooms grew themselves."

Phillip smiled broadly. "It's good to hear you say that. I would hate to design a fantastic structure only to see it ruined by lousy decorating."

"Oh," Dori stiffened. "Perhaps you'll think my taste is lousy."

"Do you own any paintings of Elvis on velvet or clear plastic raincoats?"

"No."

"Well then, you have passed the test." They laughed and drove on.

Jeremy was kneeling in the backseat staring out of the rear window at all of the new things around him. "When will see the ocean?" he asked. Dori turned to Phillip.

"Just around the next corner or so," he replied.

"I'm going swimming right away!" announced the child.

"Oh no you're not," said his mother. " There will be plenty of time for swimming. You have to help me unpack. By the way," she turned her attention to the driver. "Are you and Logan staying at the Rutledge place too?"

"I am, but just until I can get several suites and offices in the new place outfitted. Then we will all move up to the hotel. Cinnamon Inn isn't too bad. The cottages are quite attractive in a simple sort of way. The places are old and a lot of the furnishings need to be replaced. But you have to give these two a lot of credit. They hung in there during the tourist drought. Logan and I have had a talk with Howard. He told us that the last two years have been hell on them in more ways than one. They went through their savings completely. He had some big plans for the place. But those will have to wait until they recoup some of their losses. To him, our arrival beats a star rising in the East."

"What about his wife? Logan only told me that she was very flamboyant and a bit eccentric."

Phillip's mouth broke into a wide grin and he shook his head. "Boy, that is the king of the understatements. There really is no way to adequately describe her. I think that she is a borderline schizophrenic or a manic-depressive at the very least. It doesn't take a shrink to figure that out. Her mood swings are breath taking and totally unpredictable. When we arrived on Monday she hardly said a word while she was showing us the bungalows. Then that night at dinner she was animated and oozing charm and graciousness. She must have told us at least a million times how 'thrilled' she was that we had come. And she said that she can't wait to meet you, in particular."

"I am not so sure that I share her enthusiasm," Dori sighed.

"Oh, she's O.K. Just take it slow and easy."

Dori was about to ask him to explain what he meant by that when the narrow winding road suddenly emptied into a wide poorly paved street. One side was lined with shops of all kinds: bakeries, fabric stores, fish markets, fruit stands, and vegetable carts. On the other side there was a cobblestone sidewalk and a four-foot wall facing the harbor of St. Philips. Wooden-plank docks ran out from the street to the numerous fishing boats bobbing gently in the shiny water. The sea was so clear the boats seemed to be suspended in midair. Small native boys were huddled over old tin buckets cleaning the day's catch. Large, heavy black women in bright print cotton dresses would gather up the freshly cleaned and scaled fish and put them in woven baskets on their heads. Then they would cross the street and deliver their cargo to the waiting crushed-ice-laden display case at the market. The women were chattering and laughing as they went about their work.

Bicycles and motor scooters crisscrossed in front of their car. Most of the other vehicles on the road were small wooden-slatted pickup trucks filled with stalks of greenish-purple sugar cane or loaded with pale-yellow stalks of bananas. A few scrawny street dogs roamed the sidewalks eating small scraps of fish and bread dropped by the vendors.

The car rounded a sharp corner revealing another section of the harbor. Docked here were three large pleasure yachts. All three of the boats were double masted, and none were less than a hundred feet long. They were beautiful, sleek, and elegant. The smell of salt and freshly varnished wood filled the air. "The proprietors of the good life," Phillip said as he pointed out one of the largest cruisers in the harbor. Dori noticed that it was flying a French flag. Groups of young men and women, dressed in the briefest of swimwear, were gathered around tables on the deck playing some kind of dice game.

"Howard Rutledge said that there haven't been private sailing crafts in this bay for almost two years. They are a welcome sight to the local merchants."

"Do they usually stay very long?" Dori asked.

"Sometimes for a week or two, sometimes just for a few days. But either way they go ashore and spend money. After Logan gets the hotel up and running we will send a car here to bring people like these back for dinner and dancing."

"How long do you think that will be?"

"Hard to say. The things that need doing are, for the most part, cosmetic. The structures themselves are sound and have adequate facilities. I am working on a design now to join the two together in some way. Logan wants everything done fast. His lenders have only given him until the middle of April as a renovation period. After that they want the place to open, if just to catch the last two big months of the season."

Dori was contemplating the tight time schedule when Phillip turned the car onto a steep, rocky driveway. "We're here," he announced. Jeremy, who had been silent for most of the journey, suddenly became excited.

"Which one of these little houses is ours mom?" he asked as they passed by several of the small stucco and brick dwellings.

"I don't know."

"It's this one," Phillip said, indicating the last unit at the end of the driveway. He pulled the car right in front of the door. "Here is the key. Why don't you two go on in and check the place out while I unload the luggage." Jeremy was out of the car in an instant, still clinging to the small toy sailboat. Dori tried the key several times before she was able to get it to work. She had been telling herself not to expect too much, but she really wasn't prepared for what she saw.

The main area was divided into a large living room and long narrow kitchen containing a refrigerator and a small electric stove. The floor was dark wood and warped in many places, probably from the damp air, Dori guessed. The furniture looked cheap and weak. There was a small couch covered with a ghastly flower-print fabric of dubious origin. The "dining" table was the chrome and vinyl type found in roadside diners. The top was covered with dark rings where it had been burnt many times by hot pans. The walls were basically white, but in need of a fresh coat of paint. There were cobwebs in every corner of the ceiling. And small brown splotches appeared here and there on the wall where someone had smashed an insect.

She saw a door on one wall. She opened it reluctantly. A bedroom. There were two twin beds, a small wooden dresser and an exposed yellow light bulb hanging from a chain in the middle of the ceiling. There was an even smaller bedroom on the other side of the cottage. The single bathroom was equally unappealing. All of the fixtures showed their age and Dori wondered if anything even worked. Drab yellow towels hung on wall hooks by the shower. Dori touched them. They felt like sand paper.

Dori sighed and returned to the living room just in time to be greeted by an already tan and smiling Logan Hart. He was wearing sandals, white pants, and a bright red pinstriped sport shirt. "Welcome to Cinnamon Inn, your home away from home! Don't you just love the décor? Kind of conjures up images of what the maximum security ward must look like at Folsom, doesn't it?" Phillip was right. Logan was the master of the understatement.

"Logan!" Dori said, "You told me that the bungalows were 'nothing elaborate.' Well, you certainly were correct there. This place is hideous!"

"You ought to see the one I'm in," said Phillip entering with the baggage. "Makes this look like the presidential suite at the Ritz." Dori shuddered.

"Now come on," coaxed Logan. "It's just temporary until we can get things set up in our own place. Besides, it does have one thing going for it. Look." He went over to the drawn bamboo shades, which covered one whole wall of the living room. He pulled them up rapidly to reveal one of the most spectacular views Dori had ever seen. The entire length of Castle Beach stretched out below them. The sweeping expanse of the paint-box-blue sea flowing out to meet the horizon was like the view from an airplane. Dori had no idea that the Inn was up so high on the hillside.

"Come here," Logan instructed, opening up the sliding door that led to the terrace.

Dori stepped outside. She looked down below to see several more white cottages built into the side of the hill above the beach. Logan had his hand up to shield his eyes from the afternoon sun, and was pointing off to the right side with the other one. "See those buildings?" Dori squinted and tried to follow his direction. Finally she spotted two large structures, each about nine or ten stories high, set back off the beach and surrounded by shrubs and other massive clumps of greenery. "There sits the future playground of the international jet set."

Even from a distance Dori could see what Phillip had been mentioning. The places did not seem impressive now but the potential was there. Dori looked up and down the powdered sugar beach and gently rolling inlet waters. "It's beautiful Logan." She turned around and went back inside. All at once the place didn't seem as grim as it had upon her initial arrival. Phillip started to lower the shades. "Don't, she said. "That view is the only thing that is going to sustain me for the next few weeks."

Logan was carrying a magazine folded up in his back pocket. He extracted it and held it secretly to his chest. "Both of you come over here. I want to show you something." Phillip flashed Dori a look of *now what?*

"What is it Logan," teased Dori, "Miss January?"

"Hardly." He opened the magazine, which Dori saw was the most currant issue of T*own and Country*. "Feast your eyes on this!" He held a page up to them.

"Oh no, Logan, how could you do this?" Phillip stared disbelievingly at the advertisement. It read: "The Mirandan Castle Beach Hotel, in the heart of the sunny Caribbean, announces its grand opening May 1st. Enjoy luxurious accommodations, four star dining, exciting entertainment, and private beach facilities. Make your reservations early, as occupancy is limited. Contact Hart Enterprises, Harway Building, Suite #409 Fifth Avenue, New York, New York." Phone numbers and flight information followed.

"I've already had inquiries." Logan beamed.

"Oh, that is just great," snarled Phillip. "And what about 'Truth in Advertising?' 'In the heart of the sunny Caribbean?' It's more like in the toe of the West Indies."

"Oh, but I couldn't say that. It has such a remote, primitive sound to it. Frightens people off. Most everyone who comes here will let their travel agents handle the reservations. They will only have a vague idea of where in the hell the island is anyway."

"Swell," Phillip said. "We will be taking reservations for a hotel that doesn't exist."

"I know it does put the pressure on us a bit, but this will make sure that we can work in peace for the next several months without Chase Manhattan breathing down our collective necks. We'll make it."

"And what if we don't?" Dori challenged.

"If we don't, Pollyanna, then just bury me at sea. We start work first thing in the morning. The prime minister is being most cooperative. We will have all of the local labor we will need. And they have agreed to work for a reduced rate until we open. Now, Dori, why don't you unpack? I want to go over some sketches with Phil. We will be down on the lawn right below here. Come down and have a drink when you are ready. The Trents have invited us for dinner tonight. It will give all of us a chance to meet some of the ex-patriots in exile here."

Suddenly Dori realized that she hadn't seen Jeremy since they got out of the car. Phillip caught the flash of panic in her eyes. "Don't worry. He's down in the main house with Claire. He'll be fine."

"Thanks, Phillip. Incidentally, Logan," asked Dori, "where are you staying?" Logan's smile broadened.

"Oh you know how these diplomatic protocol things are. I am the guest of the prime minister at his residence above St. Philips. Naturally, I would prefer more humble surroundings." He made a sweeping gesture around the room. "But sacrifices have to be made somewhere." He gave an exaggerated sigh. Dori had to smile in spite of it all.

"Oh, get out. I'll see you later."

Dori had just stepped out of the shower, which had worked well after all, when she heard a sharp knock at the front door. She threw on her terrycloth robe and went to answer it. A large, smiling black woman was holding Jeremy by one hand.

"I'm Thelma, Mrs. Rutledge's girl. Thought you might want him up here now."

"Thank you very much." Jeremy had a scowl on his face.

"I like that red-haired lady. She's funny. She took me down to the water and I got to sail my boat. I didn't want to come up."

"Please tell Mrs. Rutledge that I am sorry Jeremy pestered her."

"Don't give no think to that. Child has been good company. I got to go now. Work for the dinner." She laughed a little. "Jimby stay with me while you up at the Governor's coming on." Dori realized the woman meant Jeremy when she bent down and gave him a playful spank on the bottom.

Jeremy sat on one of the twin beds and talked to his mother while she stood in the bathroom towel drying her hair. "That lady Thelma's skin is so black mommy. There are a lot of people black like that around here, did you know that?"

"Yes honey, I know. Remember I told you all about that before we left grandpa's house? The people on this island are a lot like the people from Africa in their coloring. What do you remember about the people of Africa?" she quizzed.

Jeremy had now stretched on his stomach on the bed, propping his head up with his hands. "God made everybody black there because the sun is so hot and he didn't want them to get sunburned all the time." He yawned. "Right?"

"Well, basically yes." Dori knew that the explanation was trivial and hackneyed. But small children thought it reasonable. "Anyway, that is why there are a lot of black people on Miranda. But remember, the color of their skin has nothing to do with the way they are inside. They are all just like you and me. The children all go to school and play a lot of same games you do and some new ones too. You will meet many of the children soon. I want you to be friendly so I can be proud of you."

Dori turned around to see how well her son was absorbing the little lecture on open mindedness and cultural differences. He was sound asleep. She went over and lay down on the bed next to his and closed her eyes. When she opened them it was almost twilight. Jeremy was still asleep. She grabbed her watch from the nightstand. She had been sleeping for almost two hours.

She heard footsteps and conversation outside her cottage quickly followed by a light knocking at the front door. "Let me guess." It was Logan's voice. " A VonFurstenberg, a Dior, a simple Calvin Klein? What are you wearing?"

Dori looked down at her attire, "how about a wrinkled bathrobe," she called through the door.

V

The winding road up the hill past Cinnamon Inn was rough and dusty. Dori's small Fiat struggled in second gear under Logan's command. "Jesus Christ!" he bellowed. "There is so much dust on the windows I can't see where in the hell I am going."

"Well, that is a comforting thought," Phillip replied. Both men were in the front seat. Both were wearing white dinner jackets, which emphasized their newly acquired tans and made them look healthy and handsome. Dori had volunteered to squeeze herself into the small back seat. She was doing her best to keep from wrinkling or tearing her blue silk cocktail dress as she bounced around on the seat.

"Really, Logan, as a guest of the prime minister I thought we would be travelling in an official limousine or your big Mercedes at the very least." Dori shot him a teasing grin, which he caught in the rear view mirror.

"Salter is on an austerity kick. He only has a few official cars: his own private chauffeured limousine and a hearse used for state funerals."

Phillip laughed, "Sounds good. At least we would all have had room to stretch out, so to speak."

"My car was supposed to arrive from New York two weeks ago," Logan said. "I've put a tracer on it but nothing yet. This lovely pile of assorted tin was the only thing greeting me at the airport when I got here."

"Logan!" Dori began, trying very hard to sound offended. "I have deep emotional attachment to this beast of burden."

"Good. Then why don't you get outside and whip it?"

Finally, the unlikely triumvirate arrived at the Governor's mansion, a large stone house high above the harbor of St. Philips. It was a massive structure viewed from the outside, at least three stories tall with an arched veranda running the length of the highest one.

Logan pulled the car up in front of a tall black man standing guard at the entrance, dressed in some kind of a military uniform with a red cummerbund wrapped tightly around his waist. With a white-gloved hand he aided Dori in making a less than totally graceful exit from the automobile. "Thank you very much." She smiled at him. He said nothing and looked straight ahead as he resumed his post by the door.

"Protocol," Logan whispered to her as he took her arm and led her up the stairs, "prevents him from speaking to you."

Phillip joined them and before they could knock, the huge, carved mahogany double doors opened. Again, another native in military dress escorted them through the entry hall into a large, breezy terrace room off to the right. There were already about ten people standing around the room drinking cocktails and talking. An elegant looking woman in her early forties smiled at the new guests and walked over to introduce herself.

"Hello, I'm Allison Trent. I am so glad that you were all able to come." She spoke to all three of them but her attention was focused on Dori. "Do come in and meet the others." She made a sweeping motion with her arm and led them further into the cavernous room. Everyone was dressed quite formally. Most of the men were in full dinner dress, and all of the women were wearing the most sumptuous and expensive of evening gowns, all of which, it was obvious, were imports from Paris or New York. A white-jacketed waiter circulated about the room taking drink orders. "Do have something," Allison Trent instructed as the man passed by.

"Yes, thank you, I will. I think I would like to try one of the local rum punches I have been hearing so much about."

"Ah, the life blood of the island!" Dori turned around to see a distinguished tall thin man smiling at her.

"Allow me to introduce my husband," their hostess began. "Victor this is," she looked blankly at Dori. "Forgive me dear, but I don't seem to remember your name."

"How do you do Mr. Trent," Dori said, extending her hand. "I'm Dorothy Dugan. I've come here with Logan Hart to oversee the decorating of his new hotel."

"Dorothy Dugan." Victor repeated the name loudly enunciating each syllable. "My, how does an Irish girl feel amidst all of these Limies?"

"Not entirely comfortable yet," she laughed. "But Dugan is my married name. My maiden name is McGee." At the mention of that an older man, quite heavy set, who was engaged in conversation with Logan and Phillip nearby, stopped for a moment in midsentence. He had his back to her. He did not turn around and eventually resumed speaking to his companions.

"Scotch Irish!" roared Victor, "That's even worse. Now we have the whole bloody British Isles represented."

Allison Trent still had a confused expression on her face. "I apologize. I shouldn't have forgotten everything. Claire told me all about you this afternoon. You're a widow aren't you?"

"Yes."

"With a little boy?" she asked, continuing to fill in the facts.

"Yes, his name is Jeremy."

"Of course. I'm not as daft as I might pretend." She gave a short raw laugh and glanced quickly at her husband.

"Incidentally," Dori said. "I haven't met Mrs. Rutledge yet. Is she here?"

"Why yes, just a moment. Claire dear," Allison called to a redheaded woman seated on a wicker chair talking with a rather plain girl. "Come over here and meet your new tenant!"

Claire stood up and moved toward them. Dori noticed that her motions were highly theatrical. She stopped several times to whisper something to different groups of people, laughing and acting coy and flirtatious, like a school girl at her first prom. Even her dress encouraged the comparison. It was a floor length multicolored chiffon with a wide skirt that billowed around her as she walked.

She put her arm out in an exaggerated fashion and took Dori's hand. "So you're the mother of that little cherub! He could be a child star you know. Those eyes!" She rolled her own widely for emphasis.

"Claire is our resident actress," announced Victor, "always in search of a new audience." Dori thought that last a cruel remark, but it didn't seem to faze its victim.

"He's just jealous, my dear. He is such a boring public speaker that Dr. Turner plays recordings of his speeches to cure his patients suffering from insomnia."

Though all in the tiny group were chuckling, there was a growing tension, which was making Dori extremely uneasy. That was why she was so grateful when the waiter appeared with her drink. The liquid in the tall icy glass was foamy. She immediately took several long deep swallows. "It's delicious," she announced.

"Ah, the famous Mirandan Pina Colada," said Victor. Better know by the natives as 'white lightening.' It is made with dark rum and a coconut liquor with the consistency of cream." Dori took another sip. She was beginning to feel the pleasant effects of the cocktail. She started to relax and excused herself, determined to meet the others at the gathering.

She sat down on a lovely English tapestry couch next to the dark-haired girl who had been talking to Claire. "Hi, I'm Dori Dugan."

"How do you do." The woman had a clipped British accent. "I'm Sara Hunnicut. I teach at the school here on the island."

"Really?" Dori smiled. "I will be enrolling my son tomorrow. He is seven."

The young woman laughed. "Well, I'm afraid that I won't have the pleasure of instructing him then, unless of course he is well beyond his level. You see, I only teach British History to the older children."

"Oh, I understand." Dori was disappointed.

"But don't be concerned. We have several native instructors for the younger pupils. They are very good. In fact, many of the children in school find that they are able to skip a level or more if they transfer to England."

The young woman seemed quite nervous and would often dart her eyes around the room, always appearing to search out the location of the host. "What made you decide to come here to teach?" For an instant, Dori thought that she saw a trace of fear in the girl's face. But it evaporated into a small smile. "I was teaching at a private girls' academy in London when I became quite ill with a respiratory infection. Victor Trent, whose daughters Ellen and Julia were attending school there at the time, convinced me to take a leave of absence and teach here for a year or two. I have been here for six months now."

"How do you like it?" Dori asked. The girl's smile broadened and became a bit smug.

"Oh, it's a very challenging experience in many respects." Her voice sounded rather strange and distant.

Suddenly she stood up, as did everyone else in the room who had been sitting. Dori also rose to her feet. Everyone was silently facing the front door when a huge, powerful-looking black man attired in a handsomely tailored tuxedo entered the room. Victor went up to him and shook his hand warmly. Then he turned to the other guests. "For the few of you who have not had the honor, let me present my good friend, the Prime Minister of Miranda, the honorable John Salter."

"Good evening to you all," the man said as he passed through the group. He stopped to exchange personal greetings with those he knew and to introduce himself to the people from the various cruisers who had been invited for the evening. Soon conversations began again and drinks were passed around once more.

Logan came up to where Dori and Sara Hunnicut were standing. "Quite a guy isn't he?" he said, plainly impressed.

"Yes he is," Dori admitted. "I had no idea of what to expect."

"A bone in his nose perhaps?" Logan teased. "He certainly isn't your every day savage spear thrower." Sara Hunnicut stiffened.

"That might be due to the fact sir that the prime minister was born on the island while it was under British rule. He was also educated in England and possesses a PhD. in history from Oxford. Excuse me please." She turned and left them, saying nothing more to Dori.

"Who in the hell is she?" Logan asked. Dori filled him in on her background.

"I'll apologize later. In a place this small I don't want to start any bad public relations."

Dori had three of the rum drinks by the time dinner was announced, and was glad that she would be eating soon. Between the rum and the traveling, she was feeling a bit lightheaded. Allison and Victor Trent led the way, followed by the prime minister. He was unaccompanied. Logan said that he had never married. He had a reputation of tiring of women easily.

The dining room was literally almost the length of a football field. The carved mahogany walls were covered with huge oil paintings of the past kings and queens of England. At the far end of the room, floor-to-ceiling leaded glass windows looked out unto the remnants of once formal gardens. The dark wooden table ran the length of the room. The top had been fashioned from one single tree, for there were no lines or breaks in its surface. Over fifty exquisite Chippendale chairs flanked both sides. Two massive tapestry-covered wingback chairs were placed at either end. Yet, ironically enough, this was not to be the dining table this evening. A smaller round table had been placed near the leaded windows. There were twelve places set, each with a place card. As Dori walked the length of the room she was gripped with a certain sadness as she looked about her. All of this faded glory. She thought about what it must've been like here during the height of British domination. She wondered if others were thinking the same thing.

Soon she found her name card at the table. She immediately saw that the prime minister would be sitting to her left. She did not recognize the name on the card to her right. Frank LeBeau. She had hoped that it might have been Sarah Hunnicut. She wanted to apologize to her for Logan's remarks.

"Allow me please." A soft voice began and she turned around to see an older, dapper-looking man with a neatly trimmed goatee pulling out her chair for her.

"Thank you very much, " she said as she sat down. He smiled at her but said nothing.

All of the women were seated while the men stood by their own chairs. Both Philip and Logan looked a bit confused, but kept their eyes on the prime minister and Victor Trent for clues as to what to do next. Finally John Salter nodded across the table to Victor and the two men sat simultaneously.

Protocol, Dori thought. For a moment there was an awkward kind of silence until the black leader raised his wine glass to propose a toast. "I would like to drink to the success of Mr. Hart's enterprise and more importantly to the prosperity of free Miranda."

Glasses were clinked and everyone politely applauded the toast, everyone except Claire Rutledge and Allison Trent who exchanged knowing glances. As the salad was being served the dinner guests began to talk privately among themselves. "And how are you enjoying your first day on our island, Mrs. Dugan?" Salter smiled as he studied Dori's face.

"Well, I really haven't had a chance to get a thorough look, but what I have seen is very beautiful. I can't get over the white beaches here. They are exquisite."

"Yes, and unspoiled. Mr. Hart has assured me that they shall stay that way."

I can imagine what else Mr. Hart has assured you, Dori thought. But she said, "And of course they will."

"And just what is your role in the scheme of things, Mrs. Dugan." His tone was more suspicious than inquisitive, as though he assumed that Dori had been brought to the island to be in Logan's bed rather than business partner. She became defensive.

"Mr. Hart has employed me to decorate the hotel since he was pleased with the work I did for him on several of his holdings in the past. Actually I was very reluctant to come. I am a fairly new widow with a small son. But Mr. Hart assured me that I might leave if I find that I don't enjoy life on the island. At any rate, I shall be returning to Vermont when the assignment is completed."

Salter's expression had not altered. He had remained smiling and interested throughout her explanation. "Don't pack before you have unpacked my dear," he said and then turned away abruptly and began to talk with Philip Graham. Dori was upset but she didn't know exactly why.

"He is a rather difficult man. But then all men of power are, don't you think? The voice had a strong French accent and belonged to the gentleman who had seated her. "I'm Francis LeBeau. And you are Dorothy Dugan." He smiled reading her place card. Dori was grateful to have someone to talk with after that rather strange experience.

The remainder of the meal passed without incident. She learned a great deal from Mr. LeBeau. He was a retired French journalist from Paris. He had come to the island at about the same time as Claire and Howard Rutledge. He had planned on only taking a holiday here, but had become fascinated with the history and the people of the West Indies. He decided to remain. "My wife did not share my enthusiasm for Miranda. I put her on a boat back to Paris. And she said to me, 'Francis this is the end!'" He waved his arms in a gesture of dramatic finality. Then he winked at Dori. "What she didn't know was that it was a beginning for me." He laughed like a small boy who had succeeded in fooling the teacher. But then for a moment, he became very serious. "Besides. I am needed here now especially." Dori had no idea what he meant, but she decided that she liked him.

After dinner, which had been a delicious blend of local fruits and spices poured over broiled chicken, the Trents led the way up the winding spiral staircase out onto the stone veranda off the third story. Gleaming white ceramic tile covered the floor. Wicker chairs and large potted flowering plants were arranged in groupings that ran the entire length of the gigantic porch. The twelve or fourteen open stone arches acted as frames for the magnificent, almost surrealistic view of the hills and the harbor. Though it was nearly midnight, the breeze filtering up from the tops of the palms was warm and fragrant, carrying the many scents of the island flowers.

A sliver of a new moon cast enough light on the beaches below that the sand became a vision of finely crushed diamonds glowing with a light of its own. And it was as if all of the stars in the universe had crowded into this one section of blue-black sky. Phillip came over to where Dori was standing. "If I pinch you and you wake up in the middle of a traffic jam Manhattan, don't blame me."

She smiled, "It all is pretty unbelievable." Brandy was served as everyone sat and relaxed, just enjoying the peace and splendor of the late evening. The guests from the cruisers were commenting on the fact that it was so wonderful to be able to come to the West Indies again. Soon the prime minister stood and motioned to one of his bodyguards, who then quickly disappeared inside the house. In a few moments the sound of cars starting below in the driveway signaled the end of the evening.

Salter left first, thanking Victor and Allison, and nodding to Dori as he passed by her chair. In a matter of moments the rest of the guests were gone also. Dori's dusty Fiat was the last car to be brought around. "They probably didn't want anyone else to see it," Logan teased. They thanked the Trents and then left. Victor had been jovial and welcomed them all once more to the island. Allison, conversely, stood in the doorway brooding and walked back into the house without saying anything.

"Quite a different group of people." Phil proclaimed on the way back to Cinnamon Inn. "But they are all kind of interesting."

"Yeah," Logan added, "and we need them on our side to generate goodwill and all that. Oh, by the way, Dori, I managed to apologize to little-miss-tight-ass. What a cool number she is. I can't figure out why she's here anyway." Dori remembered the way Sarah had looked at Victor Trent.

"I have an idea." She said, but didn't want to pursue the matter further at the moment. "Who was that heavy man you and Philip were talking to when we first arrived?"

"That was Ransom Turner, the doctor on the island. Why?"

"Well, I know he overheard my conversation with Victor and he seemed uneasy or something when he heard my maiden name."

"Maybe he's got a thing against the Scotch." Phillip said.

Logan shook his head. "I think he's got a thing for the scotch. He sure put enough of it away."

Logan pulled up in front of Dori's bungalow. "Good night, Cinderella," he said as he helped her out. "Remember, the ball is over. Work begins tomorrow."

"Yes, mein Fuehrer." Dori saluted.

She and Philip watched as Logan drove off. There was a note on the front door of Dori's cottage. "Jimby down to the Rutledges."

"I'll go get him," Philip offered. Dori thanked him and went inside and turned down the beds. She had just hit the light switch in the bathroom when Philip returned carrying a fast asleep Jeremy in his arms. Dori pointed to the bed in the far corner of the room. Philip nodded and tucked the small boy under the thin blankets. Dori walked with Philip to the front door. "See you tomorrow," he said. "Or actually a little later on this morning."

"Oh, don't put it that way," Dori frowned.

Phillip was almost to the entrance of his own cottage when he heard Dori scream. He ran back up and opened the front door. She was standing panic stricken in the middle of the bathroom floor. "Look!" She said pointing to the toilet bowl. "When I lifted the lid a frog jumped out and went into the shower."

Phillip was trying hard not to laugh. "Stand back fair maiden. This is a job for a he-man." He went into the kitchen and came back with a clear plastic bowl. He threw back the shower curtain and caught the terrified frog under the dish. He lifted the rim only slightly until he could grab the creature. Then he swiftly carried it to the front door and set it free.

"Thanks," Dori said, feeling a bit embarrassed.

"Good night again," Phillips said and left.

Dori climbed into bed and looked over at her son, who had slept through it all. How easily a child adjusts to everything, she thought. Mosquitoes were whining above her head. She pulled the scratchy sheet up around her face, remembering Salter's admonition. "Don't pack before you have unpacked." At this moment, that didn't seem like such a bad idea.

"Where have you been? As if I didn't know." Claire snapped at Howard as he walked into the bedroom. He didn't answer, but just stared blankly at his wife and disappeared into the bathroom. "Don't you ever get tired of those people, Howard? How many new stories can you tell them? How much money did you throw away tonight? It really doesn't matter because we don't have it anyhow. And they all know it. You're a fool, Howard, can't you see that?" She was standing near to the closed door now, screaming at it. Finally it opened and Howard came back into the bedroom dressed in a pair of light cotton pajamas. He climbed into bed without speaking.

Claire sat down on her side of the bed and looked down at her husband. "You are all a bunch of losers. Everyone on this island is. They couldn't make it in the real world so they came here to pretend." Her voice was dry and hoarse. She had been drinking heavily since returning home hours ago. "You think that this new hotel is going to make a difference, that you are going to ride in on Logan Hart's coattails. Well it isn't going to work. He sees you for what you are, a loser. But not me, I'm a star! I made it big once and I can do it again. I'm just waiting for the right moment. You'll see." She was half screaming, half crying.

Howard had been lying on his side with his back to her. Now he turned and looked up into her swollen red eyes and pouty face. "Go to sleep, Claire, you're not feeling well." His calm, soothing manner made her even angrier. She grabbed him by his shoulders and dug her fingernails into them.

"Don't you have any emotion left either? Has this place drained that from you too? A shell of a man, that's what you are. Just a shell!

Not like when I met you." Abruptly her manner changed and she became soft and shy and snuggled up next to him on the bed. "You know, Howie, we could go back. I'll bet you could start another store. This time near the beach, maybe even Malibu. You could teach sailing and I could commute into the studio."

Howard climbed out of bed clutching his pillow. He picked up a light blanket folded over her chair and left the room.

Claire lay back down on the bed. It was almost dawn. Soft grey morning light filtered in through the pulled bamboo shades. She watched a small lizard cross the ceiling and climb down the wall to the floor. The creatures were everywhere on the island and it was impossible to keep them out of her open-air cottage. When they had first arrived she had been mortified to find them in a drawer between folded clothes, on a kitchen table, or under her pillow. But over the years she had become immune. In fact, she had begun to treat them as pets, naming each of them and sitting for hours just watching them traverse the walls and windowsills in search of small insects.

She knew where Howard had been. Ransom Turner and Frank LeBeau had returned with them after the party. Claire had come in the house. But the man went down to the beachside bar where they continued to talk and drink and play poker. Claire had stood on the terrace watching them for some time. Their voices carried well on the gentle midnight air. They had been talking about the new arrivals.

"That Logan Hart is a real nice guy," Howard had declared. "And so is that architect he brought along with him. Seems like a bright fellow."

"We talked after dinner," Turner said while dealing. "He's got some great plans for the place. Says it's going to be ready by May. I think that target date is a bit optimistic. But we'll see."

"Mrs. Dugan is quite an attractive woman," Frank offered, "Now there's someone who could give Ms. Hunnicut a run for her money." All three of the men laughed.

Claire came back inside and closed the sliding doors. It was then that she poured herself a tall glass of rum and ginger. She had decided that she didn't like Dori right from the beginning. She was too perfect with her perfect wholesome face and her perfect towheaded child, and her perfect profession and most of all her perfect state of enviable mobility. Claire hated her because she knew that she could just come to Miranda and soak up all of this lovely local color and then leave. But Claire did not feel threatened by her arrival. She began laughing out loud at the absurd prospect of Howard trying to attract the young woman's attentions. She had seen the way Dori had looked, with the combination of disgust and embarrassment, at Howard's swaggering, bragging manner. Claire had also seen the way John Salter had studied the new guest. She shuddered. She knew that the poor, lovely Mrs. Dugan was completely unprepared to deal with what, in time, was certain to happen.

VI

John Salter waited for the three young black men to be led into his office. He knew why they had come. They were the leaders of a left-wing movement on the island. They had opposed the foreign development of Castle Beach ever since the revolution. They were idealistic and energetic, but like all devoted radicals, impatient and impractical as well. As he heard his office door open Salter rose from his desk and walked over to the open window and looked out on the gardens and a grove of thick palm trees.

"Be seated gentleman," he said without turning around. He heard scuffling as the men settled into the cane back chairs provided for visitors. He turned around to face his guests. "Good morning," he said. All of the men were in their mid- to late-twenties. Each had a tense, serious expression on his face. Charles Cliff, the unofficial leader of the group rose, unsmiling and extended his thin, sinewy hand to the prime minister

"We have come to discuss the progress of the Americans. We want to know when the operations will be turned over to the island." He always wore thick-lensed glasses that made his eyes look extremely large and out of proportion with the rest of his facial features. "You your self," he continued, "have assured our members that the enterprise shall eventually be in control of the Mirandans." Like Salter, the young man had received some of his education in England and had acquired the clipped British accent.

"Yes, and it shall be," Salter said. "But now is not the time."

One of the other men stood up abruptly and faced the prime minister. Salter recognized him as Mandy, the boy that worked for the Rutledges, tending bar and managing the changing rooms. "The Americans have been on the island for a month. They have hired our people for slave wages. And even at that there are not enough jobs to go around. We are tired of gathering crumbs from the foreigners. We have been against this from the beginning but have gone along with it because you assured us that it will be in our best interest in the end."

"And it will." Salter said, stretched, and rubbed his neck. "But what would we have? What would we gain by taking control now? If we did, Logan Hart and his architect and his decorator and his money, gentlemen, would all leave the island. We would be left with the two vacant useless structures that we had after the revolution. And the 'slave wages' you talk about are sustaining our people in the meantime. Let foreign money come in and spread itself as thickly as it wants on this island. Let them pay for our development. We will need their investments and their moral support as well. Perhaps years from now we will be prosperous enough to afford to nationalize everything on the island. But that is a long way off, if it ever comes. Each free nation needs the next, if any kind of freedom is to be maintained. If anything rash is done now, we will lose everything I'm working for, and we will be left with nothing. Is that what you want?"

The young men exchanged quick nervous glances among themselves. Then the spokesman approached the prime minister again. "No, but we don't want stagnation either. You have not kept us informed as to what you plan to do. We do not know our role in this or what we should tell our people."

Salter could not confess to them that he himself had no plan other than to try and let all of this capital investment flourish and hope that their standard of living would improve as a direct result of it. "Tell them to have faith in me and my judgment as they have before. I have worked very hard to bring this money to the island. And I shall work very hard to see that is pays off for the people."

"You know, Mr. prime minister," said the third young man, leaning forward in his chair, "I do not wish to be disrespectful, but yours is not the only voice being listened to on this island." Salter bristled, and the stiff neck he had woken up with was getting steadily worse.

"Exactly what do you mean?" Salter knew what he meant; he wanted to hear the explanation from the man himself.

"The Cubans." He said softly. "They have been talking to the Islanders. They have managed to get them frustrated and anxious by telling them that with their help things will happen more quickly. They say that under their plan no one in Miranda will be hungry or wanting in the basic necessities of life. They say that all of the foreign investors will be forced to relinquish their properties to the people."

Salter was infuriated, but attempted to control his wrath. He bit his lower lip before speaking. "And you believe that?" He looked at all three of the men, his stare intense and angry.

"We are not saying that we believe it," said Cliff, "but they are not speaking just to us. They have their infiltrators everywhere. And the people are nervous. Years after a bloody revolution they see the same thing happening that happened before: rich foreign investors come and invade the island. But then what do we get out of it? Nothing. That so-called profit sharing is a joke. The money always remains in their hands. We have told the people vaguely that everything will eventually belong to us, but that argument isn't good enough anymore. They don't understand your long-range plan. They only know that they are hungry and poor. They want swift action."

"As I told you before," Salter began having great difficulty controlling his temper, "if we try to nationalize now we will lose everything. We must wait until the hotel is a big shining success and all of the world's rich are flocking to the island to enjoy the splendor. Then and only then can we move to take it over. Don't you see? We need the money now, and will for years. We are incapable of sustaining ourselves." His voice was becoming loud and intimidating. "I thought you were with me and wanted a free Miranda that could function well and be a force to be reckoned with in the Atlantic. It will not happen if we give in to the Communist pressure. What then? Cuba will control everything from Miami to Caracas. And our island will be just another pawn in one more political game. That is not what I want for the island, or for the West Indies, or for myself." He was breathing heavily now and his pupils became enlarged with rage. "Yes, gentlemen, myself. I will not say that my motives are as totally altruistic as yours might be. I want to be the leader in the West Indies for a beginning. If we acquiesce to the Communists, that shall never happen. None of us shall ever be free again. And I refuse to be responsible for the enslavement of our people."

Charles Cliff stood up and walked over to the window. Even now, as they spoke, the loud noises of jackhammers, electric saws, and churning cement mixers could be heard operating below on Castle Beach. "But when," he turned around and faced Salter, "will we have something tangible we can point to and say, "this is ours, this all belongs to Miranda forever?'

"In time. Please understand that I share your frustrations. But you must also understand that I have been on this island longer than anyone of you have been alive. I have seen real war. I know that to achieve our ends we must work with the powerful free nations of the world. If we were to do anything foolish, we would lose it all. Our dreams of success would slip through our fingers like the sand on our beach. I also know that the eyes of the West Indies are upon Miranda. It is up to us to set an example for the others. But by selling out to the Communists, for that is exactly what we would be doing, make no mistake, we would be telling the rest of the West Indies that freedom doesn't work, that it can't work. And we would gain nothing in return. I want Miranda to be strong, and important and wealthy. And we can't do it with just cinnamon and nutmeg. We need this foreign capital and must play it for all that it is worth. You must tell the people to be patient and strong. My plan will work. If you don't defend me to them, then who will? I need your support." His tone had calmed, and he was speaking in earnest now. "I truly need your help."

He sat down behind his desk and folded his arms on the top. "Stay with me on this please. Trust me. Work with me and the foreigners and we shall achieve a new greatness for Miranda." He paused and took a gamble. "And your help shall not go unrewarded or unrecognized. Do I have your support?"

The two men looked at Cliff, who stood up and again shook Salter's hand with a firm, aggressive grip. "We shall always support what is best for Miranda. You may be certain of that."

VII

Time on the island seemed to be in a perpetual state of suspended animation. There were so many constants that days melted into one another, each dawning with the same furious burst of sunlight that warmed the sand and reflected off the endless parade of waves as they marched into shore. Dori would fix a small breakfast of fresh fruit and coffee for herself and a glass of milk for Jeremy. She tried to insist that her son eat an even more substantial meal, but ceased to argue with him when she learned that the children were provided with several snacks at school in addition to the bag lunch they brought from home.

Jeremy was thriving in the island environment. Already he was tan and his small muscles were developing well due to the daily swimming, hiking, and general exploring he had been doing. He had made friends easily with the two young Trent boys as well as with the many native children in his class at school. His teacher was an older woman, a native of the island. She had gone to England to complete her education but returned to Miranda to teach and to raise a family. Her husband had a good job managing the harvest and overseeing the warehouse operations for one of the English spice companies. Jeremy had liked her right away.

"She's really neat, mom. She's told me all sorts of stuff about the fish and the birds and the things around here. And next week she said that I get to take care of Feathers."

Feathers was a large red and yellow parrot that had been adopted by the school children as a mascot of sorts. He was fast and friendly and spent most of the day perched in a windowsill of the classroom. Mrs. Cochran had appointed a different student each week to make sure that the bird's seed cup was filled and that the area around his perch was kept clean. "In a few years Mrs. Dugan," she told Dori one afternoon, "none of these children will be interested in caring for Feathers. But now, any little job they can do around the room gives them a sense of pride and responsibility."

Dori was grateful that Jeremy was getting his turn so early in the year. It gave him a great feeling of belonging. This morning, as with all of the others since she had arrived, she sat on the terrace and watched Jeremy walk down the steep stone steps that led to the beach. There he would meet other children and they would travel the rest of the way along the sand to school. As always, when he reached the bottom of the steps he would turn and wave in the direction of his mother and she would wave back, though she realized that the sun was often in his eyes and he had trouble seeing her.

Dori sighed, smelling the salt-laden air. Things were going well. In the almost two months since she had arrived the face of the Castle Beach Hotel had changed dramatically. Crews had been working with Phillip's plans building a huge arbor that led from the side entrance of the two hotels, joining them. The arbor was filled with plants and man-made ponds swimming with exotic tropical fish. The arbor joined what had once been the two lobbies of the hotels. But at Dori's suggestion one lobby was transformed into a garden type restaurant, with an adjoining dance floor close to the beach. The other lobby was expanded to include the registration desk, small hotel shops, and the executive offices. Originally Logan had wanted to build a separate office complex down the beach but Dori had talked them out of the idea. "Why not be where you can see the operations firsthand? You can discover the problems before they are reported to you with three different versions of each story."

"And another thing," Phillip injected, "it will be a hell of a lot cheaper to transform some of the existing floor suites into offices than it would be to build a whole new structure."

Logan's tentative smile brightened. "My boy, I stand convinced."

Dori and Phillip had been working quite closely, each respectful of the others profession, consulting one another on all plans. Fortunately their tastes and ideas were fairly compatible. Dori had submitted sketches to him on her ideas for remodeling the rooms. He approved of her drawings. "The rooms are all too boxy as they exist now. I propose that we knock down the walls between the dressing rooms and the bedrooms and expand the larger oceanfront suites adjoining their terraces."

"Can you do that structurally?" Dori asked.

"No problem. And I've also thought of putting an elevator on the outside in glass. The ride up would provide quite an impressive view of the beach."

"Very dramatic," Dori said. "I love it." Dori had been keeping close contact with wholesale furniture mart and fabric outlets in New York. Several of the people with whom she had worked previously sent her brochures and fabric samples. They would be anxious to have the business. Dori had finally decided on the basic furniture and color schemes for the rooms. Last month she had wired the manufacturers to start production.

She quickly finished her second cup of coffee on the terrace then showered and dressed and drove to the hotel. As she rounded the corner past the Rutledge's bungalow she saw Claire dealing cards to Allison Trent. They were on the terrace. Without looking at her watch Dori knew that it must be nine. The women played gin rummy three mornings a week at nine o'clock. Allison waved weakly as the car sped past but Claire only looked up momentarily from the game.

Dori would be glad when she could move out of Cinnamon Inn. The rustic nature of the place didn't bother her anymore but she felt uneasy around Claire and Howard. It was Claire really. Howard was easy going enough and had actually been quite kind, taking Jeremy with him when he and Dr. Turner went swimming or fishing. But Claire always seemed to be plagued by some dilemma far beyond her ability to control. Someday she would simply radiate charm and wit, gabbing lightly about the sad state of the American theater or her fledgling days in the movies. But then, without warning, she would lapse into her dark moods, and would stay inside her house drinking and cursing the world. And Howard stoically endured the brunt of her abuse. Dori did not understand their unique relationship and tried not to give in to speculation.

She pulled her car into the makeshift parking lot at the side of the hotel entrance. Some young native men were hauling fat stumps of palm trees up to the lobby. Phillip had designed walkways and paths all over the grounds of the hotel. The stumps would be sunk into the earth, becoming flat round foot trails. He was keeping to the theme of using natural local materials in his overall design.

"Dori, thank God you're here!" Logan stood by the front door looking pale and worried. "There is a Samuel Markowitz on the phone from Needleman's in New York. Something about a shipment of bedspreads and towels."

"Oh, yes. I want to talk to him. I ordered those things several weeks ago. He probably wants to set up the shipping arrangements." Dori rushed through the door and into the makeshift office, which they all used temporarily. A native girl, who was functioning as their secretary, stood by Dori's desk holding the phone out at arms length as though it were a flailing animal.

And indeed it was. "Mrs. Dugan, if you think that I am going to pay the storage charges for the three hundred spreads, four thousand towels, and twelve hundred sets of sheets you ordered while you get your shipping permits straight, you are insane. Why didn't you anticipate these problems before? You never mentioned the possibility of an export embargo. If you had, I never would've contracted to do business with you. And believe me, when news of this gets out, you won't be able to order from the Sears and Roebuck catalog."

Dori had absolutely no idea what he was talking about, but after calming him down she got a more thorough explanation. "All I know is," Markowitz began, "that after we filled the order, a couple of men from the port authority came by to inform us that nothing would be sent to you until it could be approved by their office. 'Special regulations,' they said. Look, Mrs. Dugan," he sounded as bewildered as Dori was right now, "this is a small outfit; we were happy to get the business. But we can't afford to hold this stuff indefinitely, we need to ship it and get payment right away and I thought that you were on some kind of a tight schedule, too, down there." Dori glanced up at the office calendar. Tomorrow would be March 1st.

"Yes, we are Mr. Markowitz. I really don't know what this is all about. But I promise that I shall find out today and get in touch with you right away. In the meantime, please hold my order. We will pay all of the delay charges." Logan, who had been standing close to Dori, sighed when he heard that last comment.

She hung up and sat down at her desk, totally confused. She explained the situation to Logan, who was equally puzzled. He spent the day frantically making phone calls to the port authorities in New York, Miami, and San Juan. None of them had heard of any kind of shipping embargoes on goods traveling to hotels in the Caribbean. Yet all day long Dori was besieged with calls from most of the furniture and fabric wholesalers with whom she had placed orders. Each one had the same story. No one on the docks would touch the things headed for the Castle Beach Hotel. The longshoremen wouldn't load them and the cargo captains wouldn't allow them on board.

It was six o'clock when Logan finally gave up making any more phone calls for the day. All of the local laborers had quit working for the afternoon. Ruthie, the West Indian girl who worked for Dori, had taken Jeremy home to fix his dinner. Some of the day laborers were swimming in the water off the hotel beach area and their happy voices could be heard as they playfully called to each other, splashing in the water. Reddening rays of sun drifted through the glass of the lobby windows as the blue-green twilight snuck onto the island.

Phillip burst into the room dressed in work clothes and full of the spirit of accomplishment. "I can't wait for you to see the arbor at night. It is going to be spectacular. I had my crews string lights all afternoon. Tiny white bulbs. They look like miniature stars linking both sides of the hotel together. Really something. The depth and scope of my creativity never ceases to amaze me." Gradually he began to realize that no one was paying any attention to him and that their faces looked worn and worried. "What happened?" Logan gave him a brief rundown of the day's grim events. "Jesus Christ," Phillip sighed sitting down in a cane back rocker. "What in the hell is going on? We've got to have that stuff. We open in two months!"

Suddenly Logan exploded. "Jesus Christ! Don't you think I know that? All of my fucking classy advertising has us practically booked solid for the first two weeks. I've got to make it in those fourteen days or I don't make it at all." His face was white now and his hands shook as he spoke. He noticed and thrust them into his pockets. "What in the hell do you two care? You've both got nice safe established careers to return to. If this thing flops your reputations remain unscathed. 'It was all Hart's fault,' he mimicked.

'A real son of a bitch. He couldn't do anything right. I just felt sorry for him, that's why I went.'" Then as abruptly as the tirade started, it stopped. He sank to the small couch by his desk and put his head in his hands. "God, I'm sorry," he whispered, more to himself than to the others. "Forgive me. It's just been one rotten day. I'll straighten everything out tomorrow."

He seemed to be calming himself down. It was only now that Dori realized what an incredible strain he had been operating under. He had attempted to keep up the façade of the eccentric millionaire living out an idle fantasy, but it was clear that the success of this hotel meant everything to him. Several minutes passed with no one saying anything.

The only sounds were the voices of the frolicking natives. Their laughter and excited shrills were in direct contrast to the pervading gloom in the office. Finally Philip stood up, his entire face enveloped in a smile. "I have a suggestion," he said, "let's go out and get drunk." Logan looked up, his old self again.

"That old boy, is definitely an idea whose time has come. Dori my love?" He extended his hand. On any other occasion Dori would most likely have declined the invitation. But somehow, tonight was different. She felt that it was important for them to be together tonight, to let Logan know that they were willing to share in his failure as well as in his success.

"I feel like a house mother at a fraternity party," she said as she took Logan's arm. She called Ruthie to let her know that she would be in quite late.

"Oh, that's okay, Mrs. Dugan. Jeremy and me are doing his homework. Rithmatic." She said the word proudly. Dori winced. She had seen examples of Ruthie's "Rithmatic" when she had sent her into town for a dozen eggs and she had returned with the thirty.

But she was a sweet girl and could be trusted. This time they left Dori's Fiat in the parking lot and took Logan's Mercedes. They drove into St. Philips to explore some of the local spots. "Howie told me of a place in town they call The Buoy. It's operated by a group of English and American kids," Phillip said. "Supposedly the food is pretty good."

Logan parked by the boat harbor. He gave one of the native boys who crowded around the equivalent of fifty cents to watch the car while they were gone. The sun had set now but an afterglow remained that bathed the rich turquoise water in gold. And in the ethereal light even the small plane fishing boats looked as dignified and regal as the cruising ships.

As they walked by the harbor, fragments of conversations could be heard from the boats, some in French, some English, some Spanish. Lanterns burned brightly on the decks of the yachts as men and women sat on chairs drinking rum and brandy and discussing the following day's travel plans, or lack of them. They were just about to turn the corner and leave the harbor when Dori saw the lights from a large, lovely schooner anchored out in the middle of the bay. The ship bobbed gently. It was easily the largest, most elegant private yacht Dori had ever seen. "Why is it way out there?" She asked Phillip.

"Privacy perhaps, or maybe it's hull is too deep to come in this close."

"I can't see what flag it's flying, but it has got to be at least a hundred and fifty feet long," Logan said, then added, "a mere lifeboat." They laughed and went on their way.

Finally, after asking at least ten people, they found the location of the restaurant. It was quite a nice spot. Instead of the usual steel bands, the music emanated from a large old Wurlitzer jukebox, rigged up to take tokens that could be purchased from any of the waiters. A young American girl with a sunburned face and long blonde hair met them at the front door. "Dinner?" She asked. Logan nodded. She led them through the bar to the dining area, filled with small wooden tables and chairs. An old-fashioned kerosene lamp decorated each blue-and-white checked tablecloth. The other people in the room were probably crewmembers from the various charter boats.

Almost at once, a tall blonde boy, who could have been the older brother of the hostess, appeared at their table. "Would you like a cocktail before dinner?" He was dressed in denim pants and the blue-and-white striped T-shirt. Logan ordered rum drinks for all of them. Gordon Lightfoot music played softly in the background. The drinks arrived and Logan took a long, satisfying swallow.

"Oh, I feel better," he announced. They all did. "You know," said Philip, "this is the first time I have been in town since we got here except to shop or send cables. And just think, the whole town is named after me. But I'm more important. There are two L's in my name." Dori and Logan groaned collectively.

"This is my first time in here, too," Dori added. Logan started laughing loudly.

"Well now, tell me, Mrs. Dugan? How did you enjoy St. Phillips?" He answered for her. "Oh, I don't know. I never saw it. But I understand that it is very charming."

Phillip and Dori began laughing, partly as release from tension and partly because what Logan was illustrating was so true. Here they were in the romantic Caribbean and they had taken very little time out to enjoy it. After the third round of drinks they ordered dinner: huge stakes and big salads. Logan had learned from their waiter that all of the employees were college students from various places who had dropped out between semesters to try something else. Most of them were very involved in sailing and had reached Miranda by crewing on some of the pleasure yachts chartered out of Miami.

"Say," Philip asked their waiter, "do you know anything about that huge beauty anchored in the middle of the harbor?"

"Oh yeah. She's great, huh? Just arrived this morning. Flying a New Zealand flag. But I talked to a couple of her crew. They said she's just come down from Miami. Chartered by some heavyweight business types. Man, I would love to get a job sailing on that. Excuse me." He left their table to get a drink order for a group of French tourists.

"I really envy the way kids are today," Dori said wistfully. "The way they just pick up and go whenever they feel like it. When I was in college, nobody simply left school. The guys were too scared of getting drafted and the girls only left if they landed a husband. It seems much more logical this way somehow."

"I agree." Phillip ordered another drink. "I went straight through architectural school right after college without so much as a summer off. It was like I was being driven by some demon." He paused, thinking. "Maybe we were all afraid that if we stopped and looked at what we were studying to be, we would have found out that we didn't want to do it anyway."

"Not me," Logan said smiling, and still only slightly intoxicated. "I knew from the time I was five or six that I wanted to go into the hotel business. Whenever I had little friends come and spend the night I used to turn their beds down for them and bring them cookies and milk on a tray."

Phillip and Dori started laughing and shaking their heads at the mental picture Logan was painting for them.

It was close to midnight when they decided to head back to the car. Logan, by this time, had become quite drunk, and Phillip was not much better, so Dori was elected to drive. Yet she herself was feeling more than a little mellow. The night air was warm and seductive and they walked along the streets feeling happy, and free, and somehow, young.

When they came down by the harbor, they noticed that the big ship anchored in the middle of the inlet still had all of the lights in the salon burning and the sound of the generator hummed into the stillness.

"Some big doings going on out there," Logan said. "Maybe I just ought to swim out and introduce myself."

"I can see it now," Phillip began. "Body of drunken hotel magnate found floating in the lovely blue sea off the coast of Miranda." They were still laughing when they reached the car. Dori had forgotten all about the small child Logan had left guarding it. He was fast asleep in the backseat of the car but woke abruptly when he heard the sound of the Americans.

"I wasn't sleeping, sir," he said as he quickly scrambled from the car. "I was hiding back there in case someone tried to steal it." The boy had the imprint of the upholstery on his face and his brown eyes were heavy with sleep.

"Of course you were," Logan praised. "And you did a fine job keeping the rascals away." He gave the child someone money and waved to him as the boy darted off down the street in the direction of wooden shacks elevated on stilts above the harbor.

"I'm too tired to go back to the ministry tonight," Logan announced as Dori headed for Salter's compound. "Besides, I'm sick of the old boy checking up on me. I'll stay with Phil tonight. Okay Phil?" Phillip gave an exaggerated groan.

"I won't be any trouble," Logan promised. "I'll just sleep on the lounge on the terrace."

Dori drove up the dirt road leading to Cinnamon Inn. All of the cottages were dark, with the exception of her own. She parked the car next to Phillip's bungalow and said good night to her friends. Phillip went into his cottage while Logan walked Dori to her front door. Large moths fluttered around the yellow porch lamp. "Dori," Logan said, suddenly completely sober, "please try to get in early tomorrow. I've got to find out what has happened with our shipments."

For no reason really, except that perhaps she was tired, or she felt sympathy for him, she put her arms around Logan's neck and kissed him softly on the cheek. He moved his head and brought his face close to hers and kissed her strongly on the mouth, holding her body close to his own. Even though Dori felt little emotionally, or perhaps because of it, she did not try to prevent his kissing her once more. Then he backed away slowly still holding her hand. "Thanks," he said and turned and walked into the darkness.

VIII

Logan had not slept well. He was sitting, red eyed, behind his desk in the office when Dori arrived early the following morning. Since she had left her car there overnight, she had walked down the beach to the hotel. It had been relaxing. "Did you see Sylvia on your way in?" he asked.

"No, I didn't, but I heard noises of rattling pans coming from the kitchen." Sylvia was the West Indian cook Logan had hired to manage the kitchen. She had operated the restaurants of the last two hotels and was familiar with most of the equipment. Also, she had been quick to staff the place with reliable help. "If I don't have a cup of coffee soon," Logan said, "I might not make it through the day."

"Rough night on the terrace?" Dori went over to her window and opened it, allowing the soft morning breeze to flow through the room.

"I was afraid to close my eyes for fear that the mosquitoes would come and carry me off."

"Good morning, Mr. Logan, Mrs. Dugan. I have your coffee here. Would either of you like anything else?" Sylvia stood in the doorway, holding a large tray and smiling broadly.

"I don't think so," said Logan taking the tray from her and setting it down at his desk. "But thanks".

"Well, I am going down to the market today. I want to start pricing the melons and the vegetables. Everyone's anxious for us to buy from them, so I gotta start makin friends with the best farmers." Sylvia closed her eyes tightly and squeezed her hands into little fists like a small child wishing for a new bicycle. "I can't wait until this place is just jumping with people and I can start doing some real cooking." Then she turned to Dori. "When are the uniforms going to arrive for my girls?" Dori sighed, pouring herself a cup of the steaming strong coffee.

"Soon, I hope."

"I just can't wait for that!" said the cook, then turned and padded back toward the kitchen.

Logan anticipated Dori's question. "I've got my attorney checking with the port authorities. I'm waiting for him to call me back."

"Where's Phillip?" She asked.

"Oh, he'll be working with the crews all day. The glass elevator is being installed."

It was close to noon when John Salter's limousine pulled up in front of the hotel. "Goddamn," Logan said, looking out of the window. "What the hell does he want?" Salter stepped out of the car, dabbing his shining forehead with a clean white handkerchief.

"He's not alone," Dori added, watching two foreigners, who appeared to be American, work their way out of the backseat. One of the men was short, and about thirty pounds too heavy. He had on a lightweight suit. As he stood up he remove the jacket to reveal a sweat-stained blue dress shirt. His face was newly sunburned and peeling. He wore large, dark glasses and carried a leather briefcase. The other man was also heavyset and perspiring, but his face was more angled and intense than that of his companion. He was wearing a dark suit, and although plainly very hot, he elected to keep his coat on and buttoned. He, too, was carrying an attaché case.

Logan stood up and went into the small hall to greet his uninvited guests. "Mr. Prime Minister, what a welcome surprise," he lied, extending his hand to the black man.

"You look a bit out of sorts, Mr. Logan. You should have returned to the ministry last night rather than invading Mr. Graham's cramped dwelling." Logan was a bit disturbed, but attempted not to show it. He ignored the comment. After a long pause Salter introduced his companions. "I'd like you to meet Mr. Ramino and Mr. Mariani." The two men nodded but did not offer their hands. "They have just sailed in aboard the *Kiwi* from Miami." Though they said nothing about it, Dori knew instinctively that the *Kiwi* must be the beautiful ship they had seen the night before.

"Well gentlemen," Logan was trying to be gracious though the reason for this visit was still a mystery to him, "please come into my office and have a cup of coffee."

Once inside Logan introduced Dori to the new arrivals. Salter came over and grasped her hand firmly. "Dr. Turner tells me that your son is becoming quite a fisherman." His smile was friendly but Dori felt uneasy.

"Yes, Dr. Turner has been very kind. He has spent a great deal of time teaching Jeremy all about the sport." She averted his eyes and exchanged puzzled glances with Logan.

"And how are things progressing here, Mr. Hart?" Mariani asked, lighting a cigarette.

"Just fine. We are really well ahead of our schedule." He smiled at Salter, who sat silently.

"Really?" Mariani asked, "I don't think so." Logan's nerves were too frayed for this cat and mouse game.

"Exactly what you mean?" he asked. This time his tone was no longer friendly. At that point Ramino opened his attaché case and extracted a large manila folder.

"Mrs. Dugan, if you would be so kind as to check these inventory sheets for accuracy," he said, handing her the folder of papers. Dori opened them up and stared in disbelief at the contents: the complete and detailed mailing forms for everything she had ordered to outfit the hotel from chairs and couches, to linen and silverware. Nothing had been omitted. Without speaking she turned the lists over to Logan. He too was astonished.

"What is this!" he demanded.

"Now, let's not become impatient, Mr. Hart," Mariani said. "We have come to help you. We understand that you are having a slight bit of difficulty getting these things shipped to you."

"What do you know about that?" Logan said weakly.

"Everything," Ramino said smiling, snubbing out his cigarette in the bottom of his empty coffee cup. "You see, we arranged the delay."

Logan exhaled loudly and leaned against the back of his chair. "Why?" He asked.

"We thought it was a way to get your attention so that you might listen to what we have in mind."

Logan looked over at Salter, certain that none of these revelations came as news to him. "And what would that be?"

"Well, we know that it is very important for you to make a success of this hotel. Your bankers have assured us that a failure would most certainly result in your bankruptcy." Logan just shook his head, amazed at their depth of information concerning his financial position. "And for the prime minister, a failure of this scope would not look well in diplomatic circles. So our organization has a plan to make certain that your hotel flourishes beyond your most lavish expectations."

"How?"

"Very simple, Mr. Hart," Ramino said. "High-stakes gambling."

"But, gambling is illegal in the West Indies."

"But," Ramino continued. "As far as anyone is concerned, this will all happen without the knowledge of the prime minister. He is a very busy man, Mr. Hart. He doesn't have time to oversee the management of your hotel. He is too involved with affairs of state."

Logan was both frightened and furious. "And you sanctioned this?" He glared at Salter.

"I have no choice, as you have none either. These gentlemen have assured me that they can interrupt shipment of anything to Miranda at any time without warning. And we will be powerless to intervene."

"But what about the port authorities or the State Department. They can be told."

"Don't be naïve, Mr. Hart. Our people are everywhere. You either play by our rules or you lose the game. It's as elementary as that." Ramino almost spat out the last word.

Dori had no idea why she was being included in this discussion, and frankly she wished that she had not.

"But now," Mariani began, "both of you gentlemen will be rewarded for your reluctant participation. Think of the revenue it will bring to Miranda to say nothing of the amount of business your hotel will have Mr. Hart. We are not talking about petty ring toss. What we have in mind are backgammon tournaments. The entry fee will be one hundred thousand dollars. That is a sure method of dispensing with the riffraff. And each participant will stay here, occupying suites and spending money in the bar and in the dining room as well as buying trinkets from the natives. Are you beginning to see how everything will operate?"

Logan was numb. His mind was traveling on a roller coaster. "And your place in all of this, Mrs. Dugan," Ramino began, "will be to see that things run smoothly, that these guests are kept busy and happy."

"Mr. Ramino," Dori said, "I am an interior designer, not a social director. I was planning on returning to the states as soon as the hotel is operating smoothly."

"Of course you were, and you shall in time. But I think that Mr. Hart is going to need you in the initial stages. He trusts you. And of course, you too shall be compensated, very generously for your extra duties. I think that it would be quite unwise for you to leave prematurely, for any length of time that is."

Dori was feeling sick. What was this? A threat? A suggestion? What? But she remained silent. The three visitors stood up.

"We shall allow you time to discuss things between yourselves." Mariani said. "We feel that there is no reason to inform Mr. Graham of these plans, since he will most likely be leaving soon when his work is completed. Just call the ministry when you have reached the proper decision. It has been a pleasure meeting both of you."

This time it was Logan who did not extend his arm to shake hands. The driveway filled with dusty air as the sleek black limousine disappeared from sight. Logan and Dori returned to the office, saying nothing. Logan closed the door behind him and went over and stood by the window staring out at the settling dust. The silence was broken by the brash, rapid ringing of the telephone on Logan's desk.

"Hello, Logan, this is Jack. Listen, I don't know what the fuck is going on with your stuff. All of the shipping forms are in order. But none of the container ships will touch the crap and nobody's talking. I've shaken people upside down by their heels and I still can't get any logical answers." There was a long pause. Logan closed his eyes and rubbed his hands over them. "Hello, Logan, hello?"

"I'm here, Jack. Hey, never mind. I discovered the source of the problem at this end. I'll take care of it from here." He hung up.

"I can't go along with this, Logan," Dori said it flatly without emotion.

"Listen, Dori, I don't like it either. But there is nothing I can do about it in the meantime. They have me by the balls and you know it. I'll tell them that you are not to be involved any more than necessary.

You'll be working for me, not them, not even indirectly. I'll make sure that they understand that. I need you. You can't bail out now." She started to object. "Look I don't have any intention of keeping this deal as a steady diet, Dori. Let me organize their backgammon tournaments. Let the publicity show that the Castle Beach Hotel is a favorite watering hole of the jet set. After one season I won't have to tolerate this. The place will be able to make it on its own. And besides, I was being naïve. I knew in the back of my mind that elements of the mob were beginning to operate down here. Hell, it's been going on in the Virgin Islands for years. I just never thought that I would have to contend with them directly. We can play by their rules temporarily. Listen Dori, I have been a straight arrow all of my life. But right now, for a little while, I have no choice."

"Well I have."

"Please don't leave me now. I'm begging you. Stay for this first season, that's all. Please." Every instinct she had told her to leave, today, to walk away from this entire mess. But standing there, pale and worn out, Logan looked so tired, and vulnerable and pathetic. How different he had seemed in New York, all charm, a roving party. Yet now, stripped raw, he was a terrified child.

"I'll stay."

IX

"I'm glad that you decided to brave the trip with me," Phillip smiled as the small plane took off.

"Well, I wanted to get away for a while. And besides, after the shipping mix-up Logan wants me to oversee all of our orders personally." Dori felt a surge of relief as she saw Miranda become smaller and smaller as the aircraft gained altitude. "But I can't be gone long. This is the first time that I will have been away from Jeremy for more than just a day or an evening."

"Are you worried about him?"

"No, to tell you the sad truth, I don't even think that he will miss me that much."

"He really has adjusted to the island life hasn't he?"

"Yes."

"A lot better than his mother has I suspect." Phillip evaluated Dori's guarded expression. "I'm not being critical," he continued. "I've developed quite a case of island fever myself. That's why I decided to come back."

"But don't you have to check on some of your ongoing projects?" Dori asked.

"Yeah, that's what I told Logan. Actually, I could have done it all over the phone. But I really needed a breather."

Dori grinned slightly and shook her head. "Paradise does have a way of getting on one's nerves doesn't it?"

"It's more than that."

"What?" she asked.

"This whole thing started out to be a lot of fun. But Logan has developed an acute case of tunnel vision. All he can think of is this hotel. It has become an obsession with him."

"Out of financial necessity," Dori defended.

"Well, it's changed him. He's losing his sense of humor and a lot of his charm. To be honest, working for him is becoming a real bore. He watches over my shoulder as though I have never built anything in my life. He asks me ten times a day when something will be finished. If I didn't have this compulsion to see things through I would have quit last week. That's when he really started to come apart."

Dori was thinking of the scene in the office with the visitors from the *Kiwi*. "You don't understand," she said. "Logan is under a lot of pressure."

"I know. But he's not an infant. He's been under strain before; it's different now in some way."

The noise of the engine made it difficult to carry on a conversation for any length of time. Dori settled back in her seat and closed her eyes. She was thinking. She realized that the situation must seem more than a little odd to Phillip. She debated about telling him what was going on. At least, if he knew he would be on Logan's side. He might even decide to stay in Miranda a little while longer. But then again, why include him just because misery loves company? Why not leave him blissfully ignorant, as she wished she had remained? For some reason, she ultimately decided to tell him of the gambling operations Logan had been forced to accept.

"Holy Christ!" he said. "No wonder he's having a nervous breakdown. I have never trusted Salter. He's looking out for number one all right. How does Hart ever think that he is going to get out from under all of this?"

"Well, he figures that all he needs is one good season to publicize the place. Then he doesn't think it he will have to tolerate the illegal betting. Besides, the backers of this project hinted that they would only be staying a month or so."

Phillip sighed and shook his head. "I don't know. It seems like quite a big risk." Dori looked at him, exasperated. "Yeah, I know, he said. "He doesn't have much of a choice...still"

The constant humming and vibrating of the engine had a soothing effect. Soon, in spite of all of the things weighing on her mind, Dori fell into a sound, empty sleep.

They didn't arrive in New York until after midnight. They had changed planes three times: in Barbados, Puerto Rico, and Florida.

Yet Dori felt a new surge of energy as she waited by the baggage carousel for her suitcase. Phillip had gone out in front to hail a cab. "Look at all of these people!" Dori smiled as the driver made his way through the hectic airport traffic.

"Wonderful isn't it?" Phillip asked.

Dore laughed. "Yes."

When they reached the Plaza neither of them had the desire to go to sleep yet. They went into one of the hotel bars for a drink. It was as if both of them were abiding by an unwritten law not to discuss Miranda, or Logan Hart, or the Castle Beach Hotel. Instead, they talked about themselves, for the first time since they had met.

"So you spent your whole child in Vermont?" Phillip said as they nursed their second drink.

"Yeah, rather boring."

"Maybe to someone else, but not to me. I was an Air Force brat. My family moved all of the time, from one base to another. I went to eleven schools in five years. That lifestyle was not really conducive to making long-lasting friends."

"Didn't you ever settle down?" Dori asked.

"Kind of, for a while anyway. When I was seventeen, we were living in Tucson, Arizona. My dad was stationed at the Davis-Monthom Air Force Base there. Anyway, I fell in love with the desert. I loved all of the geographical contrasts: mountains, valleys, lakes, snow, all within an hour of each other. Tucson had it all. So when I graduated from high school I was relieved that a childhood bout with rheumatic fever kept me out of the service. That meant I could go right on to college, which I did. The University of Arizona. My father was destroyed of course. He expected me to follow his less-than-brilliant career in the Air Force. But he recovered. I have a younger brother who is a career officer, makes Jimmy Doolittle look like a traitor." He laughed, but it was hollow and sad. "I know I was a disappointment to my dad, but not to my mom. She was behind me all the way, encouraging me to go on to graduate school."

"But why architecture?" Dori asked.

A big grin spread over Phillip's face. "Have you ever seen military housing? Designed with the imagination of a flea. I used to think that I had been born in a box. My father would be so excited whenever he got some promotion and we could move from one box to a bigger box. I was sure that they could have all been packed inside each other like those wooden Russian dolls."

They spent another hour talking. Dori felt herself begin to really unwind for the first time in many days. She told Phillip about her parents and about her late husband. It was strange, and rather frightening, but when she spoke about Chris, it was with a kind of detachment that she never thought would be possible. She still had great feelings for what they had and the memories were warm and pleasant, but nevertheless, distant. Yet talking about him made her feel lonely and empty. Phillip sensed her changing mood.

"Maybe we had better call it a night?" he suggested. Dori agreed.

The suite Logan had retained consisted of two bedrooms linked by a sitting room, complete with bookcases and a fireplace. It was very much like the one she had stayed in during the time she had learned from Logan all about Miranda. Phillip walked through the arrangement. "Not a bad setup. Of course it doesn't begin to match the charms of the Cinnamon Inn. He carried her suitcase into the room while Dori sat on the bed. "I don't know if I'll be able to sleep at all without the melodious tones of the mosquitoes serenade." Phillip smiled. His blonde hair was a bit too shaggy now and he had a heavy growth of new beard. But he looked tan and happy and Dori had an aching desire to be held by him. He turned to leave.

"Don't go yet," she said softly, standing. He took his hand off the doorknob and came back into the room, close to where she stood. He had a long look into her face. Then slowly, silently, he put his arms around her and drew her to him. She rested her head against his shoulder as his grip tightened. They said nothing for several moments. Then he bent down and lifted her face to his and kissed her, gently at first, then passionately. Unlike Logan's embrace, he stirred feelings deep within her and she responded by returning his kiss with an equally hungry force.

He picked her up easily and laid her gently down across the bed. Then he stood up and stared down at her. The only illumination was coming from a small table lamp in the adjoining sitting room. In the filtered half-light the intensity of his expression was muted. "Is this what you want, Dori?" The rhythmic traffic noises sounded like surf coming onto the shore.

"Yes."

Phillip touched her hand. Then, unbuttoning his shirt, he walked across the room and quietly closed the door, shutting out the light, and the world, for a few short hours.

When Dori awoke the following morning she heard the shower running in the bathroom. Phillip was singing some popular song, dreadfully out of tune. She closed her eyes, smiled, and snuggled back into the luxurious covers. She was surprised and relieved by her feelings about what had happened—no guilt, no sadness, and no recriminations. The evening had been beautiful. Logan was wrong. Phillip had not been a disappointment in any way. He was a strong and aggressive lover. He had managed to awaken feelings in her that she had submerged for over a year. She felt more alive this morning than she had for an awfully long time. This could be the beginning of something. She had cabled her parents to meet her in town for dinner tonight. She hoped that Phillip would be free to join them.

He returned to the bedroom, wrapped in a big yellow bath towel. Dori was sitting up in bed with the sheets gathered under her arms.

"Hi," he said shyly.

"Good morning" she smiled at him. "Do you want to order breakfast from room service?"

"No" he said. "I'd like to, really. But I have to meet someone in the lobby in about twenty minutes."

"Oh, business already, huh?" She was disappointed. "That's okay. I've got to go check on the shipment of linens and reorder some more towels. Also, if I don't come back with the uniforms for Sylvia, she might start an uprising single-handedly." Dori knew she was talking too fast, but she was nervous and anxious to know what Phillip was thinking.

"Listen Dori I…"

"Yes?"

"Nothing. I'll see you later." He started toward his own bedroom. She wanted to ask him about dinner but decided against it for now.

She showered and dressed, then called and made an appointment at Charles Raymond salon for a haircut, which she badly needed. One of the drawbacks of short hair was it required a good professional cut every six weeks. It had been twice that time since Dori had had one.

She also called her wholesalers and manufacturers and set up times to see them. Samuel Markowitz brightened noticeably at the sound of her voice. "Why, Mrs. Dugan, what a pleasant surprise. So glad that all of those minor shipping problems have worked themselves out. We have already received your generous check covering the storage time on the docks."

Dori knew that Logan had not sent Markowitz any money. In fact she was going to pay him the storage fees today. Romino and Mariani had taken care of everything.

After a hasty breakfast in her room, Dori was off for the day. She had almost forgotten how exhilarating the pace of New York City could be. After she had taken care of the immediate hotel business she spent the rest of the day going from shop to shop. All of the windows in Bloomingdale's were decorated in anticipation of Easter. A huge mechanical rabbit sitting in the middle of a carrot patch waved a big furry pink paw to the crowds of children gathering outside. Dori thought about Jeremy. He would probably be swimming with the Trent boys or fishing with Ransom Turner. She wouldn't tell her father about the important role Dr. Turner was assuming in his grandson's life. It might hurt his feelings to know how easily Jeremy had shifted his affections to the new man.

On an impulse Dori bought herself two evening dresses at Bloomingdale's. She rationalized that they were actually a business necessity. She would need some dressier clothes once the hotel opened. But she knew the real motive behind her purchases. Now she had someone to dress for again—Phillip

She returned to the hotel at five thirty with her new dresses and a sample of the uniform she had ordered for Sylvia. She was trying to picture the round, jolly face of the cook when she saw the dress, a long green and yellow flowered-print cotton jersey with a scoop neck and long sleeves. Actually, the design was little more than a glorified caftan. But it was smart looking and would accommodate almost any size figure. Each one also came with a sash, for those who might wish to emphasize an enviable waistline.

Suddenly, as she was walking toward the elevator, she saw Phillip at the registration desk with an attractive, statuesque brunette woman. She waved with her free hand and made her way over to where they were standing.

"Hello," she said. "How was your day?"

"Fine. It seems that my office is surviving quite well in my absence." He was edgy. Dori smiled casually at his female companion, waiting for an introduction.

"How do you do. You must be Dorothy Dugan. Phillip has been telling me of the wonderful plans you have for decorating the hotel. I can't wait to be among the first guests." She extended her gloved hand and Dori shook it. She looked at Phillip, puzzled.

"Dori," he said, breathing deeply, "I'd like you to meet Madeline, my wife."

Dori felt a hot surge pass through her body. She felt limp. She hoped that her expression had remained unchanged. "It's very nice to meet you. I hope you will excuse me. I must go change. I am expecting my parents for dinner."

She left them, not bearing to look at Phillip. Her eyes welled up with tears. She just managed to make it to her room before she lost control. She dropped her packages on the floor and flung herself on the bed, crying uncontrollably. How could he deceive her like this? He had never mentioned that he was married. Of course she had never asked. But he had told her so much about himself that she had assumed that if he had a wife he certainly would have said something. And what kind of a marriage was it when the husband went off for months at a time? She felt embarrassed and humiliated. But her most raw emotion was one of anger. Not at Phillip really, but at herself. How could she take one night of lovemaking and start mentally building it into a relationship? She could've gone to bed with anyone of the men she had dated after Chris and it would have meant nothing to either of them. But she didn't. She waited until she thought she had the right man.

She stopped crying and began laughing bitterly. Oh the irony. Prince Charming on whom she had decided to bestow her favors was married. Logan would just love it. She looked down at the box containing her new clothes. "Grow up, Dori," she said to herself. "There is no one here to put a Band-Aid on your skinned pride and take the sting away."

She stood up and walked over to the window and looked out. Okay, she had taken a fall. She had always been one to learn the hard way. But she did learn. She could play with the big kids. She knew the rules now.

Dori managed to have a pleasant evening with her parents. They ate in a little Italian place near the hotel. It had been a favorite of her father's ever since he had been a medical student at Columbia.

"Wow, you look just marvelous dear," her mother said, admiring her daughter's spectacular tan. "Have you been coloring your hair? It looks so much blonder."

"No, the fellow who cut it asked me the same question this morning. I guess it must be the sun in Miranda. Jeremy and I take long walks on the beach almost daily. And you know me, I've never worn a scarf in my life, or a hat."

"How is my boy?" Dr. McGee asked as he poured them each another glass of Chianti. "Has he been able to make any friends?"

"A few." Dori knew what her father wanted to hear. "But he really misses his grandpa. No one will ever be able to take his place," she lied, thinking of Ransom Turner.

Dr. McGee beamed. "Well I miss him a lot too."

Dori told them of the progress that was being made in the renovation of the hotel. She casually mentioned the work Phillip had been doing. She gave no hint of the recent trouble Logan had had. She told them a little about Claire and Howard, about the Trents, and of course, about John Salter. But she painted sanguine pictures of all of them, failing to elaborate on the depth of their individual idiosyncrasies.

"How long do you think you will stay?" her mother asked as they strolled back to the hotel. Dori thought about the question.

"I don't know," she said truthfully. "For the first season at least. I promised Logan that much. The hotel will really be opening at the traditional close of the tourist peak. So we will have to work extra hard to attract guests."

Her parents walked with her to the elevator in the lobby and then kissed her goodbye. "Aren't you two going to spend the night? I booked a room for you."

"Talk to your father," Beth McGee suggested.

"Dad?"

Dr. McGee had a bashful smile on his face. "Well, I can't. I've got to get back home. Barbara Landor's daughter is visiting. She's about ready to have her first child. I promised Barbara that I would come right back after we saw you, in case the baby comes sometime soon." Dori shook her head while her mother gave her a what-can-I-do look.

"Dad, you're retired, remember?"

He laughed softly. "No, I don't remember. I keep forgetting that. Anyway, I like to drive all night, no traffic." Dori knew that it would be impossible to try and talk him out of his plan.

"Well, be careful." She apologized for not writing more frequently and vowed to send them a letter at least twice a month, and call when she could. Then they left, her dad filling a thermos of coffee for the road.

She sat down in a chair in the lobby for a moment, thinking. She had planned on staying in town tomorrow to be with her parents. But now that they had left unexpectedly she saw no reason why she shouldn't do the same. She went up to her room and called the airport making all of the necessary ticket changes over the phone.

When she hung up she sat on the bed very still, listening. No noise was coming from the adjoining sitting room. Gingerly she went over and opened the door. The room was empty. She noticed that the door to Phillip's room was closed. She returned to her own room and locked the door behind her.

She undressed quickly and climbed into bed, trying not to think of last night, but it was impossible. Her mind was overflowing with questions about what had happened and why. She rolled over and buried her face in the pillow. He would expect to see her tomorrow. They were both supposed return to Miranda together in a few days. Let him travel alone. It would serve him right, pay him back. She would leave him a short note at the desk explaining that she had concluded her business early and saw no reason for remaining. Why was she so against spending another night with him in the same hotel suite? Embarrassment, anger, fear? Did she worry that even armed with the knowledge of his married status she still might let him in her bed? She wasn't sure.

She curled up on her side and listened to the muffled street sounds, the never ending rolling tide of the city, soothing, measured, and constant.

X

In the stiff breeze, the sailboat began to lean on its side, the mainsail rippling in the wind. The deck was being washed with foam. Finally the sea proved too great an adversary and the boat filled rapidly with water and began to sink. Jeremy was knee-deep in the surf watching the drama. When at last the ship vanished from view he sighed and began to tug on the length of twine in his fingers and dragged the toy onto the sand. He picked it up and examined it. One of the small sails was missing and the captain's wheel was loose. The deck and interior cabin were filled with sand.

"Another disaster at sea, huh?" Ransom Turner bent down and took a look at the vessel. "Well, it's nothing that we can't fix. But you'll have to bring it inside where I can rinse it off and work on it."

Jeremy followed the doctor up the long grassy path to his house, a small salt-box type, several miles down the beach past school on the way to St. Philips. "Well, even if you fix it today," Jeremy said cradling the broken craft in his arms, "I'm not going to sail it this afternoon. The wind is too strong."

"Very wise decision Captain," Turner agreed. "Those are treacherous seas." He winked at the little boy and opened the screen door off the back porch for him.

Jeremy climbed up on the kitchen stool and watched intently while the doctor went about the task of making repairs. "Do you miss your mother?" The old man asked. The boy thought about it for a moment.

"A little I guess," he replied honestly. "But she's coming back pretty soon. And anyway, I haven't had much time to be sad. I go to school everyday, and then play and then I see you afterwards. It's kind of like when we lived with grandpa."

Turner looked up from his glue and string at the bright, attentive face. "Yes, I'm sure that it is." He finished his repairs and set the ship on the windowsill in the sun. "I am afraid that she'll have to stay in dry dock for several days. But then she'll be as good as new."

"Thanks," Jeremy said, climbing down from the stool. "You're just like grandpa. You can fix anything."

"Well, we are both doctors. Maybe that has something to do with it." Jeremy stared outside at the tall grass swaying in the wind. "I don't know what to do now."

"Well, Ruthie is helping Sylvia to get the kitchen ready for all of the new guests, so I promised her that I wouldn't bring you back until five. You go see if you can find any new shells for your collection." The boy took a deep breath and shook his head.

"I've got enough already."

"You might think so," said the doctor. "But when all of those tourists come to visit and they can't find any shells on the beach, they will probably want to buy yours since they are so beautiful. Most likely, you could make a lot of money."

Suddenly the little boy's eyes grew wide and excited. "That's right. I was just thinking about that. Do you have a big sack I can use?" Turner laughed and gave Jeremy a large reed basket.

"I'll fix us a snack while you're out collecting."

The child raced out the door and down to the beach. The doctor went into his study and removed several books from a high shelf. Then he reached behind them and pulled out a small rectangular box. He replaced the books and took the weathered carton to his desk. He carefully lifted off the lid and extracted the yellowing newspaper clippings. He spread them out on the blotter.

All of the clippings told the same story, but one had pictures. He studied the full photographs. How lean and young he had been. He looked at the other picture: Dr. Andrew Magee. He wondered if his colleague had aged as much as he had during the intervening years. He also wondered what McGee would do if he were aware of who had been entrusted with his grandson's care.

He folded the articles back up, following the same worn creases, and then returned them to the box. He went to his study window and watched as the fair-haired child scanned the sand for shells. Turner always knew that someday he would seek his revenge. But until Dorothy Dugan arrived on the island, he had never known that it would be so easy.

XI

"Don't you think you've had enough of those pills?" Allison watched with concern as Claire swallowed another of her headache capsules.

"It's that constant racket coming from the beach. They are pouring some concrete patios at the new hotel. Those cement mixers have been going since five o'clock this morning," Claire explained.

"Where's Howard?"

"Tagging along behind Logan Hart as usual. Makes me sick."

"Why?" Victor tells me that Howard is going to be put in charge of all of the sporting activities at the place when it opens. I should think that he would be pleased."

"Oh, he is. Now he will be able to be a child on a grand scale. God this is driving me insane. Let's go inside."

Allison shrugged her shoulders and picked up her hand of cards. They were in the middle of the game of gin rummy so she was careful not to disturb the deck, especially since she was ready to gin.

Claire cleared a place on the coffee table in the living room for the cards and pulled over two yellow rattan chairs. "Let me go see what Thelma is fixing for lunch. If it's anything interesting you can stay." She disappeared into the kitchen for a few minutes then emerged with two glasses of iced tea. "Chicken salad," she announced.

"I'll stay." Allison went on. "Victor is having some kind of a meeting in the dining room this afternoon with the plantation owners. They are going to discuss new farming techniques designed to increase sugar and banana production."

"Sounds thrilling," Claire said, settling into her chair. "Jesus Al, you changed my cards," she said re-examining her hand. "I wasn't this far behind."

"I'm afraid that you were my dear," said her opponent.

"It's this bitch of a headache." Claire drew a new card and made a tactical error, discarding the Queen of Clubs Allison needed to gin.

Claire quickly lost that game and the two following. Then they broke for lunch. "You really are having an off day," Allison said as they moved to the dining table. As Claire pulled out her chair a small lizard, resting on the seat, scurried down one leg and onto the floor. Thelma brought in the lunch: plates of lettuce and tomatoes piled high with diced chicken and a mayonnaise dressing.

"Let's have a glass of wine," Claire suggested.

"Do you really think that you should, I mean with those pills?"

"Oh Al, I'm surprised that you don't adopt me, you're so good at mothering."

Claire saw at once that she had hurt her friend's feelings. "Hey, I'm sorry. But I'm fine, honest. And a glass of white wine would go well."

By the time they were through eating a cloud cover had moved in, thwarting the sun's fury and making the terrace very comfortable. Both of the women were feeling quite relaxed and lazy. They put away the cards and just talked, stretched out on lounge chairs. Conversation flowed easily.

"What do you think of our Mrs. Dugan?" Allison asked casually.

Claire thought of the young woman, how attractive she was and how unbelievably nice. "I don't like her."

"Why?"

"I just don't like anything connected with that hotel." She closed her eyes. "Do you know that I practically had Howie convinced to move back to California with me? I could be getting some great parts in the new films now. They are searching for seasoned actresses that still have their looks."

Allison Trent was well aware of Claire's self-delusion and she went along with it. "But you would have to give up Cinnamon Inn. Now, at least Hart's operation will bring a lot of people here again. You stand to make a great deal of money." Claire propped herself up on her elbows and opened her eyes.

"And what good will that do me? I can't spend it anywhere. Besides I'm sick to death of this place. I'm drying up here. And you can't tell me that you just don't salivate at the mere mention of a diplomatic post for Victor in the home office. You don't belong here anymore than I do. Think of how wonderful it would be to live in London again." A wistful expression covered Allison's face.

"I thought that I had been hiding my disappointment well. After all, it will only be for a few more years until Salter gets things straightened around."

"Ha, isn't that what they told you when you first came to Miranda years ago? I know that you don't buy that. And let's face it, Victor is about as anxious to stay as Howie is, for different reasons of course."

Allison tensed up visibly, "You mean Sarah Hunnicut? Does nothing escape you?"

"Very little."

Suddenly, without warning, Allison burst into tears and buried her face in her hands. It was warm and she had had too much wine. She couldn't pretend any longer. Claire said nothing, but waited for her guest to speak first.

"It's true. I have had enough of this tropical nightmare. I'm tired of not having any contact with refined society. I hate the tourists. They just remind me of everything that I am missing. You don't know how many times I have wanted to swim out to one of those cruisers and just stowaway. I didn't even care where it was going. I just wanted to be out of here. The boys love it on the island. But they also know that they will be going to London for school like Ellen and Julia. They have an escape route."

She spoke in blurts, between sobs. Her face was streaked with smeared makeup. "And I am frightened, too. I never got over the terror of the uprising. Even now, at night, when I hear things rustling in the garden I think that the natives are coming to kill me. I suspect everyone on my staff. They love me and I know it. But I can't help it. They are all little sheep. Anyone could lead them to do anything. It happened before."

Claire could tell how painful this emotional disclosure was for Allison, but it had to continue. It was all part of the grand plan Claire was devising. Allison went on, "And Victor's shoddy affair with that cockney tramp." She smiled slightly, "He imported a mistress and she's not even very pretty. But it's partly my fault I know. Our lives have sort of fallen apart here. We used to be so carefree when we were first married. We both adored the diplomatic circuit. And when they assigned us to Miranda we thought it would be a great big adventure. After all, Victor had been born here. All of his memories were pleasant. But then again, he left when he was still a boy. And at first, we were happy here. But the novelty wore off. Victor still had his job and his contact with London, but I felt isolated and shut out, like I was living on the fringes of someplace."

She had calmed down now and her tone had lost the frantic cast. "I missed my friends and family. At first I went back for visits. But it was not the same. Everyone said how much they envied me, with my very own island to reign over. And I wanted them to be jealous of me so I never let them know how truly miserable I was. Even now, my friends and family think that I am happy. Only Victor knows the truth. And now you of course."

Claire brushed the hair out of her eyes, "I've always known, Al."

"I have taken my unhappiness out on Victor. I know that. But I get so frustrated. He keeps promising me that he will ask for a transfer. But all the home office has to do is merely suggest that we stay here for a while longer and Victor obliges willingly. He has become a spineless yes man. I don't know. Maybe he always was. It's very rare that we even sleep together anymore now that he has Sarah Hunnicut."

Beads of perspiration stood out on her forehead and Claire laid back down on the lounge and closed her eyes again. "Do you think that things would be better between you if you were to go back to London?" She couldn't see Allison's face, but knew that she was pondering the question.

"I honestly don't know. But if there is going to be even a small chance that we could salvage anything, we have to get away from here. And that is impossible now."

Claire said nothing. She would have to move skillfully. "What if there were to be another revolution of sorts?" Her tone was casual, her eyes still closed.

"That would do it," Allison said. "But it's unlikely, especially now that the hotel is generating so much employment. The natives are happy about that."

Claire rolled over on her stomach and dangled her arms to the terrace floor. "Not all of them are."

"What do you mean?"

This time Claire turned around and sat up before speaking. "I've been listening to some of the beach boys talking. They don't pay any attention to me of course, so I am able to hear quite a lot. Seems that certain people are not very pleased with Salter's close association with the foreign investors. It's beginning to make them nervous. Anyway, somebody's down here organizing the natives, getting them pretty upset. And they have been holding secret meetings late at night.

Allison was intrigued. "How do you know?"

"Well, several times in the past few months I've seen some of the new people meet Mandy and some of the other young workers on the island. They always gather on the beach in the dark and go off somewhere. When I asked Mandy where they go all the time he became arrogant and defensive. He said that they weren't doing anything wrong. 'Just talking with some new men' he said."

"What you think that means?" Allison asked.

"I think it means that there is a very good chance that there could be another rebellion brewing right under Salter's nose."

Allison's eyes widened and she started to bite the inside of her lip. "You're serious, aren't you?"

"Very." Claire stood up and walked over to the terrace railing. The bulky yellow cement mixers churning away looked like a herd of mechanical cattle grazing on the sand. She continued speaking with her back to her friend. "And there is something else that I am serious about. I intend to do everything I can to promote a new revolution." She was imagining Allison's expression: shock, fright, astonishment? Those would be the logical responses one could expect from the wife of a British diplomat, a woman who was extensively dedicated to the preservation of peace. But Claire was gambling against logic. Soon she heard a raspy whisper coming from the figure seated behind her.

"I want to help."

XII

The plane came taxiing down the runway at St. Philips. As she stepped from the craft, she noticed that Dr. Turner was waiting with her son to greet her. It was miserably humid. The sky was overloaded with huge, dark gray clouds. Dori bent down and hugged her son tightly. His small body was lean and strong.

"Hi, Ransom," she said standing up. "Thanks for coming. I know that my arrival is a bit unexpected." They were walking toward a yellow station wagon. It had a huge green and orange parrot painted on its side. "The Castle Beach Hotel" was printed in bold blue lettering on the front door.

Turner smiled, "Just arrived yesterday. Hart wanted you to be met in style." Jeremy was holding onto his mother's hand and skipping. "Probably a good thing that you came back a little early. I think Hart needs you."

"Why, is something wrong?" Dori asked, thinking of Ramino and Mariani.

"Nothing really, I don't suppose. But when Jeremy and I stopped by to see him this afternoon there were four trucks there unloading the stuff you ordered. It all arrived at once aboard the same cargo ship." Turner laughed and shook his head "Poor Hart, had them stack everything in the lobby until you show up. You'd think that someone as famous as he is for running hotels would know just how to handle every detail."

"That's just it," Dori said as the doctor was loading her suitcase in the back. "Logan has always had professional managers take care of the details. And he just managed the managers. He's getting a whole new perspective on the business now." She smiled, picturing Logan sitting on cartons frowning in confusion.

Jeremy was full of news and talked continuously on the drive from the airport. "Guess what? Ruthie and me have been packing things all day. Mr. Hart says that we can move into the hotel tomorrow. Our rooms are ready and everything. He showed me today. Our window looks right out where Mr. Rutledge has all of these neat little sailboats. He's going to teach me how to sail one. He promised. Right, Dr. Turner?"

Jeremy was standing in the back seat. He leaned his head over the front to get confirmation from the driver. "That's right. You'll be commanding one of those yourself in no time. Sunfish," he said in Dori's direction. "Tiny fiberglass boats, really nothing more than a canoe with a sail. Just for fun. They stay in the shallow water. The tourists love them. They can tell everyone back home that they went sailing. How are your parents?" he asked, changing the subject abruptly.

"Fine," Dori said. "Just fine."

"Did you tell grandpa all about me and Dr. Turner and all the things I'm learning?"

Dori glossed over the question. "I told him and that you were happy and had made a lot of new friends."

They drove through St. Philips. Dori scanned the harbor. No sign of the *Kiwi*. "Would you like to go back to Cinnamon Inn or right on to the hotel?" Turner asked when they came to an intersection.

She sighed. She was tired. "I better go rescue Logan."

It had started raining by the time they reached the newly paved driveway of the hotel. Turner had not been exaggerating. The main foyer was stacked to the ceiling with wooden and cardboard cartons. Dori squeezed around some of them and made her way into the office. No one was there. Then she heard heavy banging noises coming from the floor above.

"Listen, Ransom, do you mind taking Jeremy up to the cottage? Tell Ruthie that I'll be up in just a little while to help with the packing."

"That's fine." Turner smiled. "I have to stop in and see Claire anyway. She isn't feeling well. Her headaches again, you know." He spoke as though he assumed that Claire and Dori were good friends.

"Well, thank you. I really appreciate it." Again the heavy banging from the second floor. Dori went up via the inside service elevator. Phillip said that he wouldn't have the outside guest elevator up and running until he got back.

As soon as she stepped off on the second floor, Logan's voice could be heard coming from a room down the hall. "I don't know, Howard. I think maybe they go against the walls. Or maybe they just stay side by side in the middle of the room."

"Hello, gentlemen," Dori greeted as she entered the room. "You two make a pathetic pair indeed." The two men were standing in the middle of the room, with their hands at their sides, faces covered with sweat. They were glaring at several white rattan bed frames pushed into the corner.

"Thank God you're back!" Logan said with relief. "I have been searching your desk, looking for your room layouts. As you can see, all of the furniture has arrived. I've got crews ready to move it in but I forgot your decorating arrangements."

Dori opened up the small attaché case she was carrying. "Here," she said producing two large renderings of the hotel suites. "I took them with me. I was ordering some accessories from Mosley's and needed to have them."

Logan moaned and sat down on the floor. Howard looked over his shoulder at the sketches. "See, I was right," he said proudly. "They're perpendicular against the walls with a table in the corner."

"Actually," Dori injected, "the beds can go any number of ways. This is simply a classic arrangement that we can work with. If the guests want to move them around that will be fine. I can't wait to see the bedspreads and pillows."

"Well, everything is downstairs." Logan said.

"So I noticed on my way in," Dori teased. "Kind of hard to miss."

The rain was pouring down furiously. The wind blew it against the sliding glass doors with the force of a fire hose. Howard looked out on the wall of water. "I better go down and secure all of those sailboats. I think that this one is here for the night." Even above the wind of the storm Howard's heavy, lumbering footfalls could be heard as he retreated down the hall.

Dori sat down on the floor beside Logan. He looked worn out. "Well, I am glad that everything got unloaded and delivered before this started." Logan said.

"That can't be everything," Dori said. "I mean just the crates and boxes in the lobby?"

Logan had been watching the rain. "The rest of the stuff is jammed into the dining room and the storage warehouses. Sylvia is having a fit." Logan began rubbing the back of his neck. "I'm exhausted. It has been a long week." He sighed heavily. "How was your trip? And hey, why are you back already? I thought that you and Phil were coming back together in a few days. I was surprised when I got your cable. Happy, I'll admit, but surprised." Dori debated as to whether or not she should tell him about the episode with Phillip. She knew that Logan would tell her what she wanted to hear: that Phillip had behaved like a cad, that he wasn't worth it. She decided against saying anything about what had happened.

"The trip was really unnecessary for me to make actually. With the exception of the things I bought at Mosley's, everything else that I had gone to check up on had been taken care of.

Logan was aware of what she was implying. "Ramino and Mariani," he confirmed. "Our fairy godfathers, so to speak."

"Oh, by the way Logan, I have something to tell you. I'm sure you won't mind, but I think that you should know anyway. I ended up telling Phillip about this whole deal. He was bound to find out sooner or later. I can't imagine any harm it…"

"Oh Dori, I wish so much that you hadn't." Logan was visibly upset.

"Why?"

"I just don't want anymore people to know about this arrangement than absolutely necessary. Phillip will be finished here in a few weeks. There was really no reason to involve him."

Dori grabbed his hand. "I'm sorry. I just wanted him to realize what kind of an ordeal you have been subjected to lately."

"You mean, why I have been such an ogre to work for?"

Dori nodded.

"Well, he can't let anyone else know that he is aware of the situation."

Dori wanted to ask why but she was afraid of the answer.

Logan stood up and stretched. The island was still being inundated with rain. "Nothing more we can do here today. I guess you haven't seen your rooms yet?"

"No."

"Well come on." He helped her up and they took the service elevator to the top floor. Logan smiled and winked as he led her down the hall. When he came to a door not far from the end he opened it with a passkey.

"Ta da!" he said, flinging the door open wide. Dori was stunned. She could not believe what she saw. Logan had provided her with one of the choicest suites in the entire hotel: two huge bedrooms connected by a terrace and a kitchen. Each bedroom had its own bath. One entire wall of the place consisted of sliding glass doors. She had a view of the beach and of the open sea beyond. But what really had Dori amazed was the way in which the suite had been decorated: authentic Early American furniture, from pine four-poster beds to a parson's bench and an oak desk with copper reading lamps. Colorful hook rugs were thrown over wide plank hardwood floors. Patchwork quilted spreads, puffy and comfortable looking, adorned each bed. There was even a grandfather clock on one wall, and a mirrored hall tree stood just inside the front door. It was all the type of furniture Dori had grown up with and she loved it.

"Logan, how in the world…?"

"I have had this stuff ordered for months. I wanted your place to be special, not like the others. I wanted you to be happy here and to feel at home. Wait, don't say anything yet. Turn around and close your eyes." Dori obediently followed his instructions. She heard movement behind her near the windows and sliding glass doors. It was a kind of rustling sound. "Okay," he said, "You can look now."

Dori turned around and opened her eyes. She began to laugh at the same time as tears were gathering in her eyes. The whole tableaux was so incongruous but sweet. Logan had pulled down a huge shade that ran the length of the glass. It had been painted like a Currier and Ives print. It depicted children skating on a frozen lake surrounded with snow covered pine trees. There was a small cabin in the distance with smoke twirling up from the brick chimney. Logan was grinning broadly, totally enjoying himself. "Great, huh? Came from a specialty store in Boston."

Dori went over and hugged him, a platonic, but sincere embrace. "It's crazy! Vermont in the tropics, rum punch and snowmen. I love it. Really. Thank you Logan. I know that you have gone to a great deal of trouble to make this happen. You're a very thoughtful man."

"Yes, I am," he agreed happily. "And besides that, wouldn't you feel guilty leaving the employ of a man who treats you so well?"

Dori became serious. "You are really worried about this gambling thing aren't you? Do you really think that things are going to be rough?"

Logan sat down on one of the beds. "I honestly don't know. I've just got to go along with it until the hotel is established in its own right, until people like it enough that they would come with or without the betting. Mariani and his associates have other fish to fry. I'm hoping that they will lose interest after a while and that they will relocate somewhere else."

"What about Salter?"

"I don't know. I can't quite figure that guy out. He has been over here a few times. He's always friendly and his conversation superficial. He walks around giving pep talks to all of the native employees, telling them that things are looking up. I haven't sized up his role in this whole scheme yet."

As they talked the wind had slackened; it was dark and still outside. The great deluge had stopped and only a light after mist floated through the air. Suddenly Dori was very tired. "I really don't want to think about anything else tonight. I am going back to the cottage to have dinner with Ruthie and Jeremy. I feel guilty. I have been spending so little time with my son. And with the opening of the hotel in just three weeks I know that I will have even less time for him." Logan stood up and led her toward the door.

"Well, I was going to take you out to The Buoy for supper, but we'll make it another night."

"Why don't you come and eat with us?" They were walking down the hall toward the elevator.

"No, I want to recheck all of the shipping invoices again. Then I think I'll just have Sylvia scramble some eggs for me. I'm so tired I could sleep standing up."

"Have you moved out of the ministry yet?" Dori asked as they stood in the box-laden lobby.

"Yeah, I've been sleeping on a cot in the office. Phillip and I are going to be sharing a suite down the hall from yours." He stared up at the towering cartons. "As soon as all of this stuff is unpacked, I'll be able to move in." Dori felt sorry for him.

"Sleep in my suite tonight. It's all ready."

"No, no," Logan said in a martyred voice. "I wouldn't think of disturbing its pristine beauty. Here," he reached into the pocket of his pants and tossed her the keys to his Mercedes. "Take my car, I'll see you in the morning."

Dori thanked him again for her "winter wonderland" and then left. Driving up to Cinnamon Inn, she thought of her new suite once more. In this setting it was so bizarre, almost gauche, Walt Disney gone mad. But the gesture had been so dear that she decided to continue to rave about the arrangement. In time she hoped that she would be able to store all of the furniture and subtly replace it with the regulation hotel fare without hurting Logan's feelings.

Ruthie and Jeremy were sitting down to dinner when Dori arrived. Her son was happy that she was joining them. He told her all about school and about the wonderful afternoons he had been spending with Dr. Turner. Ruthie had made some kind of pork and raisin dish. It was very good. Dori had a glass of wine with her meal and was feeling better. New York and Phillip seemed years ago, rather than just a matter of days.

"I'm so excited about movin' in tomorrow, Mrs. Dugan. I'll be staying with Sylvia's girls in the bedrooms off the kitchen. But don't worry. I'll be up every morning to take care of Jeremy. And if you want sometimes I will stay with him when you are going to be out late or are busy." Dori started to realize how much she had come to depend on Ruthie over the past few months. She was more than a cook and a housekeeper. She had become almost a surrogate mother to Jeremy.

"Ruthie, you have been doing an excellent job. I am very pleased that you are happy with us." The young Mirandan smiled at the praise revealing a mouthful of white, but uneven teeth.

It was about eleven o'clock when Dori finally climbed into bed. Ruthie had finished the dishes and had gone into her room. Jeremy had been asleep for several hours. Although Dori was physically and emotionally drained, she couldn't sleep.

The next few weeks were going to be hectic. So many things to finish before the opening, so many details to attend to. She made a note to review the guest list for the first few weeks. How many would be coming for the sun and the sand and how many for the backgammon tables? She pictured Ramino and Mariani. She remembered the way they stood sweating in their expensive, tailor-made suits. And John Salter. Her feelings for him were ambivalent. He frightened and intrigued her simultaneously. She glanced over at Jeremy. He was breathing heavily with his face buried in his pillow, sleeping the deep, unbroken slumber reserved for children.

Dori went into the living room and opened the terrace doors. The mist had stopped and the clouds had cleared. A nearly full moon spilled light onto the wet sand. The air was damp and fragrant; Dori inhaled fully. She was beginning to feel sleepy and was about to go inside when a movement caught her. It was coming from the lawn below the terrace. She stepped back into the shadows and watched as a figure made its way across the grass, past the garden bar to the beach. The moonlight outlined the body as it walked. It was Mandy. Dori watched as he joined a group of other people. They were all holding candles. A dozen or more flames mingled about like fireflies converging in the night.

Then Dori saw a separate figure appear on the grass by the garden bar. It too was making its way toward the others. Whoever it was had come from one of the cottages. This person was shorter than Mandy and thinner. Dori strained to see. Suddenly, as the figure stepped into the growing gathering of lights Dori saw a pale white arm reach out for a candle. Claire! It had to be. What are they all doing?

Soft whisperings were heard. Then the group proceeded down the beach in the opposite direction of the new hotel and behind Cinnamon Inn toward the heavily jungled side of the island coast. Soon the flames became tiny specks of light before disappearing completely. Where were they going?

Dori came back inside and climbed into bed. This time sleep came, warm and comforting, like the gentle voice of a friend.

XIII

"She says that she's already heard us," one of them said. "We keep forgetting that she understands all of our talk. She says she's going to tell Salter if we don't let her in. She also says that she has a letter telling everything she knows. If anything happens to her, Salter gets the note."

"You stupid jackass" Mandy said, furious. "The Chameleon won't like this one bit." The young native stared out from the circle of candles at Claire, who was standing a discreet distance away holding a candle of her own. He left the group and came over to Claire. "What do you want with all of this?" Even in the candlelight it was hard for Claire to get a good look at Mandy's face. So she had to judge his mood totally from the tone of his voice.

"I want to help. You've worked for Mr. Rutledge and me long enough to know that I want to leave here and he doesn't. And if you are successful in any kind of trouble you are planning, I know that he will agree to leave and I can get back to Hollywood where I belong." Mandy knew nothing of Hollywood, other than it was all this American ever spoke about. He reasoned that it must be a wonderful place if she wished to trade the beautiful splendor of Miranda for it.

"Come on," he said, "the Chameleon will have to decide if we are to believe you."

Claire followed the group of natives as they made their way to the most remote section of Castle Beach, around the far end of the inlet past Cinnamon Inn. The beach narrowed abruptly and only portions of craggy rock jutted out into the ocean. The group climbed over the rocks for several minutes before turning off into the choking undergrowth. A thin path had been cleared through the thick, knotted vines. Claire stumbled several times but managed to keep her candle upright and glowing. But twice when she slipped it tilted and burning wax fell on her hand. The pain was severe, but she said nothing.

Without warning the trail widened into a large grassy clearing. Claire counted the flames of at least a dozen or more candles. As the group she was traveling in drew closer to the others she stifled a gasp as she recognized one of the faces: Frank LeBeau. She couldn't believe it. Frank LeBeau, the tedious, self-appointed historian of West Indian culture. He seemed just as surprised to see her.

"Stand over here," Mandy instructed, "with your back to the circle." Claire turned around obediently. She heard low voices behind her. It sounded as though people were arguing among themselves. She was feeling dizzy and a little uneasy. For the first time since she had decided to investigate this group, she realized that she might be in great danger. She hoped Mandy believed the lie she had told him concerning the letter to Salter.

She felt a hand on her shoulder. "Come, talk to me please. I am most interested in what you have to say." The voice had a brisk, scholarly English accent. She turned around and studied the face. She knew that she had seen him before. When? Where? She tried hard to think. He was a Mirandan. But it was obvious from his dress and manner that he had spent considerable time abroad. Then it came to her. She had seen him often with John Salter. Yes, that was it! He had become the prime minister's closest adviser during and after the revolution. Her mind was spinning. "My name is Charles Cliff," he said.

"Yes, I recognize you." Claire said meekly. His expression was sternly intense.

"Your presence here has complicated things."

"Did Mandy tell you that I have come to offer my help? I know you are planning some kind of a disturbance." The black man's lips held the trace of a smile.

"Some kind, yes," he said. "But I find it most ironic that you would wish to aid in the cause of the events that would ultimately be the ruin of all that you and your husband have worked for on this island."

Claire was bewildered. How could she convince this obvious patriot that her hatred for this place had become an obsession? How could she make him understand that whatever positive feelings she had for Miranda had died during the first revolt? How could she make him see that only by destroying Cinnamon Inn, her menacing albatross, could she ever have a hope of salvation?

"I think that Mrs. Rutledge is sincere in her desire to aid our cause, though her motives are less than altruistic." It was Frank LeBeau. "You see, Charles, Mrs. Rutledge longs to return to California. She abandoned a career there years ago to come with her husband to Miranda. And while her husband is happy here, she is not, so anything that would put an end to the possibility of their residing here would be welcome news." Claire wondered why was he coming to her defense? They had never been close friends. If anything Howard knew him better than she did. And he was really too highbrow for Howard. He was constantly discussing the political theory of Mirandan history. Howard would listen, but she knew that for the most part he found it boring. It was Charles Cliff's turn to speak.

"If you are so anxious to leave the island, Mrs. Rutledge, that you would go to such extremes as to involve yourself in internal affairs, why don't you just leave alone, without your husband?"

"I can't do that," she said with conviction. "He needs me." In her own way, subconsciously perhaps, Claire recognized that she probably needed Howard more than he needed her. She even thought that maybe she might love him still. It was hard to tell anymore. She couldn't dwell on that now.

Cliff led Frank LeBeau a few steps away and the two talked for several minutes before returning to where Claire was standing.

"Very well, Mrs. Rutledge," Cliff began. "I have no reason to doubt Mr. LeBeau. He has been one of our supporters for a very long time. He feels that you are no threat to us and that you might even be a valuable asset when the time is right." Claire felt relieved. "Your reasons for aiding our cause are petty and shallow. But it is not for me to make value judgments. We need a broad base of secret support if we are to succeed. In a matter of a few short weeks the preliminary phase of our plan will go into operation. It is imperative that you have a grasp on the overall workings of the entire structure of things."

For a moment he addressed Mandy and the group of young people assembled behind him. Claire noticed that most of them were young natives and that she had not seen them before. "Mandy, take the group to my headquarters and meet there. Drill them on the principles." Mandy nodded solemnly and quickly herded the group away, even further into the dense, strangling growth.

Cliff once again focused his attention on Claire. "It is important that the young people understand what it is they are being asked to defend. It is difficult for them to have a grasp of the important history they will be making. But if they believe that what they are doing will improve life for all of Miranda, they will be unwavering in their diligence and dedication to our cause: a united Caribbean alliance." Cliff sat down on a knotted fallen log and Claire and Frank LeBeau joined him.

"You see, Claire," Frank said in his irritatingly professorial tone, "Salter doesn't have a grasp of a United Caribbean alliance. He doesn't believe in aligning with the other islands. Charles has tried to show him that by joining forces with the larger, more influential islands Miranda will have a better bargaining position. He sees himself as a ruler of the West Indian chain. His ego will not permit him to share his authority for the good of the total."

"Our organization is operating throughout the Caribbean." Cliff said. "It has been even before the last revolution that freed Miranda. The movement seemed too radical to me at the time but Salter has been a disappointment to all of us. He has been corrupted by foreign money and promises of quick riches for himself. I am just a field chief. The real control lies with our leaders in Cuba, Haiti, and Venezuela. When the time is right the entire West Indian chain will be taken. The rest of the Caribbean will tumble in our hands like falling dominoes."

"And then," LeBeau said, "we will have total control of all passage of goods by sea between the eastern United States and northern South America. The days of the sleepy, easily exploited banana republics will be over."

"What is your interest in this, Frank?" Claire asked. LeBeau exchanged glances with Cliff.

"I love Miranda, and all of the West Indies. I always have. You might as well know, since it is a matter of public record, that I have changed my citizenship from French to West Indian. I hope to play a modest, yet significant role in a better future for my adopted homeland." He was sincere. There was no doubt about that.

"But I still don't know exactly what you were planning for the immediate future or what I am supposed to do," she said.

"You shall be told all that you need to be told and nothing more," Cliff said. "And you must agree to do what we instruct you to do and ask no questions."

"But," argued Claire, "you have already told me about the united Caribbean alliance."

Frank LeBeau and his companion laughed heartily. "My dear," said LeBeau taking her hand, "that is no secret. All of the present island leaders know of the existence of our organization. They have simply chosen not to take us seriously."

"And that will be their ultimate mistake," Cliff said. He stood up, signifying that the meeting was concluded. "We will meet here at various times throughout the coming weeks. It is not necessary that you attend each gathering. In fact there are only a certain number to which you shall be invited. I am to be referred to only by the codename of Chameleon. Mr. LeBeau is always aware of my location. If you need to see me at other than previously prescribed times, contact him."

"Why have you chosen the name Chameleon?" Claire asked, curious.

"What are the characteristics of a chameleon, Mrs. Rutledge?" Claire thought for a moment. There was really only a single significant one that came immediately to mind.

"They are able to change colors rapidly."

"Exactly, to adapt to their surroundings. That is why when you see me in the close company of the prime minister in the months ahead I will seem to fit right in place." He turned to leave. "And I suggest for now that we all attempt to emulate the chameleon, if you understand my meaning." Claire understood.

XIV

"Oh, they are perfect, exactly what I wanted." Dori was opening a carton of the bedspreads that she had designed. "What do you think?" She asked Logan, who was supervising a group of young men as they unloaded furniture.

"Terrific. But I knew that they would be."

"Such blind faith," smiled Dori. She took one of the spreads and shook it out over the cot in the office. The spread was made of heavy cotton muslin. The background color was bright lemon yellow. Small quilted parrots lined the edges. The colors of the birds alternated from red to green, to orange, to blue. In the middle of each spread was a larger parrot made up of a combination of the colors of the smaller birds. Sylvia was hovering about, oohing and aahing. Dori instructed her to get the rest of the girls and have them deliver a pair of spreads to each room.

The whole week was spent in the unpacking and arranging of the furniture, bed linens, and beach towels, to say nothing of the vast array of kitchen and dining room equipment. As well as managing the sports facilities, Logan had hired Howard to organize the bar. "I know exactly what to order," he had said. "People drink differently in the islands, long on the rum and gin, short on the scotch and bourbon." After buying the liquor for Cinnamon Inn all of these years, he had a good relationship with the best distributors in Puerto Rico. He was so enthusiastic about everything, an overgrown child, Dori often thought as she watched him dart around full of energy, grateful for this new responsibility.

Observing Howard, she would always think of how unlike he was from his troubled, moody wife. Dori said nothing to anyone about what she had witnessed from her terrace nights before. She and Claire had at best a strained relationship. She didn't want to tax it further by appearing to be unduly suspicious and meddling. She put the entire issue out of her mind. She had enough on which to concentrate.

Things were going well with the hotel preparations. They were right on schedule, remarkably enough, despite the fact that Phillip had stayed away days longer than he had originally anticipated. "Some building project he is doing on the Lower East Side has run amok," Logan said one afternoon after talking to him. "But, he will be back tomorrow." Dori glanced at the office calendar.

"I can't believe it. The day after next is Easter Sunday."

Logan smiled nervously, "Three weeks left."

"Opening-night jitters?" Dori asked.

"A bit, but you know, things are looking pretty good."

And they were. All of the rooms had been decorated to Dori's specifications: clean white rattan bed frames with those wonderful quilts, cane back chairs with brightly colored cushions, bamboo and glass tables and writing desks. But the main dining room was her real triumph. She was anxious for Phillip to see how well her decorating had complimented his architectural alterations. The room itself was large and octagonal in shape. The deep red tile floor that ran throughout the rest of the hotel was also in here. The walls had been covered totally in grass cloth. The ceiling was composed of large expansive skylights. Throughout the room lush blue green ferns hung from invisible wires. The dining tables and chairs were made of lacquered bamboo. The tables would be set with locally woven green and yellow placemats, with cloth napkins to match. The overall feeling was one of spacious, airy elegance.

"One of my better efforts," she said, giving Logan a tour of the completed project.

"Beautiful, Dori, really. Wait until some of the New York trade papers get pictures of this. Your reputation as one of the best in the business will be established permanently. Who knows, you might even be asked to pose for a centerfold in *Architectural Digest*. A first.

Dori laughed and shook her head. "I really couldn't have done any of this if you had not allowed me the freedom of choice that you did, as well as the hefty budget. Thanks."

In the large empty room their voices seemed to bounce off the walls. There was also a great deal of rattling commotion emanating from the kitchen. They followed it to its source. Sylvia was standing with her arms folded over her ample chest watching Howard as he and a few helpers installed a large microwave oven. The frown Sylvia was nurturing deepened as she spotted the new arrivals.

"I've never used one of those things," she said, pointing accusingly at the new appliance. "Mr. Rutledge has been telling me all about it. Scares me. I don't like it. Too many buttons and dials on it. It might start running this kitchen instead of me. I only need this." She gently caressed the huge eighteen-burner gas range.

"Well you can use them both, Sylvia," Logan reasoned. "I think that you will like this new one once you make friends with it."

"Harrumph!"

"I don't think that she's convinced," Dori winked.

"You try it now, Sylvia, you understand?" warned Howard gently. "Everyone on this island will be jealous of you. Mrs. Trent would love to have one of these. And if John Salter knew about it, he'd probably take it for himself."

A big playful grin swept over the cook's face. At once she became possessive toward the new contraption. "Well, you put it in proper then. If I'm going to use it, I want it put in proper. And you be careful you don't scratch it," she said, admonishing a young native. Logan laughed lightly and shook his head. Howard certainly did have a way with the locals.

For the first time since they entered the room, Dori noticed that Sylvia was wearing the new uniform she had been given. She filled it completely, but it still looked graceful and stylish. Dori was pleased.

After a fish dinner cooked at the outside patio bar and a bottle of crisp white wine, Logan and Dori took a long walk down the beach. Howard had lit the flame torches lining the walkways around the hotel. It was a beautiful sight. The air was soft and warm. Though almost nine, the sun had just set, leaving behind faint traces of gold and pink light upon the water. Small land crabs scurried along the sand and buried themselves at the waters edge. Jeremy was playing tag with some of the children of the hotel employees. Frank LeBeau and Howard were having a drink at the outside bar. It was a peaceful evening. The breakneck pace of the week had mellowed. It was evident that Logan was feeling somewhat more relaxed about things.

"I used to have nightmares that all of the guests would arrive and nothing would be ready."

"I know," Dori said, "I used to have the same recurring dream myself. It is hard to believe that it is all finally coming together."

"Yeah," he agreed, "the only real project left is for Phillip to get that outside elevator operating. I'm glad that he is coming back tomorrow." Dori stiffened slightly.

"You want to tell me about it?" Logan asked. Dori looked defensively at him. "You've been different since you returned. Whenever I mention Phillip you get uneasy. Something happened between you two." He paused and scrutinized her face. "Maybe I shouldn't use the past tense?"

Dori dug her bare feet into the powdery sand as they walked. "I really haven't worked everything out in my own mind yet, Logan. Would it be all right if we postponed this conversation?"

"Being basically nosey and starved for gossip, no it wouldn't. But Okay." He smiled as he put his arm around her shoulder. As the last remnants of daylight drained from the island they walked back in easy silence to the hotel.

XV

"Guess who came to see Victor this morning?" Allison asked. Claire was going from changing room to changing room readying them for the expected onslaught of tourists from the newly anchored Dutch cruiser.

"Where is Thelma? She promised me that Mandy would have some fresh towels down here by now. Most of the showers need new soap too. If Howard thinks that I'm going to keep this place going all by myself, then he is crazy! He's so busy playing with all of his new little toys that this dump is going to seed. And I'd let it too, except that we have started to get some letters from previous guests who want to come and stay again. And we can't live on nothing. Jesus Christ, what a mess," she said, lifting the green canvas tarp covering the bar. "No booze, no clean glasses." She spotted Mandy and several young girls ambling down from the cottages balancing stacks of white folded towels on their heads. Claire brushed tendrils of unkempt hair from her face and cupped her hands around her mouth.

"You step on it," she hollered. Mandy and the others speeded up, trying to look efficient. "And when you get through cleaning up this sty," Claire said as they came closer, "I want you to get Mr. Rutledge. Tell him that I want him here right away!"

She turned and headed in the direction of the lounge chairs set up on the lawn. She motioned for Allison to follow. "Goddamn, my head is pounding like a jackhammer," she complained, settling into a chair. "It's the humidity. That storm the other night turned this whole island into a steam bath. It takes strength just to breath." She fanned herself with a paper plate she had picked up off the grass. Claire looked up at Allison as though she were seeing her for the first time.

"Sit down, Al," she commanded. "What brings you to my Garden of Eden this morning?" Allison Trent's face was filled with anxious frustration. She sat down quickly, pulling her chair closer to Claire's, even though they were alone on the lawn.

"I've been trying to tell you," she said, exasperated. "Phillip Graham came to see Victor early this morning." Claire was massaging her temples.

"Graham? The architect? I thought he was in New York or some other civilized place."

"He was. He just got back today. He came straight to our home." Finally, Allison seemed to have Claire's full attention.

"So, what did he want?"

Allison exhaled deeply. "Well, we were out in the garden having breakfast with the boys when he was announced. He looked terrible, tired and drawn, like he had not shaved for several days, or had slept well either. Anyway, he said that he had just flown in from Barbados and had been doing a lot of thinking. He said that he needed to talk to Victor privately about something urgent. They got up and left and went into the study. I pretended to act uninterested, but as soon as the door was closed I sent the children off to play on the other side of the garden and I went around the house to the study window. Fortunately, it was open and I heard everything they said."

Claire cocked her head and grinned. "Well, Al, I'm proud of you. Eavesdropping on your husband is good for starters."

"Honestly, Claire, this is serious business." Allison was annoyed but proceeded nevertheless. "Graham said that he had learned that there was going to be high-stakes illegal gambling going on at the new hotel. He said that Hart had been coerced into accepting the situation, that he had been strong-armed by a couple of racketeers from Florida and that Salter was in on the whole deal." Claire had stopped rubbing her forehead; she was listening intently now.

"You're right, this is serious. What did Victor do?"

"Oh Victor," Allison said bitterly. "He hemmed and hawed and told him that he would speak to Salter and get to the bottom of things. Graham said that the only reason he had decided to tell him was over concern for Hart and Dorothy Dugan. He said that he didn't like the idea of their being pressured into tolerating criminal activities. Victor thanked him for informing him and told him not to worry. After that, Graham left for the hotel."

Claire lifted her arms over her head and stretched. "Graham was not supposed to know about this. They figured him for a weak sister. Dugan must've told him," Claire sneered, "while they were in bed, no doubt."

Allison was panicked. "What are we going to do?"

"The Chameleon has called for a meeting tonight. I shall tell him then. What about Victor?" She asked.

"I wouldn't worry about him. I am sure that he will say nothing to Salter. He fears him though he would never admit it. I think that he will go on as though he had never been informed. His life is easy here. London thinks that he is doing a splendid job; Salter humors him. And then we can't forget Miss Hunnicut. No, he is not about to do anything that might jeopardize his self indulgent existence."

Claire was certain that Allison was correct in her unflattering assessment of Victor's response to the situation. She moved a pair of sunglasses, which had been resting on the top of her head, down over her eyes and squinted. Howard was padding down the beach toward them.

"Look, Al, you go home and calm down. I'll take care of everything." She squeezed her friend's hand reassuringly.

Allison stood up and left, walking up the gently sloping lawn to the rock stairs that lead to the road high above the cottages. Howard was puffing by the time he reached his wife's chair.

"Isn't that Allison leaving?" he asked, catching his breath.

"Um-hum," Claire said in a disinterested fashion. "She came over to play cards but I have a horrendous headache." She scowled at him. "Which was caused by the fact that nothing is ready down here. Look." She raised her loose-fleshed arm and pointed out to sea. Several dinghies were being lowered over the side of the cruise ship. Groups of people were lining up on the deck.

"The first batch will be here in less than twenty minutes. What are you going to serve them? Salt water on ice?" She laughed bitterly at the image.

Howard squatted down on the grass near her chair. "I'm sorry. I know that I haven't been spending enough time here. But Logan really needs me at the moment."

"The indispensable beach bum," Claire said sarcastically.

Howard ignored the insult. "I'll get things set up now." He stood and walked over to the bar where Mandy was busily washing glasses. Thelma was emptying ice trays into a large Styrofoam chest.

Claire watched her husband walk away and then she put her head back against the chair and closed her eyes. It promised to be a hot day. The breeze was timid; the sun, hanging in the cloudless azure sky, beat down upon the earth with waves of violent, blistering heat. Soon the sand would be unbearable to all but the most callused of naked feet. Clair's head began throbbing. She rose slowly and headed back up the lawn toward her bungalow. Midway up the steps leading to her terrace, she turned and looked back at the beach. The dinghy had landed. Again the procession of vapid, middle-aged, overweight vacationers began its uneventful pilgrimage to the Cinnamon Inn garden bar. And again, Howard, armed with his clipboard, tagged after the men, coaxing them into signing up for his putting contest. The pink skinned women spread towels on the lawn and began lathering their bodies with heavy creams and oils.

Claire extended one hand out straight in front of her and closed one eye. From this distance it was enough to block the entire scene. She thought of the lean, handsome men she had known in Hollywood. How they had adored her. She let her arm drop to her side and stared in disgust. She resumed her climb. She knew that she must be patient. She would not have to endure the horrid indignities of this island much longer, if everything went as planned.

When she reached her cottage she took several pain pills before climbing onto the bed to lie down. Tonight the Chameleon would have to be told about Phillip Graham of course. Claire watched as a large, brown lizard on the wall across from her skillfully stalked an unwary fly. The reptile made minute, smoothly executed movements toward its victim. Finally, after a rigid, last pause, the scaly creature lashed out at its prey with a long, snapping tongue. It swallowed the fly before moving on across the plaster in search of more food.

XVI

"Look at that!" Sylvia said with amazement gazing through the door of the microwave oven. "I've never seen anything like it in my whole life. Kind of spooky, huh?" Jeremy stood up on a wooden kitchen chair to get a better view of his rapidly cooking grilled cheese sandwich.

"Neato," he said in total agreement with the cook. A small bell on the stove rang, indicating that the show was over and that lunch was ready.

"Now you watch, Jimby," she said. "This is the best part." She opened the door ceremoniously and extracted the plastic plate on which the sandwich had been cooking.

"Plate isn't even hot." She set it down in front of Jeremy who had moved to a small table in the kitchen.

"Magic," he said then took a satisfying bite out of the sandwich. "You're a good cook, Sylvia," he proclaimed. "Better than my mom."

"I heard that, young man," Dori said sternly pushing open the swinging door from the dining room.

"But you don't have the magic stove, mom," Jeremy attempted diplomatically.

Sylvia was smiling and blushing and feeling somewhat awkward.

"He's right, you know," Dori said reaching for some bread and cheese. "I'm not a very good cook. Do you think you could fix a couple more of these? Mr. Hart and I are working in the office."

"Right away," Sylvia answered happily. Dori noticed that the gas range had not been touched.

"You know, Sylvia, when the hotel is full you won't be able to cook everything in the microwave."

"I know," she said sadly, casting a disparaging look in the direction of the primitive stove.

"Something smells good in here!" It was Phillip's voice. Dori felt herself tense. She turned around with a manufactured smile on her face.

"Welcome back," she said lightly. "We were beginning to think you had lost your way."

"Wishful thinking, my dear. Hi there, kiddo," he said, turning his attention to Jeremy. "I saw Mr. Rutledge on the way in. He told me that he is going to be trying out some of the sailboats this afternoon. Said to tell you that he could use your help."

The small boy's eyes widened with excitement. "Can I go, mom?" He looked expectantly at Dori.

"Yes, but I want you to wear a life jacket."

"Okay." He wolfed down the remainder of his lunch and darted out of the kitchen through the service exit.

"Will you be wanting one of these too, Mr. Graham?" Sylvia asked, placing the freshly cooked sandwiches on a serving tray.

"No thanks, Sylvia."

"Well then," she said, addressing Dori. "I'll just take these into Mr. Hart." She picked up the tray and left.

"I'll be moving in here today," Phillip announced. "So I've got to go back to Cinnamon Inn and pack up everything. I hate the thought of examining my refrigerator. There was some cheese in there that was molding when I left. It has probably taken over the whole place by now."

Dori was deliberately avoiding any eye contact. She busied herself by pouring tall glasses of iced tea for Logan and herself.

"Sylvia told me that there were some fresh lemons around here somewhere," she said, opening cupboards.

"Here," Phillip handed her one. They were in a huge basket right on the counter in front of her.

"Thanks," she said, slightly embarrassed.

"Incidentally," he continued, "the dining room looks fantastic. And I glanced at one of the suites. Sensational. You are very talented, Mrs. Dugan."

Dori did not respond to the compliment. "Excuse me," she said, picking up the glasses of iced tea and heading for the swinging door. "Logan and I have to go over the schedule of guest arrivals. Some are coming by ship, others by plane. We have to work out the logistics of how we are going to have the hotel station wagon in two places at once.

Phillip grabbed her wrists, almost causing her to drop one glass. "Dori, we have to talk. Not now, I know. But later."

"I don't feel the necessity to discuss anything with you, Phillip," Dori lied.

"Well I do," Phillip said. "And we will." He opened the door for her. She walked briskly past him and into the office.

Logan was eating his lunch and welcomed the iced tea. Dori sat down, now totally void of appetite and faced with her sandwich.

"Phillip is back," she said.

"Oh great. There are a million things I have been waiting to discuss with him. Where is he?"

"He had to go back to Cinnamon Inn and finish packing."

Logan looked at his watch. "Well, it's probably too late now for him to do any work on the outside elevator. But I want him to get that thing working as soon as possible. I keep having visions of hordes of elegant people riding up and down in the service elevator beside a cart filled with dirty dishes."

"Logan, have you heard from Salter lately?" Dori had managed to take a few bites of her sandwich. They were like dry cubes in her throat.

"Funny you should ask that. He made one of his rare appearances here yesterday morning when you were passing out uniforms to the staff. He looked like the Cheshire cat, smiling, not a care in the world. He wanted me to tell you how wonderful everything looks. But wait." Logan paused and took several gulps of tea. "Let me see if I can phrase it exactly as he did. 'Please inform Mrs. Dugan that her decorating reflects the natural beauty of Miranda very well. Somehow she has managed from letting it become Americanized.'"

"What does he know? Most everything in this hotel came from New York and Florida. If that isn't Americanized, I don't know what is."

"I think that he just wanted to say something that sounded official and profound."

They were both avoiding the real issue. "Logan, what about Ramino and Mariani?"

Logan leaned back in his chair. "He told me that they have been in Miami for the past few weeks."

"Well," Dori reasoned, "that accounts for the absence of the *Kiwi* from the St. Philip's Harbor."

"Yeah, but they are back now."

"Oh joy."

"Salter told me that he is going to join them on their boat for a few days. They're going to sail around to some of the smaller islands to relax, ostensibly anyway. He hinted that they would be filling him in on the details of the gambling, how it's going to operate. He also gave me this before you left." Logan took a single sheet of paper out of his top desk drawer and handed it to Dori. She studied it.

"A list of names," she said. "Who are they?"

"They are among the first group of guests who will be arriving soon. They will be here for the backgammon."

"Oh," Dori sighed. "I wish that there were some way to get out of— "

"Don't say it," Logan warned. "You and I just have to have patience for the next few months, and concentrate on making the hotel a success."

"Yes, I know." Dori leafed through her desk calendar. "It is hard to believe that in just ten days this place will be swarming with people."

"Do you think that Sylvia and her girls are ready?" Logan asked.

"Well I hope so. I have been teaching them how to divide the dining room into stations and how to set and clear tables properly. I'll keep going over everything with them through next week. They are eager to learn. They are all so happy to have a job of any kind that none of them want to make any mistakes. Ruthie is in charge of running the laundry. She has got that down to a system. And Sylvia I'm not worried about at all. That kitchen is as organized as an operating room."

The wind was picking up a bit. But it was hot and blew through the open office windows. The footsteps of the hotel staff could be heard up and down the lobby as they went about completing their assigned tasks. Each footfall echoed on the tile floors.

"So few people in such a big place," Logan observed.

"Um-hum." Dori stood up and walked over to the windows. Little whirlpools of dust rose around the base of some newly planted palms. "Sometimes in college I used to stay on campus during certain vacations to finish a paper or to work on some kind of project. In a way, it was the same kind of feeling as now, being almost alone in a place that is usually overcrowded. It was a peaceful sensation for the most part but not altogether because..." she stopped.

"Because why?" Logan prodded.

She turned around and leaned against the open windows. The breeze blew her short blonde hair about her face. "Because it was an artificial calm. You could count the number of days until it would be shattered."

"Like now?" Logan asked.

"Just like now."

XVII

Small schools of radiantly colored fish swam about, scouring the pink coral, searching for food. They seemed to be unconcerned with the giant observer hovering above them. John Salter had been exploring these island waters since he was a boy. It still remained his favorite form of relaxation. He did not enjoy strapping heavy steel diving lungs to his body; he preferred to use only a mask and snorkel. He rose up out of the water for a moment to get a bearing on his surroundings. He saw that he had drifted close to shore. The *Kiwi* was floating comfortably several hundred yards away from him.

The water was shallow now and he stood up, careful to avoid any loose pieces of coral, which might be hidden in the sand. He waded onto the small beach and kneeled down to examine his mask. The strap needed tightening. Water had started to seep in during his last dive. He pulled the rubber strap until he guessed that he had taken in enough slack. He stood up and scanned the small island. It was minute really, probably no more than a mile wide and less than a half a mile long. It was just one of thousands like it in the Caribbean, a palm studded knoll in the middle of an overwhelming ocean. These small dots of land were usually uninhabited. During tropical storms many of them could be covered completely with water, some would reappear in time while others would vanish forever. But for the pleasure sailor they were like miniature ports of call, each having a shoreline replete with perfect, unbroken shells and exotic fish.

Salter put his mask back on and waded out until the water came up above his waist. Then he took a deep breath and dove down ten or fifteen feet. The water was liquid glass, clear and clean. A parade of lime-green fish filed past him. They had a bright red stripe running down the center of their bodies. He used to know what they were called. But over the years he had forgotten the names of most of these island fish.

He came to the surface and treaded water. He was closer to the *Kiwi* now. It was late afternoon. The sun was beginning to work its way down to the water line. It was almost intersecting with the top of the mainmast of the ship. The feverish yellow-orange sunlight exploded on the polished brass fixtures of the deck, engulfing the ship in an illusion of flames. Salter rolled over on his back and floated a while. He knew that his hosts would be down below in the salon playing backgammon and discussing business.

Salter had been on the boat for two and a half days and already a routine was evolving. The early morning was devoted to sailing from one location like this to the next. The seas were usually calm then. But since they were traveling fairly close in, the threat of the strong turbulence of the open water was never really a problem. Around noon, the skipper would suggest a spot to anchor. Then the steward would get out the silver and tablecloths and a light lunch would be served in the salon.

The afternoon meal usually consisted of a shellfish soup, cheeses, and fruit, often accompanied by a platter of cold cuts, bread, and a bottle of wine. The chef, an attractive-but-cool English girl, would bring up tea and cakes toward the middle of the afternoon. In between meals Ramino and Mariani would take naps or read. However, when the sun made an attempt to set, it was a signal to the steward that it was time to begin serving cocktails.

The gleaming teak cupboards of the salon housed a fragile and costly array of the finest Baccarat crystal tumblers and wine goblets. A foam buffer surrounded each glass so that even in the most vicious of storms they were protected. The steward, also English, would set up the bar while the guest dressed for the evening, usually in slacks and a sports shirt. The skipper also used this opportunity to shower and change from his sailing shorts into trousers and a long sleeved shirt. He would then join the guests for a single cocktail in the salon or on deck. If he felt the climate right for spirited conversation and easy mingling, he would stay for another. If however, he sensed that the guests were anxious to engage in private discussions, he would discreetly remove himself to the galley below. It had often been said in the Caribbean, and Salter was certain elsewhere as well, that the mark of a first-rate skipper was not in his ability to steer his ship, but in his ability to make himself scarce at the appropriate times. Of course Ramino and Mariani knew nothing about sailing. But the crew of the *Kiwi* was most experienced. Salter guessed that they were partially aware of the questionable dealings of their temporary employers. But it didn't appear to bother them. And why should it? he thought. All they had to do was keep this magnificent ship seaworthy and provide meals for its occupants. For that they each got more than a generous salary and an opportunity to sail in some of the most beautiful waters of the world.

Floating now in the warm velvet sea, Salter realized that neither of his hosts had taken even a single swim. They seemed contented to simply sit on the deck or in the salon. Passive creatures. A ship can be very confining, even one as elegant as this. Salter needed the daily swim to exercise and to relax. He wondered when talk would turn to business. He had hoped that over dinner the previous evening he would have been informed of the structure of the gambling operations planned for the Castle Beach resort but nothing had been said. Instead the talk had been of a trivial nature. However, he was certain that tonight he would find out all that he needed to know since tomorrow they would be heading back to Miranda.

"John! John!" Salter thought that he heard his name being called. He rolled over and got his bearings. He treaded water and put one hand up to shield his eyes. It was Ramino. He was leaning over the side of the ship, waving. "Come on back and have a drink. We're beginning to think that you don't like us."

"Hi!" yelled the prime minister loudly. Then he began swimming slowly toward the *Kiwi*. You're right, you fool, he thought. I don't like either of you. But I can endure you, since I must. He took long, deliberate strokes stretching his arms and kicking only slightly. He laughed to himself. No doubt he would be stabbed in his bed and thrown overboard if his "partners" knew how much he loathed them and how disgusted he was by the position in which they had him. He tried to picture their faces the day he decided that Miranda no longer needed their slimy business.

He had reached the ladder clinging to the side of the ship. Ramino extended a pudgy white hand over the side and Salter handed him the mask and snorkel.

"Thanks," he said, hoisting his large dripping body out of the water. "Magnificent fish down there. You really ought to have a look for yourself."

"I'll take your word for it."

The steward handed Salter a large blue beach towel with the name of the ship embroidered on it in white.

"Pardon me," Salter said, wrapping the towel around his waist. "I think that I shall take a shower now and dress." Mariani had come up from the salon. He was wearing a red polo shirt and white slacks. He had a drink in his hand.

"Good idea!" He said, lifting his glass. "We're already a couple ahead of you."

Salter had a quiet cabin near the bow of the ship. It had a private bath, complete with a shower, toilet, and small sink. As on all ships, the efficient use of all available space was most important. The sink in the bathroom folded down from the wall. Built-in storage units with sliding shelves held towels and terrycloth robes. His cabin also contained a double bed built into the side of the contoured wall of the hull. It was somewhat high off the ground to accommodate the chest of drawers built-in below it. Square glass hatches above his head cranked open to let fresh air in from the deck.

Salter showered and dressed and returned topside. The sun had just been swallowed up by the watery horizon; a rosy afterglow tinted the edges of the darkening sky.

"Stephen here has your rum and ginger waiting for you." Ramino said, slapping the young English steward soundly on the back. Stephen smiled through gritted teeth and presented Salter with the tall icy glass. "Thank you," John Salter said sincerely. Somehow it was important to the black man to let the crew understand that these two men were not his friends, that he found their humor tasteless and their mannerisms vulgar. He sighed and took a sip of his drink. That was impossible. At the very best, it was guilt by association. The steward left and the three men settled into deck chairs. Salter noticed that the skipper was not joining them. He soon learned why.

"John," Ramino said, sliding forward in his chair, "George and I are glad that you came on this little vacation with us. We feel that it has given you a chance to get to know us and us a chance to get to know you. After all, we're going to have to trust each other if we are to be successful." Salter nodded his head in solemn agreement.

"What Sal is trying to say," added Mariani, stirring the ice around his glass with his index finger, "is that we do trust you. We know that you want Miranda to get a lot of good press. And we can assure you that it will. The hotel is already booked solid for six weeks. We made certain of that. And everyone coming with backgammon in mind is aware of the delicacies involved in the gambling. They will be indistinguishable from the rest of legitimate guests. And the game shall only be played in a suite that we shall designate. The money will be kept in a special hotel safe. Each player must enter the game with a hundred thousand dollars. From each ante you shall receive five thousand with another five thousand going to Hart for his less than enthusiastic participation. Does that seem satisfactory?"

Salter smiled. Like hell it does, he thought. What is your cut? he wondered. His free hand was sweating; he felt it begin to draw into a fist. He exhaled deeply and calmed himself. "That seems quite reasonable," he answered. He could afford to be patient, for a while.

Stephen appeared and refreshed their drinks. Salter stood up and walked to the stern of the ship. He gazed down at the water. A series of tiny waves slapped against the side of the *Kiwi*. The air smelled of salt and varnish and rum.

"There is one slightly bothersome detail with which we need your help," Ramino said. Salter's companions had joined him.

"And what is that?" Salter hoped that he was sounding pleasant.

"Well, as you might speculate," Ramino began, "some of the guests may not have clean passports, having previously been involved in minor infractions of the law. We understand that you are quite strict about things like that here."

Salter drained his glass and threw the ice cubes into the water. "We frown upon criminal elements invading the island," he said, mocking himself. "But if you provide me in advance with the names of the individuals concerned, I shall make certain that your guests have no trouble with our authorities."

Ramino sniffed the air. "Oh boy, something smells good. I'm starving. All of this sitting around has given me an appetite." Mariani laughed heartily at the poor joke. Salter got the message. Serious conversation was over for the evening.

It must have been well past midnight when Salter awoke. It was stuffy in his cabin. And even under a single sheet he was perspiring. He got up and cranked the window above his bed open slightly. Then he lay back down, thinking. After dinner Ramino and Mariani had asked if he were interested in learning to play backgammon. When he indicated that he was not they seemed relieved, telling him that actually the game was boring and involved more luck than skill. But since the structure of the game allowed for perpetually increasing stakes, it was popular with gambling aficionados. They had all had a brandy in the salon after dinner and then retired.

Cool air was flowing in through the open window now and Salter felt better. The ship was gently rocking. The motion was soothing and peaceful. Salter had come to one definite conclusion about his new associates; they were not stupid. He would have to continue to feign a vehement gratitude concerning their involvement with Miranda. And he also decided, for the time being anyway, that he would conceal the fact that he was a master at backgammon and had been long before the game had burst into vogue.

He was beginning to drift into sleep when he heard a rasping, mechanical static. It was the unmistakable sound of a ship-to-shore radio. He was aware that the *Kiwi* was, of course, equipped with one. But he wondered who would be trying to make contact at this time of night. He sat up and listened intently. He faintly heard the skipper respond to the caller by giving the *Kiwi*'s registration numbers, longitude, latitude, and finally by stating his name.

Salter could not hear the transmission emanating from the radio. But soon however, he did hear a gentle knocking on the cabin door across the hall where Ramino was sleeping. He heard the cabin door open.

"What is it?" Ramino asked in a drowsy stupor.

"It's a call for you, sir," the captain said apologetically.

"Goddamn, at this hour!" Ramino was awake now.

Salter heard the two men proceed down the short hallway and into the captain's quarters. From then on he could only hear intervals of static followed by muffled replies from Ramino. In less than five minutes Ramino had awoken Mariani and the two men went up the stairs and into the salon.

Salter lay back down. He was thoroughly awake now and knew that sleep would not return tonight. Who had called? What did they want? Why did Ramino feel that it was necessary to inform Mariani? He sighed and rolled over. He couldn't very well go up and join them. Perhaps they would tell him about the incident in the morning. He shook his head. He knew better than that. Maybe he should simply demand to be informed. But they would only lie. So much for the "trust" they so blithely spoke of earlier.

He found that the steady rolling of the boat was now becoming irritating. He did not like this frustrating situation. Suddenly he heard footsteps on the deck. Then he heard voices, clean and crisp. His open hatch was functioning like a funnel, channeling the conversation right into his cabin. Fools, thought Salter happily. They know so little about the ship that they aren't even aware that they are standing directly above me. He rolled over silently and sat up.

"Well, what are we going to do about it?" asked Mariani, attempting to whisper.

"I haven't made up my mind completely yet," Ramino replied. "But I'll have a plan worked out by the time we get back. He will have to be eliminated naturally, and soon."

Salter heard footsteps again. The men were walking further on down the deck. Stop! Stop! he mentally demanded. He could no longer hear them. But, mercifully they turned around when they reached the stern and came back in the same direction.

"We will discuss the details with the Chameleon." It was Mariani.

Salter's chamber was quite cool now but he was sweating more profusely than before. Who would have to be eliminated? And who was the Chameleon? He felt trapped and isolated from all sources of information. He was thankful that they were going to be returning to Miranda later today. He would have to get in touch with Charles Cliff at once. If anyone knew who this Chameleon was, he certainly would. The prime minister sunk back down into his bed. He stared at the small open sliver of glass above his head, waiting for dawn and the sail back home.

XVIII

The Anglican Church in St. Philips was made of stone and rough wood. It was one of the finest churches built by the English settlers and was situated on a grassy knoll among several small saltbox houses. A few stray sheep and several goats fed on the abundant grass nearby. The path leading up to the church was a series of thin narrow strips of stone almost worn away from centuries of use.

"Easter Sunday is really not any different from most Sundays here. Church attendance is always fairly high. And since the church is open every day of the week, there is no rush by the villagers to impress their neighbors by showing up on special occasions." Sarah Hunnicut was discussing the religious mores of the Mirandans with Dori as they walked to the Easter service. Jeremy had run ahead of them to try and get acquainted with one of the meandering goats.

"You mean they do that in England, too?" Dori was amused.

"Oh yes, of course. More fashion then faith is exhibited in London churches on special holy occasions."

Dori laughed. "Vanity is universal I guess."

"As well as hypocrisy," Sarah added.

The morning was especially beautiful. The air was drier than it had been for the past several days and cool, caressing wind threaded its way to the island foliage. A single stone bell was being rung as the three reached the front door of the church.

About twenty wooden pews flanked both sides of the large building. The floor of the church consisted of boldly patterned Spanish tile in various hues of rust and blue. Dori guessed that perhaps the church had been Catholic before the arrival of the British. It was impossible to escape the constant blending of cultures here. Large bouquets of waxy, red Anthurium flowers shared space on the altar with vases of long stemmed white and purple irises. Many of

Sarah's students smiled and waved shyly as they saw her enter. Jeremy spotted several of his classmates and started for them.

"No," cautioned his mother. "You stay with us."

Sarah led the way to a vacant pew near the center of the right side of the church. As they sat down Dori saw the Trents seated several rows ahead of them. Victor was admonishing his sons to sit up straight and pay attention. Allison turned around and surveyed the congregation. Her placid expression did not change as her eyes swept past Sarah Hunnicut. Sarah was looking straight ahead at the altar. Dori felt sorry for each woman. They were really both afraid of the same thing, that if they lost Victor they would never be loved again, Sarah because she was so plain and Allison because she was growing older.

The priest entered through a door at the side of the church followed by a small group of older children dressed in the traditional red and white choir robes. The garments were so stiff with excessive starch that they crackled as the children took their appointed positions in the front pew. Sarah had explained previously that the Anglican priest traveled from one island to the next conducting services. During his absence, lay people were assigned to help the parishioners in their private worship.

The service was lovely. The choir and the congregation sang from the standard hymnal. Dori closed her eyes for one moment during a particularly beautiful selection. If she were to play a recording of this music for her parents they would never guess that it was the product of black singers in a simple island church. She was certain that they pictured her dancing to jungle drums surrounded by savages praying to exotic and terrifying idols. She also realized that she had been guilty of the same kind of stereotyping before she came. But she had grown to appreciate the special quality of these people. She was also beginning to understand Sarah Hunnicut's reaction to Logan's innocent, yet offensive, remark about Salter the night of the governor's welcoming party.

As the choir sang the recessional hymn and pews started to empty, Dori turned around to see Phillip and Logan sitting in the back with Howard Rutledge. She was upset. She had managed to avoid Phillip since he returned. She hadn't felt ready to have that talk he threatened. She took Jeremy by the hand and immersed herself in the exiting swirl of people.

Once outside, she started rapidly down the path. "Sarah?" she asked, "would you like to come back to the hotel with me and have lunch? Perhaps we could go swimming later on." Phillip could never approach her if she were with Sarah.

"Thank you for the invitation," Sarah said, smoothing out her bright print skirt, "but I really must write some letters this afternoon. My mother lives alone. If she doesn't hear from me at least once a week she gets very nervous. But the swimming does sound wonderful. Maybe another day?"

"Come whenever you can," Dori said.

They had reached the bottom of the path. Sarah said goodbye and walked off down the street to the house she shared with another teacher. Dori's Fiat was parked across the street near the boat docks. "Oh no!" She moaned when she saw what happened. The Castle Beach station wagon was parked in front of her with its back bumper touching the front of her car. And Logan's white Mercedes was parked behind her. The small car was wedged in so tightly between the two steel monsters that it would be impossible to move.

The young boy Dori had paid to watch her car was marching up and down in front of all three. It was obvious that he was happy over his increased business.

"Hi!" he said grinning joyously as she approached.

"Albert!" She said shaking her finger at him, "look at my car!"

"I know," he said proudly, "it's all safe. Just like Mr. Graham said." He was beaming. Dori was infuriated. Not at the boy but at Phillip for making a joke out of her desire to avoid him. Jeremy had climbed in the front seat of the station wagon and was playing with the steering wheel. The stall markets on the sidewalk were opening up for the afternoon trade. Fishermen were cleaning their early morning catch on the docks. Groups of young people were dancing down the middle of the street in front of the traffic. Horns were honking and bicycles and motor scooters were speeding by so closely Dori was certain they would run her over.

It had been a long hectic week and a longer four months. She was not in the mood for ridiculous games. She scanned the crowded thoroughfare for the men. Finally she spotted them moving slowly through the throngs of people. Phillip came up to her first.

"Hello," he said. "I partially apologize. This was my idea. But I have to see you. You can't go on ignoring me forever. It's a pretty small island."

"Well, I don't approve of these sophomore-ish pranks."

Logan caught that remark. "Would you prefer senior-ish pranks?" He teased.

Dori then glared at Howard. "Sorry ma'am," he said. "I just work here." He quickly got into the station wagon beside Jeremy.

"Put a smile on that face, blondie," Logan ordered, "or I won't let you hunt for Easter eggs and jellybeans this afternoon with the rest of the kids."

Jeremy had crawled over the seats into the back of the wagon and had heard Logan's threat. His face clouded over with a serious frown. "Oh please let her. She's really been good you know."

Dori couldn't help it; she burst out laughing, followed soon by the rest of the tiny group. "Okay sport," Logan said, patting the top of Jeremy's head. "I promise that I'll reconsider. What do you say you ride back with me and we can discuss it, man to man?" He lifted the boy out through the tailgate window. Howard waved, gave a honk, and drove off. Albert collected his money from Logan and said goodbye to Jeremy just as the car started to pull away.

Phillip had already seated himself behind the wheel of Dori's Fiat. She reluctantly got in beside him and handed him the keys. She wasn't angry anymore. She realized that perhaps she had been acting like a spoiled child. Phillip looked over at her radiant bronze face. "Your nose is peeling," he observed. Then he leaned over and kissed it gently. He started the car and began to drive back to the hotel. As they rounded a corner the sweeping view of the bay of St. Philips loomed before them.

"Look," Dori said pointing out to sea. Plowing through the water with all three sails swelled full by the wind was the *Kiwi*.

Sylvia and her staff prepared a delicious buffet lunch on the patio adjoining the garden dining room: fresh lobster, platters of pineapple, papaya, bananas and figs, sweet cakes and breads, scrambled eggs, bacon, and coffee. Ruthie had set the buffet table beautifully and Dori complimented her on it. "I like my new dress, too," Ruthie said spinning around to show off her new uniform.

Logan had invited the locals. He felt that it would be a nice gesture to give them a preview of the hotel before the first invasion of guests. It would also provide a dry run for the staff. Allison came with Claire.

"Where's Victor?" Logan asked.

"He had to run into town for something."

Dori thought again about Sarah's luncheon refusal.

"But that won't stop us from having a good time," Claire announced, making her way over to the bar. Mandy was mixing gin fizzes, screwdrivers, and Bloody Marys along with the usual array of rum drinks. Jeremy and the Trent boys were playing near the water's edge by the small sailboats. Some native children soon joined them. Dori squinted. She wanted to make sure Jeremy was wearing his life jacket. He was. Frank LeBeau and Ransom Turner were playing cards at a small table.

Dori stretched out on a lounge chair. She was still wearing the pink and white knit jersey wrap around dress that she had worn to church. She had wanted to change into slacks, but everyone else had dressed for the occasion so she didn't. Phillip came by with the gin fizz for her.

"Thanks," she said, taking the glass from his hand.

He pulled a chair up next to hers. "This place is really looking gorgeous." He took her hand. "The combined efforts of creative minds." Dori smiled at his remark. Logan was making the rounds talking to each guest. "He is practicing exuding charm," Phillip said.

"So is she," Dori added, looking at Claire who was all smiles and fluttering eyelids.

"We are witnessing the lighter side of her schizophrenic personality," Phillip said, "and we might as well enjoy it. Happy Easter, Mrs. Rutledge," he called. "You are looking especially well today."

"Well, how nice of you to say so. I feel marvelous. We are all so excited about the opening of the hotel. I just know it's going to be a smashing success. And I must compliment both of you on what you have done with this place in such a short time. It is a transformation, utterly breathtaking." She made sweeping gesticulations as she spoke.

"I am glad that you are pleased, Claire," Dori said. "Later on I'll take you through some of the rooms."

"That would be wonderful. I'm sure Al would enjoy coming along too." Claire looked over at Allison Trent, who had not been paying any attention to the conversation. "Right, dear?"

"Oh, oh yes, of course."

Poor woman, Dori thought. She knew where her mind was.

The afternoon went well. Everyone had nothing but good things to say about the hotel. The fact that not a scrap was left at the buffet table attested to Sylvia's cooking. Claire's good mood extended way past lunch. She was even being kind to Howard, asking him to demonstrate how one operated a sunfish. She stood on the shore and applauded his efforts. He was thrilled, performing for her like a trained seal. Most everyone went swimming. Dr. Turner put Jeremy on his shoulders while Logan and Phillip carried the larger Trent boys around. They played King of the Mountain, attempting to knock each other into the water. The men grew tired before their riders did, and proclaimed a three-way tie. The boys spent the remainder of the afternoon building forts and tunnels in the sand.

At dusk, almost everyone had left. Logan had escorted each to the front door and thanked them for coming. Mandy and his helpers were gathering wet beach towels and folding up the lounge chairs. Ruthie had come down to the beach to get Jeremy and take him up for the night. Dori was about to go inside herself.

"Don't go, not yet," Phillip took her hand. "Let's go for a walk."

They went down to the shoreline and began walking. Dori's swimming suit had dried but she was chilled. Phillip wrapped a towel around her shoulders as they walked. "There is so much that I have been wanting to say to you ever since you left New York," he began.

"Please don't. Don't tell me about your miserable, loveless marriage, about how Madeline is cold and unfeeling but that you can't leave her because it would destroy her."

"That does sound dramatic, and very convincing," he said," but it's not true. The fact is that I love my wife very much. And she loves me. And when I am through here we are going to move from New York to a small farm we own in Minnesota. Madeline writes and I have enough money now to retire for a while and pursue my real passion—painting."

Dori was absorbing what was being said. "How idyllic," she said with a voice full of sarcasm. "Why do you feel this compulsion to tell me how blissfully happy you are? Do you think that makes me feel better about what happened?"

"It should."

"Why?"

"Because what occurred that night stemmed from a need you had to try and be close with a man again. And for whatever reason you decided that I was acceptable. The fact that I could go to bed with you and still be in love with my wife doesn't cheapen the experience we shared. You realized that your desires hadn't vanished, that you were still capable of physical passion. And I honestly thought that that was what you wanted to find out. If I had known that you had thought that it was going to mean some sort of commitment, I never would have let it happen. I didn't want to hurt you, I wanted to help you."

"My, my," Dori said defensively. "Jack of all trades aren't you? Architect, painter, freelance sex therapist. Sorry, your explanation isn't good enough for me. Regardless of what you envisioned your mission of mercy to be, I deserved to know that you were married."

"Would it have made a difference?"

"I don't know. I have asked myself that same question."

It was dark now. The only lights were coming from the hotel and the far away hillside cottages of Cinnamon Inn. Phillip grabbed Dori and pushed her down on her back in the sand. He lay down close to her on the beach.

"Does it matter now?" He started to wrap his bare legs over hers.

"No," she said, pushing him away. "But you don't either." She got to her feet and brushed the sand from her body as she retrieved the fallen towel. "I expected more of you, Phillip. You know, Logan told me a long time ago that the first lover I had after my husband was bound to be a disappointment. He was right. I didn't believe it initially. But you are disappointing, in so many ways. Good night, Phillip."

She started walking back to the hotel. Then she began to run. Tears were racing down her face. They were tears of relief. She ran at the waters edge so she could feel the cool foam splashing up around her ankles. She felt free, and in control. She thought about Jeremy and the number of times he would stand against the wall with the yardstick. "Come and see how much I've grown," he would say.

"Yes," Dori said, still running, almost flying. "Come and see how much I've grown."

XIX

It had been four days since the last meeting. Claire was getting anxious. What was the Chameleon going to do with the information she had given him about Phillip and the gambling? He had no reaction when she told him. He only nodded his head and thanked her. He said that he would be contacting her later with instructions for her to carry out. She put on a loose fitting sundress, sandals, and a broad brimmed hat and went into the kitchen. Thelma was preparing to go to St. Philips to do grocery shopping.

"Thelma, I think that I would like to go into town and do the shopping this morning."

"Well, that's fine with me, Mrs. Rutledge. I have enough to do here as it is. Mr. Rutledge told me that Mr. Hart has booked too many people into his hotel. So it seems like some of his guests will be staying here. I've got to ready the cottages."

Claire had not really been paying much attention. "Yes, well that's just fine. Did you make a list of the things we need?"

"No, ma'am. I always just shop from my head."

Claire shrugged her shoulders. "Well, I guess I can do the same thing." She searched the kitchen drawers for the keys to the car and then left.

It had been some time since Claire had driven. Her recent headaches, as well as the mounting depression, had made her fairly lethargic. This four-wheeled Jeep had been Howard's idea. He said they needed it for hauling things, which was true. But she hated wrestling with the stick shift. Yet this morning, she wanted to get out. She just couldn't wait here all day for something to happen.

The dust rose up around the car as it rolled over the dirt road. Why hadn't Howard ever paved this driveway? Poor Howard, she thought. She was remembering how excited he had been yesterday when she pretended to take an interest in those pathetic little toys of his. She had been surprised that Frank LeBeau greeted her so casually and that Mandy was treating her no differently either. But then, that had been the order, to blend in.

The sun was bright and warm on her bare shoulders as she sped along past the circular entrance of the Castle Beach Hotel. The huge front doors were opened wide and the crews of workers were busy polishing the tile floor of the lobby. She drove on toward town. It was simply a few days until the first guests arrived. "You seem genuinely excited about all of this," Howard had said as they walked home down the beach the previous evening.

"I am," she had said honestly, taking his arm. "I am very excited about everything." Howard mistakenly took that to mean that Claire had undergone a change of attitude.

She rounded the last corner near the harbor and turned onto the main market area. The fruit and vegetable vendors had especially attractive and abundant selections of produce today. She surveyed the stands as she searched the curb for a parking space. When she located one, she parked and got out of the car, being certain to take her big wicker shopping basket with her. There were crowds of shoppers milling about the stalls and tables. She managed to maneuver her way through the masses.

She bought melons, oranges, strawberries, onions, celery, and red peppers. Then, she headed across the street to the docks where she bought some fresh whitefish and juicy crab. Her last stop was the bakery. She wanted some hard rolls for lunch. There was a crowd around the counter there as well. She set her shopping bag down and took off her hat, fanning herself with the brim. She gazed idly out through the window. She looked again. Across the street Frank LeBeau was standing by her car. She picked up her groceries and left. She hurriedly crossed the street.

"Hello, Claire," Frank said easily as he took her shopping bag and loaded it into the back of the Jeep. Claire studied his face. Was this just an accidental meeting? But it couldn't be. He was waiting for her, wasn't he? "Are you finished with your shopping?" he continued.

"Well, not really. I was going to get some things at the bakery but there was such crowd. It can wait."

"Nonsense," he said. "If you don't stand in line all of the good breads will be gone. Come along. I'll wait with you. I could use a sweet breakfast roll myself. Once one is ten pounds overweight, why not make it eleven?" He laughed and patted his ample stomach.

Claire bought several loaves of bread, a spice cake, and some roles. Frank selected a big fruit-filled turnover. They returned to Claire's car.

"Why don't you sit down here and talk to me while I devour my roll," he suggested, pointing to one of the many stone benches found throughout the city. She did. "Oh this is so delicious," he said, "you really ought to have one." He nibbled at the confection delicately, savoring each morsel. "Claire, I spoke with the Chameleon this morning. He wants you to do something for him."

"What?" she asked expectantly.

"He wants you to ask Logan Hart if you can work at the hotel desk on a part-time basis, to take reservations, answer phones, sort mail, things like that."

"What!" Claire was amazed at the request. "Why?"

"He wants you to be in a position where you will have easy access to the hotel offices. I don't know what he has planned at this point, but I am certain that this is a strategic part of it."

Claire was livid. "Who does he think I am? Some groveling little chambermaid he can order around? I am not going to beg Logan Hart for a job. My husband is already on the payroll. What are we supposed to be? The reliable live-in couple? We happen to have a hotel of our own to run, you know?"

Frank calmly finished eating his turnover during Claire's tirade. "It doesn't have to be like that at all. Just tell Hart that since you have had experience at managing reservations and keeping books, you would be happy to volunteer to train some of the native girls."

"But Dori is doing that," Claire protested.

"Well, I am sure that she would welcome some assistance. And remember," LeBeau said brushing the crumbs from his lap, "the contributions we make will hasten our individual objectives." Claire agreed to try and get the job. But she was less than pleased about the idea.

XX

"I have no idea," Cliff said shaking his head. "Where did you hear this name being mentioned?" John Salter told him about his short cruise aboard the *Kiwi*. He had no alternative at this point. He explained to his aid about the gambling operations soon to begin organized by Ramino and Mariani and sanctioned by him.

"But it is only to be a temporary arrangement. I will tolerate it just long enough to secure the capital and the favorable publicity we need to keep Miranda going."

"I see," Cliff said quietly. "Perhaps this Chameleon person is the one they work for. I would guess that individuals involved in this type of illegality must protect their identities from the authorities."

Salter pondered the explanation remembering the talk on the boat concerning passports. It seemed logical. "Then you don't believe that it has anything to do with someone on the island?"

"I doubt it, sir, but I shall investigate it thoroughly."

Salter felt relieved. "Has there been any indication of militant organizers around recently?"

"No, your support is strong. I have convinced the people that your motives are good and that they will lead us to prosperity. I can assure you that the Cuban and Haitian insurgents have lost their foothold here." He smiled broadly at the prime minister. "You are favored to be elected president of the organization of West Indian Islands in the fall."

Salter put his arm around the young man's shoulder in a paternal gesture. "And you shall be with me. I believe in rewarding loyalty."

Salter accompanied his aide to the front gates of the ministry where a guard let them out, then returned to his office. He was fortunate to have Charles Cliff on his side. The people listened to him. Salter sighed. In the same way he himself had been listened to once. He couldn't blame the islanders. Things had been slow since the revolution. Economic strength did not come easily. But, if he were successful in bringing more foreign money to the island as well as political support for his new democracy then things would get better. Then why did he have such a gnawing feeling of insecurity? He would be glad when all of this was over.

XXI

Skaters whirled around on the frosty ice. Snow settled in the tops of the pine trees. Smoke rose in gentle rings from the chimney of a near by farmhouse. Dori gave a strong tug on bottom of the shade and Vermont neatly rolled itself around a wooden cylinder at the top of the window. The New England shade was the only part of Logan's original decor that had remained in the room. Dori had convinced him that as much as she loved everything, if any other guests were to see her suite they might feel that hotel employees were receiving special privileges and accommodations. Logan found that explanation reasonable. So all the furniture was moved into the storeroom with no hurt feelings. And Dori redecorated the room exactly as the others in the hotel.

She looked down at the beach below her room. Howard was busy with his sailboats as usual. Jeremy was walking down the beach to school with several native children. The week had evaporated. Tomorrow the guests would descend. Dori showered and dressed quickly.

Logan and Phillip were both in the office when she arrived wearing a pair of bright yellow cotton slacks and a crisp print blouse.

"Good morning gentlemen," she said lightly. Ever since the night on the beach with Phillip she had not found it difficult to work with him. She was actually almost indifferent to his presence.

"Welcome to the zero hour," Logan grinned.

Phillip was on the phone but he gave her a casual wave. "Yes, that will be fine," he said into the receiver. "No, I prefer that it be direct. Yes. Thank you. I will." He hung up. "Plane reservations," he said, "I'll be leaving the day after tomorrow." Dori displayed no overt reaction to his announcement.

"Well sport, we'll miss you around here," Logan said. "But I know that greater duties call. Hey, I won't let you set one foot off this island until you get that outside elevator working."

"I'm on my way," Phillip said, standing up. "Just needs a little adjustment and it will be ready. Thought that I would unveil it tonight at the staff dinner."

"That's a great idea," Logan smiled. "It will give everybody a chance to ride in it before the guests come. After that it's back to the service elevators."

Claire entered as Phillip was leaving. "Well," she said happily, "I have assigned all of the guestrooms. I placed the keys in the boxes and I have already checked to make sure that each room is made up and fully equipped." She was smiling and looked delighted with herself.

"That's wonderful," Dori praised. "I can't tell you how glad I am that you offered your services to us. I know that I couldn't have done it alone."

"Happy to help." She glanced at the clock on Logan's desk. "Oops, I must be off. I am giving some of the slower girls another lesson in filling out the reservation forms." She exited with a childish skip out of the office.

Logan had a stack of papers in his hand. He slapped them down on his desk and laughed out loud. "She is too much," he concluded.

"Don't laugh." Dori defended. "I really meant what I said. She has been a fantastic help. I don't know what has caused her sudden change, but I am grateful for it."

"Howard is beside himself," Logan said. "Told me that he has never seen Claire so zealous about anything since she was trying to make it in Hollywood."

Suddenly Dori was aware of a new piece of office furniture. "What's this?" She asked staring at a huge steel vault.

"It's on loan from Ramino, it's a hotel safe of sorts. It will be used to store the backgammon money."

"For a while," Dori said wistfully, "I was beginning to think that this was just another beautifully spectacular island resort hotel. What an ugly reminder that it isn't." She said, putting her hand on the cold gray box.

"You know, you don't realize how lucky you are be having such great weather for the opening tomorrow," Howard said as he mixed himself a drink at the bar. "Usually this time of year is pretty iffy. Lots of storms. This must be a good omen." Dull smoke was rising out of a hole in the ground where Mandy and some of the other employees were roasting a pig for the evening dinner. "Say, this party is a great idea." Howard continued. "Good P.R."

"Well everyone has worked hard. They deserve a break." Logan said.

It was almost sunset. Dori felt exhausted but relaxed. Everything was in order. The kitchen was ready. The various menus had arrived from the printer in San Juan. The bar was stocked. And most importantly, the employees seemed comfortable with their assigned responsibilities.

"Where is Claire?" Howard asked, looking around.

"Oh, I told her not to work anymore," Dori said. "But she insisted on finishing up some last-minute details."

Logan's desk chair had been facing the water. He suddenly stood up and turned around, folding his arms in front of him, appraising the hotel as though he were seeing it for the first time. "Not bad" he said softly, "not bad at all."

Mandy came by with a tray of drinks. He was dressed in the orange and yellow pinstriped shirt and white cotton pants Dori had ordered. All of the male employees would dress in the same manner except for the beach boys. They would wear white cotton bathing trunks with the Castle Beach parrot insignia on them. Thelma and the girls were busy setting up the buffet tables. Logan motioned for them all to stop and come over to where he was standing. The boys cooking the pig also came. "Pour them each a drink, Mandy, and then get one for yourself." The group was growing larger. Soon Claire came out from the lobby, and Phillip stopped puttering with the elevator for a moment. When everyone had been served, Logan proposed a toast. "Every one of you helped build the Castle Beach Hotel. You should each be as proud of yourself as I am of you. Thank you." He raised his glass as the crowd cheered.

The evening was grand. The steel band played and everyone danced to the rhythmic, pounding music. John Salter, the Trents, and Dr. Turner joined them all for a dinner of roast pork. Sylvia served them outside at several small circular tables. Dori sat next to the prime minister. But this time it did not become an unpleasant experience. For some reason Dori now found him extremely easy to talk with. Perhaps it was because they both shared the secret of the impending gambling operation. Yet neither of them tried to bring up the topic.

"I love the steel band music," Dori said. "It is such a unique sound. It is really hard to believe that such lovely music can be produced from such simple things as discarded oil drums."

"Our people are very inventive. This music form is truly West Indian. Other people have copied it. But I can guarantee you that you shall never hear it played so well as you do in these islands."

Dori looked at the circle of whirling native dancers. They were jumping and writhing and swaying to the beat. "I must say, they dance very much like American teenagers."

Salter threw back his head and laughed loudly. "The influence of rock 'n roll is global."

Dori had not realized until now what a relaxed, easy manner this strange man had. She told him a little of her background and of her childhood in Vermont.

"It has been a long time since I have seen the snow." Salter admitted. "Once when I was a young student in England I went on holiday with some boys from school to Switzerland. We did a bit of skiing. It was marvelous, though I spent more time falling in the snow than gliding over it. I would like to give the sport another try sometime. It intrigues me. Vermont sounds like a lovely spot for skiing." He saw Dori's attentive beautiful smile fade abruptly. He was bewildered. "Have I said something to offend you? If so, please allow me to apologize."

"No, really. I am the one who should be apologizing. I am sorry." She explained quickly, and unemotionally, that her husband had been killed in a skiing accident. Salter changed the subject.

"Tell me about your parents. What does your father do for a living? Hunt bears and chop trees I imagine."

Dori smiled. "Not all the time. He is a..."

"Doctor," interrupted Ransom Turner, who was listening to their conversation from the next table. He was extremely drunk. "Dr. Andrew McGee. Right?" His head was weaving slightly and his gaze unsteady. Dori had known that he drank quite a bit, but she had never seen him like this.

"Yes, that's correct. Did Jeremy tell you about him?"

"Jeremy didn't have to young lady. Your father and I go way back." He flung out his arms wildly knocking over his drink on the table. He didn't seem to notice. "The great Andrew McGee. Why don't you go ahead and ask your precious daddy about me! I'm sure that he hasn't forgotten me, no matter how hard he's tried." He laughed bitterly, "And oh, how he must have tried."

Victor had been watching the exchange and came over to table. "Ransom, why don't you let me take you home? You have had a bit too much to drink."

"Oh I have, have I?" The doctor became belligerent.

"The punch is very strong," Trent said humoring him. "Come on and let me drive you home. A good nights rest will make you feel a lot better."

By now most everyone was witnessing the scene. Dori was waiting for Turner to become totally unruly, but abruptly his attitude changed and he was docile and submissive. "Okay Victor. I don't feel good anyway. And I'm not having any fun."

Victor helped him stand and the two proceeded to the front of the hotel. They had taken only a few steps when Turner said loudly, "After you drop me off you can go visit Sarah. You're the teacher's pet. Ha ha." Victor said nothing but kept leading the drunken man toward the car. Automatically, heads turned in Allison's direction. She had pretended not to have heard the remark. She knocked her napkin to the ground and busied herself in the process of retrieving it. The tension was thick and no one seemed to know how to break it. But Phillip, who had seen none of this, appeared from the shadows. He was jubilant.

"Ladies and gentlemen," he announced, "for the evening's entertainment I shall present a one-man show to boggle the mind, thrill the senses, and ignite the imagination!" There was a long pause. "The elevator is working!" he added dramatically.

Everyone laughed and applauded. His timing had been perfect. "If you shall all turn your chairs in this direction," he instructed, pointing to the corner wall of the main hotel building, "I shall give you a demonstration of my greatest engineering accomplishment since I coerced Logan Hart into giving me a bonus."

He disappeared into the thick garden foliage and emerged at the base of the elevator. At the same time Frank LeBeau whispered something to Claire and she immediately got up and walked through the arbor and into the lobby. Just then Phillip turned on a switch. Immediately the glass elevator was outlined by hundreds of tiny white lights, identical to the ones he had used in the trellised courtyard linking the two sides of the hotel. The overall effect was breathtaking. He climbed into the elevator for the maiden voyage.

"What a view he is going to have from there," Logan said. "Maybe I ought to charge the guests an admission fee."

The graceful glass capsule glided slowly and majestically up the side of the building. Dori watched respectfully. Phillip's ego was immense. But in his profession, he did have the talent to match. All eyes followed the delicate carriage on its journey to the top and down again. Watching it produced an almost hypnotic effect on the viewer. The sparkling glass oval surrounded by the darkening tropical evening produced a magical feeling. Phillip took it up once more. It seemed to float to the top like a shining bubble of iridescent air. But then suddenly, as it began its descent, there was a loud snapping sound and it plummeted to the ground, almost exploding as it hit the cement patio. Shattered glass flew for yards and shorted out lights and exposed wiring hissed and snarled.

For an instant no one moved, overcome with shock. But then everyone rushed toward the crash. Phillip lay facedown in a crumpled heap at the bottom of the elevator. His hand was riveted to the controls, which had broken loose from the electrical panel. Sparks flew from them and they growled like an animal gone berserk. "Oh my God!" Logan said when he realized what happened. "Don't go near him!" He screamed as he ran around the side of the building.

Dori had turned away and covered her ears. In a matter of seconds, the horrible hissing and sputtering had stopped. The broken, flickering elevator lights went out, as did all of the rest in the hotel. The kerosene torch lamps lining the paths through the gardens provided all the light that was left. Dori turned around. Logan walked back slowly and joined the group. Salter and Howard had entered the remains of the mutilated elevator and lifted Phillip up and carried him to a clearing on the patio where they laid him down.

"He's dead." Howard said, vocalizing what everyone was already thinking. "Electrocuted," he added softly.

"I cut the power," Logan said. "But it was too late."

People sat or stood, paralyzed by the ordeal. Dori felt as if she were being suffocated. She had to escape. She couldn't bear it. She would not let death make a martyr out of her again. She ran through the darkened hotel lobby on her way to the parking entrance. The door to the office was open. As she ran past, she thought that she saw a shadow moving in the room. But she just kept running. She jumped into her car and felt frantically under the front seat for her spare set of keys. At last her fingers touched the small pieces of metal and she was off.

She didn't care where she was going; she just needed distance from what happened. Tears rolled down her cheeks and she brushed them away with her hand. She passed many small dirt roads that fed into this main island thoroughfare. Small houses along the way blurred as she sped by. She drove for almost thirty minutes. She knew that in a few more miles she would be coming into St. Philips. She didn't want to go there. She didn't want to see the people happily partying aboard their yachts. She didn't want to hear the music coming from The Buoy.

She slowed down as she saw a road coming up on her right. She turned into it, determined to follow it to the end. It was bumpy and clouds of dust rose up in front of her headlights, making it almost impossible for her to see where she was going. But she didn't care. She kept driving in low gear until the road came to an abrupt end in front of a grove of rubber trees. She turned off the motor and just sat in the car, listening to the building breeze. Where was she? She laughed bitterly. Well she couldn't have gone far. After all, this was an island.

She left her headlights burning and got out of the car and began walking. To the left of the rubber trees was a small path. Dori could make out the silhouette of some kind of a building ahead. She began walking toward it. The path grew steeper but she continued. She came to some big stone steps. They were the entrance to the structure. She climbed them, nearly out of breath when she reached the top.

The building had spaces for doors and windows, but no wood or glass. It had to have been abandoned for a long time. Dori was remembering Halloween in Middlebury. All of her little friends would dare each other to go into the deserted old Griffith barn. But no one would. It was dark and empty and it could be haunted. But now, Dori walked into the ebony darkness willingly. She had learned over the years that people, not places, are the haunted things.

She walked slowly through each room. They were all empty. But in the last there was a small winding staircase. She grabbed onto the railing and followed it to the top where it emptied into a small round room with a peaked roof and a space for a door. The opening connected her with a large balcony. Double metal railings ran around the circumference of it. This had to have been a lighthouse at one time.

The wind was gaining momentum. She walked around the balcony and looked out. She hadn't realized how high up she had come. On one side she could see the harbor of St. Philips. There were many newly arrived yachts reclining in the inland waters. She walked around to the opposite side. Far below her and back to the left she knew was the expanse of Castle Beach. The lights had probably been turned back on by now. She shuddered and started to turn away. Then she heard something. She stopped and listened. It was more than the wind. It was the sound of an engine, a car engine. Soon she saw a pair of headlights far below her, winding their way up the same road she had taken. She could not make out what kind of car it was or even the color. But it sounded large and powerful. She was shivering. She was only wearing a sheer white eyelet cocktail dress.

The car stopped behind hers and the motor and the lights were turned off. It had to be Logan. He followed her? She waited. Suddenly her own car headlights were extinguished. Whoever it was must certainly have taken this path many times if they felt confident enough to traverse it in total darkness. Dori felt her way back down the winding stairs and through the vacant rooms to the front entrance. The soft gusts of air had matured into slapping winds that whipped the tops of the palm trees viciously.

There was a clearing just at the base of the high stone steps of the lighthouse. Dori saw a moving shape approach her from the distance.

"Logan?" she called loudly, but her words were rendered mute by the wind. She kept calling, as the hulking figure grew steadily closer. "Logan!" Then she heard the sound of the voice that she least expected.

"No Mrs. Dugan, it is John Salter." He mounted the final steps and joined her by the entrance. "Just a minute!" he said loudly to be heard. He disappeared momentarily around the outside of the building. He came back minutes later carrying a small wooden crate. "Come back inside," he instructed, ushering her into the building. Though there were no doors or windows, the stone walls deflected the harsh direct force of the wind. Salter set the box down on the floor and opened the lid. He pulled out some kind of an oval object. It was difficult to tell in the dark just what it was. Dori heard the striking of a match. Quickly Salter hovered with the match over the object. In a moment he moved away and the room was bathed in a glowing light. "I always keep a kerosene lamp out here," he said, looking up at her, smiling softly.

"Do you come here a lot?" Dori was puzzled.

"Victor and I used to play here as boys. It was an operating lighthouse then. An old British sailor and his wife lived here. They would let the island children climb up onto the balcony and look for pirate ships. I come up now just to get away and think." He took off the jacket to his uniform and spread it out on the ground and motioned for Dori to be seated.

"No thank you," she said.

"Very well." He picked it up, shook it out and draped it gently over her shoulders. She did not protest.

"Why isn't the lighthouse used anymore?"

Salter sat down on the ground in a corner of the room. "Oh it really wasn't needed. Actually, it was only used during times of war, when it was necessary to spot ships of battle. Since it was one of the earliest buildings on the island it has not been torn down. It does have a certain historical value. But," he said sadly, "it is dying from neglect and exposure. I can't be expected to do it all you know?" He seemed to have addressed the last remark to himself. The wind was whirling and screeching through the empty rooms.

"Is this the beginning of a hurricane?" Dori was concerned.

Salter listened for a moment studying the patterns and velocity of the shifting air currents. "No, I doubt that it will even bring rain. At any rate, it should be gone in the morning. Uncertain winds are always a part of life on an island."

Dori was shivering and her skin was pale. Salter stood up and took her by the hand, leading her to the corner. "Please sit down. You won't get the full brunt of the wind here." Dori obeyed. She sat down and curled up next to the stone wall. Salter sat next to her. Their shoulders were touching. He had not let go of her hand. Neither of them spoke. They listened to the wind venting its fury as it passed above them. The air would be sucked out of one side of the room only to be blown in from another empty window or doorway. The lantern would flicker, but tenaciously hung on to its small flame.

After some time, it was hard to gauge how much, the ranting air moved on, having grown tired of this small, but sturdy victim.

"Hart will telephone Mrs. Graham with the news," Salter said. Dori's eyes had been closed. At once a picture of the tall, lovely, self-sufficient woman Dori had met in the lobby of the Plaza came into her mind. Widowhood was still too new to Dori to try and imagine how any other woman would react to it.

"Do they have children?" she asked, without opening her eyes.

"Hart mentioned that they have two daughters."

"He never mentioned a family to me," she said. She was feeling sorrow for Phillip's wife and children. But simultaneously she was still harboring contempt for the way he had treated her. Or had she made too much out of it? Her mind was tired, and in shock over the event. Strange thoughts came to her and she had no defenses at the moment with which to screen them. Had Chris ever had a casual affair while they were married? She thought about it. Of course not. She had never asked him. It was unnecessary. She thought again of Madeleine Graham, smiling at her in the hotel. Dori was certain that she had never suspected Phillip either. Wait! she thought. What am I doing to myself? He is dead. They are both dead! I don't care if Chris had a million lovers. I loved him. And nothing will change that. And nothing will change it for Madeleine Graham either. Suddenly all the resentment she had felt for Phillip flowed out of her as quickly as the wind had left the room. Something inside of her dissolved. She saw Phillip's crumpled body lying at the bottom of the elevator. But the body had Chris's face. Then she saw Chris's body on the stretcher being lifted into the ambulance. But this time the face belonged to Phillip. She turned to Salter, her eyes filling with tears. "Everyone dies," she said. "And they can't change the things they did or didn't do. They leave and they take your feelings with them. I can't love one dead man and I can't hate another." She was half screaming, half crying now, on the verge of hysteria. "It's so hard to be left behind. What are you supposed to do with yourself?"

The black man lifted her up and cradled her on his lap. She put her head against his chest and cried. He rocked her softly back-and-forth wrapping his muscular arms about her. In a few moments she had stopped sobbing. She tried to compose herself. She stood up quickly, straightening her dress and running a hand through her tousled hair. Salter looked up at her. The light from the lantern at her feet delicately etched her face in muted gold. Her eyes were wet and gleaming. Her cheeks were flushed. The low oval neckline of her gown exposed just a trace of her firm, round breasts.

It was still now. Not even the slightest breeze remained. "The wind is capricious here," she said, in a voice that she hoped would indicate that she had recovered. Salter got to his feet and came over to her as though he had not heard what she had said. He put his hand under her chin and lifted her face to his. He kissed her tenderly on the mouth. Then he took her in his arms and kissed her again, deeply, with a passion that almost overwhelmed her.

"You are a rare and lucky woman," he whispered, holding her body close to his and stroking her hair. With her head against his chest she could feel the rhythm of his breathing. "You are not ashamed to admit that at times life frightens and confuses you. But you are too harsh with yourself. We are all aimless travelers, confronted by things that mystify us. Yet most would rather pretend strength than acknowledge weakness."

Dori looked up into Salter's face, at the lines of his sculptured, rugged jaw. His brown eyes were intensely penetrating. She remembered the night she had met him at the Trents. He seemed so invincible. Even now, there was only the hint of vulnerability about him.

"I followed you here because I saw how afraid you were. He said. "I didn't want you to be alone."

"Why?" she asked. He grabbed her hands and drew her close to him again. His jacket fell from her shoulders to the ground.

"Because I want you. And I want you to need me." He bent down and kissed her on the neck then he reached behind her and unzipped her dress. But he did not try to and remove it. Instead he stood back caressing her cheek with his hand as he drew away. Then he undressed. His body was tight and fierce looking. Dori felt a sensual throbbing begin within her own. She knew that the decision must be hers. She could turn and go and nothing more would ever be said of this.

She took several steps closer to him, then reached up and pulled her dress down, letting it fall in a circle about her feet. She stepped out of it and spread it on top of the rest of the clothes. The lantern was burning low, almost out of fuel. Soon the light would be gone. What was left of this night was theirs to give to each other. She knew that dawn was crouching just hours away.

XXII

Where was he? Claire didn't like waiting. She had been sitting on the terrace since six this morning. She stood up and scanned the beach below her once more. He should have been here by now. She lit a cigarette. Howard wouldn't like to see her smoking. She had given up the habit years ago. But she was nervous. And anyway, Howard wouldn't be back all day. He and Hart were taking Phillip Graham's body to the port authorities before putting it on a plane bound for New York. And then there would be the guests to meet.

Her head was throbbing. She went into the bathroom and opened up the medicine cabinet. "Shit," she said looking at the empty pill bottle. With the shape Turner had left in last night he wouldn't be good for anything until at least noon. She went into the kitchen and poured herself a small glass of scotch, then returned to her vigil on the terrace.

She knew what had happened to Phillip Graham had not been an accident. She had known that it was going to happen but she had not been told how. The horrid scene of the shattered elevator and the snapping, hissing wires kept coming into her mind. It was sickening. And then she thought of the moments in the office. Had Dori seeing her? No, she couldn't have. She had been too distraught. And it was pitch black. At the very worst she saw only a form, a shadow. She couldn't identify a shadow.

Claire glanced down at the large manila folder resting on the card table. She had done just what she had been told to do. Cliff would certainly have to start trusting her now. She looked out again. Frank LeBeau was walking slowly down the beach toward the garden bar of the Cinnamon Inn. His small black dog was well ahead of him trotting along the shoreline, stopping occasionally to sniff and paw in the sand. Claire sat her drink down and extinguished her cigarette on the terrace floor.

She picked up the manila folder and started toward the steps. She was feeling a bit dizzy and hung on to the railing. They met halfway across the lawn.

"Here," she said, thrusting the package at him, wanting to be rid of it.

"Did you have any trouble?" He asked.

"If I had had any trouble," she snapped, "I wouldn't have it, would I? "

"Take it easy, Claire," he said, "everything is going to be fine. The Chameleon will be very pleased."

"Well, when am I going to know what this is all about?" She asked. "Why does he want these anyway?"

"Just be patient. He will tell you when he feels it is important for you to know." He turned and left, strolling easily back down the beach, calling the wandering dog to his side.

At twilight, Howard Rutledge waited at the airport for the fifth and last plane arriving from Barbados carrying the final group of guests bound for the Castle Beach Hotel. He was exhausted. Already, he had transported close to sixty people and their luggage to the hotel, giving each group a short history of the island, answering a plethora of routine questions, and in general welcoming them to Miranda.

As he drove along in the brightly colored station wagon he would glance in the rearview mirror at his human cargo. They were such a strange conglomeration of people: older, obviously wealthy matrons on holiday; young couples, married and not, here for surf and sun and a great deal of sex; middle-aged couples who were spending a large portion of their life savings for the fling they believe they deserved; and a great number of lonely people, traveling unaccompanied, in search of something. Howard had seen them all before when the Cinnamon Inn was flourishing—the contented and the despairing, the aging and the ageless. They were all living testimonials to the plight of the human condition. And to Howard, they were frightening reminders of how difficult life could be in the real world.

He drove swiftly around the curving roads, naming various flowers and birds for the benefit of any interested tourist. His shoulders and back ached, more from tension then from driving. It seemed like days since he and Logan Hart watched the casket carrying Phillip Graham being unceremoniously loaded onto a plane heading for LaGuardia.

Hart had not taken it well. He had made certain that Mandy and the others helped clean up any traces of glass. The faulty wiring had been repaired. Sylvia and Ruthie had put some potted plants and bright flowers in the service elevators to make them look more appealing to the visitors. The remains of the shattered exterior elevator were dismantled. Hart said that he would contact the engineering contractor from Martinique to take charge of the reconstruction. And by daybreak there was little evidence that anything out of the ordinary had taken place.

But Hart was uneasy, to say the least. "The guests will find out what has happened. You can't keep the electrocution death of one of the most prominent American architects a secret." He had been pacing up and down in his office all night.

"Accidents happen," Howard assured him. "This was unfortunate."

"To put it mildly," Hart added.

"The people have other things on their mind. They are coming here for a good time. The death of the Pope wouldn't put a damper on things for long."

Hart shook his head in sad agreement. "You're right. People are basically self-centered. They might be sorry for Graham one minute and then demanding that the elevator be repaired the next. Jesus Christ, what a business!"

Howard was now driving through St. Philips. The passengers were remarking on the beauty of the harbor and asking questions concerning the various sleek yachts anchored offshore. But one man in the back was strangely silent. He studied everything with an analytical eye, yet did not make any comments. Howard had thought that he was strange from the moment he stepped off the plane. He was met by Charles Cliff, Salter's aide, and immediately ushered through the normal passport security check. Howard reasoned that he must be some kind of a VIP. He was carrying a small briefcase on his lap. Since he hadn't spoken, Howard could not tell what nationality he was. But he had a rather tan complexion and dark, brooding eyes. Howard guessed that he might be Spanish or Mexican.

At last the car swung into the circular driveway of the hotel. Mandy's staff was waiting with gleaming brass luggage carts. Howard parked and opened the doors for the guests. Then he went into the lobby to check on all of the reservations. Claire was not behind the desk with the clerks. He really didn't expect her to be. She was terribly upset over the accident last night. Howard knew that she was probably home in bed, sleeping. He hoped that she hadn't been drinking, or taking too many of those goddamn headache pills at the same time.

He went into the office. Logan was sitting behind his desk. He was white, except for the great puffy circles under his bloodshot eyes.

"Man," Howard said, "I thought that I was tired until I looked at you. Why don't you drink a bottle of rum and go to bed? Everything is under control here. The last of the guests have arrived and are being tucked into bed right now."

"Where is she?" Logan said flatly, staring straight ahead. Howard knew he was referring to Dori.

"I don't know. Maybe she is up with Claire."

"No, I've tried there. Claire said she hasn't seen her since the accident, neither has Sylvia or Ruthie or any of the staff. Allison still has Jeremy. She said that she will keep him until I hear from Dori." He stood up and walked over to the window. "Where in the hell could she be?" His eyes were closed and he rubbed them. "Where in the goddamn hell could she be?"

"Here I am Logan." He whirled around and opened his eyes. Dori was standing in the doorway with John Salter. The look on her face said it all. Dori wanted to explain everything to Logan, to tell him all that had happened to her. But she couldn't. She didn't understand much of it herself. So she just apologized for making him worry and then excused herself. She said good night to John in the lobby. "Thank you for…"

"Don't," he put his fingers to her lips. "Just smile at me now." She did and then left.

Dori went into the office and called Allison Trent. Jeremy got on the phone and asked if he could please stay another night. "We've built this really neat fort in some big trees and we are pirates!"

Allison assured her that he would be no problem. "Actually," she said, "the boys play much better when Jeremy is around. They don't have time to fight with each other. And remember I told you that I wanted to keep him here so you can concentrate on the hotel opening."

Dori thanked her for taking care of him and said that she would be there first thing in the morning to retrieve him. When she hung up, Howard had left and Logan had closed the door. He was staring at her as though he had never seen her before. She couldn't read his expression. "You don't know what you are doing, Dori."

It was going to be a lecture. "Please don't be angry with me, Logan. Maybe you're right. Maybe I don't. Maybe I am just a fool. But I couldn't be making any greater mistakes than I did when I thought that I was being wise."

"Oh yes you could. What do you know about this man? What do you know about his past, or even his present for that matter? He uses people."

"Don't we all?" She said defensively. "Oh Logan." She sighed and went over and hugged him. "I don't want to know everything. I've made that mistake before, demanding to know everything about someone. I know enough. I know that I have never met anyone like him. I have never felt anything like I feel when we are together. It's hard to be logical here; we are all so isolated. We make up our own rules."

"Or excuses," Logan injected.

"I'm not going to fight with you, because everything you are saying could be true and probably is. This thing happened so fast. I can't explain it and I can't deny it either. I have taken a man I hardly know as a lover. I guess I should be shocked at my behavior. I keep waiting to be. But I'm not. I'm through judging myself for a while. I need what he offers me. For now that is good enough. There will always be time for regrets."

Logan shook his head. "Somehow I never pegged you for an existentialist. I didn't think that was your style, but God knows that I am in no position to cast any stones. Just be careful. I happen to care about you."

"I know, and thank you."

"Back to matters at hand," Logan said. "There is a great deal of hotel business that needs discussing, but not tonight. I think I'm going to take Howard's sound advice and dive into a bottle of rum and then go to bed."

"Okay," Dori smiled gently at him. "I promise to work twice as hard tomorrow to make up for staying away today."

He escorted her through the busy lobby to one of the service elevators. "Sleep well," he said, then turned and walked quickly away.

XXIII

George Ramino went up on the deck of the *Kiwi* when he heard the engine sound of the dinghy. He looked out and saw a small skiff churning through the water toward the side of the ship. Already the gassy fumes from the outboard motor filled the air. Lanterns burning on the masts served as a guiding beacon for the tiny boat. It drew up close to the side of the *Kiwi*. The engine sputtered for a moment and then stopped. Charles Cliff maneuvered the boat up next to the lowered ladder. "Here we are, gentlemen," he announced to his passengers.

"Watch your step," cautioned Ramino as the first man began to ascend the ladder. Mariani was standing nearby holding a flashlight on the wooden rungs as an added help to the new arrivals. "Welcome aboard," Ramino said, extending his hand to the first man, and then to the second. They each shook hands with Ramino as well as with his companion.

"Let's go down below where we will be more comfortable," Mariani said. He led the men toward the salon entrance. Cliff secured the boat and then followed the others below. Though he had been aboard the *Kiwi* several times before, the sumptuous beauty of the salon always awed him. The walls were all carved, polished teak wood. Each lighting fixture was solid brass. Oriental carpets adorned the floor. Tonight, there was a decanter of brandy on the table surrounded by five crystal snifters.

"Please be seated," Ramino instructed. "I trust that you both had a pleasant trip," he added, pouring brandy for his guests.

"It was without incident, if that is what you mean." The speaker was the man with the dark complexion Howard had observed riding in the back of the hotel station wagon. His accent was very definitely Spanish.

"Well, I assured you before you came that you would have no passport problems," Mariani said proudly. "Attention to details is of paramount importance."

"Very good. I surmise that is why you roused us from our beds tonight." This time it was a tall, gray-haired man who spoke. His accent was an unusual blend of Spanish and Italian.

"That is correct," Ramino said. "But before we go further, I should like to make proper introductions all around. Charles," he said, "I would like you to meet Ramon Delgado and Simon Ochoa. They have played in competitions worldwide, but under aliases better known than their real names. And fortunately for us, they have never allowed their photographs to be taken at the tables. So, to their prospective opponents they will be virtually unknown."

Charles smiled and nodded, sipping his brandy. Light from one of the wall lamps reflected off of the thick lenses of his glasses. Delgado, the short dark man, held his brandy snifter up to Mariani for a refill. "Mr. Cliff introduced himself when he met us at the dock this evening. We are both well aware of his part in things. But all of the information we have been getting is piecemeal. I would feel more comfortable, as I am sure would Mr. Ochoa, if you would elaborate on the logistics of the games." Simon Ochoa shook his head in agreement. His thin, fragile physique made him look the part of a scholar rather than of a professional gambler.

"As you wish," Ramino said, standing. "For your own protection, you shall know only that which is germane to your tasks here. Sal," he glanced over at Mariani who quickly stood up and disappeared down the stairs leading to the cabins. He returned a short time later carrying two briefcases, identical in shape, but of different colors. He set them down on the table and snapped them open. Each was filled with neatly arranged rows of bills in various denominations from one hundred to one thousand dollar bills. The men unemotionally appraised the contents. Ramino closed the lids.

"Each contains one hundred thousand dollars," Ramino said. "All of this has been laundered in Switzerland. It comprises the collected funds from our various supporters throughout the Windward Islands, as well as large contributions from private sources in Haiti and Cuba. Tomorrow this money will be deposited in the hotel safe in your names, to be used by you at the backgammon tables. Since our contact with you must be kept at a minimum, you shall be allowed to use your discretion when determining the stakes of the betting. We have total faith in your mastery of the game."

"But," said Mariani, "we do suggest that you tease your opponents at first, losing small sums of money by careless errors that will give them a false sense of security."

Delgado and Ochoa exchanged a knowing glance. "I understood Mr. Ramino to say that you both have unfailing faith in our mastery of the game," Ochoa said, unsmiling.

"Forgive me," Mariani apologized. "I am sure that you are aware of all the available techniques. I vow no more kibitzing."

Ramino spoke. "You shall receive one hundred dollars for every thousand dollars you win. Our goal gentleman, is to obtain an additional five hundred thousand dollars by the end of June."

The room was quiet. The electric generator hummed rhythmically in the background. The *Kiwi* rocked gently in the calm midnight water. It was Delgado who broke the silence. "And what of our opponents? With what working knowledge are they operating?"

"I was coming to that," assured Ramino. "We have chosen all of the participants very carefully. Each of them will be gambling with money they have no legitimate right to be risking. Thus, when they lose large sums, as we are hoping they will, each shall be forced to go elsewhere to recoup or disguise their losses. Their frustrated recriminations, of necessity, will be of an internal nature. And even if the impossible were to happen and one of them were to discover the patterns in the games, and the connection between the two of you, they would still have to keep their suspicions to themselves since they can ill afford unsavory publicity."

Mariani opened a small attaché case and extracted several typewritten sheets. "We have prepared dossiers on each of your opponents. We suggest respectfully," he added, "that you study them carefully. We hope that they will give you a better understanding of the strengths and weaknesses of each of the players."

He handed copies of the sheets to both men. "We have also," said Ramino, "taken the liberty of preparing false dossiers for both of you, in case you are asked routine questions concerning your background or occupations."

Delgado read his fact sheet and chuckled. "I am quite impressed with myself: professor of nuclear physics at the University of Madrid. Where would a college professor get a hundred thousand dollars?"

Ramino smiled, "Let them worry about that all month."

Simon Ochoa seemed somewhat less pleased with his resume. "Italian industrialist based in Mexico City. I loathe Mexico City and know nothing about industry. But I shall make a valiant attempt to conceal both facts."

Cliff handed Ramino the manila envelope he had received earlier from Frank LeBeau. Ramino excused himself for a moment and went below to examine the contents. He smiled and sighed deeply—Philip Graham's complete blueprints to the Castle Beach Hotel.

They concluded their discussions and went up on the deck. Charles Cliff jumped down into the dinghy and after several tries, started the motor. Delgado climbed down the ladder carefully, holding onto the railing with both hands. Ochoa handed him the folders of papers and then followed him into the boat. But he paused a moment to direct a question to his hosts. "I don't know what your cause is or for whom you work; I don't want to know. I want to make my money and be on my way, but just tell me this. If it is so important that you have all of your needed funds by the end of June, what happens in July?"

Ramino, who was in the process of lighting a cigar, stopped. He looked quickly at Mariani and Cliff and then directly at his interrogator. "Everything," he answered softly, and tossed his match into the water.

XXIV

The dining room was already crowded when Dori came in for breakfast the next morning. She sat down quickly at a table close to the entrance and watched the proceedings. Things were running quite smoothly considering that this was the first full day of operations. The Mirandan waiters in their crisp white pants and colorful striped shirts paraded in and out of the kitchen carrying big trays of fresh fruit, steaming platters of sausages and scrambled eggs, baskets of roles, and pots of coffee. The seated guests appeared to be enjoying themselves. The food did look appealing. The combination of red tile floors, clean tan bamboo tables and chairs, and hanging tropical ferns gave the whole room a breezy peaceful feeling.

Dori took a rapid, visual inventory of some of the guests. There was a long table filled with people in their fifties and sixties, each wearing a name tag provided by the travel agency that had arranged the tour. There were women loaded with heavy straw purses and men carrying every variety of camera imaginable. Dori was able to hear enough snatches of their loud conversations to realize that they were from somewhere in the south, perhaps Tennessee or Kentucky. While eating a lumberjack breakfast, the women talked about that stringent diets they would go on the minute the vacation was over.

Seated at other tables throughout the room were couples in their twenties and thirities, some with children, some without. Most of the couples were extremely well groomed and attractive. There were also groups of older women traveling alone, or young girls, off on holiday. The only table that seemed the least bit odd was one in the back near the veranda that led to the beach. Two men and a woman sat studying their menus. One man was probably about thirty, while the other was much older, perhaps fifty-five or sixty. The woman with them was elegantly dressed in a Kelly-green silk pantsuit. Her straight black hair was pulled back tightly into a bun. She appeared to be in her late forties. For some strange reason she looked vaguely familiar to Dori.

"May I join you?" It was Logan.

"Of course."

He sat down. His eyes were red and the lids puffy. He spotted a waiter and called him over. "Get me a Bloody Mary, will you? Right away, please. What a day to be nursing a hangover," he said to Dori when they were alone. "But maybe it's better this way, it's hard to get upset about anything when I feel so lousy." He rubbed his temples.

"Still mad at me?" Dori asked.

He dismissed that suggestion with a quick wave. "No, you're a big girl. I can't worry about you. It's some other things."

"Like what?"

His drink arrived. The waiter also poured Dori another cup of coffee. "Like this Ramino thing," Logan said, stirring his drink with the stalk of celery sticking out of it. "He and his sidekick darkened my doorstep first thing this morning. They deposited an incredible amount of money in the safe, said they would be back later with the other antes. Joy. Every time I sit down at my desk I feel like a Brinks guard." He took a bite of the celery stalk. "Oh," he groaned, "the noise sounds like I am chewing rocks."

"Who has the combination to the safe?" Dori asked.

"Well I certainly don't. I don't want to have it." He covered his eyes with his hands. "See no evil."

"When are the games going to start?"

"Jesus, Dori, you make it sound like we are heralding the beginning of the Olympics. But what the hell, in a way I guess we are." He took a few long swallows of the spicy cocktail. "Today, I guess, this afternoon, in a ground floor suite. They want to be near the booze and the money, I suppose. Ramino said that we are welcome to watch the matches if we want to, Salter as well." A waiter came by with coffee for Logan.

"Have you met any of the players yet?" Dori asked.

"Well no, not exactly. But Ramino filled me in on who they are. One guy is some nuclear scientist in Spain. Then there is a fellow from Mexico City." He scrutinized the tables. His eyes rested on the same group that had intrigued Dori. "See that guy?" He said, nodding at the young man. "Son of Jules Cavanaugh, president of Cavanaugh cosmetics. Ramino said that the kid is a compulsive backgammon player. Said that he borrows company funds to feed his habit. His old man keeps bailing him out. But if the stockholders got wind of it, there could be big trouble. That other man is Martin Gibson, a New York investment counselor. Guess what he does with his clients' money?" Logan asked rhetorically. Dori couldn't believe what she was hearing. "And that aging vamp with them," Logan continued, "is none other than Morgan Talbot."

"The actress?" Dori asked, amazed. "I knew that I had seen her. She used to be very popular. She made all of those sappy, predictable romantic comedies with Nicky Barnes."

"Well, she is into a whole different racket now. She founded some quasi-religious sect named, get this, The Profound Life Improvement Institute. She's got a large following on college campuses. But the only thing that really seems to be improving is her bankbook. Ramino said that the papers are printing stories that she has come to the West Indies to proselytize and conduct seminars. Incredible, isn't it?"

"Very," Dori said, shaking her head.

"Well," Logan said finishing some coffee, "I am going to try and put the whole thing out of my mind for the time being. I do have a hotel to run. Which reminds me, will you make sure that the band is ready to play tonight? And also, please post a notice that the dinner will be served around the outside bar, buffet style. I want to go down to the beach this morning and make certain that Howard is careful about who he allows to use those sunfish. I don't want any more accidents."

Dori had a sinking feeling at the obvious reference to Phillip. "It was so horrible, Logan." She stared at the sediment in the bottom of her coffee cup.

"It's over," he said quickly. "The story appeared in the New York papers yesterday. I've received some calls of concern and sympathy from a couple of my associates. And a few reporters have called to check the details of the incident. But other than that, nothing."

"If only there had been something that could've been done."

"The medical examiner from Martinique confirmed that he died immediately from the shock. I told Phillip that I didn't think that he knew enough about electrical wiring to work on the elevator. I wanted to call in someone else. But he wouldn't hear of it."

"That was Phillip," Dori observed

"In any case," Logan added, "our own great Dr. Turner would have been of little help."

Dorothy thought of the drunken doctor's strange diatribe. "John and I talked yesterday about Ransom. He doesn't seem to think that he knows my father as he insisted he did. John thinks that Jeremy must have told him about my dad and he just blurted out all of that for no particular reason, other than to interrupt our conversation."

"Still, I don't think that it would do any harm to write to your dad and ask him what, if anything, he knows about Turner. Howard said that even he and Claire don't know much concerning Turner's background." Logan drained his glass. "Well, the jolly innkeeper is off," he said standing.

Dori watched with admiration as he made the rounds of the tables, introducing himself to those he hadn't met the previous day and greeting by name those he had. He passed by her table on his way outside. He stopped short, as though just discovering her. He reached down and took her hand and grinned broadly. "Allow me to introduce myself. I am Logan Hart, host to racketeers and conventioneers." Dori laughed as he winked and walked out through the lobby to the beach.

Jay Cavanagh was the first of the players to arrive at the designated suite. Mariani told him that the games would begin at four o'clock but he wanted to drop by early and get a feel for the place. Like most competitors, he believed that the arena of play was equally as important as the sport.

His hosts seemed rather irritated to see him when they responded to the knock on the door. "Mr. Cavanagh?" Mariani said, a little surprised. "You are an unexpected visitor. I believe that we arranged for the time of four this afternoon for the commencement of the games."

"Yeah, I know," said the young man. "But I just wanted to come by and have a look at the place, since I plan on spending a great deal of time here."

Mariani smiled tightly. "I am glad that your optimism abounds. Perhaps it will serve as a safeguard against your early elimination in the tournament."

"Listen," Cavanaugh said, taking off a terrycloth beach robe and tossing it across the back of a chair. "I didn't come halfway around the world to be snaked out."

"None of the players did," said Ramino emerging from the kitchen area. "I can assure you that they are all equally intent upon winning."

"Well then" grinned Cavanaugh, "it ought to make for exciting afternoons." He walked around the room examining the three-game tables. The black and red leather backgammon boards were already set up. He liked the place. It was very much like his own room, minus the bed. He looked out of the terrace windows to the beach beyond. It had a better view. His room was on the opposite side of the hotel and faced the entrance road instead of the water.

He sauntered into the small kitchenette and opened up the refrigerator. He was happy to discover that it was well stocked with all necessary cocktail supplies. He enjoyed nursing a tall bourbon and soda during play. But unlike many of his previous opponents he never drank to the point where his judgment would be impaired. "Well gentlemen," he said finally, retrieving his robe and heading toward the door, "everything seems to be in order." He glanced down at his ornate gold watch. "Guess I have time for a short swim before the kickoff."

"Indeed," Ramino agreed, opening the door for him, "some vigorous physical exercise makes one better prepared to endure tension."

Cavanaugh paused in the doorway leaning against the frame. "Whose tense?" He asked and walked off down the hall.

It was a little after two. The last of the lunch crowd was just leaving the dining room. The waiters were rapidly clearing tables and carrying trays of stacked dishes into the kitchen. Lingering smells of fruit and coffee hung in the air as Cavanaugh passed by on his way to the lobby. He went into the small gift shop next to the front desk. It carried the standard sundry items found in most hotel stores: a limited supply of basic over the counter medicines and suntan oils, newspapers, chewing gum, cigarettes, and a few dated magazines. A rack of postcards depicting various scenes around Miranda caught his attention. He examined all of them. There were some with an aerial view of the harbor of St. Philips, or shots of the natives working on the lush green banana plantations or in the sugarcane fields. There were even photographs of the ministry and the British government house. But there were none of the Castle Beach Hotel. Too new, he reasoned. He bought a bottle of suntan lotion and a pair of cheap sunglasses before starting for the beach.

He paused in front of the open door to the business office. He saw Logan Hart sitting behind his desk, reading something. "Guarding the money?" Cavanaugh said, eyeing the safe.

Logan looked up. "The lock on that monster is guard enough. How are you enjoying your stay here?" He asked pleasantly.

"I'll be able to give you a better idea sometime later on today." He smiled out from behind large black lenses. " You gonna come up and watch me wipe 'em out?"

"Perhaps, but I am not really too familiar with the game."

"Nothing to it actually, a little skill and a lot of luck. But better than cards." He reached into the pocket of his robe and pulled out a package of cigarettes and lit one. He discarded the used match on the tile floor. Logan watched, saying nothing. "The one singular advantage backgammon has over every other game is that it is virtually impossible to cheat."

"How is that?" Logan asked, genuinely interested.

"Because everything is out in front. Both players know exactly what spot the other is in. And since both players need a variety of numerical combinations throughout play, loading the dice serves no purpose. But the betting is the best part." He took a deep draw on his cigarette. Already a long gray mass was collecting at the end. Logan casually handed him an ashtray. "You see," he continued, "any time during the game either player can challenge his opponent by using the doubling cube, which automatically doubles the bet. If the opponent rejects the challenge, the challenger automatically wins." Logan was trying to follow his explanation but it was obvious from the puzzled expression on his face that he was having some difficulty with it all.

"Hey," Cavanaugh said, "just come today, Hart, and watch. You'll catch on." He started to leave. "Incidentally, why don't you get rid of that horrible supply of goo you are carrying in the gift shop? If this is supposed to be a first-class joint, better get in a line of Cavanagh Cosmetics. I'll arrange it." Again the big toothy smile. He finished his cigarette and dropped the butt on the floor and left, whistling.

Claire sat under a beach umbrella watching the people. The sand was crowded, even during the heat of the day. Groups of children, newly introduced and now good friends, played by the water's edge while their parents swam or sat near the outside bar enjoying the rum punch. Other guests, determined to acquire an instant and enviable tan, lay on the large Castle Beach Hotel towels sacrificing their pasty skin to the savage rays of the sun. Tonight they would wear loose fitting clothes and display their blistered flesh in a rite of passage familiar to all island tourists.

The sun, flaming in a cloudless sky, reflected off the water with an almost blinding light. Howard was in his element. Claire looked on in disgust as he cheerfully dispensed snorkels, masks, fins, and other oceangoing paraphernalia to eager visitors. One by one he would walk them down to the water and demonstrate the correct use of the equipment. Then he would stand onshore and share their meager efforts. Claire was reminded again of how easily pleased her husband was. His tastes and desires were so simple.

She brushed the hair out of her eyes and retied the scarf that was holding the bulk of it back from her face. Even in bed, Howard's passion was so quickly aroused and so easily satiated. From the beginning, Claire had known that she was a much more complex individual than was her husband, that he would never be able to totally satisfy her physically or emotionally. But that hadn't mattered. In fact, that was part of his initial appeal and perhaps it still was. She did not want him to understand her completely. That would make her too vulnerable to manipulation. He was never a threat to her own fragile ego. She never had to worry that he might overshadow her in any important area. And he was loyal and in the beginning had encouraged her to pursue her career in film. She closed her eyes. If only they had held out a little longer instead of moving here. If only they had left before Hart had come down to the island like the Pied Piper with all of his grand plans. Now even her own hotel was thriving on his overflow of guests.

She opened her eyes. Howard was showing a young man how to operate one of the small sunfish. How she hated the waiting. When would Frank tell her what the Chameleon had planned? After all, she had proven that she was trustworthy. She did steal the blueprints from Phillip Graham's desk. And in the confusion of the hotel opening, no one had even missed them. But what did Cliff want them for? She had to find out.

She reached into her big canvas purse for a cigarette. A woman brushed against her chair. "Excuse me," she apologized as Claire sat up. Claire knew the face immediately. It belonged to Morgan Talbot. Her heart began to beat faster and she felt her entire body start to quiver. Morgan Talbot! She had been writing her own ticket in Hollywood when Claire was still trying to become an extra. Claire remembered sitting in the bleachers outside of the pavilion housing the Academy Awards waiting to catch a glimpse of Morgan Talbot and Nicky Barnes. They had both been nominated for their starring roles in *The Bride Takes A Holiday*. Neither of them won and it was to be the final picture they made together. But it had been a wonderful movie. Claire had seen it dozens of times.

Her mind was reeling. She would have to meet Morgan Talbot. Perhaps they would even have some mutual friends back on the West Coast. Even if they didn't, Claire knew that a single word from this star would get her back into pictures. She got up and walked over to the bar, where Morgan was sitting at a table by herself. "How do you do, Miss Talbot," Claire said graciously, extending her hand. "Please let me introduce myself. I am Claire Cambert Rutledge. My husband and I own the Cinnamon Inn." She pointed down the beach to the cottages nestled into the hillside.

"I am happy to meet you. Would you like to join me?"

Claire sat down smiling. "Have you ordered?"

"No, I haven't been able to attract the bartender's attention as yet."

"What would you like?"

"A tall gin and tonic would be lovely."

Claire called to Mandy and snapped the orders at him. She hoped that her new companion was impressed. "It takes forever to understand these natives," she confessed with a definite air of superiority. "I've been here twenty years and they still puzzle me."

"What a beautiful place you have chosen to live, Mrs. Rutledge."

"Oh, call me Claire, please. On an island nobody stays on a last name basis for long." The drinks arrived and Claire insisted on paying. "Are you here for vacation?" she asked.

"Yes, in part. I am also here on business."

Claire was intrigued. "Are you studying a new script?"

Morgan Talbot threw back her head and laughed. "How sweet you are. No, I haven't made a picture in years." Claire looked disappointed. "But I have not been idle. I have founded a new organization. Perhaps you have heard of it, the Profound Life Improvement Institute?" Claire thought for a moment before shaking her head that she had not. "Well you will. It's nationwide already. I am lecturing all over the United States and establishing new chapters everywhere. I am here to do a bit of fundraising." She took the wedge of lime resting on the rim of her glass and dropped it into her drink.

"What is it that your Institute does exactly?" Claire asked.

"I try to teach people the essence of a happy life. It is a method that I have developed over the years. It is a philosophy that has emerged from my reading and meditation. Not a true religious philosophy. Actually, I teach that only by accepting one's self and others totally, complete with flaws, is one able to recognize and enjoy real happiness and fulfillment. I teach it through reality therapy."

"Oh," Claire said, still disappointed. "Do you keep any contact with Hollywood?" She asked hopefully.

"Oh yes, of course. Some of my biggest supporters are actors I have helped during times of personal crisis. They have come to one of my seminars when their careers were floundering. I have helped them to understand the simple secret to contentment. After they grasp the concepts they are better able to change the destructive patterns of their lives and achieve success, personal and professional."

Claire had become mesmerized by Morgan Talbot's long, red, and perfectly manicured nails as she drummed them on the side of her glass. Claire ordered them both another drink and then told her long story to the new listener, explaining that she would be returning to California in just a matter of time, and of her desire to resume acting.

"Is your husband as anxious to return as you seem to be?" She asked.

"He will be," Claire answered.

Morgan Talbot smiled. Her face was still so gorgeous, clear and void of lines and wrinkles. Her glossy black hair was laced with gray. But even that seemed to add to her overall beauty. She rose to leave. "Well, I must be off. Shall I see you at the buffet tonight?"

"Yes," Claire answered eagerly.

"Splendid. Perhaps we can discuss your aspirations at greater length." She said goodbye and walked off briskly toward the lobby.

The combination of the gin and the heat and the sheer euphoria Claire was experiencing transformed her into a giddy child. She took the empty glasses back to the bar and gave Mandy an extra-large tip. Then she collected her things by the red and blue beach umbrella and raced barefooted down the hot sand toward Cinnamon Inn. She had only a few short hours to sift through her portfolio and select the best photographs of herself to show to Ms. Talbot.

XXV

"No, no, Jeremy, more like this." John Salter ran past the boy to the spot where the red and black soccer ball rested. He kicked it vigorously and it flew through the air coming down yards away, rolling over and over in the grassy field.

"Okay," Jeremy said, running after the ball. Salter came over and sat down next to Dori on a stone bench. "I used to play cricket and soccer here on this very green."

"It must hold a great deal of memories for you," Dori said. Salter thought about the day he had met Bradley Trent, Victor's father.

"Yes, it does."

They watched as Jeremy ran along it kicking the ball ahead of him. Several times his foot would miss the target altogether and he would fall backwards into the grass. But that made him even more determined to succeed. He would attack the ball furiously, as though it had a life of its own. Salter laughed, enjoying the spectacle. "That boy is not a quitter." He looked over at Dori, who was smiling at her son. Her bright lovely face was tan and glowing. She smelled faintly of gardenias. "You are very beautiful," he said, matter-of-factly.

"I am glad that you think so." Suddenly she was feeling awkward.

"Are you regretting anything? " he asked.

"I didn't know how I was going to feel when I saw you again. That is why I decided to stop by the ministry after I left the Trents.

"And what is your reaction to me today?"

"Unexpected, in a way. When I saw you coming toward me down the hall I felt as if I were greeting someone I have known for a great deal of time. Even now, it is hard for me to realize that we were practically strangers just days ago."

"Time is protracted here," he said taking her hand. "Please don't worry, Dori. What we are experiencing is very new, for both of us. We must be patient and accept our feelings as they come, the good and the bad. Let it be enough that we are special to one another." He kissed her softly on the mouth.

Jeremy had grown tired of the solitary sport and rejoined his mother. "Can we go back to the beach? Mrs. Trent said that there are a lot of children staying at the hotel now. I can show them how to sail the boats."

They got up and walked toward Dori's car. "You be on your way," Salter said, "I will see you later at the hotel."

"Are you going to watch the backgammon?" Dori asked.

"Perhaps. Of course the game shall mean little to me." He started up the path toward the ministry. "I never learned to play."

"The first pairing off will be alphabetical," Mariani announced when all of the participants had arrived. "The one with the last name closest to the beginning of the alphabet shall play the person whose last initial appears closest to the end. Thus you, Mr. Cavanaugh, will play Miss Talbot. Mr. Delgado will be matched with Mr. Ochoa. And you, Mr. Gibson," he added smiling at the handsome gray-haired American, "shall play the winner of the first set. And we shall proceed from there. Is that satisfactory to you all?" A bar had been set up in the corner of the room. Jay Cavanagh was already mixing himself a drink.

"How many games in a set?" he asked.

"Five to begin with," responded Mariani. "The sets will increase in length as elimination occurs. Today each game shall be worth five thousand dollars. And until each player has had an opportunity to play with every contestant, the doubling cube will not be used."

This time it was Martin Gibson who spoke. "Your rules are a bit restrictive, don't you think?" Mariani shrugged his shoulders and walked over to the bar.

It was Ramino who answered the question. "I can assure you that the guidelines have been set up for your own protection. We feel that you deserve the opportunity to assess the ability of each player before you begin risking large sums of money."

"I find that very prudent," Morgan Talbot said.

"Okay, okay," Jay Cavanagh was getting anxious. "Let's stop talking and start playing." He took off his blue blazer and hung it over the back of a chair. Then he arbitrarily sat down at one of the game tables. "This okay with you, Morgan?" he asked.

"Fine," she said, put off by his instant and uninvited familiarity. Martin Gibson pulled out her chair and helped her to be seated. "Thank you, sir," she smiled politely, and then glanced disparagingly at the brash young man seated opposite her.

The rest of the players took their places. Mariani, Ramino and Martin Gibson floated, observing the process at each table. It was clear from the beginning that Jay Cavanagh was intensely competitive. Several times during the first game he made foolish moves, without thinking ahead. He would curse his mistakes, and make amends by studying his succeeding moves at great length.

He won the first game but lost the next two. His facial expressions and the entire way he sat in the chair reflected his volatile moods. When he was winning his posture was erect. Sometimes he would drape one arm over the back of his chair, looking almost bored. But when he was in the process of losing he would huddle over the game board, with both elbows resting on the table, his hands against his forehead. He was oblivious to any outside distraction. Oddly enough, regardless of how he was faring, he never looked at his opponent. It was almost as though invisible forces were rolling the dice and moving the pieces on the opposite side of the board.

Quite conversely, Morgan Talbot's expression changed little throughout play. From looking at her one would find it difficult to guess whether or not she was being successful. Gibson concluded, after watching both of the players for some time, that Cavanaugh was surely the more skillful of the two, sometimes making almost brilliant calculations that required advance speculation on each possible move available to his adversary. But Talbot was a thorough, plodding player, consistently conservative yet lacking imagination and finesse.

He was pleased to learn, after watching Delgado and Ochoa, that neither of them would prove to be too great a threat. They both made the classic opening moves, and played strictly by the book. Both of them made many amateurish blunders repeatedly in the course of a single game. How odd that they should be willing to risk such large sums of money at a game which they both played so poorly.

Gibson smiled to himself; the tightness he was feeling in his shoulders began to dissipate. He would not question this lucky turn of fate, but rather prepare to reap the benefits. Hopefully, his winnings here would counteract the beatings he had been taking in the market and his clients would still hail him as the financial guru of Wall Street.

Slowly the afternoon dissolved into dusk and dusk into twilight. Delicate fingers of pink light penetrated the terrace glass and reached into the recesses of the room, like spreading watercolors. The mingling sounds of shouts and laughter coming from the beach vanished, soon to be replaced by the feverish pounding of the steel drums.

It was close to nine o'clock when both tables finished the last game in the second set. Jay Cavanagh had won both sets, sweeping the last one five to zero. Ochoa and Delgado split the games, each winning one set. Things had gone smoothly. Ramino was pleased. "We shall keep track of each of your winnings," Mariani said.

"You're just making work for yourselves, fellas," Cavanaugh said as he stood up and stretched, "I'm keeping track of my own." He smiled, breezy and confident, grabbing his jacket and tossing it over his shoulder. "I'm gonna find Hart. Why in the hell didn't he show up today? I was fantastic!"

Logan was wearing a white dinner jacket and looked very much the proprietor as he strolled by the long buffet table examining the inviting array of dishes. Sylvia is out doing herself, he thought and smiled. There were at least seven crystal bowls filled with various salads, some featuring tropical specialties such as papaya and mango. There were large quantities of fresh breads, platters of roasted beef and broiled chicken, steaming lobster and cracked crab. At one end of the table two young man, dressed in white chef's hats and aprons, stood behind gleaming stainless steel chafing dishes, ready to serve eager guests succulent offerings of teriyaki shrimp and cilantro rice.

It was a happy coincidence that several photographers representing influential international travel magazines had arrived this morning. They were busily snapping pictures of the food and of the carefree guests as they lingered over the groaning board heaping their plates with samples of everything. Tables had been set up all around the garden bar. Some early diners had already finished their meal and had taken to the dance floor. They whirled about, uninhibitedly, attempting to integrate current disco dance steps to the pulsating music of the steel band. The tiny white lights Phillip had installed in the foliage twinkled like low hanging stars.

Logan had invited the Trents as well as Claire and Howard to join them. He had told Dori to extend the invitation to John Salter and to Sarah Hunnicut as well. On the way to his table Logan spotted Ransom Turner sitting at the bar. He felt a sharp pang in the pit of his stomach. He would not allow anything to spoil this festive atmosphere. He asked Mandy for a rum punch and then sat down next to the doctor.

"Hello, Ransom." Turner looked up from his drink and glared at Hart, but said nothing. "I'm afraid that I'm going to have to insist that you leave, unless you can promise me that you will not cause any more problems."

Turner stood up. He was on his way to becoming quite drunk again. "Oh, I'll make you a promise alright. I promise that I have just begun to cause problems. But don't worry. I'm not staying. This place is a dump anyway." He threw some money on the bar and left, weaving and bumping into several people on his way to the lobby.

Logan breathed a heavy sigh and took a swallow of his drink. What has happened to that guy? When he was sober he was charming, witty and interesting. Drunk he was bellicose and full of hate. A true alcoholic, Logan thought, what a waste.

For the most part, the rest of the evening was light and relaxing. Claire Rutledge seemed to be in especially grand form, dressed ostentatiously in a long red velvet gown despite the heat. She had sought out Morgan Talbot and had insisted that she join the group, constantly embarrassing the woman by introducing her as the crème de la crème of Hollywood society.

"Do you know that Morgan has founded a nonprofit organization totally devoted to helping people discover true happiness?" Claire asked, full of pride.

"Well, it's not entirely nonprofit," the actress said softly.

Logan winked at Dori. "Yes Claire, we have heard about Ms. Talbot's fine crusade."

"But she is still very active in films." Claire spoke for her guest as though the woman needed an interpreter.

Morgan, who was seated next to Howard, said. "Your wife tells me that you are both very anxious to return to California. She said that you previously managed athletic teams."

Howard was uncomfortable and stared disappointedly at Claire. "I owned a small sporting goods store." He said simply.

"Why Howie, you are so modest!" Claire snapped, "Small store! Associated Artists it didn't think so. They paid us a tidy fortune for it. Anyway, he will buy another one when we move back, perhaps attached to a health spa or something."

"Again, I must correct my wife," Howard said. "She has wanted to return for years. But there really isn't any point to it now since business is booming here, thanks to Logan."

Claire sat back in her chair, folding her arms in disgust. "Well, we will just have to wait and see how long business booms won't we? You never know, it could end tomorrow and we would all have to leave." Allison Trent looked on with alarm as Claire spoke. Their eyes connected and Claire recovered. "But Mr. Salter does seem to be running the island quite nicely now. And prosperity is the order of the day."

"Don't sound so disappointed, Claire," Salter said. I hope you and your husband will stay with us for many more years. You are both practically honorary citizens." Howard beamed while Claire forced a thin smile.

Victor Trent had not been listening to the conversation. He was watching Sarah Hunnicut, who was now dancing with some young flashy American. Victor looked on anxiously as they spun around, clinging to each other.

"Who is that?" Allison asked, voicing her husband's question.

"Jay Cavanaugh," Logan said, "the cosmetic heir."

"Quite handsome, don't you think?" Claire asked Allison, enjoying Victor's frustration.

"Very," Allison said.

"He is a pompous ass," offered Morgan Talbot authoritatively. She realized that everyone at the table was waiting for an explanation. "We met briefly," she added rising to leave.

"You're not going?" whined Claire.

"Yes, I really am awfully tired. And I have some business I must conduct tomorrow." She said good night to the gathering and proceeded across the crowded dance floor in the direction of the arbor. Claire reached under the table and extracted a worn cardboard portfolio held together with frayed red satin ribbon tied at the top. She ran after the actress catching up with her as she was about to enter the lobby.

"These pictures of me are from some of my very old films. I was hoping that perhaps you could look at them in your spare time and tell me what you think?" Claire's eyes were so wide and pleading and pathetic that Morgan agreed. Why not support her harmless fantasy?

Claire returned to the table in a state of joyful frenzy. "This afternoon Morgan begged me to show her my portfolio." She gave a haughty look at her husband. "She seems to think that I have a classic beauty, just what they are searching for these days."

Sometime, a little after midnight, the band stopped playing. The sad remnants of food left languishing on the buffet table were cleared away, and most of the guests had gone to their rooms for the night, contentedly exhausted. Some stragglers sat together quietly on the beach enjoying the balmy air. Howard invited the group at the tables to come back to Cinnamon Inn for a nightcap. All but the Trents declined. Dori guessed that neither Victor nor Howard relished the prospect of being alone with their wives at the moment.

Logan stayed at the table, eager to talk with Dori and Salter privately. "Did either of you watch the backgammon this afternoon?" he asked. They both replied that they had not. "Well, I was planning on it, but at the last minute I had to drive the station wagon into St. Philips to pick up several more hams and a side of beef." He grinned slightly. "We're still a bit unorganized here."

"Do you think that it would be wise if we watched?" Dori asked. "I wonder if it might not annoy the players?"

"I don't give a damn if it annoys the players," Logan said loudly. "I don't want things to get rough. And with the kind of money being tossed around, it's bound to happen unless we keep a lid on it."

Salter shook his head in agreement. "Unfavorable publicity would be bad for the island as well as for the hotel."

"How long do you think it will be necessary to put up with all of this Logan?" Dori asked.

"I don't know for sure. I am booked for two months in advance. When I am booked for six I'll breathe a lot easier. Maybe then."

Salter made arrangements for his aide Charles Cliff to pick him up at one. The limousine was already waiting when he walked with Dori through the quiet lobby. They were both extremely careful to avoid any physical contact in public. They had agreed that for many reasons it would be best. But the strain on each of them was tremendous. "Will you come back to the ministry with me?" Salter asked as Cliff opened the car door for him.

Dori hesitated. "Well, Ruthie is with Jeremy. They are sound asleep by now I'm sure."

"Please. I'll bring you back soon."

Dori climbed in beside him. He held her hand discreetly on the ride from the hotel. But even that contact was enough to arouse her. Cliff parked the car in front of the iron gates. He opened the door for them. Salter asked him for the keys. "Thank you, Charles. I'll be driving Mrs. Dugan home shortly."

"Yes, sir." Cliff said. "Good night." He walked down the path to his own separate quarters away from the main residence. He paused in the shadows and looked back. Minutes later the lights burning in the second story bedroom went out.

The young black man just stood, gazing intently at the darkened space for a long time. How would the natives feel if they knew that their prime minister was expending all of his energy making an American woman his mistress? This was the same man who had preached so often about keeping the island for Mirandans. It was clear that Salter's talk of nationalism had been nothing more. He had become corrupted by his proximity to such rampant capitalism. Cliff opened the door to his small dwelling and entered, seething. He was filled with a renewed dedication to his mission.

At that exact moment John Salter was thinking of nothing but the lovely young woman in his bed. Once in the room they had both quietly and quickly removed their clothing. John had scooped Dori up and laid her down on the turned back sheets. He climbed onto the bed and straddled her. Without saying anything he slid his powerful arms down her body and parted her legs open wide. He slipped a hand between them and his fingers tenderly explored her soft wet sex. Dori shuddered and a deep throbbing began in her loins.

"Please John," she pleaded, "come inside me now." She stroked his massive erection and guided it into her. He groaned at once and began thrusting.

She wrapped her legs around him and put her hands on his buttocks squeezing. "Harder, deeper," she whispered repeatedly into his ear like a mantra and he obeyed. What had began as gentle lovemaking had become an act of sheer animal lust. He pounded into her and her legs tightened around him. The deeper and faster inside he came the more she wanted until finally both of their bodies reached a beautiful agonizing climax.

They were drenched in sweat and panting. John rolled on his back but almost immediately gathered Dori in his arms, kissing her forehead and stroking her damp hair. Neither one spoke. There was so much to say and so much to be left unsaid. Dori didn't trust her words right now. John pulled the top sheet over them. "Sleep a little while," he said softly. "I'll have you home before daybreak."

XXVI

The room was virtually silent. Only the constant low hum of the air conditioner and the muted voices of children frolicking on the beach penetrated the otherwise soundless vacuum. Logan Hart and John Salter stood over the game board. Dori looked on from a distance, as did others gathered there. Jay Cavanagh was seated opposite Martin Gibson. They both were drawn and tired. It was the tenth day of play. The betting had proceeded from sets to individual games. A great deal of money had changed hands. At one point Gibson was on top, using the betting cube effectively enough to almost double his initial investment, winning close to seventy-five thousand dollars from each player. But as with most games based principally on chance, a player's luck changes without notice; it was happening to Martin Gibson.

Over the last three days he had lost all but fifty thousand dollars, most of it to Delgado and Ochoa, the men he thought would be so easy to defeat. And now Jay Cavanagh had challenged him with the doubling cube. If he refused the challenge, the game would stop and he would forfeit his original stake. If he accepted and won, he would still have his initial investment plus another hundred thousand from Cavanaugh. He would be back in the money again. But if he accepted and lost, he would be left with nothing, and no chance to recoup his losses.

He closed his eyes and massaged his temples, thinking. Many of his clients in New York were under the impression that he had come to the Caribbean looking for additional capital investments for them. If he lost this money he would be forced to disclose to them the sad financial shape of his company, due to previous gambling fiascoes as well as to his series of unstudied, careless market speculations. He had no choice. He accepted the challenge.

Dori watched intently. By now she knew the basics of play. The object of the game was to bring all of your men from your opponent's side of the board to your own, and then, by rolling the dice, remove all of your men from the board before your opponent did. At this junction both players seemed evenly matched, having five outstanding men on the other's side.

Cavanagh rolled: a one and a three. He elected to move one man four places. Gibson rolled: a pair of fours, doubles as it was called. He breathed a grateful sigh. This meant that he could move a total of sixteen places on the board. He chose to move four men occupying a single slot four places, bringing them on his side of the board. Salter cringed, a stupid move. This left his remaining man exposed to attack by one of Cavanaugh's, since a lone man in a slot could be taken and forced to start over. Cavanaugh rolled, producing the perfect combination to allow him to capture Gibson's one remaining man. At this point the outcome of the game was agonizingly predictable. By the time Cavanaugh's last man was removed from the board, Gibson was white and shaking.

"Well ol' man," Cavanaugh said, standing and scratching the back of his head. "Better hotfoot it back to New York and start fleecing your suckers again if you want to play anymore backgammon with me."

Gibson's nerves were raw; he swung at Cavanaugh, hitting him directly in the face. Blood started gushing from the young man's nose and he pushed his assailant to the ground before Salter and Ramino could restrain him. When he calmed down a bit they let go of their hold on him. But again he lunged at Gibson, still on the ground.

This time Salter brought Cavanaugh to his knees with a swift karate movement. Dori, who was bringing a towel and ice to help stop the nosebleed, saw what happened. She gave the stunned Cavanaugh the things she had brought. But she was looking at John Salter. She had never imagined that he could be violent, regardless of the situation. This abrupt display of physical force startled her.

Logan helped Gibson to his feet. Then he turned to Cavanaugh, who had slumped into a chair and was nursing his injury. "I want you out of my hotel."

Let's not let our tempers get the best of us," Ramino said, glancing at Hart. "I am sure that Mr. Cavanaugh will be able to wind up his business in a few more days."

"You bet!" The now crimson towel he was clutching to his nose muffled his voice. "I'm on a winning streak. The rest of you better watch out." He stood up, still guarding his face, and started to leave. "Loser," he said, passing by Gibson.

The following morning, at dawn, Martin Gibson walked out of his terrace onto the deserted beach, and proceeded slowly and methodically to the water's edge. He was naked. He walked into the calm early-morning sea and began swimming, with strong, determined strokes. And he just kept on swimming.

It was not until late afternoon that his body washed up on shore near the rocks where the sand ends by Cinnamon Inn. Two native girls, selling their spice baskets to the tourists from the cruisers, were the first to spot the body, floating face down in a small tide pool.

The news reached Logan Hart as he was about to accompany some new arrivals into the dining room. He excused himself and went immediately to Gibson's room. There was a Do Not Disturb sign hanging from the door handle. He opened the door with a passkey. On a table next to an unmade bed he found an envelope. Inside was a note in which Gibson confessed that he had been using clients' money to finance his gambling habit for years. He detailed all he knew about the illegal betting going on at the hotel, including the names of all the participants as well as the names of all of the organizers. Finally he asked forgiveness from his wife, children, and associates for what he had done as well as for what he was about to do.

Logan put the note back into the unaddressed envelope and thrust it into his pocket. When he reached his office, he used the intercom system that had been set up between the hotel and the *Kiwi*. Finally he was able to contact Ramino. He rapidly explained to him what happened.

"Where is the body?" Ramino asked calmly.

"It's in the storage room that houses the air-conditioning equipment. I'm calling the port authorities at once."

"Don't," was all that Romeo said, but his meaning was explicit. "I'll take care of everything. Go back to your guests and say nothing."

Logan, hating himself, did as he was told. He tried desperately to make small talk with the tourists, answering all of their questions concerning the recent renovation of the hotel and about his plans for the future of it. But throughout dinner he kept glancing into the lobby for a sign of Ramino or Mariani. Finally, Mandy came to his table with a message.

"Excuse me sir, but there are some gentlemen here to see you." Logan got up from the table and went into his office.

Ramino and Mariani were there with Salter. "Well," Logan said, "what have you done?"

"See for yourself," Mariani said, stepping away from the window.

In the parking lot, a long, rough wooden casket was being placed into the back of a pick up truck. "Mr. Salter has given us a clearance to fly the body directly to Puerto Rico where a medical examiner of our acquaintance will perform an autopsy. He will fill out the necessary certificates indicating that Mr. Gibson, unaccustomed to such strenuous physical activity in such high heat and humidity, suffered a massive heart attack while swimming and drowned." Ramino sat down behind the lower desk. "The hotel will issue a brief statement expressing deep regret over the sad incident and will cable sympathies to the bereaved family."

"Where is this note you mentioned?" Mariani asked.

Logan went over and unlocked the top drawer of his desk and took out the letter, written on hotel stationery. He handed it to Mariani, who read it and then passed it to his companions. When Ramino was through reading it he crumpled it up into a ball and placed it in the ceramic ashtray on Logan's desk. Then he struck a match and lit it. The paper burst into high flame, which then quickly died down. The note became a billowing cloud of fine ashes. Ramino picked up the container and emptied the remains out the window, where the tiny particles caught on the breeze and vanished.

XXVII

The days folded over each other, like the waves—merging, dividing, changing contour, but ultimately remaining the same. A month had passed since the opening of the Castle Beach Hotel. The resort was flourishing. Already articles had appeared in papers from Los Angeles to Manhattan speaking of it in a series of superlatives. The most prestigious of travel agencies were contacting the hotel to book tours well in advance of the prime season in January and February.

Logan Hart was relieved and pleased with the way things were going. Despite the "accidental" death of Martin Gibson three weeks earlier, the backgammon had continued without further incident. Most of the original players had gone. Jules Cavanagh had grown tired of constantly wiring his son additional funds, so Jay was forced to leave with little more than forty thousand dollars. He was no more graceful in defeat than he had been in victory.

"It's worth all of the dough I have lost just to get off of this bloody island." He smiled to Hart in the lobby just prior to leaving for the airport. "It's a bore," he amended his statement, "with the exception of that great piece of English tail. Tell Miss. Hunnicut that it was a ball." He climbed into the back of a local shuttle taxi while laughing at his crude joke.

A mid western cattleman had taken Cavanaugh's place. A real estate broker from Beverly Hills replaced Gibson. Logan was not certain how much Morgan Talbot had lost before she elected to quit the game. But unlike Cavanaugh she did not leave the island. She moved into the guest quarters of Claire's cottage at Cinnamon Inn. Allegedly her purpose was to help Claire brush up on her acting technique. Logan figured it was a task Morgan happily endured in order to enjoy the free accommodations and a few more weeks in the tropical sunshine.

Logan had been attending many of the backgammon sessions, as had Salter and Dori. It was evident that a pattern was emerging. Ramon Delgado and Simon Ochoa were the only players who consistently ended up victors. Logan hadn't been keeping score, but he reasoned that each of them must have won close to two hundred and fifty thousand dollars beyond their initial hundred grand entry fees.

Of all of the gamesmen who had come and gone they were the most obscure. Both of them were extremely private individuals, and were never seen taking advantage of any of the numerous recreational facilities the hotel had to offer, be it the aquatic sports or merely the garden bars and scheduled dances. But Logan knew one thing about them: they were backgammon wizards.

John Salter also knew it and it concerned him. He had had an uneasy feeling about both of these men from the very beginning. There was too much of a calculated methodology in their play. Their moves and betting techniques were too brilliant for amateurs, especially amateurs with their given backgrounds. When Salter had attempted to engage Delgado in conversation concerning his work at the University of Madrid, he was extremely vague. Salter had often visited Spain during the time he had spent touring Europe in his school days. When he asked Delgado about certain spots around the University or families who had been well known in local society he was met with blank stares and had to content himself with the explanation that Delgado's work in the nuclear field was all consuming. But if it were, then how did he get to be so proficient at backgammon? Was it really merely a hobby?

He had the same misgivings about Ochoa. He, too, was reluctant to speak about his occupation in Mexico. And though neither man socialized with one another, Salter got the distinct impression that they had met previous to this occasion. The prime minister listened to the wild parrots outside of his bedroom window. They were there on this balcony railing every morning screeching and chattering to the dawn. Salter rolled over on his back and folded his hands behind his head. It was June. The anniversary of Mirandan independence was next month. That meant that he would have to host a meeting of the Organization of West Indian Islands here in Miranda. He took a deep breath. The timing was good. Thanks to the new surge in tourism the unemployment was down. The people were contented enough. Perhaps he should choose that occasion to announce his plans to expand foreign investment on the island. A bold move like that would be quite impressive. That might assure his election as president of the group in the fall.

He got up and walked across the deep rugs to his marble-floored bathroom. He opened the shower door and turned on the hot water, watching as the steam began filling the room. He would discuss his plans with Charles Cliff this morning. He was certain that the young supporter would be happy with his decision. He turned on the hot water handle until the central stream was the perfect temperature and then got in. Perhaps in time, with the additional foreign capital, Salter could nationalize certain businesses on the island. No, if he did it he would have to take everything. Hart would be devastated by the move of course, and for that John Salter was genuinely sorry. Oh, but why should he even speculate about it? Miranda was not ready for step like that, not now.

He tilted his face until the full force of the water stung it like a million tiny needles. He thought about Dori. He knew that whatever they had now was due to a unique set of circumstances. In actuality they had very little in common but their need to be close. Salter realized that his need was almost purely physical. But over the weeks he had come to understand that this basically primal relationship had become highly convoluted to Dori, engulfing her entirely. She was trying valiantly, he knew, to abandon herself to the strictly sexual side of the affair. But she was failing miserably. Her puritanical upbringing had taught her that a physical relationship must be linked with deep, enduring love.

John Salter had neither the time nor the desire to pursue anything even close to that. If he had, he would have done it long before now. Over the years, he had not intentionally avoided commitment. It was simply that his most compelling drive was for power and political authority. It still was. But he suspected that Dori was convincing herself that she was in love with him. It was her way of obtaining an emotional equilibrium.

He turned off the water, grabbed a towel hung over the door and began drying himself. American women, he thought, for all of their talk of liberation, are still little girls seeking approval.

XXVIII

The big mail truck lumbered along the terminal roads at the Miami airport. The young bearded man behind the wheel adjusted the windshield wiper lever to the highest setting to combat the onslaught of the heavy rain. The thin rubber blades swept back and forth across the glass clearing it for a few precious seconds.

"Shit!" yelled the driver as a taxi cut in front of him to get close to the curb outside of the American Airlines terminal.

The mail truck maneuvered its way in between two parked cars and the driver got out. He ran inside and collected the three waiting mail sacks at the post office substation. He dragged them back outside and lugged them around to the rear of the truck. The steel arm holding the rear doors together was stuck. The young man struggled against it in the blinding rain, keeping his shoulder under the stubborn lock.

Finally, a porter waiting just inside the terminal witnessed the driver's plight and came to his aid. Together they were able to unjam the rod and open the doors.

"Thanks," said the grateful man, his bearded face dripping with water.

The porter waved and ran back inside the building for shelter. The driver hoisted the drenched canvas sacks into the truck and slammed the doors shut. A rain coated policeman, who stood in the road conducting the congested traffic, motioned for the mail truck to get out of the passenger-loading zone.

"Screw you!" the angry driver muttered to himself as he climbed in behind the wheel. His wet hand gripped the gear knob. He thrust the engine into first and drove off, skillfully weaving his way back into the mainstream of traffic exiting the airport.

In the back of the truck the mail sacks jiggled with the movement. The water, with slow determination, worked its way into the canvas of the three most recently loaded bags. Inside was the small blue envelope Dori had addressed to Dr. Andrew Magee, Maple Farm, Fairlee, Vermont. By the time the satchel would be emptied at the main post office for sorting the wet, smearing ink, would be completely illegible.

XXIX

"Yeah Jack, I understand," Logan said shaking his head as he spoke on the phone. "I meant to get back long before this, but things have just kept piling up. Maybe in July or August." He stood up and eyed the office calendar. "No, I'm sorry, but I can't possibly see how I can make it much before then."

He walked nervously about the room, cradling the phone in his arm. "Jesus Christ, what do you think that I pay you for? If there are problems with my other hotels, then I expect you to solve them, not to come whining to me." He apologized immediately. "Listen, forget I said that. I know that you've been doing everything you can. Just hold on a little longer. The pace should get a little less hectic here in a month or so." He nodded in agreement to whatever was being said on the other end of the line. "No question about it, Jack. You were right to bring it to my attention."

Dori walked into the office. Logan held the receiver to his ear by pressing it against his shoulder and threw his hands up in the air in a gesture of futility. "Right, Jack," he said, placating his listener. "I'll get back to you soon, promise. Bye."

He hung up and sunk down in the chair behind his desk. "I feel like I have just fought a wrestling match with an alligator."

"Who in the world was that?" Dori asked.

Logan reached behind his neck and rubbed the top of his back. "My attorney, Jack Gloom-and-Doom Flynn. Said that my place in upstate New York and the one on Hilton Head are going to hell in a hand basket, managerial problems among others. Damn it, I gave him authority to hire and fire, but he won't exercise the responsibility. He says that I have got to get back and take charge of things."

He glanced over his shoulder at the silent, ominous safe. "Just a perfect time for a trip, don't you agree?" he asked sarcastically.

Dori was glancing at some requisition orders Sylvia had submitted. "You're not going to leave, are you?"

Logan stood up and walked over to the window. "No. I can't yet, not until this gambling thing is all over. All this hotel needs is another Martin Gibson episode. Mariani told me that they had only chartered the *Kiwi* until the middle of July. He said that they would be moving on."

"To the bigger fish you hoped that they would be off frying?" Dori asked, reminding him of his previous statements.

"Yeah, right. Only now I don't know. He hasn't made any noises about leaving and the players keep coming and going every day. Since I don't even have the combination to my own safe I have no idea how much money has been won or lost, or is even hanging in the balance. I hate this feeling of being out of control of the situation."

"What about the reservations, Logan?" Dori asked, joining him at the window. "You have your six month backlog. You don't need to go along with this anymore. Simply tell them both that you have fulfilled your end of the bargain, even to the point of covering up a suicide."

Logan looked at her in amazement, his eyes growing wide. "How did you know?"

"Oh Logan, anyone who had been in the room that afternoon and saw what Gibson was going through would know that he didn't drown by any freak accident."

Logan took a deep ragged breath and returned to his chair. "What should I do?" He folded his arms on the top of his desk. "I simply can't demand that they leave…can I?

"Well, not exactly like that," Dori said, "but you could hint that for the sake of everyone concerned it might be better if they moved on before someone in authority got wind of what was transpiring."

Logan rolled the prospect over his mind. "Yeah," he finally nodded, "I suppose that it could be done delicately, with finesse."

Suddenly Dori got a big grin on her face. "If only Jay Cavanagh were still here. He was such a people person." Logan groaned and then he too smiled.

Rain had begun to fall when Delgado and Ochoa reached the *Kiwi* shortly after dark. Charles Cliff had provided both of them with rubber slickers to shield them as they rode in the open skiff to the ship. This time they were both a bit more adept at negotiating the rope ladder and climbed up the side hurriedly.

Their hosts were waiting to greet them below in the salon.

"Good evening, gentlemen," Mariani said cordially. He was wearing a deep burgundy-colored velvet smoking jacket. He was pouring brandy into a large snifter. "Storm brewing?" he asked Cliff.

"I don't think so," said the young man, wiping his eyeglasses dry, "just a good rain."

"Well, sit down everyone," Ramino invited. "We shall have our well-deserved celebration despite the weather." He pressed the buzzer beneath the carpet with his foot. In a moment the English cook came up the stairs from the galley carrying a tray of elegant looking hors d'oeuvres: caviar, smoked salmon, various cheeses, and fruit. There was also a basket of warm French bread on the table.

The steward followed with a chilled bottle of champagne. He extracted long stemmed crystal glasses from the cupboard.

"Oh, you two have spoiled us," Mariani said condescendingly to the crewmembers. "What are we ever going to do when we have to leave the ship?" He patted the young girl's thigh in a lecherous fashion. She ignored the crude advance and returned quickly to the galley.

Mariani laughed heartily. His guests were not particularly amused by his antics. "Well," he said, suddenly in a voice full of business, "let me propose a toast to our illustrious associates who have helped us shear the golden sheep and thereby furthering a noble cause."

, They raised their glasses and drank. Then Ochoa toasted his counterpart. "To your brilliance."

Delgado amended the accolade. "To our collective brilliance."

The bottle of wine was gone shortly. Ramino was about call for another one when Ochoa stopped him.

"None for us please. We would simply like to collect our winnings and be off. We are taking the first flight leaving the island tomorrow."

"Very well." Mariani withdrew too long envelopes from the inside pocket of his smoking jacket, handing one to each man. Two hundred thousand dollars apiece," Mariani said. "Not bad for six weeks of work."

The two recipients counted their money. Ochoa smiled, "Much more than a college professor could earn in that time, don't you agree, Ramon?"

"Without a doubt," Delgado answered, placing the money in a small briefcase he had brought with him to the boat.

Ramino and his partner walked the men to the entrance of the salon. It was still raining. But it was a soft, easy spray. Cliff noticed that both Mariani and Ramino seemed to be highly inebriated. He was disappointed in them. "Have a good flight," Ramino said. "Perhaps we shall meet again when your services are required."

The two gamblers got into their rain gear and quickly climbed over the side of the ship into the dinghy. Mariani called Cliff aside. "Come back after you get them to shore." His voice had lost the soft jovial tone he had been using. His words were sharp and crisp. Cliff realized at once that the man had been feigning his drunken posture. He nodded that he would return and then quickly jumped into the small boat and started the motor.

In an instant he was flying across the top of the water toward the dock at St. Philips. He deposited his passengers and returned rapidly to the *Kiwi*. The atmosphere inside the salon with decidedly different now than it had been just minutes before. The main table had been cleared of all glasses and trays. In their places were two big blueprint sheets spread out over the entire surface. Cliff recognized them at once as Phillip Graham's plans to the Castle Beach Hotel renovation. A small hanging lamp had been pulled down over the drawings. The two men hovered above them, giving careful study to each one.

"Come here, Charles," Ramino said, appraising the thin, serious black man. "Didn't you say that John Salter will be hosting the annual meeting of the OWII next month?"

"Yes. In honor of the anniversary of Mirandan independence."

"Where do you think this meeting will be held?"

Cliff thought for a moment. "Most probably in the cabinet room at the ministry."

"What do you think it would take to get him to change his mind about the location?"

"I'm not really sure. Why?"

"Because we think that it would be far better if he were to hold this meeting at the Castle Beach Hotel, in the main dining room. It has been decided that if we are to make a positive statement pointing to the fact that foreign capitalism is eroding all of the islands and that the new power will not tolerate further exploitation, what better way of illustrating that than by destroying the newest shrine to American imperialism? And with it will go all of the money hungry island government heads. I think this will mark the start of a spiritual cleansing of the Caribbean." He was watching the young man's face for a reaction.

Cliff understood the reasoning behind the plan and agreed with it. "How do you propose to accomplish this objective?" Cliff asked.

It was Mariani's turn to speak. "Look," he said pointing to the blueprints. "Thanks to the success of our backgammon venture, we have the funds to turn our ideas into reality. Soon we will bring a team of demolition experts to Miranda. They will pose as hotel employees: gardeners and maintenance men. They shall wire the entire hotel with explosives in such a way that with the ignition of one timing device, it will crumble in its place."

"And," Ramino added, "we want it to happen when Salter is addressing all of the island representatives. And what a perfect occasion. Finally, the anniversary date of Mirandan independence will have some meaning. The hotel will not explode outwardly, but it will simply collapse, symbolizing death of the old structure of government from within, destroyed by its own inherent weaknesses. Its demise will symbolize a new beginning for all of the people in the Caribbean."

"Most of the hotel guests will be in St. Philips for the parades and dances, so the number of innocent victims shall be kept at a minimum. In any event, they must not be our primary concern now. Those, which of necessity will die accidentally, will become martyrs, having been sacrificed for a cause greater than a single life."

"And you" Ramino said, "shall be the new voice of authority and reason on Miranda."

Charles Cliff felt himself begin to quiver and shake with excitement. His mind was alive with the thought. The plan was glorious, inspired, utter genius. Salter had earned his fate. He had his chance to bring equality to the people of Miranda but he had failed. He was not visionary anymore. He was too slow to act. He had lost the fire of revolution. He had become too addicted to easy pleasures.

"Our plan rests with you, Charles," Mariani said. "You must convince Salter to conduct the meetings at the hotel. We shall be waiting to hear of your progress. His commitment to the idea must be made soon."

Cliff said goodnight and left. The rain had stopped as he motored slowly back to the harbor. A half moon darted in and out of the passing clouds, casting flashing streams of silver light on the rippling water swirling up around the dinghy. The air was humid and warm. But Charles Cliff was shivering. The time had come. He was being subjected to the ultimate test. Had he been able, over the months, to generate enough trust that Salter would abide by his mere suggestion? Would he be curious? Cliff knew that if the prime minister even suspected that he was involved in any conspiracy his life would be snuffed out as easily as one kills snake, or a chameleon for that matter, he thought.

XXX

Salter looked about the room. The backgammon tables were set up as usual. Several of the new participants were engaged in play. But the feeling in the air was not the same that it had been on previous afternoons. At once Salter realized the reason why—Ochoa and Delgado were missing. He spotted Ramino and Mariani sitting on the patio enjoying a cocktail. He walked past the game tables and opened the French doors.

"Good afternoon," he said, stepping out into the bright sunlight. Ramino was wearing an open-necked short-sleeved shirt and bathing trunks. His associate was dressed in a similarly casual fashion. How different they seemed from the dark suited men they were when presiding over the betting.

"Hello, John," Ramino said standing and extending his hand, "how nice to see you. It's a beautiful day. After the rain last night we were not expecting such a cloudless sky."

"Where are Ochoa and Delgado?" Salter asked, ignoring the small talk.

"Oh," Ramino said, sitting back down. "I'm afraid that they were both forced to leave this morning. Since they were actually on holiday, the number of days they were able to spend with us was limited. But they did depart much richer men." He laughed and Mariani joined in "Actually," Mariani said, "you and Mr. Hart will be pleased to learn that after the present players conclude tomorrow or the next day with the sets in progress, we will be moving on as well. Mr. Hart prudently reminded us this morning that he has done exactly as he promised by allowing our operation to go on as planned for this length of time. He kindly invited us to leave and we have agreed to do so. We don't like to spend too much time in any one place. Federal officials do have their ways of getting a bit too close." He shielded his eyes from the sun as he spoke, looking up at Salter. "But," he

223

added, "we both appreciate all that you have done to make our stay on the island comfortable."

Something was bothering the prime minister. "Why are you not observing play today?"

Ramino answered. "The remaining stakes are so low that frankly it is hard for us to take a serious interest. Already our mind is on our coming dealings in the Mediterranean."

"Well," Salter said, "let me be blunt. I did not like the way you moved onto my island and threatened both Hart and myself with financial and personal ruin. We had no choice but to acquiesce to your demands. But I strongly suggest that you never attempt anything like that here again. And also, since I have been playing tournament backgammon from the age of fifteen, it was obvious to me that Mr. Ochoa and Mr. Delgado are professionals. The percentage of winnings they gave to you for allowing them to victimize amateurs must have been substantial." He glanced in through the shaded windows at the tables of seated gamesmen. "I trust that it shall not be necessary for us to have further dealings prior to your departure."

Ramino stood up and faced the black man. "Believe me, Mr. Salter, no one will be happier than I when our business on Miranda is concluded."

Howard Rutledge was walking down the beach past the garden patios of the ground floor suites. He spotted Salter and waved to him. "The wind is great. What about coming down and watching a couple of the sunfish race?" His strong voice carried well. Salter waved back, indicating that he would be coming. He stepped down from the patio onto the sand. He walked quickly along the beach to the waiting boats rolling in the waves near the shore. The men on the patio watched him go, saying nothing. But Ramino, who had been toying with a pencil, snapped it between his fingers and threw the pieces to the ground.

Salter stood by the water's edge and watched as young beach boys raced the sleek, small boats around in the inlet. The boats would lean far to one side in the wind and the skillful sailors would traverse the slick decks, defying gravity, as though their feet had suction cups. Their bodies were strong and agile. Again Salter was reminded of what a natural resource Miranda had in her people. He knew that with the coming of the anniversary of independence the active young political voices on the island would again cry for nationalization. How could he convince them that they must be patient? The time was not yet right, if indeed it would ever be.

The prime minister still longed for a symbiotic rather than parasitic relationship with foreign governments and corporations. And he knew that many shared his dream. The world was small, and growing smaller. There was no longer any logical incentive for any country to exploit another, regardless of the difference in size. Usable land and abundant natural resources were scarce. A new drive to conserve and cooperate must be born. He had remembered reading about the concept of a "global" village. It was an idea that stressed the inter-relationship and inter-dependence of all men on one another.

The sun was angling sharply toward the horizon. Howard had wadded out into the water to help bring two of the boats in for the night. Salter rolled up his pant legs and walked into the water to meet him. "That was quite an exhibition you put on," Salter praised the sailors. "Judging from the way you handle those boats one would think that you had been born on them." The young boys looked at the prime minister, smiling at the compliments.

"Yeah," Howard said, slapping one on the back good-naturedly, "I wish that I could do that well. But," he laughed, "I need a bigger boat. These things practically sink when I'm aboard."

The natives tied up the boats and ran off down the beach in search of another way to vent their ceaseless energy. The older men stood, side by side, and watched as the boys took highflying leaps over the unsuspecting tourists lying on the brightly colored beach towels.

"You know," Howard said, longingly, "I used to run like that, maybe faster." He glanced down at his hefty paunch. "And I would eat just as much as I do now and never gain a pound." He sighed and shook his head in resignation. "Age does have a way of taking you by surprise, doesn't it?"

"Nonsense," Salter said, "you could still out match any of the men on this island for brute strength and endurance. And those are qualities that only come with age and perspective."

At once Howard's dismal expression brightened into a big grin. "Yeah, you are right, ya know? I never thought of it quite that way before."

Salter laughed, "Age also has a great capacity to rationalize."

The two men talked a bit more and then parted, Howard to help Mandy check the scuba equipment for a few waiting guests, and Salter to talk to Hart.

The air-conditioning system generated a cool breeze in the lobby. The door to the office was open. But only Dori was there, seated behind her desk. She smiled softly when she saw Salter walk in.

"Hello," she said, getting up, "what brings you here? Were you looking for me?" Her voice had an expectant lilt.

"Well actually, this moment I am looking for your employer."

"Oh," she said, sitting back down.

"But then I want to see you," Salter added quickly.

"That's better," she said. "Logan was just here; he went to check on the number of new arrivals today."

"And departures?" Salter asked.

"What do you mean?"

"Oh, I guess that you haven't heard of the unexpected good fortune brought down upon our heads today."

"No, what?"

"I have learned that both Ochoa and Delgado left this morning."

"Well," said Dori, "then that explains why Ramino came in here last night and took a big chunk out of the safe."

"That explains it, " he agreed.

"Then you mean that the gambling is over? Will they be gone now?"

Salter nodded. Dori ran over and hugged him. "I am so glad. Ever since that horrible thing with Martin Gibson, I've been so worried."

Logan walked in and saw the two embracing. He felt awkward and embarrassed. But he was too far into the room to leave without being noticed. Salter pulled away from Dori.

"Hart," he said," have you heard the news?"

"Yeah. I have just been talking with Mariani. He thinks that they will be leaving in a day or two. Then we can start running a normal hotel around here. And," he added, glancing at the wall calendar, "I can go to New York for a few days. I've got some business problems that I have to work out. "

"Nothing serious I hope?" Salter said honestly.

"Everything is serious to attorneys and accountants," Logan smiled, "but I don't think that it is anything I won't be able to handle."

The phone rang. Logan answered it and handed the receiver to Dori. "It's Ransom Turner, for you." Both of the men were as surprised as Dori by the identity of the caller.

"Hello, Ransom," she tried to sound abrupt, and offhanded, but her curiosity was overwhelming. "Why did you wish to speak with me?"

The voice at the other end of the line had little resemblance to the harsh, vindictive one she had heard weeks before. "I would have come to see you personally, Mrs. Dugan, but Mr. Hart does not want me to come to the hotel anymore. And he has every reason to wish that I stay away. My behavior has been less than exemplary. I do apologize." He was soft-spoken and sounded extremely sad and contrite.

Dori motioned for Logan to pick up the extension. He did.

"You see," Turner continued, "I have had a slight drinking problem over the past few years." Logan rolled his eyes upward at the use of the word *slight*.. "And it caused me to say ridiculous things and become quite argumentative. But I am trying to learn to control it."

"I think that is very wise, Ransom," Dori said, her tone softening. "People don't like to be around you when you are so unpredictable and belligerent."

"But Mrs. Dugan, I really miss the time I used to spend with Jeremy. I never drank when I was with him." Dori tried to remember a time when he had been drinking while with Jeremy. She couldn't. "I don't know why I said those things about your father. I don't know anything about him except what I have learned from you and your boy."

It had been a month since Dori wrote to her father asking about Turner. From that time she had received a couple of letters from him, neither mentioning the doctor. Turner must be telling the truth. "I wish that you would allow him to visit me again. I promise to take good care of him. I always have."

Dori looked at Logan, who shook his head as if to say, *It's your decision.*

"Okay Ransom. I guess that perhaps I have been a little too harsh. I know that Jeremy has missed seeing you too. If you like, I will tell him to go to your house tomorrow after school. Then I will pick him up there later in the afternoon."

"Oh thank you, Mrs. Dugan." Turner said. "I have been making him a new mast for his sailboat. It's all ready now."

They said goodbye and Dori hung up. "Well I am glad that that situation has straightened itself out. This is proving to be a good day for resolving a lot of things."

The phone rang again. Logan answered it. It was the airport requesting the hotel station wagon. "Howard is busy at the beach," Logan said after Dori suggested him. "I think I will go and meet the new crop myself." He reached under his desk and pulled out a yellow hat with the green and orange parrot embroidered above the name of the hotel. "How do I look?" He grinned and put it on.

"Like a zookeeper," Dori teased.

After Logan left the room, Salter closed the door and came over closer to Dori. He lifted her out of her chair and pulled her close to him. He kissed her deeply, moving his hands down her back and over her slender hips.

"Let's go to your suite," he whispered.

"John, I think that we ought to talk."

He ignored her remark and simply kissed her again, voraciously. "We will," he said, leading her towards the elevator. And he knew that they would, in time.

"Oh I think that this weather is totally divine. I don't know how you could ever tire of it, either of you." Morgan Talbot speared another piece of fresh papaya with her fork. "It's a paradise, really." She put the fruit into her mouth. " Yummy. I could survive on this alone."

While the visiting actress devoured her salad, Claire and Allison only picked at theirs. The three women were having lunch at The Buoy in St. Philips.

"Paradise is in the eye of the beholder." Claire said, eating the pineapple from her rum punch. "I would trade all of this for a chance to ride down Sunset Boulevard in Howie's blue Chevy convertible."

"And what about you?" Morgan asked, motioning to Allison, "for what global spot are you yearning?"

Allison, who was toying with a glass of white wine smiled weakly. "Plain, foggy London, I'm afraid."

"Well I think that you both are utterly mad!" She finished the last bit of fruit on her plate.

"Didn't you say that you think that I have real talent?" Claire pleaded. "Isn't it natural for me to want to resume my interrupted career? After all, Morgan, maybe I would have chosen this life too if I had had a chance to really excel in my chosen field first like you did, if I hadn't been so foolish and sold out before my big break came. Now you don't want to make movies anymore. But I do." Claire's eyes began to fill with tears, like those of a frustrated child.

"Don't get upset, dear." Morgan soothed, "or you will get one of those nasty migraines. I think you are absolutely right. One should have the freedom to pursue one's goals, regardless of what they are. After all that is the basis of happiness." She chipped polish from one of her nails. "True happiness that is. What is your goal?" Again she directed the question to Allison Trent.

"To save my sanity, and perhaps my marriage," she answered candidly.

Suddenly Claire spotted Frank LeBeau at the bar, ordering a drink. He was alone. She excused herself for a moment and joined him. "Where have you been?" she demanded. "I have gone half crazy wondering what has been going on. Have you seen Clif—the Chameleon?"

"Don't get upset with me," LeBeau said, paying for his beer. "You know where the meetings are."

"Yes, but I haven't been able to get away. Besides, you said that you would let me know when you wanted me to do something. It has been weeks since I got those plans for you, and you still haven't told me what you wanted them for."

"No," LeBeau said, staring straight ahead, "and I probably won't. The fewer people who know the plan, the better."

Claire was indignant. "Is that to say that I can't be trusted? You know, I could have blown this whole thing wide open a long time ago. But I didn't, because you said that something was going to happen soon. Well, I have been patient for about as long as I can."

LeBeau finished his beer in two swallows. He set the glass down on the bar, slowly, deliberately, and then turned to Claire for the first time.

"Don't threaten me or the Chameleon." His voice was restrained, tense. His face looked as though he could fly into a rage at any moment. "You have done what has been asked of you and you have done it well. But for now, you're part in this is finished. You'll be contacted if you are needed again. Things will occur according to a certain schedule. And if you should find yourself becoming edgy and anxious, just think about Phillip Graham. He died a miserable death. But then he was ready to go to the authorities with the information he had. I am sure that you would exercise better judgment than that." He put a tip on the bar counter, and walked out.

Claire returned to the table, trying to disguise her nervousness. "Why don't we all go back to Cinnamon Inn and play some cards?" All of the ice had melted in her drink, but she finished it anyway.

"What did Frank have to say?" Allison asked. "Still trying to convince you that the French are the true owners of Miranda?"

"Something like that," Claire said. She glanced at the bar where they had been standing. "But I never take him seriously anyway."

XXXI

Arsenals of huge white clouds invaded the blue afternoon skies, signaling the coming of rain. Sunbathers gathered up their beach towels and magazines and retreated to their rooms or to the comfortable shelter of the thatched canopy over the garden bar. There they would stay, drinking and talking and playing cards until the daily showers came and went, like a giant with a watering can marching across the island. After the temporary seizure of the sky, the clouds would evaporate. The sun would quickly regain control, drying out the sand in minutes.

This was late June in the West Indies. The daily rains became a ritual, eagerly awaited by tourist and resident as well. There was something cathartic about witnessing nature's volatile shifts in mood. It also provided a short respite from the intense heat.

John Salter sat in his office drinking a tall glass of iced tea. He was working on his address for the upcoming OWII meeting. The windows were open and the heavy drops of rain splattered on the thick, waxy leaves of the rubber trees growing near the building. The pungent sensuous aroma of gardenias scented the air. It was difficult for him to concentrate on his work. He kept thinking of Dori. Despite his original intentions, their relationship had become extremely intense. And it was not simply a physical attraction anymore. When they were not together he found himself missing her, her clean beauty, her sense of humor, and her probing, interested mind. He even found himself speculating on what it would be like to live with her on a permanent basis. She seemed to have adapted quite well to life on the island, and had expressed no severe longing to return to the United States, for purposes other than to visit her parents.

He was not ready to admit that these feelings were love. It was, however, an emotional attachment that he had never expected to feel. And he did not know exactly how to deal with it.

A sharp knock on his office door derailed his thoughts. "Come in." The door opened and Charles Cliff stepped inside.

"Good afternoon, sir."

"Hello, Charles," Salter said smiling. "I'm glad you are here. I wanted to talk to you about my speech to the organization next month. I'm working on it now," he said, lifting up the papers on his desktop. He motioned to the young man to be seated. "Listen to this, will you?" he asked, standing with one of the sheets in his hand. He read from it a passage that emphasized the need for all of the islands to work together to bring more foreign investment to the Caribbean to provide more employment for the people. "The island governments must be in harmony with one another in encouraging the United States and Great Britain to bring more business and industry to the island." He was quoting from the text of his address. He continued. "We are dependent upon them for capital and technology and they on us for labor. Hopefully in time we will not have the need to rely on them so heavily for survival. But we must maintain cordial relations with all countries. And we must let the free world know that we need their military support as well as their financial backing to protect our ever-threatened fragile democracies. It is not enough that they simply applaud our freedom, they must help us to guard it."

Cliff, filled with disgust at the words he was hearing, shook his head in agreement whenever Salter looked up from the page.

"What do you think?" Asked the prime minister.

Cliff's nerves were raw. Now was his opportunity. He must grasp it. "It is an extremely powerful speech, sir. It will be well received."

Salter sighed and rubbed the back of his neck. There were rings of perspiration under the arms of his short-sleeved shirt. The methodically whirling ceiling fan could not combat the heavy humidity in the room.

"Good, I am glad that you feel that way. Now the only thing left to do is ready the guest quarters."

"I think that they are all in order, sir. I instructed the staff to do some repainting and make some minor repairs where needed."

"Fine, but what about the cabinet room here? Since I plan on preparing a copy of my address for each member at the conference, I think that we should install individual reading lamps at each place.

The lighting in that room has always been bad, even on the brightest of days." He looked at his watch. "And most probably we will be meeting during the afternoon rains."

"I have been giving the meeting place some consideration lately," Cliff began. "Perhaps, in order to stress your message of this strength brought to the island by foreign investments, the meeting should be held at the new hotel. It has been bringing the island a great deal of favorable publicity lately." Cliff struggled to keep his tone matter of fact.

Salter walked about the room pondering what had been said. Then he came up close to the young man's side. His brown eyes grew wide and penetrating. "Charles," he asked, "was this idea yours alone?"

Cliff felt the blood drain from his face. Did he know? What had he discovered? "Yes, sir, it was."

Salter tossed his head back and emitted a loud laugh. Then he put his arm around Cliff. "Well, it is brilliant. My only regret is that it is not mine." Cliff grew limp with relief.

"But it is now, sir," Cliff offered.

"So it is," Salter said, patting his aide on the back, "so it is."

Dori tossed and turned on her bed while the afternoon rain fell outside the window. The gambling had finally ended and Mariani and Ramino had sailed away aboard the *Kiwi*. Logan had decided that he couldn't put off the trip to New York any longer. He had caught a plane to Barbados this morning. He had left Dori in charge of things until he returned.

The responsibility sounded ominous at first. But actually, the hotel was practically running itself at this point. Sylvia was in total control of the kitchen and the staff of girls. Claire was still helping out behind the desk occasionally and Howard, Mandy, and their helpers took care of the beach area. It was Dori's job to supervise. She was grateful that everything was running so smoothly and prayed that things remained routine, at least until Logan's return.

She looked over at Jeremy. He had decided to nap on the extra bed in her room. His breathing was heavy and rhythmic. Dori studied his face. It was tan and freckled. His blond hair, like her own, had become almost white with the constant exposure to the water and the bleaching sun. She guessed that he must have grown four inches since they arrived on the island. She was always having to take him in to one of the few clothing shops in St. Philips for new T-shirts and shorts. Her father would be pleased with what the island life had done for his grandson.

She wondered, however, what his reactions would be to the changes in his daughter. Could he understand what was happening to her? Did she understand it herself? She sat up on the bed and looked out of the window. The rain had almost stopped. She got up and walked outside onto the terrace. A fine mist floated through the air like snowflakes. She looked down. People were starting to return to the beach. Colorful beach umbrellas went up. A few children were swimming again and Howard was hoisting the sails on several of the small boats.

She came back inside and lay down on the bed once more. She knew that John Salter had an overpowering effect on her. She lost her inhibitions when they were together. He made love to her violently, losing himself in the act. Often, she had been frightened by his total lack of restraint. Yet, at the same time, his zealous passion intoxicated her and she felt helpless. And she, too, would completely abandon herself to the moment.

It was like being caught up in a dark fantasy, attracting and repelling simultaneously. She had never before been involved in a relationship that existed solely from day to day without thought of the future. It was a relationship constantly involved in the process of destroying and renewing itself.

She was also finding that when they were together she seemed to lose her identity, becoming what he wanted, willingly. He held a fascination for her that could not be explained. At times she would find herself wishing that she had never come here. At other times she would be filled with suffocating panic at the thought of ever leaving this place, or of leaving this enigma of a man.

She closed her eyes. In a few hours she would have to dress and act as hostess in the dining room. She drew a deep breath and rolled over on her stomach. Surely this limbo would end...but the waiting...the waiting.

XXXII

"God dammit, I expected you to come waltzing in here looking like Clark Gable with a tan. Instead, I get a walking corpse. You're not a very good ad for your resort." Jack Flynn ushered Logan Hart into his 5th Avenue office.

"I just run the place, Jack, I'm not a guest there." Logan was exhausted. He had missed two of his connecting flights from Barbados and Miami because his plane out of San Juan was late. He had just arrived in New York at eight thirty this morning. It was close to ten now.

Flynn called over his intercom, instructing his secretary to bring them some coffee. Logan collapsed into a comfortable brown leather wingback chair. Flynn went to a large file cabinet in the corner of the room and opened a drawer. He extracted some folders.

"Well, I hate to be the one to tell you, but you have been busting your ass for nothing."

Logan sat up straight. "What the hell is that supposed to mean?" The secretary came in and poured them both hot coffee and then left, having been asked to hold all calls for the duration of the meeting.

"Look, Logan, I have been handling the books for you since you went off on this cockeyed adventure. I've been the one fending off the bankers with a chair and a whip. But you are about to be swallowed whole."

Logan was drinking the scorching coffee rapidly. He was so numb from lack of sleep that if the liquid were burning him he showed no signs of feeling pain.

"Look," Flynn said, spreading balance sheets over the top of his desk with his big, freckled, Irish hands, "the figures don't lie. Your place in the Adirondacks isn't drawing the crowds anymore. Madison Westin has built a huge spa near your lodge and the people are flocking to it. The rustic mountain cabin concept is dying a fast and furious death. People want to be pampered now while shown the way to youth and beauty. The easy way that is. They would rather sit all day in a Jacuzzi drinking straight carrot juice then follow some bowlegged trail guide through the woods. Who knows why it happened? The fact of the matter is that it has. Since you have been in the Caribbean that place alone has lost over five hundred thousand dollars."

Logan stared at the sheets of paper, looking for something that would tell him that this weren't true.

"Logan, the manager kept insisting that the entire staff be kept on, regardless of the expense. He was waiting for you to tell him to let people go. I asked you about it lots of times when we talked. But you just kept telling me not to worry, that you would take care of it. Well, it seems to be taking care of itself."

"Hey Jack, I don't need to be scolded like a petulant child. It's my money were watching go down the hole here."

Flynn sat on the top of his littered desk and stared at his client. "I do think that you need me to come down hard on you. I don't think that you grasp the seriousness of the situation."

"I'm beginning to, believe me." Logan bent over in his chair and rested his head in his hands. He was so tired he was almost punchy.

"The worst is yet to come," Flynn warned. "Hilton Head is all but out of business. The weather has been so lousy there this season that nobody has been doing much of anything. Golf is dead. But your place has suffered the most. No one is coming there anymore. The reason is psychological really. Everyone has been reading about Castle Beach. They all know that you are pouring your energy, talents and resources into it. They feel that the other Hart developments have become little more than poor relations to you now."

"But why?" Logan asked. "Other corporations have hotels all over the world and none of them seem to suffer."

"That is just the point, Logan. Corporations have hotels, not individual flesh and blood people. You are recognizable. You used to stay at both of your places off and on all year long. Suddenly you leave for the tropics, abandoning your old hotels like tired wives and running off in pursuit of a new golden haired mistress."

Logan groaned, "Please skip the poetic analogies." He thought for a moment. "Well, what if I sell both hotels and just concentrate on the one in Miranda?"

"I thought of that too, believe me. But right now there are no buyers. And besides, even if there were, the selling prices you could get at the moment wouldn't even cover your losses."

The attorney poured himself another cup of coffee. Then he pressed against a piece of redwood paneling in the wall. It slid back to reveal a small, but fully equipped bar. He reached for a decanter and laced his coffee with some brandy. "You want any?" he asked Logan.

"No, I think that I would pass out."

"Logan, the next thing that I have to tell you is the most difficult." Flynn stirred his coffee. "I know how much this new place in Miranda means to you."

"I don't understand how any of this could happen," Logan said. "How could everything have gotten away from me like this?"

"Well you went at this full bore, and frankly, your ego got in the way. You spent far more on the renovation and decorating than you had originally contracted for."

"Well, I know," Logan said apologetically, "but things like that always happen. That's to be expected."

"Logan," Flynn said sternly, "you are not hearing me. The final figures came in yesterday afternoon. You have incurred bills amounting to three times what you had intended to spend. If your holdings were flush, I might be able to swing it for you, but now...." He took a big swig of the brandied coffee.

"But now what?" Logan asked nervously.

"I worked it all out on the office computer. Even if your resort down there were to be booked solid for the next five years, which is most unlikely, deducting operating expenses, you would still be far in the red."

Logan was listening, trying to grasp the magnitude of what was being said, but it was almost impossible for him.

"What are you saying?"

"I think that you ought to bailout. As it is, technically, you are in a position to declare bankruptcy. Your liabilities far exceed your assets. We might even be able to salvage one of your places here."

Suddenly the impact of what was happening hit Logan. He thought of all the work he and Dori had put into Miranda. He thought of Phillip Graham's death, of Ramino and Mariani, and of Martin Gibson.

"No," he said standing. "I will never do that. Do you think that I could stand by and watch Madison Weston or Paradise Inns swoop down like vultures to pick the carcass of what I have built, what I've sacrificed for?"

"Isn't that exactly what you did in the beginning?" Flynn asked.

"No," he reconsidered. "Oh, I don't know. Maybe that was what it was originally, but not now. This place has become so important to me. It's my dream. It's a living dream. I made it come true." His voice grew hoarse and frantic. He stood up and grabbed the lawyer by the shoulders. "Oh you ought to see it, Jack. It is so beautiful. It rises up on the beach like a Phoenix."

For an uncomfortable instant the lawyer thought Hart was going to cry. But he didn't. Instead he turned around for a moment to regain his composure. When he faced Flynn again he stood straight and his jaw was set resolutely.

"When must final decisions be made concerning all of this? I need time."

"Yes, of course. It's a big step. And believe it or not the banks will be quite patient about everything."

"And why shouldn't they be?" Logan snapped angrily. "They will get everything back one way or another." He asked Flynn for copies of all the pertinent information. He wanted a chance to study everything before he made a single move. The thought of bankruptcy was abhorrent to him. Somehow he would find an alternative. He just needed a little time.

He said goodbye to Flynn, promising to call him within thirty days to let him know what he had decided to do. It was noon when he stepped outside of the building and hailed a cab to take him to the Plaza. He sat in the back of the taxi with both rear windows open. His lightweight suit was sticking to his skin. June in New York—hot, muggy, and dirty. The fumes from a stalled bus in front of them billowed into the car. Logan fought the urge to vomit.

As soon had as he checked in at the desk, he went up to the suite and showered. He put on the thick hotel terry cloth robe and lay down on the bed. He was certain that he would lapse into a drug-like sleep. But nothing came. His mind was wide-awake and fought the rest his body so desperately craved. On an impulse he decided to call his ex-wife. He knew that she was married to that professor creep with patches on the elbows of his corduroy jacket. But he didn't care about him. He needed to talk to Elaine. He was curious about the children. They had both written him from college in the early spring. But neither had mentioned their summer plans.

Logan sat on the edge of the bed and looked up the number. Maybe the kids would like to go back to Miranda with him for a while. The phone rang about five times before it was answered. Unfortunately, it was Elaine's new husband who picked up the receiver.

"Hi ya, Malcolm. This is Logan. May I speak with Elaine?"

"Low-gann!" Malcolm said, dragging out the name. "Are you calling from the depths of the Atlantic?"

Logan gritted his teeth and tried again. "No, I am in town on business for a day or two. May I speak with Elaine?"

"Just a moment. I think that she is meditating now, but I'll check." There was a loud bang in the receiver as Malcolm set the phone down. Logan was sure that he did it deliberately. He waited for almost five minutes before he heard Elaine come to the phone, huffing, out of breath.

"Hello there," she said brightly. "Sorry that I took so long, my breathing exercises you know."

"No, I don't know," Logan said, "but I am sure that they are very beneficial."

"Oh, they are. You really ought to try Bikram yoga."

Logan shook his head. "Listen Elaine, I am calling to find out what Robin and Alex are doing. I thought that they might like to go back to Miranda with me for a while." There was no response, only the sound of vigorous breathing.

"Elaine!"

"Oh, sorry. I was doing some deep knee bends. Can't break the rhythm. Now let me see. I'm afraid that you are too late. Both of the kiddies are gone for the summer." Logan hated the way Elaine always referred to the children as "kiddies." They were both in their twenties, for God's sake. "They are in Hawaii for six weeks," she continued, "one of Robin's little friends at Bennington lives on Kauai, sounds marvelous, doesn't it?"

"Elaine, their own father owns a resort in the middle of the Caribbean. Why in the hell did they go to Hawaii?"

"Well don't get mad at me, Logan. Robin wanted to be with her friends and Alex said something about the surf being better in Hawaii."

"I see," Logan said. "Since when has Alex become such an authority on island waters? Oh never mind. Goodbye Elaine."

"I'll tell them that you called."

Logan hung up the phone and lay back down. He wished desperately that Dori were here. She had a unique way of making him laugh even when things were at their worst, and they were now. He was remembering the day he had shown her her rooms at Castle Beach. How they both had laughed knowing how silly and ridiculous and fun it all was. He also remembered the night he had kissed her outside of her cottage at Cinnamon Inn during the time they were having all of those shipping problems.

Of course all of that was before John Salter had come into her life. It was hard for Logan to be objective about that affair. Salter had mesmerized her. He possessed a charismatic power and knew how to use it. And Dori was so vulnerable. The combination frightened Logan. Between the shark and the minnow, the victor is always the same.

XXXIII

The young couple was so sunburned. The new skin on their noses was red and fiery. Claire could tell that their faces must have peeled at least twice. She was working behind the reservation desk for the afternoon, helping Dori out while Logan was away.

"I'll bet that hurts," she said as the woman handed her the key to their room.

"Oh yeah it does, but the weather has been so beautiful that neither of us could stay out of the water."

"Anyway," said her husband, "this is been the vacation of a lifetime. We blew all of our wedding money to come here but I don't have a single regret."

"Well that's good," Claire smiled.

"Except one," the wife said, "that we have to leave."

Claire checked them out and called for the hotel station wagon. "Be sure to come back," she said as they drove away. How she longed to be escaping to the airport with them. She returned to the lobby. Howard came in from the beach area.

"Hi, honey," he said cheerfully, "are you busy?" He was dressed in the regulation Castle Beach shirt and shorts. Claire studied his appearance. He reminded her of the man who used to run the Ferris wheel at the summer carnivals in Charlottesville.

"Why," she asked without interest, "what do you want?"

"Frank is down at the garden bar. He wants to know if you can join us for a drink. I'm through for the day."

Claire sensed that LeBeau must want to tell her something. "That would be lovely."

A plump, pleasant-looking native girl was sorting mail into boxes behind the desk.

"JoAnn?" Claire asked, "Will you watch things here for me for a little while?"

"Yes Mrs. Rutledge," smiled the girl.

"Now are you sure that you know how to fill out all the forms and things?"

"Yes I do," she said proudly.

"Well good." Claire lifted a hinged section of the reservation counter and stepped out from behind it. She was smiling and humming happily. Howard took her arm.

"My you seem to be in good spirits all of a sudden," he said.

"Do I?" Claire asked shyly, in a little girl's voice. "Then it's just because I'm with my handsome Howie." Her tone was mocked sincerity, but Howard didn't mind. He would rather have her this way than to see her in one of her dark, bellicose moods.

LeBeau was sitting at the bar, arm wrestling with Mandy when they joined him. "Whew," said the Frenchman, "there is something to be said for pouring liquor all day. It builds up the muscles. This fellow has beaten me three times in a row."

He climbed off the stool and led the way to a table. Mandy came over to take their drink orders. Claire requested a rum and coconut punch and Howard a beer. Claire kept wondering when LeBeau would have a chance to deliver his message. The three of them sat and talked about the seasonal rains, the variety of guests, and about the parades planned in St. Philips for the celebration of the anniversary of Mirandan independence.

"I understand that all of the schoolchildren will be putting on some kind of a play," Howard said. "Jeremy told me all about it." He laughed. "He said that he is going to play the part of Columbus sighting Miranda for the first time." Frank LeBeau shook his head and smiled.

"My how we alter history. Everyone knows that Ponce de Leon was the first man to see the West Indies." He winked.

The wind was starting to pick up now and was whirling sand around in little circles on the stone floor of the open-air bar. Frank looked past Howard's shoulder out to sea.

"Howard, I think that one of your boats is drifting away."

Howard turned around in his chair and surveyed the shore. "Dammit, you're right. I thought that I had all of those tied up." He glanced at the bar to see if Mandy could take care of it but he was busy mixing drinks for a large group of guests who had just arrived.

"Excuse me," Howard said, getting up, "I'll be right back." He took long strides down to the beach.

LeBeau rested his elbows on the table and stared at Claire. "Who runs the hotel laundry?" he asked.

"Well, Ruby is in charge, but the other girls help out."

"Do you?" He asked.

"Frank, I am not a domestic."

"Claire," LeBeau was getting annoyed. "What I am asking is do you have access to the laundry area?"

"Sure, I do my own clothes there sometimes, why?"

"I want you to get six of the uniforms that the men wear."

"Why, can't Mandy do it?"

"The Chameleon feels that he would look too out of place if he were caught rummaging around in the laundry room."

"Okay, I'll get them, but why do you want them?"

"Just get them, Claire, and bring them to the meeting tomorrow night. I can assure you that if you assist us now, it will hasten your return to California."

Claire said that she would bring them to the meeting just as Howard was returning to the table.

"Strangest thing," he said, sitting down. "The lines holding the boat had come completely untied in the wind. Never seen anything like it." He shook his head and finished the rest of his now warm beer.

Jeremy walked around the dining room showing his collection of shells to tables of guests having breakfast. Dori spotted him on her way into the office. She motioned for him to come to her.

"Honey, what are you doing?"

"I'm trying to sell all of the super shells that I've been collecting near Dr. Turner's house. Look!" He dug his hand into the pocket of his shorts and pulled out a fistful of coins. "See all of the money that I've made!"

Dori bent her knees and squatted down so that she could address him at eye level. "Honey, you shouldn't bother people while they are eating. And besides that, the shells here on the island are free to those who want to collect them."

"Yeah, but if they don't, then they can buy them from me. Mine are all perfect, no broken ones at all."

"I know." Dori realized that she would have to try another approach.

"But think of all the poor island children who are trying to sell things to the visitors. They need the money to buy food for their families. You just spend your money on candy and things from the gift shop. So you see, if someone buys a shell from you, maybe they won't have enough money to buy anything from the other children."

She watched Jeremy's face. He had a big frown creasing his forehead. His lower lip was curling into a pout. But then abruptly his expression changed into a big grin.

"I know. I have got a better idea. I'm going to save 'em. When we go back to visit grandma and grandpa I can sell 'em to the kids around there. I'll bet you that I could make a lot more money!"

It wasn't exactly the response that Dori was hoping for, but it did solve the problem for the moment. She gave him a kiss and sent him off to school. She had decided that she liked the practice of having school for half a day in the summer. It kept the children from getting bored or from losing the skills they had acquired during the regular term.

She was more than a little surprised to see Ransom Turner waiting for her in the office.

"Hart isn't back from New York yet is he?" The doctor asked nervously.

"No, but I am sure that he will welcome you here again if you have learned to control your behavior."

"Oh, I have. Haven't touched a drop since Jeremy started coming to visit me again."

Dori had to admit, he did look well, better in fact then she had seen him look since she had first met him.

"Well, I am glad, Ransom." She sat down behind her desk. "What can I do for you?"

"Well, I have come to discuss Jeremy's upcoming birthday. He told me that he will be eight on the tenth of July."

Dori was embarrassed. It was only two weeks away and she had forgotten it.

"I would like to give him a party if I could," Turner said. "Nothing real fancy. I'll just have some of his school friends over to my house for cake and ice cream and a few games." He had an excited smile on his face and his eyes brightened as he spoke. Dori was very moved by the gesture.

"I think that is a wonderful thing for you to want to do; I've been so busy here I confess that I haven't planned anything yet. I know that Jeremy will be thrilled. You mean a great deal to him. When we had our misunderstanding and he didn't see you for a while he was miserable."

"He is a fine little boy," Turner praised. "Curious, intelligent, polite, a joy to be around. He has filled a real void in my life, I can tell you that."

The phone rang. Dori answered. "Yes," she said. "We didn't expect it to arrive today. I'll have to check the storerooms and confirm the amount of space we have. I'll call you back shortly." She hung up. "I'm afraid that my day has begun," she said, standing. "All of the new items I have ordered for the gift shop have arrived in St. Philips, three weeks early!"

"Don't let me keep you," Turner said. "I can imagine what a responsibility it must be to try and run this hotel by yourself."

Dori started out of the office. "Thanks again for offering to have the party for Jeremy."

The doctor followed her out of the room and waved goodbye in the lobby. He got in his car and began the drive back to his house. There was so much planning to do. He laughed out loud delightedly, and tightened his hands around the steering wheel. In just two little weeks they would pay for robbing him of all those years. Oh, and how dearly they would pay!

XXXIV

The shirts were folded neatly and stacked in four different piles, according to size. The same procedure prevailed for the white pants. Ruthie and the other girls who normally ran the laundry had gone to the dining room to clear the breakfast dishes. Claire quickly collected six shirts and six pair of pants and stuffed them into a large straw basket she was carrying. She walked rapidly away from the room and onto the beach in the direction of Cinnamon Inn.

Howard was just coming toward her. "You are up so early," he said. "I was hoping that we could have breakfast together."

"Well, I had things to do. I took some towels to be washed." She said pointing at the basket.

"Hey, great. Give me one of them will you? The back of my neck has been getting so burned I think that I had better cover it up today." He reached for the basket. Claire held it away from him.

"These are for our cottages. Logan Hart isn't the only hotel owner around here you know?"

"Don't be angry with him," Howard said. "After all, he is the one bringing us all of the business."

"Our beloved patron saint," Claire said and walked off.

Howard watched her leave. He wanted to run and catch her and tell her of the surprise he was planning. He knew he couldn't yet. But soon.

The meeting began exactly at ten o'clock. Luckily Claire was able to get away easily. Howard had taken the Castle Beach station wagon into St. Philips to pick up Hart at the airport. Claire had convinced Morgan to ride along. As was customary Claire walked around the sharp rocks where the beach ended below Cinnamon Inn and waited for Frank LeBeau, then together they maneuvered their way over the craggy terrain to the spot where the Chameleon was standing.

"I've brought the uniforms," Claire said, turning them over to the black man.

"That is very good," he said. Tonight, a partial moon supplemented the meager candlelight. Cliff addressed Claire directly. "We are very pleased with the contributions you have made to our cause. But, your participation ends at this point. Just know that in a very short time your desires shall also be served."

Claire wanted to tell him that she had had it with all of the mystery. She wanted to know what was going on. Then she thought of the guarded warning LeBeau had given her that one afternoon at The Buoy. She simply said, "I hope you are right." Mandy led her back over the rocks to the point where the beach began. Then he left.

Claire climbed the grassy hill by the changing rooms and then the stairs that led to her terrace. She went into the kitchen and poured herself a rum and ginger, then took it back outside. The nightly music of the steel bands at the hotel could be heard drifting through the air. Claire's mind was turning. The blueprints, the uniforms. What was being planned? They said that she would know soon. She took a deep gulp of the drink. It stung her throat and she coughed severely for a moment. It was the waiting. The waiting was the hardest part.

At about the same time Logan Hart's plane was touching down on Miranda, the *Kiwi* was dropping anchor outside of Fort de France, Martinique. It was late evening, but even out in the harbor the music and traffic noises could be heard. The steward readied the dinghy. Ramino and Mariani came up on deck. They were both dressed in somber colored slacks and short-sleeved cotton shirts.

"When you leave us at the dock," Ramino said, stepping into the small skiff, "you may all have the evening free." The captain and the cook were standing on deck.

"Thank you, sir," said the captain.

"In fact," Mariani added, "we won't be ready to sail again for about a week. And while we are here we will be staying at La Petite Chalet."

"That will be very good, sir," the captain said. "It will give us some time to repair some of the worn rigging."

"And I need to go into the markets to purchase more fresh fruits and vegetables," said the cook. "Also," she looked at the steward, "I think that we need to take on some more freshwater."

"Yeah," Romeo agreed. "I took a shower this afternoon. No pressure at all."

"Well, we will take care of everything while you are on shore," assured the skipper. "Just send word if you need anything from the ship." The steward lowered two small suitcases into the boat and then climbed in beside the men and started the motor.

"Oh, one more thing," Mariani said, "when we are ready to sail again we will be bringing six more with us." The crew looked surprised. "It will just be for a few days," Ramino added. "They will all be men." He leered at the attractive English girl. "Certainly you can take care of six more men, can't you honey?"

"The ship can accommodate twelve comfortably, sir," the captain said. "Your guests shall be welcome."

The steward pushed off and sped the men toward the lights of the docks. The young English skipper put his arm around the girl and watched the small boat vanished into darkness. "I will be happy to get rid of those two."

"You are not alone in that thought. When is their charter schedule to be over?"

The lean blonde man bent down and straightened out the twisted rope ladder. "It ends July twelfth," he said "thank God."

The streets of Martinique were filled with French speaking people, some were dark, and others were quite light skinned. Many of the residents were originally from other islands in the Caribbean. There was a blending of people here. The streets were extremely narrow and paved with cobblestones. Most of the buildings had a flat stucco exterior and were pressed close together. The majority of them had three or four stories.

The hotel in which Ramino and Mariani were staying was in such a building. Their rooms were on the fourth floor. They were small and cramped, but otherwise adequate. There was a message waiting in Ramino's room. He read it. "Panella has already arrived," he announced to his companion. "He is waiting for us at the restaurant down the street, Chez Francine."

Mariani clutched the handle of a brown leather briefcase. "Let's go," he said.

Even at eleven o'clock the streets were filled with people. There were many small nightclubs in a row along the main thoroughfare, such as it was. Far down on the right they spotted the sign, buzzing in yellow neon lettering, with several letters only partially illuminated. They climbed a flight of steep stairs before emerging into a small, but pleasant dining room. Since neither of them had had personal contact with Panella previous to this occasion, they searched the room for a man dining alone.

At last Ramino spotted a large man with a full beard sitting alone at a table on the open-air terrace. In a moment he saw them and walked through the dining room. "Are you gentlemen from the *Kiwi?*"

"We are." Mariani answered.

"Well, welcome to Martinique." He had a decidedly French accent but looked almost Germanic. He glanced at the satchel in Mariani's hand. "I'm glad to see that you are ready to conduct business. But first," he led them to the table, "we shall dine. The food here is marvelous." And it was.

The three men stayed, enjoying the evening until the last of the patrons left and the owners were closing up for the night. Some of the waiters were turning chairs upside down and stacking them on the tabletops.

"I'm afraid you'll have to leave now," said a frail woman who had been tending the cash register all evening. Panella stood up and smiled. He reached into his pocket and gave her the local equivalent of a fifty-dollar bill.

"We would like to stay just a while longer."

"Very well," she said and retreated discreetly into the kitchen with the money.

"I have your men and your required ammunition."

"Where?" Ramino asked.

"Near the docks. Finish your brandy and come."

They lingered several more minutes and then followed their new guide through the winding streets into a dark foreboding area of town to a small, dilapidated wooden structure.

Panella knocked on the door. A short young black man opened it cautiously. When he recognized the face of the caller he relaxed a bit and opened the door wider, to accommodate the new arrivals. The men stepped inside. There were five other men in the room in addition to the one who had responded to the knock. They were all black, all young. And they all had the intense expression Ramino had seen so many times behind Cliff's thick glasses.

Panella introduced each of them. Then he displayed the ammunition crates of dynamite and some elaborate timing devices.

"All of these men are highly trained in the use of explosives. They need only to study the blueprints of the targeted area for several days to discover the stress points. Then they will be prepared to wire it perfectly for demolition." Mariani looked at each man.

"I am confident that they will be very successful." He opened the attaché case and turned over the money to Panella. Then he spoke to the anxious men. "We have five days to prepare before we set sail for Miranda. It will take us three days of traveling to reach the island. That will give you only three days to plant the ammunition. Will that provide you with a sufficient amount of time?"

René, the leader of the group nodded his head. "It will be plenty of time."

"Well," Ramino said, "I suggest that we all get a proper night of rest. I regret that it might be the last one we shall have until this assignment is completed."

They thanked Panella and then left, walking slowly back to their hotel. Each man was absorbed in thought. But their minds were obsessed with the same thing: the beginning of the death of imperialism in the West Indies was only an agonizingly small number of days away.

XXXV

"I never thought that it would come to this Victor. I never wanted it to. I honestly felt that what we had would be enough, but it isn't. I can't endure just having snatches of a relationship with a man I know will never be with me constantly. Being alone is better than what I have now." Sarah Hunnicut was sitting on the edge of the bed, wrapped in a sheet, watching Victor dress. Tears were forming in the corner of her eyes. "I'm going back to London. And then I am going to try and get a teaching job in Scotland or Wales, or Australia, or anyplace else. I have already written and asked for a replacement here."

Victor stopped buttoning his shirt and came and sat down next to her. He wanted to comfort her. He knew that now was the time that he should beg her to stay, or tell her that he would ask Allison for a divorce so that they could be married. But something strange had happened. The night he had seen Sarah dancing with the American, Jay Cavanagh, he was amazed to find that he had been unable to muster up the slightest bit of jealousy. Even when he tried to picture them making love it did nothing to his emotions. Yet, when he imagined Allison being intimate with another man he grew livid with rage and an all-consuming jealousy. It was then that he had begun to realize what he must have been doing to his wife, almost flaunting this affair in her face. But it wasn't until this moment that he realized how very much he still loved her. He also felt such shame that he had taken advantage of this young woman for his own pleasure.

"I am sorry if I have made you unhappy," he said honestly. "I had no intention of causing you pain"

The red-faced girl looked up at him. She stroked her disheveled hair with one hand. "You are not in love with me are you?" she asked softly.

"No." Victor braced himself for what he was certain would be an emotional outburst. She was entitled to it. But it didn't materialize. Instead she stood up and grabbed her robe off of the chair and slipped into it.

The window of her small bedroom was open, though the curtains were closed. A gentle breeze ruffled them letting in flashes of the afternoon sunlight. She appraised Victor coolly. "Well, that makes my leaving so much easier."

She stood by the door and watched Victor finish dressing. And she walked with him silently through the living room to the front door. She opened it for him. "Goodbye."

"Sarah...I"

"Goodbye Victor."

"Goodbye."

The Englishman kissed her on the cheek and walked down the steps to his car. She closed the door behind him and dropped to her knees, weeping, not because she loved him, but because she didn't. They had both wasted so much time fooling themselves and each other.

Allison was sitting on the veranda watching the big Norwegian cruise ship resting in the water off Castle Beach. She had never had too much faith in Ransom Turner. That was the reason she had taken one of the island ferries out to the cruiser. She wanted to confer with the ship's doctor. He only confirmed her darkest suspicion: she was pregnant.

On the ride back to shore she had been numb. How could this be happening to her? She was almost forty-three years old. Her twin daughters Ellen and Julia would be starting at the Sorbonne in the fall. The boys were almost ready to go off to Eaton.

"There is nothing to be particularly concerned about, Mrs. Trent," the physician told her. "Your general health seems to be very good. Just watch your weight and be certain to exercise properly and everything should be fine."

Fine! she thought, How could anything be fine? Even now as she sat there with a small glass of sherry she knew that Victor was spending the afternoon in bed with Sarah Hunnicut. She set the glass down and began to sob, deep wrenching sobs. Victor, he would be paralyzed by the news. She knew that he would feel obligated to stay with her now, even though she suspected that any day he would be coming to ask her for a divorce. He would stay with her out of pity and out of a sense of duty. She couldn't bear it.

Suddenly she heard the unmistakable sound of Victor's car pulling into the circular driveway below. She walked over to the open arched wall. The boys were with him. They spotted her and waved.

"Hello, mother," Brian yelled. "Father saw us walking up the road and felt sorry for us so he stopped."

"What a good Samaritan." Allison was trying desperately to sound casual.

The guard opened the door for Victor. He stepped out and came into the house. Soon she heard his footsteps coming up the spiral staircase. He joined her on the balcony.

"Where are the children?" Allison asked.

"Oh," Victor turned around, "I thought they were right behind me. They must have run off to play somewhere." He drew a chair up close to hers and sat down. "It is just as well, I want to talk to you alone for a moment."

Allison felt a sickening tightening in her stomach. This was it. She picked up her sherry glass and wrapped cold fingers around the stem.

"I haven't been exactly certain of my feelings until today," Victor said. "But now I know for sure." Allison stood up and walked over to the railing. She had her back to him. She could not watch his face as he told her he was leaving. She prepared herself for what was certain to follow. "Allison I have seen Sarah for the last time. I realized that I don't love her. I don't think that I ever did. And I know now that I have never ceased caring for you. I cannot make up for all the agony and humiliation I have caused you. And an apology would be so beyond in adequate I only pray that you will try, in time, to forgive me and that we might be close again as we once were. But if you choose to leave me now I will understand and will make no protest although I will be broken hearted."

Allison hadn't moved since he began speaking. Victor walked over and stood behind her. He placed his hands tentatively and tenderly on her shoulders. "Please tell me what you are thinking? Is it too late for us?"

She swung around and faced him. Tears flooded her eyes. He put his arms around her and she buried her head against his chest. It was like a damp, evil shroud had been lifted from her body. It would take time, she knew, to heal from this. But at this moment she knew that she would, that their marriage would. She clung to him for several minutes, saying nothing. Then they kissed with a hungry passion that they used to know.

He took her by the hand and they walked silently through the long rosewood paneled hall and up a few steps to their bedroom. They both quickly undressed and climbed into the big four-poster bed. The distant voices of the children could be heard in the garden far below.

Allison now felt that the new life she was harboring was a sign that she and her husband were being given a precious second chance. Victor rolled over and took her in his arms. She was anxious to tell him, and she would soon. But this glorious moment of reunion must belong to them alone

XXXVI

Something was wrong. Dori knew Logan too well not to notice. It had been a week since he had returned from New York. He just glossed over everything when she had asked him what Flynn had to say. And he kept referring to having "minor operational problems" with his other holdings. But his entire demeanor and attitude were different. He was constantly lost in thought.

He would stand by the windows in the office and stare out into the gardens. Often Dori would go on some errands for several hours, only to return to find him still standing, staring. And his wonderful, spontaneous wit had become submerged somewhere to be replaced by a cynical bitterness she had not seen before. When she told him of Turner's touching offer to host Jeremy's birthday party he said, "That quack would use any occasion as a celebration to get drunk." And he seemed to have lost his all consuming interest in the hotel. He wandered around the lobby and the dining room as if he were the only person there, failing to acknowledge the greetings of friendly guests and employees.

He no longer cared to check the progress of the reservations or did any public relations work at all to encourage the additional tours and conventions. In short, he had become another person.

One afternoon John Salter and Charles Cliff came to the office to discuss plans with Hart for using the dining room as the site of the OWII meeting the following week.

"It will be a good thing for the hotel," Salter said after proposing the idea. "By having the meeting here it will show the rest of the Caribbean, as well as any potential foreign investors, that Miranda has prospered and will continue to do so precisely because of the infusion of outside capital. And," he turned to Cliff, "we only touched on this vaguely before but I feel I will use the occasion to ask democratic foreign governments with interests in the West Indies to start coming to the aid of all free islands in their efforts to squelch communist inspired uprisings." Cliff nodded in approval, hoping that his utter contempt for the remarks did not show.

Logan agreed to allow the meeting to be held there. "But what about security?" he asked.

"I will be taking care of that," Cliff said abruptly.

Logan saw that the prime minister seemed satisfied with the arrangement.

"Well then that is fine," Logan said. "Now, will you both please excuse me? There are some urgent business matters that need my attention."

The two men left. Dori was sorting the mail at the desk when she saw them leaving through the main entrance to Salter's waiting limousine. He made no attempt to stop and talk with her. Perhaps he had not seen her. Dori put down the letters and went after him. But by the time she got outside his car was pulling away. Had he seen her? Probably not. She shrugged her shoulders and returned to her task.

Sometime later she went into the office. Logan was at his desk hovering over some columns of figures.

"Are those the inventory lists of the things that arrived for the gift shop? Oh Logan, just wait until you see all of the fantastic things I have bought!"

"That seems to be what you do best, spending other people's money." Logan regretted the remark the moment he made it.

A shocked and deeply hurt expression consumed Dori's face. She walked over and looked directly at him. "I think that you had better explain that."

Logan folded his arms and put his head down on his desk.

"Never mind. I didn't mean it. You of all people have to know I didn't mean it. I'm just tired."

"O.K." she said. "But that just isn't a good enough explanation. We all get tired, but that is no excuse to lash out at the people around us. You accused me of having changed after I came back from New York. Well, you have too. The only difference is I snapped out of it. But you haven't. What is going on with you Logan?"

He looked up. Suddenly a terrified expression swept over her face. "It's Ramino and Mariani isn't it? The authorities have discovered everything, the gambling, Martin Gibson?"

"If only it were as easy as that," Logan said, only half joking. He stood up and stretched. "Okay, you have been with me on this wild escapade from its inception. I suppose there is no reason to keep the truth from you now. Come on." He took her hand and led her out of the office. "I'll tell you everything, but not here. Let's go to the terrace bar and get a drink. We can walk down to the beach and watch the sunset. As long as I'm here I might as well enjoy it."

They sat in orange-and-green-stripped canvass sling back chairs near the shoreline. A cluster of American teenagers, newly arrived with their various sets of parents, had organized a spirited volley ball game further on down the beach. Jeremy was happily serving as their mascot of sorts, running to retrieve the ball when it landed out of bounds.

"Important man there," Logan said as they watched from a distance.

"Listen," Dori said smiling, "I am sure that he thinks that he is captain of both teams."

They were each drinking a strong coconut rum punch served in tall frosty glasses. Logan extended his legs out in front of him and closed his eyes for a moment.

"You know, I think that I might like being a guest here."

He had stalled long enough. "Tell me what's happening, Logan."

He sat up. "Remember when Jack called last month and told me that everything was going to hell in a hand basket?"

"Yes."

"Well, he wasn't just being cute and colloquial. It's true."

"What do you mean?"

Logan told her the whole complex story explaining his two only possible options.

"Sell Castle Beach?" She was still disbelieving.

"Or go into bankruptcy."

"Oh Logan no!" She grabbed his hand. "You have worked so hard."

"So have you," he added.

"How could this happen?"

"It's simple actually. I allowed my mania over this crazy dream of mine to run my life. I forgot to pay attention to the hard fact that, in this world anyway, dreams must be built on solid financial foundations. I did everything wrong. Me! The fellow who was criticizing everyone else's poor management. I spent way too much time and money on this place. I ignored my other holdings. I have leveraged myself so high it's a wonder that my nose isn't bleeding. Any Econ 101 student could have seen that I was headed for disaster. But not me. All I could see was this hotel, rising out of the sand like a jewel." He finished his drink.

They sat silently for quite a while. The setting sun had performed its spectacular feat of dropping, like a flaming red star, into the sea. The twilight sky was a swirl of grey and purple afterglow. The aroma of seasoned pork, roasting over the outdoor pits, filled the air. Dori looked around. The beach was practically empty. She hadn't even noticed that the volley ball game was over and that everyone had left.

"What are you going to do?" she asked.

Logan began to fold up his chair. "I don't know. Hey!" he said with an achingly sad smile, "Guess where my kids are right this minute? They're in Hawaii." Dori looked surprised. "Yeah, Hawaii. I was going to bring them back here with me but my daughter wanted to be with her band of girlfriends and my son doesn't think that the surfing here is so great." He started to laugh. "Can you believe it?" Without warning his raucous laughter dissolved into a wrenching sigh. He dropped the bent canvas lounge chair in the sand and began walking away from Dori down the beach. She did not try to go after him. She knew from experience that some pain is impossible to share.

XXXVII

To the people of Miranda, July twelfth was more important than simply a day in which to celebrate the anniversary of their independence, since for the majority of them daily existence had changed little from the days of British control. They still worked the plantations for low wages, or ran small shops in Saint Philips catering to the tourist trade, sporadic as it was. But human nature told them that it surely must be better to be autonomous then to be dominated by another government. So, regardless of the fact that they were living the same lives they had always known, they tried to feel better about themselves. Thus July twelfth was a time to celebrate life.

The shops and spice factories, along with the banana and sugar plantations closed for a week in preparation for the parade through the streets of St. Philips. Many of the neighboring islands joined in the spirited rejoicing. The yachtsmen of St. Vincent sponsored a sailing regatta to the island. Ships from Bequiay, Union, the Tobago Cays, and Curacao would join the procession into the harbor. Visiting heads of state of the larger West Indian islands would motor into port aboard their private cruisers. Then they would be met ceremoniously by the prime minister as well as by Victor Trent, who represented England during the weeklong festivities.

Steel bands would set up in the streets and play continuously day and night. The local taverns and restaurants remained open twenty-four hours a day. Tourists from the large cruisers poured into town to be caught up in the joyful frenzy.

On July seventh the Trents hosted a dinner at the government house for John Salter. The guest list included the visiting dignitaries, Claire and Howard and their friend Morgan Talbot, Logan Hart and Dori, Ransom Turner, and Frank LeBeau. There were also several Mirandan men and their wives. The men were the local presidents of the British owned factories and plantations.

Over cocktails Allison remarked that of all the people invited only Frank LeBeau had been unable to attend. That pleased Claire. She was certain that he must have been organizing something for the Chameleon. She felt tense and nervous. She sensed that whatever it was they had been planning would happen soon. Ransom Turner was on his best behavior. He drank nothing but club soda with lime and kept his conversation light and trivial.

Dori was struck with the tremendous change that had come over the Trents since she had seen them last. Victor was genuinely warm and attentive to his wife, and she clung to him happily. Her face was radiant. The poorly disguised hostility that had existed between them before had vanished. Something told Dori that their change of heart was sincere and not simply manufactured for this diplomatic occasion.

Waiters floated through the room with trays of delicious canopies and other exotic hors d'oeuvres. Aside from the invited guests, several guards accompanied each government official. They all stayed a discreet, but watchful, distance from their employers. Charles Cliff stood in a corner away from the others. Twice he was offered champagne but refused. He observed the proceedings with a detached interest, pausing several times to clean his thick lensed glasses with a handkerchief he had in his uniform pocket.

Claire seemed preoccupied and extremely high strung. She darted about the room talking with clusters of people just for a moment before moving on. Howard and Morgan were engrossed in some kind of personal discussion, since they would cease speaking whenever Claire approached. Dori could not imagine that they had any romantic interest in each other. Still, it was strange.

Logan stood by Victor and John as they spoke to the assembly of officials. The major topic of discussion was the impending conference to be held at the hotel on the twelfth. Dori could tell that Logan's mind was not focusing on what was being said. She agonized for him, but knew that the decisions he had to make must be his own.

Salter was not revealing to anyone the nature of his address. But he teased the crowd by hinting that it would be a major statement concerning the future of Caribbean commerce. Several times he would glance over at Dori and then look away quickly before their eyes could meet. She was sitting with Ransom Turner in a corner of the large living room near a grand piano. He was telling her all of the things he had arranged for Jeremy's party.

"He is going to be so surprised," Turner said. "I just told him to come over to my house for the afternoon. He doesn't know that all of his little classmates will be there. I've planned a treasure hunt and lots of other games."

"This is really so sweet of you Ransom," Dori said.

"Well, I can bet that you are going to be busy with all of your guests."

"You're right about that. The hotel is overbooked as it is. Even Cinnamon Inn can't house anymore for us."

Dinner was announced. According to protocol, John Salter was to go into the dining room first, since the party was being given in his honor. He looked around the crowd until he saw Dori. Then he walked slowly over to her and held out his hand. She was amazed and a little bit confused but she took it anyway. Together they walked past the open mahogany doors into the dining room. Dori could feel the eyes of everyone on them as they travelled to the table. This time the long formal table had been exquisitely set for the event. It looked lovely. Each of the forty or so place settings displayed heirloom Wedgwood china and ornate sterling silver. There were three long-stemmed crystal goblets of descending size at each place. Small white porcelain figurines held handsome manuscript name cards. Dori saw that she was to sit along the right side of the table next to Logan and Howard. But, before she could be seated, Salter moved the place card next to his near one end of the table.

Allison handled the situation quite gracefully, motioning to the rest of the guests to move down one space until the vacant chair was eventually filled. Dori was extremely embarrassed. But Salter was not the least bit self conscious about his actions.

When all of the guests were seated Victor rose to propose a toast. "I have had the distinct pleasure of knowing John Salter since we were both children here on Miranda. I have watched him rise to great heights of power and authority.

He has dedicated himself to the betterment of the island people. July twelfth shall be his personal day of triumph. And I hope that it will serve as a reminder to the rest of you that although Miranda is now free, largely through the efforts of this man, she has maintained strong economic trade relationships with many of the independent countries in the world. And it is for this reason that she will flourish. To John Salter, my associate and my friend."

He raised his glass of chilled champagne. The dinner guests all stood in honor of the black leader. Dori studied John's face as she drank to the accolade. He sat in a serious and humble pose. Only once did he look up to Victor and smile warmly. He was in his element, receiving the praise and recognition of his assembled peers. His jaw was set straight and strong.

During dinner Dori spoke with the president of one of the neighboring northern islands and with his wife. They were both very charming people as well as being highly versed in international affairs. Like John Salter they had been educated in Europe, but were native to the island. Their parents had worked side by side on a sugar plantation.

Several times during the meal Dori saw Logan staring at her. She could not detect what he was thinking.

"Are you having a nice time?" John leaned over and asked.

"Yes, very. It is a wonderful evening. You are very well liked and respected here."

"By you also?" he asked.

"Yes," she smiled, "by me also."

After dinner the party moved to the third floor terrace. Snifters of cognac were brought out on silver trays. Again, Dori noticed that Turner had nothing. She was pleased. Claire and Allison had been talking during the last part of the meal and continued their conversation on the way up the stairs. Morgan Talbot joined in the discussion at intermittent intervals, injecting a few well-spaced oohs and aahs. But for the most part, she had been centering her attention on a less than receptive Logan Hart.

"Now, don't you think that some of the hotel patrons would be interested in a mini-course in my revolutionary philosophy? I mean, after all, let's face it—the kind of people who can afford to stay at your place must certainly be somewhat jaded and bored with life. That's why they keep travelling. They are searching for inner peace. I can show them how to find it. They will thank you." She was wearing a beautifully tailored long jade-green raw-silk dress. As usual, her black hair was lacquered into a stiff topknot.

"With all due respect, Miss Talbot," Logan began, "I really don't imagine that my guests come to Miranda for inner peace. I think that they come for a good time. And it is my job to see that they get it."

"Well, it is very distressing that a place as gorgeous and serene as this should be devoted solely to such hedonistic pursuits." With that pronouncement she swept another glass of brandy from the passing tray and a large handful of after dinner mints from a near by enamel bowl.

Salter was circulating among the visiting dignitaries, personally welcoming each of them to the island and scheduling appointments to meet with each of them individually prior to the general conference on the twelfth. Dori was standing near the open arched wall of the balcony watching the lights from the cruise ships. In the past few days the harbor and inlet bays had become filled with boats arriving for the activities. From this distance their illuminated decks looked like strings of iridescent diamonds. And the full moon commanding the still night sky spread a light that enveloped the island in a magical glow.

Soon the sounds of engines could be heard starting below. Chauffeurs stood expectantly by the vehicles waiting to ferry their officials back to their yachts or to the ministry for the evening. Salter approached Dori as the guests were preparing to depart.

"I must leave now with the others. Will you meet me at the lighthouse in an hour? There is something I must talk with you about."

"Why don't you come to the hotel?" Dori asked, puzzled.

"No." The prime minister shook his head emphatically. "Please do as I ask."

"Alright."

He turned away and walked down the stairs with Charles Cliff, thanking Victor and Allison profusely, and bidding goodbye to the rest of the guests. Dori rode back to the hotel with Logan. Claire and Morgan came with them. Howard was driving some of the lower level officials into St. Philips in the hotel station wagon.

"Allison certainly looked lovely tonight," Dori commented.

"Why shouldn't she? She just pulled off the greatest coup of all times," Claire said miserably.

"What do you mean," Logan asked.

"Our Mrs. Trent is pregnant. And she has convinced Victor that having a baby at her age is a delicate procedure that should be closely monitored by only the finest of physicians. So they will be moving back to London in about a month. Victor spoke this morning with the home office requesting an immediate transfer due to a medical issue."

"Claire!" Morgan said, "I'm disappointed in you. We promised Allison that we wouldn't say anything. Victor does not want to tell Mr. Salter until after the conference."

"Don't worry," Logan said, looking at Dori, "we won't mention this conversation again."

"Well, I am thrilled for her," Dori said. "And I would think that you would be too, Claire. She has been your friend for years."

"Nobody makes friends on this island," Claire said, slumping further down in the back. "They just try to keep their number of enemies at a minimum."

When they reached the hotel, Logan offered to drive Claire and Morgan up the hill to Cinnamon Inn.

"No thank you," Claire said. "I think that I will walk down the beach. I need the air."

"I'll go with her," Morgan said, taking off her shoes and holding up the hem of her dress. "I need the exercise."

Dori walked into the lobby with Logan. The Mirandan girls behind the desk waved to both of them.

"How is everything going?" Logan inquired.

"Pretty okay," said one of the girls, "except Sylvia is real mad. Six of the men's uniforms are missing, there aren't enough room service carts left, and her fancy stove broke."

Logan put his hands up over his ears. "Stop. I don't want to hear anymore." He motioned to Dori. "Come on, let's go see what we can do to get in the way. Dori glanced nervously at her watch. "What is it?" Logan asked.

"Logan, I'm sorry, I really am, but I have to meet someone soon."

He led her away from the desk. He knew without asking who it was. He looked at her and then said, "Don't worry about it. I can handle things here." He left, walking briskly through the dining room toward the kitchen.

Dori went up to her suite and changed out of her blue sleeveless evening gown into a pair of slacks and a light cotton top. She moved quietly, careful not to awake Jeremy and Ruthie who were asleep in the other two bedrooms.

Salter's car was already there when she reached the end of the old lighthouse road. The powerful moonlight drenched everything in a strong white wash hue. The deserted stone building looked so stark and blunt in this kind of harsh exposure. She got out of her car and followed the narrow footpath to the stairs at the base of the structure.

"Hello." John stood in an empty doorway.

"Hello, John." He was still in full military dress. "I'm sorry if I kept you waiting."

He escorted her inside to the main room on the ground floor. Dori smiled. He had lit the old kerosene lamp. It burnt softly in a corner. He came close to her and took her in his muscular arms kissing her fiercely.

"You looked lovely tonight, more beautiful than any of the women there."

"Thank you."

"Come with me, " he said, taking her by the hand and leading her slowly into another room and up the circular staircase to the turret at the top of the lighthouse. They walked outside onto the small platform.

"Look," he said, with a wide sweep of his arms, "all of Miranda is at your feet." And from this vantage point it truly was, from the glittering harbor of St. Philips, to the hillside lights of Cinnamon Inn and everything in between. It was obvious that Salter was filled with special pride in his island this night.

"It is magnificent," Dori said.

Salter came and stood by the ornate iron railing next to her. He was looking out to sea.

"It is a perfect gem. But only one of many. All of the islands in the West Indian chain are as spectacular as this in their own unique way. And when the various leaders you met tonight convene later in the fall to elect someone to represent all of the islands collectively, I want it to be me. And that is only the beginning. I will be the single most influential and important voice in the entire Caribbean within the next decade."

Dori examined his countenance in the moonlight. The softness had left. It was now all sharp angles and hollows. And when he spoke, it was as if he were thinking out loud. His tone was restrained but determined.

"When you sat next to me at dinner this evening, what did you notice about the women who accompanied the other members of the organization?"

Dori thought for a moment. Suddenly she realized the answer he wanted her to give.

"They were all natives of their various islands."

Salter's expression became even more intense. "Yes, they all are. It was very important that you saw that for yourself. That is the reason I chose you to be my dinner partner."

"But why?"

"Because I wanted you to understand that regardless of what is happening between us, there can never be a lasting role for you in my life."

"Have I been asking to have a permanent part in your life?" Dori was hurt and angry.

"Not yet," he said, "but you would have in time. You are not the kind of woman who can live for the moment, though you have been trying to be. You need a foundation to build on. And it can never be with me."

Dori felt her face grow hot and flushed. "Why are you telling me this now?"

He came close to her but held her away from him by her shoulders. "Look at me!" he commanded. "It's not you that I am telling. I am telling myself." His eyes were swelling with tears. "I can't allow myself to love you. Someday your wishes might color my judgment. The West Indies is in trouble Dori. Even now, there are countless radical groups forming throughout the Caribbean, dedicated to overthrowing our fledgling democracies. They would like to take control of the islands one by one. My sworn duty is to see that it doesn't happen. I must be totally devoted to insuring that end. Everything else must be excluded from my life. It just has to be that way." He let go of her shoulders and dropped his arms to his side. "I wanted to tell you here. This is where we began and this is where we must end. We have come full circle, like the moon. Goodnight."

He left her out on the walkway, descended the stairs, and started down the path toward the cars. Dori watched as he vanished into the thick growth farther on down the hillside. Soon she heard his car engine start followed by the sound of wheels running over loose stones as they turned around and headed back down the hill. Dust rose in the air, to be spotlighted by the prying moonlight for an instant before settling back down on the ground.

She waited for her tears to come, but they didn't. She was still absorbing all that John had told her. As yet she had not been able to articulate her own feelings about their affair even to herself. Intellectually, she knew that she should have been prepared for this kind of abrupt ending. John Salter was an abrupt man. Yet emotionally, she was ill equipped to cope with this sharp parting. She refused to react to anything he had said. Not now.

She left the light house and walked slowly back to her car. The numbness was leaving her. The ramifications of what he had said were beginning to sink in. He loved her. She had sensed that tonight. But he was a highly disciplined person, capable of denying himself something in order to attain what he believed to be a greater, more valued goal.

Dust rose up around the car windshield. She saw something in her headlights at the point where the narrow dirt side street joined the paved road around the island. She came to an immediate halt. It was Salter's car. He had gotten out and was leaning against the front of it. He came over and opened Dori's door. She stepped out.

"Don't talk," he said, grabbing her and kissing her savagely several times. When she tried to break away he held her body close to his.

"John," she was finally able to ask, "did you mean everything you said to me out on the tower?"

"Everything," he said.

Dori's instincts told her to get in her car and drive away quickly, to leave this paradox of a lover. He had already set the stage himself. It should be easy. But even as she pushed him away her body ached to be held and possessed by him one last time. He led her to a small field hidden from the road and filled with tall grass. There he undressed her slowly and methodically, caressing her skin as though he had never touched it. And soon, making sweet sad love in the moonlight, they held reality at bay for one last time.

XXXVIII

In the predawn mist the *Kiwi* rounded the corner past the crowded harbor of St Philips. The sleek ship was low in the water because of the added cargo of men and of crates of ammunition. Ramino and Mariani stood on deck and observed the congested bay as they passed. Only the small fishing trawlers were beginning to maneuver their way through the obstacle course in an effort to reach the open sea. There were yachts of every size and description resting in the water. From the array of flags it could be determined that some had sailed north from Trinidad, and others south from the Virgin Islands.

Mariani watched in silence. He knew that at this moment some of the men sleeping peacefully aboard their official ships would be dead within days. The thought neither elated nor depressed him. It was simply a necessary fact if their plan were to be successful.

Below the deck of the *Kiwi* the six demolition experts prepared to leave the ship. They were changing into the uniforms of Castle Beach employees. Both Ramino and Mariani were confident that the men knew exactly what was expected of them. Each one had committed to memory the blueprints of the hotel. Each man had been assigned the task of wiring a particular section of the development. All of the feeder wires would be connected to a main time fuse which would be set to go off at precisely three o'clock on the afternoon of July twelfth, two hours after the conference had begun in the dining room.

Soon they left the harbor behind them and headed around to the other side of the island behind Cinnamon Inn. The crew began to lower the sails. They worked swiftly, drawing the heavy canvas sheets and tying them securely to the masts. From this point on, the *Kiwi* motored slowly through the calm, glassy ocean as tinges of sunlight outlined the horizon, signaling the arrival of morning.

The ship was passing in front of the Castle Beach hotel. The men below deck looked out of the salon windows at their target. Each man solemnly appraised his objective in silence. There was almost an air of reverence in the room. In time, the hotel disappeared behind them, as did the long expanse of white beach.

Now, only craggy rocks were visible against the base of the island. The tide broke over them in foaming white assaults. Ramino walked to the bow of the ship. He held binoculars up to his eyes and scanned the shoreline. In a few moments he spotted Charles Cliff and Frank LeBeau bobbing in a small outboard just yards beyond the rocks in the water. Cliff started the motor as soon as he recognized the *Kiwi*. Mariani motioned to the skipper to cut the engine and drop anchor.

"Gentlemen," Ramino said to the six men waiting on deck, "this is the Chameleon," he introduced Charles Cliff who was pulling up in the boat. "From now on you shall receive your instructions from him. His companion is also dedicated to our cause of liberation. He shall assist you while you are on the island. We shall not meet again until Saturday when our mission is over. We will reconvene at the ministry at that time."

The men were taken ashore in groups of three. Then Cliff made additional trips to pick up the crates of dynamite. The men on shore unloaded the boxes and disappeared with them into the underbrush. Soon Cliff waved both arms in a gesture indicating that all was well. Then he and Frank LeBeau also vanished into the deep foliage.

For Ramino and Mariani, all that remained was the waiting. The sun was climbing steadily higher in the sapphire sky. As yet, there was very little breeze.

"It's going to be one hell of a hot day," Ramino said, heading to the salon for breakfast.

"Yeah," Mariani agreed, following. "But maybe it will rain this afternoon, cool everything off," he scanned the shore one more time before going below, "for a while anyway."

"Jesus, I feel like I am throwing an orgy," Logan said as he spoke to Howard outside the bar. "I can't believe that we need more booze. I already have a corner on the rum market. Man, when they celebrate something down here they put the rest of the world to shame!"

Howard shook his head, smiling, and continued to check the liquor inventory sheets. "The tropics make alcoholics out of everybody, for a while anyway. The tourists are the worst. You would think that they couldn't have another drink anywhere else on earth ever again. I've seen it before. They all feel like they have to get their money's worth out of their vacation."

"Does that include spending it in a constant state of semi-consciousness?"

"Yeah," Howard said, "for a lot of them."

"Well," Logan said signing and initialing the sheets, "it's their livers. Guess you had better go into St Philips and stock up before the lunch crowd stumbles in."

"Right-o," Howard said and left.

Logan sat on a bar stool and looked out at the beach. The daily ritual was beginning again: the older women sitting on brightly-stripped towels spread out on the sand, pink, spongy flesh protruding from tight one-piece bathing suits, young women herding children around by the water's edge, hoping that they still look alluring in their modified bikinis, and the adolescent girls, wearing the briefest of swimwear, stretched out on the raw sand, bodies tight and glowing, confident that they would always be this young and this sexy looking.

, Logan noticed how different things were for the men. Regardless of their ages they all strutted up and down the beach like peacocks, believing fully that they could have any woman they wanted. They all spoke of being in their prime, whether they were young or old, fat or thin. They engaged in every sport available and attacked it vengefully, determined to be the master. They were all gladiators defending their egos against the lions of failure or rejection or time.

Suddenly Logan realized that the analogy applied to him as well. He could not endure the prospect of losing Castle Beach. Yet he had gone over the balance sheets a million times, attempting to arrange some kind of alternative to bankruptcy, which would force him to sell his dream, this very real part of himself. As yet he had come up with nothing. Flynn was awaiting his decision. He would have to make it by the first of August.

He got up from the stool and walked back to his office. He noticed that several new palms were being installed outside, close to the side of the lobby. Mandy was helping a couple other young men lower them into the ground. Logan couldn't remember if he had ordered them or not. Perhaps Dori had. At any rate, they produced a nice effect. "Wonder how much those things cost apiece?" he thought out loud as he entered the building.

Dori was behind the desk filling out reservation forms.

"Where's Claire?" Logan asked.

Dori smiled slightly. "I have an idea that she probably took to her bed ever since she heard the news about the Trents. Morgan has come over here several times and told me that Claire has been in a rotten mood for days now. But she also said that she and Howard are cooking up some kind of a surprise for her. They are going to wait until the independence dance here Saturday night to reveal it."

"Do you know what it is?" Logan asked.

"I have no idea. But I hope it cheers her up."

Logan shook his head. "That woman can make a career out of her depressions."

"Speaking of surprises," Dori said, "tomorrow is Jeremy's birthday party at Ransom's house. Jeremy only knows that he is to go to the doctor's house after play rehearsal at school. I told him that there might be a cake. But he doesn't even suspect that all of his friends will be there. In fact, you and I are invited too."

Logan brightened. "I haven't played a good game of pin the tail on the donkey in years. What time?"

"Well, the party starts at three. But Ransom thinks that we ought to wait a couple of hours before we show up. Let the kids have some time to play by themselves. We will come just when they are ready to serve the cake and ice cream."

"Oh goody, goody" Logan said, clapping his hands, "the best part!"

Dori laughed. "Oh, you really are impossible."

"Maybe," he admitted, "but it's nice to see you laugh. You haven't done much of it recently."

Dori's smile faded. "Excuse me, I have some billings I have to straighten out."

"Dori I…"

"Excuse me."

Logan shook his head and went into his office, closing the door behind him.

"Mommy, wake up. It's raining." Jeremy climbed up onto his mother's bed. "Does this mean that there won't be any play practice or cake with Dr. Turner?"

Dori propped herself up on her elbows and looked out of the window. The morning sky, though blue, was filled with rolling grey clouds. Rain poured down on the beach. There were small white caps out on the water. But the sun was still penetrating the clouds at regular intervals.

"No honey," Dori said, sitting up and holding her son on her lap. "This is just like the little storms we get in the afternoons. It will be gone soon, probably even before you finish breakfast."

The worry evaporated from the little boy's face. He squealed and bounded off the bed. "Then I am gonna get dressed and eat right away."

"Hey, wait a minute mister," Dori said, "don't I get to give you a birthday kiss?"

Jeremy padded back and stood by the bed. Dori leaned over and hugged and kissed him several times. "Happy birthday, my great big eight-year-old. If you look under the bed I think you will find something there for you."

Jeremy got on his knees and lifted up the bottom of the spread. He pulled out a big box wrapped in the gift paper from the hotel shop. He tore through the paper and opened the lid of the box.

"Oh neat!" he exclaimed, extracting a rubber facemask and a snorkel. He put them on. Then he dug further into the box to find a pair of swim fins. He kicked off his slippers and tried them on. "They are just my size!" His happy voice was muffled through the snorkel. "Boy, wait until Brian and Henry see this stuff! Thanks, Mom." He hugged her again, removing the snorkel but not the facemask. He walked around the room flapping his rubber, webbed feet.

There was a knock on the door. "I understand that a very old man lives here!" It was Logan. Dori slipped into a cotton robe and answered the door. He was holding a big covered birdcage by a wire ring at the top. He grinned broadly and walked into the room. "Here, frog man, happy birthday!" He set the cage down on a table. Jeremy ripped off his mask and carefully lifted the cover on the cage. Inside, on a wooden perch, sat a brightly colored parrot. The bird screeched loudly in greeting.

"Oh boy!" Jeremy was in ecstasy. "Can I keep him?"

"He is all yours," Logan said, "if it is O.K. with your mom." They both looked at Dori.

"Hey, I'm not going to be the villain in all of this. You may keep him, but you have to feed him and take care of cleaning his cage yourself."

"Famous last words," Logan teased.

"This is the best birthday ever. Thanks, Mr. Hart."

"Look, Jeremy," Dori said, pointing to the window, "it has stopped raining already."

Jeremy threw his hands up in the air. "Yeaaa!" He grabbed the birdcage with both hands and ran with it into his room scattering sunflower seeds everywhere as he went.

"Oh," Dori said, exasperated, "How could you do this to me?"

"Nonsense," Logan said, "don't you know that having pets teach children a sense of responsibility?"

"Hmm," Dori said, unconvinced. "Where did you find him anyway?"

"Howard told me about this old native who lives in St Philips. He catches them when they are young and tames them. The one Jeremy has will even ride around on his shoulder."

"Oh wonderful," Dori said. "My son, the Caribbean pirate." They both laughed at the image.

"There you go again being happy," Logan said.

"Logan, please."

"Alright, alright, I'm leaving." He backed toward the door.

"Wait a minute. I do want to thank you. I know, better than most, that you have so much on your mind, things far more important than a little boy's birthday. I really appreciate it."

"What do you mean?" Logan asked. "I have my ulterior motives. You can give Jeremy a head's up. I plan on winning all of the games and prizes this afternoon." He winked and left.

Dori spent the morning with Sylvia planning the buffet menu for the evening of the twelfth. "Remember that all of the guests staying at Cinnamon Inn will be coming too."

"I know," Sylvia said. "I've got both main refrigerators full of salads and roasted chickens. We are also going to barbeque three pigs outside. Things are under control."

"Well, at lest you won't have lunch to worry about that day. We are sending around notices to all of the guests that Mr. Hart will be hosting a luncheon for them at The Buoy in the honor of independence."

"Well, that's nice." Sylvia smiled. One of her front teeth was missing. Dori knew that she had a bridge. But she had complained to Dori that it bothered her. So she usually kept it in her apron pocket, inserting it only for special occasions.

"It's more than nice. Charles Cliff demanded that all of the guests be out of the hotel between noon and four o'clock. The prime minister will be meeting here with the other island representatives."

Sylvia looked bewildered. "I forgot all about that. Will I have to serve them lunch?"

"No," Dori said. "In fact Mr. Hart wants all of the hotel employees to come into town for lunch too. There are going to be tables set up all along the street just loaded with food."

"Well, I'll come, that's for certain. It will be nice not to have to eat my own cooking for a day." She laughed loudly for several minutes. Then she caught sight of her toothless grin in the bottom of a pan hanging over the gas stove. She dug a hand down into the pocket of her apron pulling out the bridge and put it back into place. "I hate this thing!" she announced.

Frank LeBeau strolled around the gardens of the hotel. He knew the point at which each exterior charge was to be buried. They had each been embedded in the soil laden root structure of the newly planted palm trees. This morning he had observed two of the young men at work by the French doors off the dining room. They were pretending to repair some of the stone steps leading from the terrace to the beach. They were in reality digging new holes, filling them with dynamite and then covering them with additional slabs of stone, creating new steps. By working in broad daylight they attracted little attention.

LeBeau looked up to the top floor of the hotel, trying to imagine what it would be like to watch the entire thing crumble in a matter of seconds. The image made him tingle with excited anticipation. He looked at his watch. It was almost noon. In just a little over forty-eight hours the new order would be taking over in Miranda. He thought about Claire. He couldn't tell her exactly what was going to happen of course. But he did feel sorry for her. The waiting must be agonizing for her since she didn't know what was to take place, or when.

On an impulse, he decided to walk down the beach to Cinnamon Inn and see how she was. He was not prepared for what he found. She was sitting in the middle of the living room floor of her bungalow. She was wearing a ruffled white lace dress, much too youthful for her. Her badly dyed hair spread around her shoulders like red straw. Scattered about her on the floor were faded glossy portfolio pictures of her taken at least twenty-five years ago.

Morgan Talbot had let LeBeau in. "I don't know what is happening to her," she said, "she has lost touch."

"Hello, Frank," Claire said happily, looking up at her visitor. "I haven't seen much of you lately. But then I have been so busy. I'm waiting right now for my agent to call. You know they are remaking *Gone With The Wind*. And it has been whispered that I have a good chance to land the part of Scarlet O'Hara. It's all still very hush hush of course, so don't breath a word of it." She put a finger up to her lips. She had been drinking or taking pills or both and her movements were sloppy.

It was the pressure, LeBeau was certain of that. He got down on his knees and grabbed her hands, looking into her vacant eyes. "Claire, it will all be over soon. I promise. All of this agonizing waiting will be over soon."

"Oh I know," Claire said brightly, "my agent should be calling just any minute now. He just loves to keep me on the string. Once I land this part I just might have to fire him."

Morgan came over and told LeBeau that she thought it would be best if he left. "She is really very tired. Howard says that she gets this way sometimes when she is very upset and hasn't rested. I am going to see if I can persuade her to take a little nap." LeBeau left, shaken.

"If your agent calls dear, I promise to wake you," Morgan coaxed, "but you really need to lie down for a while. You need your sleep. If you do get the part, you will have to be on the set very early tomorrow."

"Of course, you're right, Morgan." Claire said, getting awkwardly to her feet. "You are such a good friend." She walked unsteadily to her room and lay down on the bed. Morgan pulled the shade over the window and left.

Her attitude toward Claire had changed over the weeks. At first she had found her to be an unbelievable annoyance, a conceited, bitter, never-was, who mistreated her gentle husband unmercifully. But during the time she had spent with her she had begun to get a sense of the real Claire Rutledge. She was a pathetic creature who needed understanding rather than condemnation and ridicule. Morgan saw a great deal of herself in Claire, and it frightened her. When she had come to Hollywood she had had the same dreams of stardom shared by all naive actresses. Fortunately, she had been able to fulfill a large number of them. She wondered how she would have reacted had she been always left on the fringes like Claire, forced to live vicariously through the seemingly glamorous lives of other people who had made it. Would she have been able to accept failure any more gracefully than did Claire?

She debated whether or not to tell Claire what she and Howard had planned. She decided against it. She tiptoed back into the bedroom. Claire was fast asleep, exhausted by her frenzied despair.

Jeremy looked ridiculous dressed as Columbus. But Dori applauded his efforts as he rehearsed his role in the Independence Day pageant.

"Look, look I say!" Jeremy shouted on cue. He raised his arms and pointed off into the distance. His long velvet sleeve fell over his hand, reminiscent of the Sorcerer's Apprentice. "Like a jewel the land rises out of the sea! We have discovered heaven!" Dori clapped for him as well as for the rest of the children as they practiced their parts.

When the rehearsal was over Jeremy changed out of his costume into shorts and a red-and-white-striped T-shirt. He gave his velvet robe to the teacher for safekeeping. "Goodbye Mom. I'm going to Dr. Turner's house now."

"Have a good time, honey," she waved as he ran out the door. His teacher came over and spoke to Dori for a moment.

"He is certainly very excited about something." She said.

"He is eight today."

"Oh," said the woman smiling, "well, that explains it."

Dori was about to go back to the hotel when she saw Sarah Hunnicut walking down the hall to her classroom carrying several cardboard boxes.

"What are you doing in here on such a gorgeous day like this?" Dori asked, following the young woman into the room.

"Hi, Dori. I'm packing. I'm leaving today." She was taking books down from a wooden shelf and stacking them in boxes, sealing each lid with heavy shipping tape.

Dori was stunned. "Leaving? Going where?"

"Back to London, for a while anyway, then somewhere else. There is no reason for me to stay here anymore. Perhaps there never was."

Now Dori understood the Trent's recent behavior.

"I'm sorry. I will miss you. I know that we had just started to become friends, but I really will miss you." Sarah put down her tape and scissors for a moment.

"Thanks. I always thought that we could have become good friends too." Then she grinned. "But there is no reason why we still can't. I'll give you my mother's address in London. She will always know where I am. If you ever decide to pop over, please ring me up." She wrote out the address on a slip of paper and handed it to Dori.

"Thank you. I will. Good luck, Sarah." She gave her a brief hug.

She left her there in the small classroom and walked out of the low building to the dusty parking lot. She folded up the scrap of paper upon which the address had been written and put it in her pocket. Why did people, even casual acquaintances, always feel the need to reassure each other that they would stay in touch? She knew that she would most likely never see Sarah Hunnicut again. They both knew it. Yet, instead of simply parting, they carried on this charade. Dori had done it before in college, at graduation, saying goodbye to people while vowing to maintain close ties. And she had seen it at the hotel:

the mad exchange of addresses and phone numbers as guests checked out and bid farewell to other guests. Why did people find it so hard to admit that most relationships in life are of a transitory nature? Why can't they just let go? She suddenly thought about herself and John Salter. Goodbye did not come easily on any level.

XXXIX

It was close to five o'clock when Dori and Logan got in the car to drive to Turner's house and join the birthday party. Dori had noticed that for the past few days Logan had avoided the subject of what he was going to tell Flynn, and when. She wondered if he were any closer to making a decision about what to do with the hotel. She eased into the topic.

"We have been having to turn down reservations all week," she said nonchalantly. "Seems that Mirandan Independence is the equivalent to the Fourth of July and Mardi Gras all in one."

"Don't leave out New Year's Eve," Logan offered.

"That too. I think that the hotel is being very well received. Everyday there is some new tour group trying to book a trip. And many of our guests say that they want to come back next year. I can't imagine that you will ever have a vacancy problem. In fact, your operation is enough to keep Cinnamon Inn alive." Logan was driving. He had been listening intently to what Dori was saying. He knew exactly what she was trying to do. He shook his head.

"It won't work, Dori, but thanks. I am aware of how well Castle Beach is doing. Maybe if it weren't taking off like this it would be easier for me to accept the truth."

"Which is?" Dori asked quickly.

"Which is," Logan sighed, "that Flynn is right. I have created a beautiful albatross. If I had curbed some of the elaborate spending that went into the renovation I might be in better shape now."

"But Logan," Dori insisted, "don't you see that if you hadn't done the hotel exactly as you have it would have been just another Caribbean resort, and the people wouldn't be flocking to it. I remember when we were in New York. I said you wanted to build a monument rather than a hotel. And you did. But that is what makes it the spectacular creation that it is."

"A monument to stupidity," Logan said.

He rounded a corner and took a sharp turn to the left onto a narrow dirt driveway, which led to Turner's modest wooden house tucked privately away near a small cove. There were tall, colorful wildflowers growing in abundance around the property. There was also an arbor covered with deep purple Bougainvillea. A footpath led around the side of the house to a set of old wooden stairs ending at a screened in porch. Dori followed Logan up the stairs.

It struck both of them as strange that there were no sounds of children playing outside. The door to the house was wide open. They walked in slowly. No one was in the kitchen, and there was no evidence of any party preparations. Dori went quickly into the adjoining living room, then the study, then and the bedroom. No one was in the entire house. She returned hurriedly to the kitchen and opened the small refrigerator: no cake, no ice cream, and no party. She was gripped with a kind of panic she didn't comprehend.

"Maybe they are all down at the beach, " Logan suggested.

"Of course," Dori said, the hysteria receding. "I'll bet that Jeremy couldn't wait to show off all of his new swimming gear."

They went out through the open kitchen door and around a stand of tall grassy weeds to the beach. Dori took off her shoes and carried them as she began running toward the shore. A strong breeze had come up and was rippling the shallow water of the tiny bay. She put her hand up, shielding her eyes from the glare of the late afternoon sun. She scanned the shoreline over and over again for a sign of Jeremy or the doctor. Nothing. The entire expanse of sand was deserted.

She turned around to Logan, who was right behind her. "Where are they?" she asked, no longer able to hide the concern in her voice.

"Let's go back inside," Logan said. "Maybe he left us a note. He might have taken them all into St. Philips to watch the parade preparations. After all, he knew that we were coming. I'm sure that is why he left the door open."

They returned to the house. Logan searched the kitchen and the living room. Dori focused on the bedroom and the den. The bedroom was dark and drably furnished. There was a small nightstand near the bed. It held a reading lamp and a tiny vase, holding some wilted wildflowers but there was no note. She went into the den, which contained floor-to-ceiling book shelves filled completely with hardbound medical journals.

On her first pass through the room she hadn't noticed the small desk in the corner of the window. The shade had been pulled down. The dark furniture was almost lost against the walls. She raised the shade, flooding the room with light. She had just started to examine the top of the desk when she saw something that startled her. Arranged neatly, side by side on the desk blotter, were two old and yellowing newspaper clippings. One contained a photograph of her father, taken at least thirty years ago. Another picture was that of Turner, taken at about the same time.

She picked up the clipping with her father's picture and held it close to the window. She read the faded text of the accompanying article:

> Today, a guilty verdict was announced in the much publicized mal-practice suit against Dr. Ransom Turner, a surgical resident at New York City's Cedar Sinai Hospital. It had been asserted that Dr. Turner operated while under the influence of alcohol. The patient was thirteen-year-old Carolyn Stone of Brooklyn Heights. The surgery, which involved a delicate fusion of vertebrae to correct a spinal curvature, resulted in the girl's total paralysis from the waist down.
>
> Dr. Andrew McGee, a resident in pediatrics at the same facility, observed the surgery. The defending attorney conceded that it was McGee's withering testimony that lost the case for his client.
>
> The court awarded the patient damages in excess of five million dollars to be paid by Turner's insurance company, Harrington Life. Turner was also required to forfeit permanently his right to practice medicine in the United States.

Dori's hands were ice cold and trembling. She read the other article that said much the same thing except to add that Turner felt he was being made an unfair example of by the medical profession, and that Andrew McGee testified against him in an attempt to prevent Turner from getting the post of chief pediatric resident at the hospital.

The article said that he planned to leave the country, but vowed revenge on the individuals responsible for ending his medical career.

She heard footsteps behind her and turned around. Logan was standing in the doorway holding a half-empty bottle of cheap scotch. "This was on the living room floor by the couch," he announced. Then he looked more closely at Dori. "My God, what's the matter? You're shaking all over!" She said nothing but handed him the well-worn newspaper clippings; he read them hurriedly.

Dori searched the top of the desk once more. There was a Bible. She picked it up and opened it to a place marker—Chapter Twenty, Verse Five: "I the Lord thy God am a jealous God, visiting the iniquity of the fathers upon the children unto the third and fourth generation of them that hate me."

"Oh Logan, what is happening? What does this mean? Why didn't my father write and warn me about him? He never mentioned him in his letters."

"I hesitate to say this Dori, but maybe he never got your letter."

Dori sunk down to the floor. "My God, Logan, you know what Turner is like when he drinks! Why didn't I call my father right away after that ugly scene he made? Why did I ever let Jeremy come back here again? Where are they?"

Logan kneeled down and put his arms around her and helped her to her feet. "Now is not the time for hindsight. Our main concern is Jeremy. Turner could not have left the island in this short amount of time. He has pulled his phone out of the wall. Let's go back to the hotel and call Salter. He can have all outgoing flights checked, and he can authorize patrols to investigate all of the ships in the harbor. Turner is a familiar figure around here, and so is Jeremy. They can't go far without being noticed."

They sped back to the hotel in silence, each occupied with thoughts too frightening to share. Logan had the accelerator pushed to the floor the entire way. At one point two farmers were herding a group of pigs across the road. Logan swung the car onto the bank of a hill to avoid hitting them. As he drove on he could hear the men cursing and shouting at him. When they reached the hotel his shoulders were in a tight knot.

Dori leapt out of the automobile before it had come to a complete stop and flew through the lobby to the office. She picked up the phone on Logan's desk and called the ministry. The receptionist was far from cooperative.

"I'm sorry, Mrs. Dugan, but the prime minister cannot be disturbed. He is in a private conference with the representative from Trinidad."

Dori was possessed by rage and fear and began screaming incoherently into the telephone receiver. Logan came in and quickly grabbed the phone out of her hand.

"This is Logan Hart. I must speak with John Salter at once. It is an emergency." He looked over at Dori. She had regained a bit of her composure. She was slumped in the chair behind her desk. She was pressing a fist against her mouth to keep from dissolving into total hysteria.

"John," Logan said into the phone, "I need your help right away." Logan quickly explained the situation to the island leader. Then he said, "Thank you. I know Dori will feel much better now." He hung up. "He is going to have some men monitor the harbor and the airport. There is no way Turner can escape."

"But Logan, maybe he has no intention of leaving. Maybe he is just going to take Jeremy off somewhere and..." Her voice caught in her throat.

"Don't say it!" Logan commanded. "Salter is going to send some people out to search the island. He told me to get Howard to work on it as well. He knows the island almost better than any native." Logan came over and took Dori's hands in his.

"We will find them. Try not to worry. Do you think you would feel better if you spoke to your Dad?"

Dori stood up and went over to the window. "No. I realize now that he must not have received my letter. If I call him, he will just worry. And he can't do anything from that distance anyway."

"Right," Logan said, "might as well wait until we locate Jeremy. Then we can call him. He will probably want to wish his grandson a happy birthday."

Dori was fighting back tears. Logan put his arms around her and hugged her tightly. He just held her gently for a few minutes, neither speaking.

Finally he said, "I think that you better go upstairs to your suite and wait for a while. Turner may try and contact you through your direct line."

"Okay," Dori agreed, and walked slowly out of the office. The lobby was filled with guests heading into the dining room for dinner. Their light, airy banter only served to magnify Dori's consuming sense of desperation. She went to her room and went out on the terrace. She saw Logan walking rapidly down the beach toward Howard, who was folding up some lounge chairs and carrying them back to the canvas equipment tent. They talked briefly. Then Howard grabbed two of the beach boys to finish the task and he ran off down the sand toward Cinnamon Inn.

Logan went inside the hotel. Dori lay down on her bed and waited. Traces of orange light from the rapidly descending sun filtered in through the windows. But soon the light disappeared and hardened into darkness. In the next room Jeremy's new feathered pet chattered and squawked, demanding attention. Had it really only been this morning that Logan brought the gift? Time was losing its hourly significance. It was just becoming a series of elongated caverns filled with experiences.

Though her nerves were raw she began to escape into a half sleep, injected with troubled dreams. She saw Chris and Jeremy running happily along the beach, flying a kite. But then she saw that they had stopped laughing and smiling. Their faces became twisted in terror. John Salter, Phillip Graham, and Ransom Turner were coming after them with shiny weapons in their hands. Dori tried to run after the three men and make them stop but her movements were painful and slow. And when she attempted to scream no sound emerged.

She awoke suddenly to the sound of a child's voice in the hall. Jeremy! She rushed to the door and threw it open. A startled young woman walking down the hall with two little girls stared at Dori as she stood in the corridor.

"I'm sorry," Dori apologized, "I thought I heard my son." The other woman said nothing, but turned away.

Dori couldn't stay in the suite any longer. She returned to the office. Logan was there with Howard. "And there has been no sign of them at the airport?" Howard was asking when she walked in.

Logan looked up. "Were you able to get any rest?" he asked.

"A little."

"Well, I think that you ought to have something to eat," Logan insisted. "I am going to call the kitchen and have Sylvia send over a plate."

"Logan, I can't eat anything. My stomach is in my throat."

"Well, I am going to order something for you anyway."

He was just about to pick up the phone when it rang. Dori's heart jumped.

"Hello?" Logan said. "Hello?" he quickly nodded to Dori indicating that it was Turner. She raced to her desk and picked up the extension.

"Ransom, what have you done with Jeremy? Let me talk to him!" She was almost yelling.

Logan put his hand over the mouthpiece. "Go easy, Dori," he cautioned.

Turner sounded drunk and belligerent. "Oh, I am giving little Jeremy a birthday party, don't you remember? Right now we are playing cowboys and Indians and I have got him all tied up." The doctor laughed and then began coughing into the phone.

"Have you hurt him?" Dori asked, her voice under control.

"Oh no, not yet."

Logan whispered to Howard to go and see if the hotel switchboard operator could trace the call.

"What do you want Turner?" Logan asked.

"Oh, I don't want anything, except for Andrew McGee to suffer as I have. I waited and waited for that jury to reach a verdict. And when they did it almost killed me. And I have been dying a little bit every day since then, and so will the little boy, until he is all gone."

Dori put her hand to her mouth and gasped, dropping the receiver.

"If you so much as touch that boy," Logan blurted out.

"Oh, I don't intend to touch him. He is going to die all by himself. And it will be Andrew McGee's fault." Again the coughing and hoarse laughter.

"Mommy?"

"Quick!" Logan called to Dori, "It's Jeremy."

Dori grabbed the phone. "Sweetheart, are you okay? Where are you?"

"I don't know where I am. Dr. Turner has made me wear a blindfold and sit all day. And there was no party. He's acting mean and I'm hungry." The child began to sob.

Turner's voice came over the phone again. "And he is going to get hungrier and hungrier." Then he hung up.

Howard came back into the office and shook his head." She couldn't trace it."

Dori stood, shaking violently with fear staring across the room at Logan. "He is going to starve him to death!"

Logan still held the mute receiver in his hand. "We'll find him."

Men searched the island all night long for the doctor and the boy. Salter assigned Charles Cliff the task of managing the hunt. Cliff assembled the men and provided them with detailed maps of the island sectioned off into pie shaped slices. He sent three men to explore each section. He also announced that he would take the responsibility of investigating the rugged terrain behind Cinnamon Inn. He could not afford to take chances on one of the other men accidently discovering the storehouses of ammunition.

He met Frank LeBeau at the secret retreat shortly after midnight and told him of the recent developments.

"You made a wise choice to cover this area yourself," the Frenchman praised. "We wouldn't want a ridiculous slip up to spoil everything that we have planned and worked for."

Cliff examined the crates of ammunition. Most of the dynamite had been removed. The only thing left was the elaborate timing device.

"Rene is going to install this last," LeBeau explained. "That will be the most delicate part of all. But I have great confidence in his ability."

"As do I," said Cliff. "Where are the men?" he asked.

"Oh, they come and go. They are most likely using this opportunity to work. There must be such confusion at the hotel now that their activities will be unnoticed."

Cliff smiled. The night air was warm and sultry. "What do you think about Turner?" he asked.

"I have always thought that he was psychotic," LeBeau said. "But he's smart. They won't find him. If I know him, he is probably hiding right under their noses."

He was. Shortly after Jeremy arrived at the doctor's house in the afternoon the old man blindfolded him and led him down the beach and up a grassy hill to a cave he himself had dug into the side of it. Turner had been working on the project for weeks. It was long and rather narrow, but tall, close to eight feet. He had stocked the dirt shelter with provisions: food, liquor, and water. He had candles, matches, and blankets. Earlier in the day he had driven his car away from his house into the thick underbrush by the side of the road. Then sometime after ten he lit a candle and led Jeremy, still blindfolded, to the car. They drove into St. Philips, but turned off before they came into the center of town. Turner knew that some of the dock warehouses had pay phones. With shipping operations all but suspended during the week of celebrating, he knew that the chance of being spotted was slight. He parked near the phone and dragged Jeremy with him. The telephones were not enclosed in booths but hung in metal boxes on the side of the buildings. It was from here that he made his call to the hotel. He then went directly back to the cave.

He had allowed Jeremy to drink water, but gave him nothing to eat. When the child asked to go to the bathroom Turner would take him to the entrance of the cave and let him relieve himself in the brush.

By midnight Jeremy had cried himself out and stopped begging to be taken back to his mother. Exhausted, he fell sound asleep on the dirt floor of the cave. Earlier Turner had removed the blindfold but had tied the boy's hands and feet. Now, however, he covered him with a blanket, not out of concern for the child's welfare, but because he wanted to stretch out the agony everyone would be feeling. If the boy were to contract some serious illness, he could quickly die. That would not be good enough.

Turner himself slept fitfully from time to time throughout the night, waking long enough to take a drink from one of his bottles of scotch. But close to dawn he heard voices not far from the cave. He knew that men must have certainly been searching for him. Most probably they had gone first to his house and were now exploring the nearby area.

The child awoke to the noise and was about to call out when Turner jumped on him, gagging his mouth with a corner of the blanket. He kept the boy very still for several minutes. Soon the voices became fainter as the group moved on.

Dori had stayed in the office all night long, hoping that Turner would call again. But the only calls that came in were from Howard, or Victor Trent, who had joined in the search. No news. A physician, who was a guest at the hotel, came in at about seven in the morning, at Logan's request, to give Dori a mild sedative and instruct her to try and get some rest. At first she refused, but as the pill began to take effect she reluctantly agreed to lie down.

Logan took her upstairs to her suite and sat with her, waiting for her to fall asleep. She was physically and emotionally drained.

"He said that it was the best birthday morning he had ever had." She began to sob violently, wearing herself out. And with a deep ragged breath, mercifully sleep came at last.

Logan quietly let himself out and returned to the office. He too was exhausted. And despite all that had happened, he still had work to do. He went into the dining room and ordered breakfast: fruit, scrambled eggs, bacon, toast, and coffee. He felt a little better after he had eaten.

John Salter and Charles Cliff came to the hotel around noon. Unfortunately, they had nothing new to tell him about Jeremy.

"How is Dori?" Salter asked.

"Sleeping, thankfully."

"Well, then I won't disturb her. But please let her know that we are all doing everything we can. My men have searched everywhere, as Charles can tell you. Still no sign of them. But they will turn up, I am certain. But now," he said, changing the subject, "I'm afraid that the matters of state must go on. Tomorrow the conference will be convening here. I would like to go over the seating arrangements with you."

"Fine," Logan said, lacking enthusiasm.

The three men went into the dining room and planned out how the chairs and tables would be placed for the meeting. Salter wanted all of the tables to be put end-to-end and covered with white linen. He wanted everyone to be seated together along the sides of the tables. He would sit at one end with Victor Trent sitting at the other.

"I will require a microphone when I deliver my address," Salter said.

"I'll see to it that it is available," Logan assured him.

Salter seemed satisfied, as did Cliff, with the accommodations. They left to return to the ministry, where Salter had planned to meet privately with more of the various island dignitaries.

The day wore on at an excruciatingly slow pace. By four o'clock the afternoon rains had come and gone, leaving behind damp heavy air thick with the aroma of tropical flowers and wet sand. Dori attempted courageously to go about the business at hand. She went into the kitchen and discussed the plans for decorating the hotel for the independence dance the following evening.

"I want you to have the girls collect all of the Anthuriums they can find in the garden," she told Ruthie, who was helping Sylvia in the kitchen. "I want vases of them at every table, enough so that each woman can take some back to her room after the party."

"Yes, mam," the young black girl said, slicing carrots.

Dori saw that the girl's eyes were red and swollen from crying. "Don't worry, Ruthie," she said, "they are going to find Jeremy." The girl dropped her knife and threw her plump arms around Dori and hugged her. "Just any minute now," Dori whispered, to both of them.

Howard let some of the beach boys run the water equipment concession while he continued to look for Turner. He went to find out if Claire or Morgan had seen or heard anything since he told them yesterday about what had happened. He was disappointed to see that Claire was still in one of her strange moods. Today she was dressed in a long-sleeved black leotard and matching tights. She had some kind of jazz music on the record player and was spinning about awkwardly. Morgan was out on the terrace reading.

"Dance," Claire said when she saw Howard, "takes the grace of a swan and the strength of a pachyderm. I happen to possess both. And when I return to Hollywood I may even open a dance studio. It will give me something to do in between pictures."

Howard was grateful that at least she knew where she was and that evidently she had not been drinking for a while. She was just indulging in fantasy now. She resumed her twirling around the room, inventing movements to the music. Howard went past her to the terrace.

"Have you heard anything about the boy?" Morgan asked, looking up from her paperback.

"No, in fact I was taking a chance that maybe you had seen something."

"I wish I could say that I have. Anyway, Claire is calming down. I think that she will be ready for our surprise soon."

"Well not today," Howard said. "I have got to get back. Poor Hart is about to collapse." He left the terrace and walked back through the living room.

"Turn the record over, will you, Howie?" Claire asked in an irritatingly infantile tone of voice. Howard looked at her. He was disgusted. But he was too tired to argue. He flipped the record over and threw the needle on. It skipped across several bands before resting in the middle of a song. He left, slamming the door.

Claire rushed out on the terrace. She waited until she saw him come down the stairs on onto the lawn.

"Temper! Temper!" she shouted over the railing. He didn't turn around.

Dori spent the evening in the office, still waiting for perhaps another call from Turner. She left the door to the office open, so she could watch the activity in the lobby, in case someone might be looking for her.

At eight o'clock the steel band began as usual pounding their drums wildly while the tourists, seized with the spirit of celebration and lubricated thoroughly with rum, formed a human chain, singing and swaying their way through the foyer and arbor to the garden dance floor. Logan left Dori's side for only brief intervals, just long enough to act as the gracious host, springing to the music with the most influential of dowagers and glad handing visiting tycoons. But he would quickly return to the office to see if Turner had attempted to make contact.

By eleven thirty they had still heard nothing. But close to midnight the phone rang. Dori ripped the receiver from its cradle even before the first ring had been completed.

"Hello?" she said frantically.

"Dori, is it you?" John Salter asked.

She shook her head at Logan who was getting ready to pick up the extension. "Hello, John. Forgive me if I sounded sharp. But I was hoping to hear from Turner. He called earlier last night. But we haven't heard anything since then."

Salter was sympathetic. "I have been hosting a very important dinner for all of the leaders who will be attending the conference tomorrow. If it were at all possible, I would be with you."

"Thank you, John. I realize the pressure you are under. And I appreciate your concern."

The prime minister said goodnight and hung up. Dori came out from behind her desk. The fluorescent office ceiling lights were beginning to give her a severe headache.

"Logan, do you mind if I turn these lights off for a few minutes?" she asked, standing, poised by the main switch at the entrance.

"No, go ahead," he said. "The glare is getting to me too."

She shut the door to the lobby and flipped the switch. At once the room was transformed from the ravaged nucleus of activity to simply a large dark space filled with forms and shadows. The wall length windows at the far end of the room caught the fluttering lights from the garden torches. The vibrating light hit the glass in bold flashes giving the illusion of a small relaxing fire glowing in the corner. It was a tranquil mirage.

Logan sensed its therapeutic effects at once and pulled his desk chair into the middle of the room facing the windows. Then he lined Dori's chair up next to his. They both sat down and just stared out of the windows into the night. For a long time neither of them said anything. They merely sat and listened to the throbbing music and the happy whoops and shouts from the garden dance floor.

"Do you know," Dori asked, "that I would like to go out and scream at all of them to shut up and go away?"

Logan took a chance at comic relief. "I'm afraid that would weigh heavily against you on your employment record."

Dori looked straight at him, astonished by his lack of sensitivity. But then his intentions became obvious to her. She took his hand and held it close to her face and kissed it softly several times.

"Sweet Logan," was all she said.

Suddenly Logan jerked his hand away. "Don't move," he whispered. "Look out the window."

Dori squinted. At first she saw nothing. But then slowly a shape became evident crouched by the base of a large palm tree. It was a man. He was wearing one of the standard hotel uniforms. He glanced furtively several times behind him in the direction of the dance floor around the side of the hotel. He was carrying some large object, wrapped in a beach towel. At one point he stared directly into the office windows. But since the interior lights were out, he could see nothing, yet he himself was silhouetted against the darkness by the light from the burning torches some distance away.

Dori and Logan sat stock-still, waiting for the man to make his next move. Slowly he unwrapped the towel from around the square parcel he carried. In this light, and from this distance, it was impossible for either of them to distinguish what the object might be. But then the man knelt down and began to paw away the dirt from around the tree trunk. He was using some kind of trowel apparatus for digging.

Logan had no idea what the man was doing, but the entire operation seemed bordering on sinister. He had not remembered seeing the man's face before. Aside from that, none of his employees did any landscaping during the night. And even if he were to be engaged in a legitimate enterprise, there would certainly be no need for all of the secrecy.

When the man's back was turned toward the window Logan dropped from his chair to the floor and crawled on his stomach to his desk. Carefully he reached up and pulled open the lower right hand drawer and extracted a small pistol.

Dori had not been following his progress across the room for fear of causing a movement that could be noticed by the man working outside. Thus when Logan returned to his seat by a series of protracted crawls, she was stunned to see a gun in his hand. She had known that Ramino had given him one to protect the safe during the backgammon tournaments, but she had never seen it. She said nothing.

Outside the man was still digging. Finally he stopped and glanced over his shoulder several additional times before carefully lowering the square shaped object into the newly dug hole.

All at once, without warning, Logan leapt to his feet and rammed his chair through the floor length window. There was an explosion of glass. For a brief moment the man outside was rigid with shock. It was during this precious passage of seconds that Logan jumped through the flying bits of glass and dove upon the man, knocking him to the ground. Logan buried the muzzle of the gun in the back of the man's sweating neck.

"My hand is trembling," Logan said directly into the man's ear. "If you make a single attempt to move your head, I will pull this trigger."

The man lay flat against the ground breathing heavily. The shattering window had been no competition for the raucous thundering of the steel drum band. And the dancing went on uninterrupted by events just yards away.

"Dori!" Logan called. Dori had been collapsed against the back of her chair but came out through the jagged hole in the wall of windows.

"Logan, you're bleeding badly," she said, looking at his arms and hands.

"I'm okay. Please. Just go quickly, but calmly, and find Howard. He might be on the beach or wandering around by the dancers. Make up any excuse to bring him here but don't sound alarmed. And don't run, walk!"

Dori left, strolling casually through the lobby. She was wearing a print skirt with big side pockets. She slipped her hands into them to conceal the fact that she was shaking. She smiled at the mingling guests as she passed by. Once outside she increased her pace a bit getting down to the shoreline. The evenly spaced torchlights illuminated the beach. She saw couples, and groups of young teenagers, sitting in the sand or wading at the water's edge. But Howard was nowhere around.

She started running to the dance floor forgetting, for an instant, Logan's instructions. She had slowed down to an easy walk by the time she reached the garden bar. Mandy was serving a big rum punch to Frank LeBeau who was sitting on a stool.

"Hello," Dori said lightly, "have either of you seen Howard anywhere?"

"Have they found your boy?" Frank asked.

"No, I'm afraid not yet. But I am confident that they will very soon. Logan wants Howard to take the station wagon into St. Philips. Four of our guests arrived this morning without their luggage. Some mix-up in Barbados. But it's all here now. We just got a call from the airport. Poor Logan. You would think that it was his fault that these people misplaced their bags. They have been causing a mild harangue about it all day. I think he is more thrilled than they are that it has been located."

Frank took a sip of his foamy cocktail. "What a business. It would drive me crazy."

"There's Howard," Mandy said, nodding his head in the direction of the beach.

Dori turned around. Howard was lumbering toward the bar. He was soaked. "Some fool kids took one of the sunfish out without permission. Capsized it right away. I just had it out with their folks. I know a few smart alecks who won't be doing a lot of sitting for a while." He laughed. Then suddenly he remembered the boy. "Jeremy!"

"No, Howard," Dori said, "nothing yet. But Logan wants to see you right away. Come on." They started toward the lobby.

What a treat you've got in store, LeBeau smiled after them, then focused his full attention on his drink.

Once out of sight of the bar Dori rapidly whispered the details of what had happened to Howard. He burst through the office door and ran out of the broken window. He took the gun from Logan, who got unsteadily to his feet and stood aside. Howard pulled the thin young black man up with one hand and marched him back into the office. He held the gun on him while Logan examined the contents of the hole. He didn't know much about explosives, but he could certainly recognize sticks of wrapped dynamite and a timing device. He didn't touch any of it. But he quickly glanced at the detonation clock. It was set for three p.m., July twelfth. He covered it over with loose dirt and then returned to the office.

His arms and hands were soaked with freshly dried blood. But luckily, all of his wounds were superficial. Dori had gone into the linen supply closet and brought back washcloths and towels. She wet several cloths from the pitcher of water on Logan's desk and washed the dirt and blood from his cuts.

298

Logan took the gun from Howard and told the frightened black man to sit on the floor in the far corner of the room, which he did.

"Howard," Logan said, "I know that we have replacements for this glass in the basement storage units. I want you go get a couple of your boys, ones you know," he added, looking at the stranger in the hotel uniform. "Get this window repaired immediately. It has got to be done before daylight. And say nothing of what has happened. And then please, just stay here. You can sleep on the cot until I contact you."

"Okay," Howard said. He went at once about the task of chipping away the remaining slivers of glass still clinging to the window frame.

"Come with me," Logan instructed Dori. Then he proceeded to take the man out through the broken window again, around the far garden path running in front of the hotel to the side service stairs. They climbed many flights before arriving at the top floor and Dori's suite. They had passed no one on their way. Dori quickly took the key from her pocket and opened the door, then closed and locked it once they were all safely inside.

"No one will bother you tonight. Everyone knows about Jeremy. So your room will not be disturbed." Again he had the man sit on the floor in a corner. "Call Salter," he said.

Dori placed the call. Again she got the same ministry receptionist she had the previous afternoon. "This is Dorothy Dugan," she said calmly. "I want to speak to the prime minister at once." This time she got no argument from the woman. Salter must have said something to her after the last episode.

Soon she heard John's voice, full of sleep.

"Dori, what is it?"

"It has nothing to do with Jeremy," she said and handed the phone to Logan.

"Salter, get over here right away." Logan commanded. "Dori will meet you in the lobby."

"Hart, I have got to get some rest. I have an important speech to give tomorrow. If it has nothing to do with the boy, then I can't possibly see why I—"

Logan cut him off. "Come at once." There was a desperate urgency in Hart's voice that made Salter uneasy. "If any of your guests see you leave, just tell them that it has something to do with Turner. But come! And come alone." He hung up.

Dori went down to the office to wait. Howard and two young beach boys were already in the process of replacing the window. When Dori saw the familiar headlights of Salter's car pull up in the driveway she started out to meet him.

"Howard," she asked as she left, "if by any chance a call comes in for me here, please have it transferred to my suite." Howard, helping the boys lift a large pane of glass into place, nodded that he would.

Dori met Salter outside and led him around to the side and up the stairs. She knocked on the door of her suite. "It's Dori, Logan." He opened the door and they came inside. Salter stared in shocked disbelief at what he was seeing: Logan, bloodied and holding a gun on a hotel employee.

"What is this?" Salter wanted to know.

Logan explained what had happened, that he had discovered the man outside the office planting a box of explosives. "He doesn't work for the hotel," he said indicating the man sitting in the corner of the living room. "Somehow, he managed to get a uniform."

Salter's face became rigid and hard. But there was fear in his expression. He grabbed the mute terrorist crouching on the floor and dragged him to his feet. Then he hit him several times across the face. Dori turned away. The interrogation had begun. The man resisted answering questions about what he was doing here or who had hired him, until Salter took him out on the balcony and began to shove him over the railing.

"You see, you are useless to us if you fail to provide us with information. It would serve our purposes better to simply throw you to your death and then wait and see who comes to identify you." He pushed the horrified man further and further over the railing until all that separated him from a violent death were the large arms of the prime minister.

"The Chameleon," he blurted out, barely able to speak.

Salter hoisted him back onto the terrace where he crumbled to the floor. Salter's mind was racing. He had heard that name before, aboard the *Kiwi*, with Ramino and Mariani.

"Who is this Chameleon? What is his name?"

"I do not know." The man spoke with a Cuban or Haitian accent. Salter hit him again. Already the young man's mouth was swollen. "I don't know his name. We were just told to call him the Chameleon."

"We?" Salter said.

"There are six of us."

"What does this Chameleon look like?" Salter asked.

Dori and Logan were standing a few yards away watching the scene.

"He is Mirandan."

Salter's jaw tightened and he gritted his teeth.

"Young, old, black, white, what?!" He hit the captive once more. There was a loud crack like a bone had broken in the man's face. He screamed out in pain. Dori thought that she was going to be sick.

The man sputtered his reply. "Young, very black, very serious, big thick glasses." Salter relinquished his tight hold on the man's throat. Then he turned slowly to Logan and Dori. They all knew who he had identified.

"Charles Cliff," Salter said in appalled amazement. "Charles Cliff," he repeated.

For the next few hours the questioning continued. They learned of the plot engineered by Ramino and Mariani and implemented by Cliff and Frank LeBeau. By four in the morning Dori couldn't take it anymore. She went into Jeremy's room and lay down on the bed. Where was her little boy?

Logan called down to the office and asked Howard to come up to the suite. He told him to bring some strong rope. He then turned his attention to Salter.

"I want him to stay here as guard. You and I must go down to the office and talk." Salter agreed that Howard could be trusted with the information. Logan went into the hall bathroom and finished the job of cleaning his cuts.

When Howard arrived Logan told him everything they had learned.

"We must decide what we are going to do," Logan said.

"I can't believe that this is happening," Howard said. "All of this." He tied the prisoner up and agreed to stand vigil over him. But the man was hardly a threat anymore. He was so battered he simply crouched in a corner groaning.

Logan and the prime minister locked themselves in the office and closed the curtains over the newly installed windows. Salter was devastated.

"I knew that there were groups of malcontents circulating through the islands attempting to organize take overs and rebellions, but somehow I thought that Miranda was immune." He laughed a dry, bitter laugh. "And Charles Cliff, my trusted protégé behind it all."

His expression became angry and he pounded a desk with his fist. "I have been trying to tell the American and British government officials that the Caribbean needs their military support to resist these terrorists. But ever since Grenada and Nicaragua no one wants to get involved in the dirty job of defending small democracies. So they fall, one by one, a coup here, an assignation there. And bit by tiny bit, ostensibly insignificant countries become controlled by radical factions with diverse ideological agendas. But the foreign governments don't care until it begins to hit them in the pocketbook. That is all they understand. Oh, certainly they will help Israel and also placate the Arabs. Conflicts in the Middle East command their attention. They must try to keep peace to maintain their supply of oil. And Africa, naturally they will come to the aid of Africa. Their corporations are there. And it's too damn big to simply ignore. So they send their arms and their money and their diplomats.

"But what about Miranda or the other islands in the West Indies? They stormed Grenada and that's that? All is well? Do they really think that there is no use in getting involved in the internal struggles of such after thoughts of countries? Because what do we offer the world: sun and sand, rum and spices, a stalk of bananas? That is surely not enough to worry about. But they don't get the big picture." Salter's face was covered with sweat and his eyes were bulging from their sockets. "There are new groups of revolutionaries who have designs on all of the islands in the Caribbean. Their ultimate aim is to have total control of the Atlantic Ocean between Florida and Venezuela in order to permit the trafficking of God knows what. And believe me, they are financed by the worst political and criminal elements in your country."

Logan's back was in a knot. Salter went on. "The Americans cheered when Miranda gained its independence from England. They hailed it as the end of colonialism and the dawning of freedom for a proud people. And they encouraged trade and tourism here. But they really don't take us seriously. We are but an amusement park for America and Europe as well. They have no idea of our strategic, political potential."

Logan was listening earnestly. Salter had a right to be angry. Everything he was saying was most likely correct. But at this point the diatribe was becoming too philosophically abstract. He was about to tell him exactly that when a strange look came over the black man's face.

"Wait a minute," Salter said, thinking. "Perhaps there is a way to use this impending disaster to our advantage."

"What?" Logan said, incredulous.

"Do you have casualty insurance on the hotel?"

"Of course, as extensive as one can get operating in a foreign country. But why?"

"Listen to me, Hart. Dori told me about your precarious financial situation." Logan was embarrassed. "Don't be angry with her. She is just very concerned about it."

"Yeah well, we have more important things to discuss right now."

"You are not hearing me," Salter said. "Why can't we allow the demolition to go off as planned?"

"What!" Logan yelled and stood up. "Are you crazy?"

"No, I'm not. We will let the plan go on as scheduled. However, we will remove everyone from the hotel, and at the last minute I will move the conference to the ministry. And if what that pathetic man upstairs said is true, and I think that it is, he is too frightened to lie, Cliff will be aboard the *Kiwi* with Ramino and Mariani at the time of the demolition. They will be watching it from offshore. Let them believe that it has gone perfectly. When they come to take possession of the ministry we will be waiting for them, all of them. Their plot to kill all of the conservative West Indian leaders will be exposed to the world.

Perhaps the United States will begin to see the real force being wielded down here and will do something about it, to make sure that it doesn't happen again. A plan of this magnitude is enough to make them a little bit frightened, and England, too. Remember, Victor Trent is to be attending the conference. They had planned on killing him also, to say nothing of the guests of the hotel."

Logan was staring in total disbelief at Salter. But the prime minister would not be deterred. "And you will lose the hotel that you were going to lose eventually, but this way you will collect enough insurance to salvage some of your holdings in the states and have enough left over to pursue new ventures."

Logan's mind was reeling. The scheme was the most bizarre thing he had ever heard. The music from the dance floor had stopped several hours before. But the sounds of a few tired, happy guests walking through the lobby on their way to the elevators came drifting in through the closed office doors. Logan shut his eyes and messaged his forehead. His entire body was aching from tension and exhaustion. And now, the cuts inflicted from the shattering glass were beginning to painfully sting and throb.

He thought of Flynn waiting in New York. He would be thrilled if a "lucky" tragedy like this were to happen. Logan would be able to save both his money and his face. He could hear the lawyer already on the cocktail circuit: "Poor man, what a bad break, just when the place was really gaining momentum. Hotel had made him a millionaire several times over. What a jewel! But he will do it again. Not a quitter, that boy!"

Logan started toward the door. He turned back to Salter. "Dori has been with me from the time this whole place was just a wild daydream. She deserves to be consulted. Wait here."

He left the prime minister and went back upstairs. Howard was sitting on a chair watching the young captive asleep on a rug.

"You think that you will be able to hold out for a few more hours?" Logan asked. Already the sky was beginning to lighten. "Would you like me to spell you?"

"No, I'll be fine. I'll let you know if I need a break."

"Thanks, Howard. You have really been great through all of this."

Logan slowly opened the door to Jeremy's room. Dori was lying down, staring at the ceiling. She turned on a bedside lamp when she saw Logan. It cast a soft amber light on her face.

"Dori, I have to talk to you about something."

"Jeremy!" She sat up straight and swung her feet over the side of the bed.

"No, but try not to worry so much. I know that he will be found safe and sound very soon. I just know it. This is about the hotel." Carefully he explained everything Salter had said to him to convince him to go through with it.

"Why are you talking to me about it?" she asked.

"Because I need your advice."

"It would solve a lot of your problems."

"I know. No one would ever discover that I failed down here."

"Except yourself," Dori said.

"I was hoping you would say that. I have been thinking. I don't know if I could live with all of it."

"Well, Logan, that is something only you can decide."

Suddenly the phone rang in the next room. Dori leaped off the bed and rushed to answer it. She picked up the receiver. It was Turner.

"Just wanted to see how everybody was. Worried I hope. Your little boy is asleep now."

"Ransom!" Dori screamed into the mouthpiece. "Why are you doing this?"

"I told you why. It's just a little matter of retribution. An eye for an eye you know. It's your daddy's entire fault. Just remember that." He was slurring his words badly. That meant that he had been drinking continuously since the kidnapping.

"Is Jeremy alright?"

Turner began laughing. "Oh, he's fine. But he is a little bit hungrier than he was yesterday." Turner began laughing and coughing.

"Please let me speak to him."

"I told you, he is sleeping," Turner snapped. "Anyway, he's not with me."

Logan grabbed the receiver from Dori's hand. "Turner," he began, I thought you might like to know that Dori's father has just arrived to be with her. Howard is driving him back from the airport right now."

Dori looked at him, confused. She started to take the receiver from him. He shook his head and motioned for her to step back. At first he thought that Turner had hung up. But then he heard the congested breathing.

"Well, goody for all of you. I don't ever want to see that son of a bitch again. But I am glad that he is here to worry and to wring his hands and feel guilty." The line went dead.

Logan held Dori's hand and guided her back to Jeremy's room.

"Why did you do that?" she said.

"I have an idea. I am going to go ahead with Salter's plan. I am going to let the hotel go."

"But what does that have to do with what you just told Turner?"

"I am taking a gamble that once he learns about what has happened to the hotel, he will come out to investigate. After all, if he thinks that both you and your father have been killed, then his plan of revenge will be meaningless." Logan had left the connecting door to the bedroom open. Howard had heard the conversation.

"That is a hell of a way to try and flush him out," Howard said.

"Howard," Logan said, "for a number of complex reasons I have no alternative. And I am sorrier than I can say."

"I understand," Howard offered weakly, "I guess."

Howard didn't understand any more than Logan did what was happening. But the times were not calling for insight, they were demanding action. Logan returned with Dori to the office and told Salter his decision, as well as what he had told Turner.

They all spent the remainder of the hours of early dawn making plans to evacuate the hotel. All of the guests had been invited to a luncheon Logan was hosting at The Buoy. Dori produced a brief flyer instructing everyone that they must be out of the hotel by noon. The notice said that due to the complaints of mosquitoes and small lizards in some of the rooms, the entire hotel would be fumigated between the hours of twelve and four. No one would be allowed to remain in their rooms or to be within a quarter mile radius of the hotel.

Salter assured Dori and Logan that he would be able to take care of his side of the arrangements without giving Cliff any reason to be suspicious.

"I will bring all of the conference guests here at one o clock. Then I'll dismiss Cliff. That will give him time to join the rest of his conspirators aboard the *Kiwi*. While they are coming around the bay to be in a position to view the demolition from a safe, off shore, distance I will simply move the conference back up the hill to the ministry. You can join us there at two."

Salter left the hotel just in time to change into his full military dress. He was scheduled to lead the independence parade through St. Philips. It began at ten in the morning and was followed by a series of plays, more street dancing, and more feasting.

Cliff was waiting anxiously in the prime minister's bedroom when Salter walked in. "I've been very concerned. What detained you so long last night?"

"Hart thought he had spotted Turner and the boy. But it wasn't them, just some guests. Naturally, Mrs. Dugan was quite upset. I stayed on to be with her." Tell him what he wants to hear, Salter thought as he began to undress. Let him think that you spent the night making love. It will only add to his false sense of security.

"Oh yes, of course," Cliff said. "This must be an extremely difficult time for her."

"Extremely," Salter said. He tried very hard not to have too much direct eye contact with his underling. He had been able to keep the hatred and loathing he was feeling for this man from his voice. But he was not certain that he would be able to banish it from his eyes.

"I will start your shower for you," Cliff said. "As you can see I have already laid out your clothes for this morning's activities."

"Thank you, Charles," Salter said, slipping into a bathrobe. "I really don't know what I would do without you." He smiled at Cliff and stepped past him into the steaming shower, dropping the robe on the bathroom floor.

XL

Dori and Logan were the first ones to eat breakfast in the dining room that morning. They both had to force any food down at this point. It all tasted like cardboard. But they were smart enough to realize that they could not expect to operate on little more than sheer adrenalin for three solid days.

"Logan, there is so much that should be saved from the hotel," Dori said, heaping sugar into her coffee.

"Forget it," Logan said, "I have thought of that too. But we can't let ourselves start thinking about everything that is going to be destroyed. I don't know if I could go through with this if I did. Just pack a small suitcase for yourself and Jeremy, and put them in the back of my car." He sighed. "I just keep telling myself that if this thing will bring Jeremy back safely, it will be worth it. His return will be enough to negate any pangs of guilt I might feel over what I am doing. And do you know, the more I think about it, the more convinced I am that it will work. Turner is a vindictive man. That's true. After all, he saved those newspaper clippings for all of these years. He has probably been planning this horrific event since we first arrived on Miranda. Making your father suffer means more to him than harming Jeremy. And the reason he won't let himself sober up is because if he did, he would realize how futile all of this is, and how fond of Jeremy he truly is. It will work, Dori, believe me!"

Dori looked across the table at Logan. These past months on the island had taken a sever toll on him, to say nothing of just the past few days. He was haggard and thin and looked more than his forty-five years.

"I do believe you," Dori said, and drank from her second cup of sweetened coffee. "I have to."

They took breakfast trays up to Howard and the captive. Both ate eagerly, though the young black man seemed to be in extreme pain. One side of his face was terribly swollen from the repeated blows Salter had inflicted.

"Howard, we have got to get him out of here soon, " Logan said. "You too. But where can you go?" They all thought for a moment.

"I've got it," Howard said. "Because of the celebration in St. Philips today, I won't be issuing any fins or masks. And the sunfish won't be used. If you can get a laundry hamper up here, I can put him in the bottom and cover the top with beach towels. Then I can wheel it out to the equipment tent. I'll stay in there with him until," he paused, "until it's over."

"Is that place safe enough?" Dori asked.

"Oh yeah, it's far enough away."

Logan arranged for the hamper. Together he and Howard lifted the black man into the bottom of it and arranged hotel beach towels loosely over him. Howard made certain that the prisoner was fitted with a gag before he wheeled the canvas hamper out into the hall and onto the elevator. Logan accompanied him while Dori went to distribute the newly printed flyers in the dining room.

On their way down to the beach, Mandy came over to talk with Howard. Neither Logan nor Howard knew of his involvement in the overthrow.

"Good morning," Mandy said. "What have you got there? Let me help you."

Logan and Howard exchanged brief glances. Both were debating whether or not Mandy should be told. Logan was about to tell him when Howard said, "No thanks, just a bunch of beach towels. You're gonna have your work cut out for you tonight at the outdoor dinner. How are the pigs coming along?"

"I am on my way to check the pits now."

"Well, after you do that," Logan said, "I want you to take the day off. Go into town. The Buoy is serving lunch today on me."

"That includes drinks, too," Howard added. "It will give you a chance to see what a mixed drink is supposed to taste like." They all laughed and then Mandy went on his way.

"I don't even trust him anymore," Howard said. "He's been pretty thick with LeBeau lately. And didn't you say that this guy you captured said that LeBeau is in on it?"

"Well, he didn't know his name, but he described him perfectly," Logan admitted.

Howard unzipped the tent and they wheeled the container inside. Fins, masks and snorkels were stacked against one wall of the tent with beach mats and sun umbrellas against another.

"I think that I am gonna keep him in here," Howard said, indicating the hamper. He removed a few of the towels and checked on his captive. The gagged and bound man stared up at him defiantly. Howard draped one large towel across the top and folded up the rest and put them on the floor.

"I guess you are going to have to drive some of the guests into St. Philips since I had better stay here."

"Okay," Logan agreed, "that's fine. I'll check back with you from time to time before I leave at noon." Then on an impulse he asked, "How is Claire? We haven't seen her lately."

Howard heaved a big ragged sigh. "She is in one of her moods."

By now Logan knew exactly what that meant. "Would you like me to see if she and Morgan would be interested in coming into town for the day?"

"Thanks sincerely, Logan. But I think that Claire is better off at home when she gets like this. Morgan is taking care of her."

Logan left and went back into the lobby. He glanced at his watch: ten o'clock. Dori was already herding guests into the island cabs.

"When you get to The Buoy," she instructed, "just tell them that you are from the hotel. Everything will be free." She winked at one of the older men. "Now I expect to see you dancing in the street when I get there."

The man chuckled and kicked up his heels a bit, while his wife stood nearby smiling. "He hasn't stopped dancing since we got here," she said.

Some of the guests were more reluctant to leave. Three teenaged girls, all daughters of the same exasperated couple, stood in the lobby complaining.

"I don't want to go watch some ridiculous pagan ritual and be pressed against all of those sweaty people," one of them said. "I would rather stay here and work on my tan."

The father shared Dori's frustration. "Don't ever let them tell you that travelling is broadening," he said. "At least not at their age. We have taken them practically around the world and their favorite place is still the pool at our country club in Dayton, where they and their equally privileged pals can spend afternoons ordering diet Cokes and talking about how bored they are. Spoiled brats."

But eventually they, too, were coaxed into the station wagon and driven into town. By eleven thirty everyone but the kitchen help were out of the hotel. Logan rechecked all of the rooms to be sure. Sylvia, Ruthie, and some of the other girls were setting up the tables in the dining room as Salter had requested, in one long row, covered with white linen cloths.

Logan hooked up a microphone at one end of the table and was in the process of testing it when Charles Cliff entered the room.

"Everything looks perfect," he proclaimed happily.

I'll bet it does, Logan thought. Dori watched as the young man smiled and walked around the room. She couldn't fathom this man. For all he knew he was about to be responsible for the deaths of nearly twenty people. The number would have been much greater if they had not cleared the guests from the hotel.

Dori, of course, was aware of the violent nature of terrorists, driven by their rigid ideologies. It was impossible to read any newspaper in the world without being horrified at the lengths to which dedicated revolutionaries would go in the name of a cause. But being directly involved in the process was an entirely different experience.

"Well," Cliff said after he finished touring the room, "the delegates shall be arriving soon. I think that this address will be one of the prime minister's most effective. I am sure this day will be remembered for years to come. Good afternoon." He strolled out of the dining room and through the lobby. Logan just shook his head in astonishment at the calculated ruthlessness of the man.

At noon, Dori got in her car accompanied by Ruthie while Logan, after checking once more with Howard, took Sylvia and the rest of the girls into town with him. He was driving the station wagon, since he had allowed a group of guests to drive his Mercedes into St Philips. It was the only way he could think to get his car safely away from the hotel. Somehow, he felt that he had to salvage that much. As the station wagon pulled out of the circular driveway it passed the first of the limousines carrying Salter and his guests.

The native girls chattered excitedly on their way into town about all of their boyfriends who were going to dance with them. They were all dressed in what Logan imagined to be their finest clothes: long flowery printed skirts and white blouses with lace jackets. When the car rounded a corner he looked back in the rear view mirror at the hotel. For a moment his eyes welled with tears. He quickly blinked them away. His throat tightened and was dry and ached. But he bit his lip and drove on.

He had never seen St. Philips look so spectacular. All of the lampposts had been decorated with flowers and paper streamers. The yachts in the harbor bounced from side to side and their masts, strung with bright red and yellow balloons, looked like giant metronomes swaying rhythmically to the music that came from everywhere. People ran through the streets in wild costumes, waving banners proclaiming the anniversary of Mirandan independence. The remnants of the morning parade participants were still in attendance. Choirs sang patriotic songs and school children reenacted their play many times. Dori felt her heart began to pound when she saw one of Jeremy's classmates dressed in the velvet robes of Columbus.

"Please, God," she whispered, "protect him and bring him home to me." She parked her small car behind the station wagon on the dirt road leading to the church. Ruthie scrambled out to join her friends. They all vanished into the crowd together. Logan came over and took Dori's hand. Out of nowhere, Albert, the little boy who always watched the cars, appeared. Logan gave him some money.

"This time, don't let anyone park so we can't get out."

"Not me!" he said, taking the money and winking.

Dori smiled at him. He was a little older than Jeremy. She looked out into the throngs of people. Where was he? They made their way slowly down the street through the milling crowd. Several times when Dori became separated from Logan a party-going Mirandan would grab her and begin dancing her around in the street. But eventually she would manage to break away.

Finally they reached The Buoy. Even though the restaurant had a large dining room and deck, they were not adequate to take care of the onslaught of people comfortably. The platters of food had been set up on tables around the room. People were sitting and standing, holding their drinks and plates, trying to figure out how to eat. But they all seemed to have caught the spirit of the moment and the atmosphere was happy and relaxed. The food looked as delicious as it was abundant: lobster, crab and shrimp stuffed into huge avocado halves, grilled steaks and chicken, every kind of island fruit and vegetable, and loaves of freshly baked bread.

Logan succeeded in getting around to greet many of the hotel guests. Dori stood near the entrance with Allison Trent who had come while Victor was attending the conference.

"If only there were something I could do for you now," she said sincerely to Dori.

"There is," she said. "Please pray for Jeremy's safety." Dori bit down on the inside of her cheek to keep from breaking into sobs.

"I have been," Allison assured her, grabbing her hand and squeezing it for a moment.

Dori noticed that the pouting teenage girls had found an unexpected pleasure: three young American boys who were working at The Buoy. The girls were all smiles and charm now, giggling almost constantly. Dori wondered briefly if she had been as silly at their age. She glanced at her watch: one o'clock.

Everyone was seated at the places designated by Salter. Victor Trent looked down from the long table at the collection of West Indian leaders and representatives. It was quite an impressive assemblage. He was grateful that John had included him in the conference. He understood that his appearance here was taken as a token gesture, but he appreciated it never the less, even more than the prime minister might know, since this would be Victor's last official function. He had just received conformation that his request to return to the home office had been granted.

Salter tested the microphone. It was working properly. Charles Cliff stood by the door until Salter signaled that he was ready to begin. Then Cliff nodded politely to the man he thought he would never see again and left the dining room, closing the double doors behind him. Salter began his prepared address in case Cliff had lingered outside. He hadn't.

Once he shut the doors, Cliff raced out of the lobby and took off down the beach, running wildly. He passed beneath Cinnamon Inn and climbed over the rocks near the water's edge. In his haste he fell several times on the seaweed-covered terrain, scraping his hands and legs. But in less than twenty minutes he was at the site of the small boat. LeBeau had already started the motor in anticipation of his companion's scheduled arrival. Cliff hurried out into the water to meet him. He climbed over the side. The lenses of his thick glasses were drenched with water by the time he got in and sat down across from the Frenchman.

"Perfection," was all Cliff said, smiling broadly.

They travelled quickly out to the *Kiwi* and got on board, securing their boat behind the yacht's own dingy. Once inside the salon, Cliff related to an anxious Ramino and Mariani how well everything had gone. Ramino instructed the captain to motor out about a mile and a half and then drop anchor in front of the Castle Beach Hotel.

"I can bring her in a lot closer than that, sir," the skipper said. "That ground is clean, no rocks at all, and fairly deep water almost to shore."

"I said a mile and a half out!" Ramino snapped. "This vessel is still chartered to me until five o'clock today. And those are my orders."

Ramino wanted to position them far enough away to watch the demolition through binoculars, but not close enough to be recognized in case Salter or Hart were anywhere around. They were both too familiar with the *Kiwi*.

Mariani uncorked a bottle of champagne. This time Cliff, who normally abstained, joined in the toasting to the venture, gulping down the bubbling wine.

"Where are Rene and the other dynamite men?" Ramino asked.

"In seclusion about the island," LeBeau said. "I gave them instructions yesterday to meet us this afternoon at the ministry at five o'clock."

"Very good," Mariani said, lifting his glass.

Suddenly Cliff began laughing uncontrollably.

"I fear that our gallant young friend does not tolerate alcohol well," LeBeau smiled.

"It's not that," Cliff said. "I am just thinking. This morning Salter said that he didn't know what he would do without me. And now he is walking around in what will soon be his coffin with the rest of the capitalist puppets. He is telling them that the West Indies must seek American and English military aid if they are to turn back the tides of revolution. And he didn't know what he would do without me."

This time the joke was shared by all.

XLI

As his guests listened in horrified silence Salter explained what had happened during the night, as well as what was going to happen within a few brief hours. Then sedately, according to the plan that had been quickly adopted, they filed out of the dining room, through the now-empty lobby and out into the main parking area. Limousines drove them back up the hill to the ministry. Salter escorted them all into the small cherry wood paneled meeting room. There he went into a further explanation of why he was not going to halt the planned destruction of the hotel.

"If I were to let it be known that their plot had been discovered, our chances of capturing the leaders of the organization would be remote. As it is now, they will walk into this room voluntarily in just a matter of hours. We shall then be able to discover if their network of support is as vast as I suspect it must be.

"All of you are aware of the fact that our pleas for military support from the United States, and yes, Victor, from England also, have fallen on deaf ears in the past. Perhaps after today they will listen."

Salter sat down. The large wooden ceiling fans spun monotonously around and around overhead, circulating the warm humid air throughout the room. All of the delegates were in shock and subdued with personal thoughts. Each of them now realized that if it had not been for a quirk of fate, they would never have seen their homes or families again. Salter studied the men—frightened children, all of them. He reluctantly included himself in this designation. Coming face to face with the prospect of one's eminent mortality humbles the most powerful of rulers.

One by one, in a spontaneous outpouring of gratitude, the representatives stood up and came over to the prime minister and embraced him warmly. They each assured him of their financial and moral support during the difficult time that would most certainly follow today's events.

Victor was the last to approach the prime minister. The two men looked deeply into the eyes of the other. Salter saw a towheaded boy running awkwardly behind him on the cricket field. And Victor was remembering his strong, but kind, playmate and tutor. The tremendous affection and loyalty each man had for the other transcended words, so no words were spoken. But Victor extended his hand and John grabbed it with both of his and the two men embraced briefly. Then Victor returned to his place, his heart filled with a strange kind of joyful sorrow.

Ransom Turner was running out of liquor. Returning to his cave in the early dawn hours after completing his call to the hotel he had stumbled into two bottles of scotch and they shattered on the floor, sacrificing their precious contents to the dirt. And now, sitting just inside the mouth of the rock shrouded den, Turner cradled in his lap the only soothing libation that remained: a bottle of warm bourbon, more than half empty.

The doctor's face was drawn and filthy. Dried dirt and saliva clung to three day's growth of grey stubble. His red eyes were sunken pockets in his head, and were surrounded by puffy, ashen flesh. He had eaten little of the crackers, cheese, and fruit stored in the back of the hollow. But Jeremy had been given even less to eat, having been allowed only a small overripe banana a day and some water. He was weak, and slept most of the time. When he was awake he would cry and beg the doctor to take him to his mother. Turner would always refuse. And if the child had irritated him enough, he would slap him several times across the face and order him back to his blanket, where the boy would cry himself to sleep.

Jeremy was sleeping now. It had been an exceptionally hot morning. The sun penetrated the leafy covering at the opening of the cavern until the temperature inside the musty hole became almost unbearable. That was why Turner had moved closer to the front, dragging the boy on the blanket as he went. But now the cooling afternoon rain was offering a brief respite from the inferno.

Turner took another deep swallow of the bourbon. The inside of his mouth was raw from the alcohol and dotted with canker sores. But the prospect of sobriety was more frightening to him than was any pain brought on by these minor afflictions. So he continued to drink. Ever since Hart had told him that Andrew McGee had arrived in Miranda, Turner had become a man possessed.

"Right now that bastard is only a few miles from here." He was practically spitting his words. "I'll bet he's sorry now for ruining my life. I told him that he would pay. He didn't believe me then. Ha! He should have known that I don't make idle threats." He nudged the sleeping boy. "I don't make idle threats, ya know!" he yelled, drooling.

Jeremy opened his eyes and stared up at the ranting, ugly creature who had been his friend. The child was dehydrated and his lips were chapped and bled often from tiny cracks on the surface. He tried hard not to cry since the tears that hit his mouth would burn and sting his lips. He knew from what the doctor had been saying that his grandpa was at the hotel with his mother. How he wished that they would find him. He wondered if they were taking care of his new parrot. He hadn't even given him a name yet.

Jeremy was drifting back to sleep when Turner said, "Get up! I think that we will go pay a little unexpected visit on your ol' granddad." He had his mouth close to the child's face and his putrid breath made the boy gag. Turner ran back into the far recesses of the cave and returned with his car keys and a rifle. He put the barrel of the gun against the back of the boy's head.

"He watched me when the verdict was read! Now it is my turn to look at his stupid face when I pull this trigger." He put the gun down to his side and untied the child's feet, but not his hands, which were bound behind him.

He marched Jeremy out of the cave and into the rain. They walked for a while in the wet sand before turning up a grassy path, which led to the doctor's small French car hidden in the tall weeds.

"Get in!" he ordered, opening the passenger side of the automobile for Jeremy. Then he went around and got in behind the wheel. At first, when he started the engine, the tires just spun around in the newly formed mud. But he threw the car into reverse and backed out of the holes.

By the time he reached the main road the rain had stopped. He finished the last of the bourbon and tossed the bottle out of the window into the weeds. He was fighting a bout of exhaustion. He strained to keep his eyes open as he was weaving his car down the road. He made Jeremy slump down in the front seat in case they passed anyone who was aware of the situation. But the road was deserted. He passed not a single car on the way to the hotel.

"I might even have a little drink with your ol' grandpa before I kill you. Just for old time sake. What do you think about that?"

Jeremy could not come to terms with the thought of dying. He still wasn't exactly sure what happened when you died. He was only convinced of one thing: that after you die you just go away somewhere, disappear like his father had done. He didn't want to do that. And he didn't want to be shot with a gun. He imagined that it must hurt an awful lot. He began to cry softly. His arms and shoulders were aching from being held in one position for so long.

"Shut up!" Turner snapped as they pulled up in front of the hotel. He didn't seem to notice that there were no cars in the parking lot other than his own.

He got out quickly and went around to the other side and commanded the boy to get out and walk ahead of him into the lobby. Turner kept the gun at the child's back as they entered the hotel. He looked around cautiously. The lobby was empty—no one behind the desk, no one seated in the chairs or on the couches. He dug the barrel of the rifle into Jeremy's back.

"Go on!" he said, indicating the dining room. He pushed the child aside and kicked the doors open and stood back. Nothing. He looked in. There was just a long row of tables and chairs. The swinging doors to the kitchen were open. He listened. No noise.

He went to the large French doors at the far end of the dining room. Even through the potted plants on the patio he could see that there was no one on the beach. It was hard for him to think clearly. Where was everyone? Then it came to him—the office! He grabbed the boy by the shoulders and rushed toward the hotel office. Again he kicked the door open and entered with the rifle pointed at the child's head. The room was empty.

Turner was confused and furious. "Andrew McGee, where are you?" he screamed. He threw Jeremy into a chair. Then he removed his own leather belt and used it to strap the boy in. The restraint was unnecessary. Jeremy felt sick and dizzy and had no energy to try and run away. Turner grabbed the rifle and started running through the halls opening doors with the passkey he had taken from Logan's desk.

"I know you're hiding in here somewhere, you coward!" he yelled in every hallway. "I was going to let your grandson die a natural death, but not anymore. I'm gonna kill him. Don't you want to see that, you son of a bitch!"

He ran through the arbor to the other wing of the hotel to continue his search. But soon this frenzied exertion had exhausted him. He returned to the office coughing and wheezing. Jeremy looked up at him with terrified eyes.

"I must think," Turner said out loud, slumping into a desk chair. He looked at Logan's open calendar. "It's Independence Day. The hotel guests are probably all in St. Philips. That explains why they aren't here. But what about Hart and the rest?"

He put his head down on the desk and closed his eyes briefly. His temples were throbbing. He sat up and opened his eyes again. Suddenly he caught sight of a notation on the calendar that he had missed before. Blocked in the slot reserved for afternoon appointments it read, "Salter addresses visiting delegates."

"Of course!" Turner shouted, euphoric, "that's where they are, Jeremy! They're all listening to the man! Let's go up to your place. We will wait there to surprise them!" The child was shocked to hear the doctor call him by name. He hadn't used it since he took him away.

Turner unstrapped the boy and led him through the lobby to the elevator. When they emerged on the top floor he unlocked the door Jeremy indicated was his. Once inside, Jeremy walked quickly through the living area to his bedroom. The parrot and his cage were gone. It was finally all too much. Jeremy threw himself on his bed and started sobbing loudly. Then he grew angry.

"I want to see my Mom and my Grandpa and my new parrot! Why are you so mean to me! I hate you! I hate you!"

Turner was taken aback by this outburst. The child had been so passive up to this point. He came near the bed and stood over the little boy.

"Well, I don't hate you. You are just an essential component of my grand plan to extract my much deserved revenge." Jeremy breathed a ragged sign and rolled over, burying his face in his pillow. Turner put his hand out to pat the child's back, but caught himself.

"I need a drink! Isn't there any booze in here?" He stormed out of the room. Jeremy heard him opening doors all the way down the hall. "Ah ha!" he heard him shout from a distance. Then he came back holding a bottle of brown liquid. "Pretty high-class people staying here. This is the good stuff!"

He drank eagerly directly from the bottle, swallowing hard. Some of the liquor spilled down his face. Jeremy, mercifully, had fallen to sleep. Turner sat down in a rattan chair and drank, holding the rifle between his knees. He looked outside. The clouds had vanished and the sun was beginning to beat down again upon the empty beach. "Must be about two o'clock," he mused, yawning.

Dori and Logan left the party at The Buoy and drove to the ministry. They took the small Fiat, for the time being leaving the Mercedes and the station wagon in St. Philips. Logan drove. They rode in virtual silence, each consumed by their own thoughts. They were met at the entrance by one of the limousine drivers, who drove the car quickly into the huge garage housing the official automobiles. He parked the car and closed the massive metal garage doors, concealing all of the cars from view.

Salter came out of the conference room to greet them. He looked tired and nervous. "I have explained everything to the delegates. They are all in agreement with the steps we are taking. Let's go into my office and wait privately."

They walked down the long marble hall, past the closed doors of the meeting room to Salter's office. His secretary was sitting in the outer chamber. She got up and opened the door for them.

"May I get anything for you, sir?" she asked the prime minister. He looked at the others. "No, I don't think so, thank you."

They went inside and shut the door behind them. There was a long couch by the window where Dori and Logan sat. Salter paced slowly about the room, glancing at his desk clock every few minutes. They all felt the need to speak. But at the moment there was nothing to say.

Like the conference chamber, Salter's office was cooled only by ceiling fans. Dori leaned her head against the back of the couch and stared at the spinning blades. Their rhythmic whirling and soft steady rasping noise had an almost therapeutic effect on her nerves. She just closed her eyes and listened.

But the hiatus in the tension was broken by the ringing of the phone on the secretary's desk. She responded to the caller in a soft voice and then knocked on the office door and stepped inside.

"Excuse me, sir, but there is a man on the phone who wishes to speak to Mrs. Dugan."

Dori sat bolt upright. "It's Turner," she said, her stomach twisting in knots.

"Put the call through right away," Salter said, handing the receiver to Dori. Her hands were ice cold.

"Hello, Ransom," she said. "How is Jeremy?"

"I want to see your father," he said, ignoring the question. "Where is he?" He started coughing, almost choking. "Maybe he is not even here at all!" He was yelling now. "Maybe Hart lied!"

"Where are you calling from?" Dori asked, hoping that in his stupor he might let his location slip.

"Wouldn't you like to know?"

"May I please speak to Jeremy, just to see that he is okay?"

"No!" Turner said angrily." He's fine. But he won't be for long. Where is your goddamn father!"

Dori was trying to think of something to say when she heard her son's voice in the background, yelling. "Mom, where are you? Do you have my parrot? He's not here in my room anymore!"

"Shut up!" she heard Turner scream. Then the line went dead. Dori dropped the receiver and then turned around. She looked as though she were about to faint.

"Oh my god, Logan, they're at the hotel!"

Logan raced for the door. Salter put his arm out to stop him.

"It's twenty to three. You won't make it."

"Yes I will!" Logan said. "If I leave right now! I know exactly where the timing device is buried. I can do it!"

Dori was calling the hotel, but it was no use. The phone would only ring in the office or at the switchboard, not in the individual suites or rooms.

Logan tried again to get past the black man.

"No," Salter said. "I'm afraid that I can't let you go."

"What!" Logan screamed. He raised his fist to strike the prime minister, but before he could make a move, Salter's powerful hand flew at his neck horizontally striking him on the collarbone and then behind the head. Logan dropped to the floor, unconscious.

Dori was trying to climb out of the window behind her when Salter tackled her from behind. When she struggled and started to scream he slapped her hard across the face twice and threw her down on the couch. Although she was in pain and shock and beyond sleep deprived she whirled around and rushed at Salter, head down, and hit him square in the abdomen. He *whooshed* as the air was forced from his lungs and for a moment was a bit disoriented. But then, regaining his composure, he grabbed Dori roughly and pinned her arms behind her back.

"I tried to tell you that my primary responsibility is to Miranda, that I must insure her freedom at all costs." He emphasized the *all*. "I said that I could not let anyone influence me, not even you. If I am to discover who is at the bottom of this movement, the plan cannot be interrupted. If they knew we were on to them, they would scatter the earth like cockroaches. I hope that someday you will be able to understand that your son is being sacrificed for the greater good."

Dori jerked her arms free from his grasp and just stared at him, incredulously. "He's just a little boy, with his whole life ahead of him. How can you possibly let this happen? I hope you die," she said. Then she added, just because she wanted to, "I hope you and your dreams of West Indian leadership die too."

"You had to ask about that goddamn bird," Turner said, grabbing the frightened boy by the shoulders. He led the child through the open terrace door and then raised his rifle in the air. "Look," he instructed, "I think I see him flying over there." With that he began shooting wildly.

"No!" Jeremy yelled, coming after him, "Don't shoot my parrot!" The child began crying violently and looked over the railing. He could see his small pet nowhere.

In the equipment tent Howard Rutledge had almost fallen asleep. But the shots startled him. He walked outside of the tent and gazed in the direction of the hotel. He scanned the rows of patios and terraces. The harsh sunlight reflecting off the sand made it difficult to see anything. But then, some piece of shining metal caught his attention. It was on the top floor. He squinted and put his hands around his eyes to shield them from the glare. Suddenly he felt his knees grow weak. It was Turner with a rifle. And cowering beside him on the terrace was Jeremy.

Howard quickly ducked behind the tent so that he would not be spotted. He looked again. They had gone inside. Now was his only chance. He was not wearing a watch and had no idea of what time it was. He raced across the sand and around the side of the hotel to the service stairs. He bolted up one flight after another, gasping for breath when he reached the top. He paused for a second before opening the door into the hallway. His breathing could not be so labored or he would be discovered.

He worked his way quickly but silently down the hall, pressing himself against the wall. The door to the suite was open. From the sound of Turner's voice Howard could tell that his back was to the door. He rushed in and jumped the doctor, taking control of the rifle as he did.

"Come on, Jeremy!" he screamed. "We have to get out of here! This place is going to blow up any minute. Jeremy! Run down the stairs and away from the hotel. Run down the beach as fast as you can! Run and find Claire! For an instant the child just stood, motionless. "Now, Jeremy!" Howard screamed, and the boy ran past him, out of the room and down the hall to the stairs.

"Get up, Turner!" Howard ordered, tossing the rifle aside. The doctor lay still. Howard bent down and rolled him over. Then he put his ear to the doctor's chest. He had passed out.

Howard hoisted the dead weight of the man over his shoulders and started out the door. He looked down the hall at the elevator. He decided against it and went for the stairs.

Down on the beach Jeremy was running with his hands still bound toward Cinnamon Inn. He was sobbing when he came upon Claire and Morgan who were strolling down the sand toward the hotel.

"What's happened?" Claire asked as she bent down to embrace the exhausted child. Morgan worked briskly to untie his hands. Through his stifled sobs they were able to make out very little.

"Dr. Turner is in the hotel. He has been mean and hitting me. He thinks he saw my parrot and tried to shoot him!" He was gulping air. "But Mr. Rutledge found me. But he's still there."

"Well good for Howie," Claire said lightly. "I guess they are through spraying for bugs now."

"We are on our way to see him right now." Morgan added. "He and I have a surprise for Claire. You come on with us. We will get you all cleaned up and give you something to eat," she said. "And then we will find your mother. Everything will be alright now, honey."

The women continued walking toward the hotel, each holding one of the boy's hands. "But the hotel is going to—" Jeremy didn't have time to finish his sentence. Suddenly a rumbling, like an explosion deep within the earth shook the ground. And then the three watched in stark horror as the hotel disintegrated before their eyes, crumbling to the sand, floor on top of floor. Like a jigsaw puzzle, it just came apart. Grey clouds of fine powder billowed up around the falling fragments of concrete, glass, and steel. And then it was all over. The hotel was reduced to worthless rubble.

Howard had gone down three flights of stairs when, like an accordion, they all collapsed on top of him. He died instantly. And buried with him, crushed under mounds of cement and glass was Ransom Turner, and all of his hate.

Aboard the *Kiwi* the four men watched solemnly at the culmination of their months of work.

"Congratulations, gentlemen," Ramino said. "This is a remarkable victory. But it is only now that our real task must commence. Claiming Miranda is our first step in achieving total control of the Caribbean."

The crew watched in transfixed disbelief at the sight of the devastation. But they said nothing. They were in a very precarious position. Though they knew now exactly what had happened, and who was responsible, they had no actual proof. They would be unable to implicate these men in any kind of a criminal trial. This maddened and frustrated the captain. But he also realized it was probably also the only reason none of them would be killed.

The *Kiwi* motored quickly around the side of the island into the harbor of St. Philips. The steward readied the small ship to shore boat for them. Cliff took Ramino and Mariani into port and then came back to get LeBeau and some luggage. They left the small vessel tied up at the dock. They all glanced around. The celebrating was going on uninterrupted. LeBeau hailed an island cab. They all got in. "To the ministry please."

Logan had come to and was trying to comfort Dori. She had stopped crying and was frantically trying to find a way to escape and get to her son. Salter had gone into the conference room to wait for Charles Cliff and the others. He had instructed his guards not to allow Mr. Hart or Mrs. Dugan to leave until he had given them permission.

"They might see you," he explained to his captives "and realize that there is something wrong. You will have to remain here until after they have come," he added when he posted the guards.

Logan was devastated. He felt responsible for Jeremy's certain death. He stood up from the couch and made Dori lie down. Then he sat on the floor beside her and stroked her forehead. Again Dori lost herself in the swirling fans. Logan watched her face. She was in deep shock. For that, at least, he was grateful. Momentarily, it was a shield against reality.

The cab dropped the men off in front of the ministry. Cliff was the first to get out. "Has the prime minister returned from the conference yet?" he inquired of the well-rehearsed guard at the door.

"Mr. Cliff, you don't know what has happened?"

"No. I have been attending the celebrations in St. Philips. What has happened?"

"The prime minister, Victor Trent, and all of the delegates have been killed. And the Castle Beach Hotel has been completely destroyed. Some kind of sabotage."

Cliff and the others feigned great shock and remorse. "Are you sure?"

"Yes, sir. The bodies are being recovered now. The rest of the staff is waiting in the conference room for your instructions."

"Yes of course," Cliff said, at once full of authority.

"Does anyone have any idea what occurred?" Lebeau asked.

"No, sir. No one but the prime minister and his guests were there at the time. It was a massive explosion of some type."

"Well," Cliff pronounced, "whoever is responsible for this horrific crime shall not go unpunished." The guard opened the door and let the men inside.

"I am expecting some additional men to be joining me shortly," Cliff told the guard. "Will you please show them where we are?"

"Yes, sir," replied the guard, closing the door after them.

They walked briskly down the hall to the conference room. The double doors flew open even before Cliff had touched the knobs and the four revolutionaries were staring into the face of John Salter. Behind him at the table sat the rest of the West Indian Island leaders. And standing behind them were their aides, each shouldering a high-powered firearm focused on the new arrivals.

"Do come in, gentlemen," Salter said between gritted teeth. "We all have so much to discuss since we have learned all that we can from your comrade." In one corner of the room lay the still bound and gagged body of Rene Busschard, a single bullet through his head.

After Mandy and the rest of the demolition experts arrived, a guard came and released Dori and Logan. The Fiat was waiting in front when they walked outside into the bright afternoon sunshine. Logan helped Dori into the car and he climbed in and they drove off. The auto wound quickly around the road from the ministry. He dreaded passing the smoldering remains of the hotel, but he had no choice since he must get Dori to Cinnamon Inn to rest and to make the phone calls that must be made.

Logan tried not to look as they neared the palm-studded entrance of what had been Castle Beach, but his eyes, as well as Dori's, were drawn to it. The total devastation was staggering. It was as though a massive bomb had been dropped on this single spot. Everything around it was untouched. Even the rows of delicate, bright Flamboyant trees lining the driveway stood straight and tall, unharmed.

Logan drove on, brutalized by what he had seen. In minutes he turned off the main road to the Cinnamon Inn cottages. He pulled up in front of Claire's bungalow. He got out and knocked on the door. There was no answer but it was unlocked, so he went in. He opened the door to Morgan Talbot's room. Both of the twin beds were made. He turned one back and then went and brought Dori inside.

"I want you to lie down. Then I am going to go back into St. Philips and find the doctor who has been staying at the hotel. I'll return as soon as I can."

Dori sat up. "Don't leave me, Logan! You can't leave me." She clung to him tightly.

"I won't, Dori, I won't." He held her close rubbing her back gently.

"I don't want to see the sun anymore. Close the curtains."

Logan got up and went to the window. Perhaps if he did draw the shades she would get some desperately needed rest. But when he got to the window he stopped short. Coming down the beach was Morgan Talbot with her arm around Claire. And following behind was Jeremy, tired and dirty but alive! On one shoulder of his tattered T-shirt perched the green and yellow parrot Logan had given him.

"Dori," Logan said, "Come here. I want you to look at something."

"I can't, Logan. I don't want to see anything."

He went over and grabbed her by the hand, pulling her reluctantly to her feet. He led her into the living room and out onto the terrace. "I am sure you are going to want and see this Caribbean pirate. Look!" He pointed to the beach.

Dori lifted her head. She gasped, "It's Jeremy!" She flew down the stairs by the side of the cottage and darted across the lawn onto the sand. Logan watched with joy and relief as she scooped her young son up in her arms, parrot and all.

XLII

The news of the thwarted take over attempt, as well as of the execution of all of the insurgents, spread rapidly throughout the Caribbean and around the world. All of the major airlines scheduled emergency flights to evacuate anxious tourists from the island.

Dori and Logan had been staying at the Trents for a week. Jeremy had been eating well and sleeping a great deal. He was recovering nicely from his terrible experience. He did not seem to have sustained any lasting emotional scars from the ordeal, though it was still too early to tell. But in their conversations Dori was convinced that her son had a clear grasp of what had happened.

"I felt kind of sorry for Dr. Turner," Jeremy said at one point.

"Why?" Dori asked, keeping her tone casual.

"Because he was so lonely. He wanted to make everybody unhappy just like he was. But you can't do that, mom. You can't make everybody unhappy just because you are."

"That's right, honey, you can't."

"And anyway," Jeremy said, holding the parrot on his hand, "he was really sick all the time, coughing and everything. I bet he wouldn't have said or done all of those mean things if he had felt better."

Howard's death had saddened everyone, especially when the circumstances surrounding it had been learned. A funeral was held at the small Episcopal Church in St. Philips. Logan went with the Trents while Dori stayed with the children. She felt that Jeremy had been too close to death too often. She wanted him to have only happy experiences now. But she and Jeremy said a prayer together for Howard, thanking him for saving Jeremy, and as it turned out, his parrot as well. Howard must have moved the bird to the equipment tent with him long before the explosion. That is where Claire and Morgan had found it.

Victor Trent reported that Salter did not attend the funeral. "No one has seen him all week, he has tripled the guards around the ministry and has requested the use of armored cars from Barbados. He won't be taking any chances in the future."

Dori had spoken with her parents twice since the twelfth. She told them only that she and Jeremy were fine. She did not mention Turner's name. There would be time enough for detailed accounts of the past grim events.

Allison had been busy all week packing crates of china and crystal to be shipped back to England. Dori had helped her. Logan had been spending the time attempting to get certain things in order. He had spoken with Flynn on several occasions over the last few days. As Logan had predicted earlier, the attorney was elated over the turn of events. "Man, I'll try and start a fire under our insurers right away, so to speak. Wow! What a settlement!"

Logan decided to wait until he got back to New York to break the news to Jack that he did not intend to collect. He had told himself earlier that if Jeremy were returned safely then he could take the insurance money without guilt. But he had not figured on Howard's death, or even Turner's for that matter. He knew that without the money it was going to be rough. He would have to declare bankruptcy and hope he could salvage something.

Soon Jeremy had put on a few pounds and was rested to the point where Dori felt that it would be safe for him to travel. Logan made the arrangements. "We leave tomorrow," he announced at dinner that evening. "I am afraid that all of the big extra commercial flights are over. We are going to have to take the mail run to Barbados."

"Oh that won't be so bad, "Victor said. "We are leaving the day after tomorrow. No telling the contraptions we will have to fly before we get home to London."

The four of them were sitting at the small circular table at the end of the dining room. It was the one at which they had dined the first night Dori had arrived on the island. The help had all left, so Allison was managing alone. They were having a very plain meal of salad, soup, and bread, but it was more than adequate.

"What will happen to this house after you leave?" Dori asked.

Allison looked over at Victor. "I really don't know," he admitted. "The head office will not be sending any more representatives here, for a while anyway. Salter is going to have to make his desires more firmly known. And if he wants British and American military aid, he will have to provide some assurances that he will not move to nationalize any foreign businesses on the island. He can't have his cake and eat it too. At any rate, I suppose this house shall remain vacant until the crown decides what, if anything, to do with it."

They finished dinner and Logan and Dori walked outside in the gardens while Allison continued to pack. Victor was playing some kind of board game with the boys on the third floor balcony. Laughter and shouts could be heard drifting down on the gentle evening air.

"What time do we leave tomorrow Logan?" Dori asked.

"The plane is scheduled to take off at eight in the morning."

"Well then, let's go and say good bye to Claire. Howard saved Jeremy's life. I want to express my eternal gratitude and tell her that we will never forget his self sacrifice."

Morgan let them in. Like Allison, Claire too was in the process of packing. But she seemed composed and genuinely glad to see them.

"Claire, I don't know what to say to try and tell you what I thought of Howard. I will never forget what he did." Dori began to cry, but stopped herself quickly.

"He loved Jeremy," Claire said in a matter-of-fact manner. "As you know we never had children of our own, and Howard missed them. He was a wonderful child himself in many ways." She smiled and looked calm and subdued. And she was. Fortunately, her mind had completely blocked out any recollections of the indirect role she had played in her husband's death.

"Do you know the surprise Howie and Morgan had planned for me?" Dori shook her head that she did not. "He was going to send me back to California with Morgan for awhile, to concentrate on my acting career, to see if it is really something I want to do again. He was going to stay here and manage the cottages. But there is nothing to manage now since everyone has left the island. And it will probably remain that way for some time." Her tone was not bitter. "Morgan suggested that I close down the place for at least three or four months and go with her to Los Angeles. And do you know what?" She got a mischievous grin on her ragged face. "I'm gonna do it! Howie would be so proud of me."

Dori and Logan said goodbye again and walked out in front. Morgan followed them to their car. Big brown moths twirled around the yellow porch light.

"Claire needs a great deal of professional help. And I am going to see that she gets it." Morgan said. "Of course, I will also make sure that she attends several of my seminars. I still think they would have been a hit at the hotel."

Logan smiled and shook his head. "We'll never know."

"Maybe at one of your places in the states then?" she said.

Logan started thinking about all of the health and meditation farms Flynn had said were crowding him out. "Come to think of it, Morgan, you just may have something there. Look me up if you get to New York."

The woman beamed. "I'll make it a point to get there."

"You know," Dori said during the drive back to the Trents, "Somehow I have a feeling that Claire is in good hands."

"Me too," Logan smiled.

Victor drove them to the airport the following morning in the hotel station wagon. "I'll drop this and the other two cars off at the dock for you and arrange for shipping."

"Thanks, Victor," Logan said. "I really appreciate it. I may end up having to live in this beaten up wreck for a while."

Jeremy was in the backseat carrying the parrot in a cardboard box full of holes.

"You might have some trouble getting that bird through customs," Victor warned Logan. "They are pretty strict about things like that."

"If I can't pull enough strings to bring a handful of feathers across the boarder," Logan laughed, "then I really have lost my touch. I already have an idea. We can give him a sleeping pill and Dori can wear him as a hat."

Dori was sitting next to Allison on the seat with Jeremy. She just shook her head at Logan's suggestion. But she was glad to see that he had regained his wonderful sense of humor. The Trent boys were in the tailgate section lying on the few suitcases that were left to make the trip.

They rounded the last turn and the airstrip came into view. Dori's heart flew up into her throat. Parked by the small, twin-engine plane was Salter's limousine. The prime minister, flanked by two hefty, uniformed guards, stood in front of it.

Logan turned around to Dori. "Are you going to be able to handle this?"

She knew that it was his way of asking if she wanted him to stay with her.

"I'll be fine," she said softly.

Victor swung the car around near the other side of the plane. It looked like it was only going to be the three of them on the flight, along with some canvas mailbags. The children jumped out of the car and ran over to examine the airplane. Victor and Allison went with Logan to the small wooden terminal to check the tickets and reconfirm their connecting flights.

Dori stood alone. Salter left the guards and walked up to her.

"I checked to see what flight you would be taking. I wanted to say goodbye."

Dori looked up into the face she thought she had known so well. His once soft brown eyes had been honed into sharp points of light, displaying no emotion. His lips were drawn into a tight slit across his face. He had become a stranger. "Our first good bye was much better than this, John. That is the one I will remember."

She turned and walked away. Soon she heard the heavy car door shut and the engine start. When she looked again, the car was out of sight.

"Hey, mom," Jeremy called from the door of the small plane. "The captain said that I can ride with him in the cockpit!" Brian and Henry Trent were extremely jealous, which only added to Jeremy's triumph.

Logan came out of the terminal. "Well, Dorothy, said the wizard, have you had enough of the Land of Oz?" He smiled gently.

"Yes," Dori said, "I think I have."

"Everything is all set," Logan said. "I guess this is it."

He shook hands with Victor and Allison. Dori kissed them both lightly on the cheek and thanked them for everything.

"Take care of yourselves and send me a picture of the new arrival," Logan said, grinning.

Victor laughed. "Oh I am sure that if Allison has anything to say about it the London Times will run a special supplement devoted to the birth of our new baby." He squeezed his wife's hand playfully.

Allison called the boys to her side. The pilot signaled that he was ready to take off. Dori climbed the short metal steps to the plane. Logan followed. Jeremy was already happily fastened into the seat next to the captain. Soon the small craft taxied rapidly down the short runway and rose quickly into the air.

After achieving a little altitude the pilot swung the plane around in a gradual circle. They were passing over the island on their way out to sea. Both Dori and Logan looked down at the long bleached-white stretch of sand that had been the focal point of their lives over the past months. Even now, crews of workers were still carrying off the last stone and gravel remains of the hotel in a caravan of large trucks.

As the plane travelled farther out to sea and climbed higher and higher the spectacular emerald green and turquoise blue of Miranda faded beneath them. Logan kept his face turned around toward the window for a while. When he finally looked back Dori could see that his eyes were clouding over with tears.

"Have you got anything to read," he shouted to the pilot over the engine noise, "except other peoples' mail?" he smiled.

"Yeah, there are a couple of newspapers around there somewhere."

Logan searched the seat behind his. "Ah!" he announced after he got up and looked around. "I'm in luck, yesterday's *New York Times*." He sat down next to Dori, opening the paper and putting it up close to his face. He turned a few pages, supposedly reading.

"Dori wondered if perhaps he were crying when suddenly he said, "Hey, here we go!" He dropped the paper to his lap. A big grin consumed his face. He began reading from the classified section. "Listen: 'small New England hotel for sale, close to skiing, lakes, mountains and hiking trails, year around recreation area. Ten cozy cabins and a small lodge. Needs some redecorating and professional management.' Remember when I accused you of spending your life wading around in buckets of maple syrup?" Dori nodded. "Well, do think there is room in there for another couple of feet?"

She leaned over and kissed him warmly on the mouth, surprising both of them. "Um hum," she said, and kissed him again. "I think maybe there is."

EPILOGUE

Dori stood on the back deck of the house, looking past the birch trees to the boat dock and the lake beyond. The water was still and glassy, rare for a late summer afternoon when the breeze usually picked up. She was listening for the putt putt sound of the outboard motor on the small Boston Whaler Jeremy had taken out earlier with some of his friends.

He was almost sixteen now and would be a high school junior in the fall. Where had the time gone?

When Dori returned from the West Indies she moved back in with her parents to get her bearings, and had planned on going back to New York, eventually. But then her parents announced that they had made the decision to move to Arizona.

"I've endured my last New England winter," her mother proclaimed happily.

Dori tried to talk them out of it but stopped when she saw how excited and eager they were to start this new chapter in their lives. But it was at the same time that she realized, surprisingly enough, that she did not want to leave Vermont.

With the money she had saved plus the money her parents gave her from the proceeds of the sale of their farmhouse and property she was able to purchase a smaller place on a beautiful lake. And she took over running her mother's shop, The Quilted Pine, tweaking its inventory and adding to its already growing line of collegiate clothing. She doubled revenues the first year and they just kept growing. She was even toying with the idea of adding a small inn to cater to the visiting families and friends of students attending the many colleges dotting Vermont.

That wasn't the only major change she had made in her life. Her reminiscing was interrupted by the familiar sound of the Boston

Whaler nearing the dock. Suddenly she felt strong arms hug her from behind. She turned around and kissed her handsome husband.

"Honestly, Logan, you're like a Chippewa Indian the way you can sneak up on someone."

He laughed. "I've learned a lot living in these woods." He looked down at the dock and saw Jeremy and his lanky buddies crossing the lawn and heading up to the house. "Hmm," he said. "I better fire up the grill. I'll get some burgers going before they start eating the bark off the trees."

"May I help light the barbeque?" asked a little blond girl of about eight as she walked barefooted to where her parents were standing.

"I wouldn't think of starting it without you," Logan said, bending over to place a kiss on the top of his daughter's head. He turned around and started walking back inside toward the kitchen.

"Hurry up, Miranda, let's cook dinner."

www.ingramcontent.com/pod-product-compliance
Lightning Source LLC
Chambersburg PA
CBHW022205010726
47493CB00002B/427